CW00470828

A MYTHICAL IRISH TALE

And the quest to get back home

Book 1

Declan Michael

This is a work of fiction. Names, characters, places, and incidents either are the product of the author's imagination or are used fictitiously. Any resemblance to actual persons, living or dead, events, or locales is entirely coincidental.

Cover by Rachel543

Edited by Declan McGrath

Bio wrote by parizaadd

ISBN 978-1-7392962-2-3

For more information, email: declanmmichael@gmail.com

Website www.declanmichael.ie

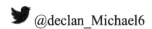 @declan_Michael6

Dedication

To Linda and Garon for believing in me.

Thank you!

Also, to those who inspired it, but won't get to read it.

Thank you too!

CONTENTS

A MYTHICAL IRISH TALE

And the quest to get back home

CHAPTER ONE

THE WEDDING DAY

oday was no ordinary day for Garon as he woke from a long night's sleep. It was the 2nd of March, and his uncle Joseph was getting married today, so Garon would get to see his two favourite cousins, Dillon and PJ.

Garon was 17 years old with a slim build and of average height. He had pale skin and mousy brown hair parted at the side. He ran downstairs in his pyjamas and hugged his mam like he did every morning. His mam Lynne was the same height as Garon, with a medium build and shoulder-length brown hair.

"What's for breakfast, mam," asked Garon

"Oh, it's your favourite love, it's bacon and eggs," said his mam.

"Where is dad?" asked Garon.

"Oh, he's gone to the shop for his newspaper and fresh bread," said his mam

"Dad and his fresh bread," Garon said as he and his mam giggled.

Right on cue, his dad Daniel arrived at the door and said, "Oh, the smell of this fresh bread is amazing."

Garon and his mam giggled even louder while his dad sat at the table and said, "The two of you never change."

Garon's dad was also of medium build, but was a few inches taller than him. He had combed back slightly greying brown hair. Garon liked to mock his dad by calling him captain fantastic after Reid Richards in the fantastic four.

All three of them then sat down for breakfast. His dad said they needed a good feed as it would be a long day ahead, and that it would be the evening before they ate again. After they had all showered and put on their best wedding day clothes, it was time to set off for the church. Garon wore his favourite black chinos, a white shirt, a teal jumper, and black trainers. He also had his favourite teal headphones.

His dad told him to leave the headphones behind, but his mam said he wouldn't wear them in the church. With that, she gave Garon a little wink, and they smiled at each other. His dad just shrugged his shoulders and carried the overnight cases to the car for their overnight stay in the hotel where the wedding was being held.

They lived in a small town called Clondalkin, and the church was only a short drive from their house. The town is a suburban town and is believed to have been founded by Saint Cronan Mochua as a monastic settlement. Three main focal points stood out to Garon as he saw them daily for as long as he could remember.

The round tower, saint Brigid's well, and the local church.

The round tower was founded in the 7th century by St Mochua and is one of only four remaining round towers in County Dublin. Thought to have been built around 790 AD, and stands 27.5 metres high, and still has its original cap. It is believed to be the slenderest of all the round towers left in Ireland today.

St. Bridget's Well. Legend has it that St. Brigid came to the site and baptised pagans at the well. The well is believed to have curative powers. A piece of rag dipped in the water and used to wipe the face was said to cure people with eye complaints.

The church was built in the Gothic revival style and had a belfry with a vestry at the rear. As you enter the Parish Church, your attention is immediately drawn to the stained-glass windows over the High Altar. Starting from the left, there is Saint Laurence O'Toole, dressed in his bishop robes and vestments, ready to say Mass. He also has on his pallium the white cloth over his shoulders with the stripe hanging down in front. An Archbishop may only wear the pallium when in his own diocese.

Next there is the virgin, Mary. She is shown with the moon under her feet and wearing a crown of twelve stars on her head. The next section shows Saint Joseph holding a rod with lilies growing from it in his right hand. Finally, there is Saint Patrick, who is shown as a bishop with his mitre and crosier. He wears a cope, (the outer vestment worn at ceremonies) other than mass. He holds a shamrock in his right hand and there is a dying snake under his feet.

When they reached the churchyard, many cars and people were already there before them. Garon's dad said, "Oh, I can see some of the family is here already."

There was his mother, Deirdre, a widower who was accompanied by his brother Joseph, who was getting married. Next to him were his other three brothers, Gary, Dermot, and Jason, with their wives, Lisa and Molly and Julie.

The carpark was full of Garon's cousins and lots of other relatives Garon didn't know. Joseph didn't have any kids, but Gary had two kids, Dillon and Lucy, while Dermot had four kids: PJ, Derek, Chris, and James. Then there were Jason's twin daughters, Jessica and Clodagh, but Garon only had eyes for Dillon and PJ as they were his two favourite cousins.

Dillon was Gary's oldest; he was 18 years old and 6 foot tall with blond hair parted at the side and had the type of smile that would light up a room. He was dressed in clothes similar to Garon's with grey chinos and a black shirt. He also wore black trainers and had his favourite black headphones around his neck. Lucy was 16 years old but never seemed interested in the older boys. Derek, Chris, and James, who were all roughly the same age, always played together.

PJ was Dermot's oldest he was 16 years old and the same height as Garon. He had a quiff in his dark blond hair and liked to sport a small goatee to show off his manliness. He had a cheeky smile that always got him out of trouble. He wore a cool trilby hat with mirror sunglasses and a white tee shirt with black jeans and black trainers. He was also wearing his favourite red headphones around his neck.

When Garon got out of the car, he didn't even have time to say anything to his mam and dad as he had made a beeline for Dillon and PJ. The boys all embraced each other with one big hug, which seemed to last an eternity.

The boys were well-suited as a team. First, you had Garon, the group's thinker and brains. Then you had Dillon, who had great charisma and was a brilliant talker, next you had PJ, who was a loveable rogue, he could pickpocket anyone and be forgiven if he was caught as his cheeky smile and way with words got him out of many tricky situations.

Dillon spotted some girls and told the others to follow his lead before approaching them and flashing a smile. "Would you like to make sweet music with me?" he asked. "Well, cousin Dillon, would you think that's appropriate?" came the reply. A blushing Dillon apologised for not knowing them before PJ chirped in, "But he's only asking you to be in a band with him". Garon slapped PJ on the head before grabbing his trilby and throwing it at Dillon, who ran off with it. PJ ran after the boys as they teased him by holding his hat in the air and passing it to each other.

When the boys got bored, they returned the hat before PJ disappeared and returned, showing the others what he had found. He opened his hand, producing the wedding rings. "You plonker," said Garon. "You robbed them from my dad. There won't be a wedding today if you don't give them back".

PJ made his way over to Daniel and held out the rings, saying sorry. "Why you little," said Daniel before Lynne cut across him, saying, "Mind your language in the churchyard, Daniel".

In the meantime, everyone was waiting for the bride and bridesmaids to arrive. Suddenly everyone was told to get into the church as Aoife (Joseph's bride-to-be was nearing the church).

Joseph and Daniel (Garon's dad) made their way to the altar, as Daniel was the best man. They spoke to Father Murphy, the priest who was already at the altar in his full garments, waiting to welcome the bride and groom and the congregation to the service. Suddenly the music here comes the bride began playing, and the bridesmaids started walking down the aisle. There were three bridesmaids in total.

The bridesmaids each wore sleeveless full-length Lilac dresses with a slit down the side and carried bouquets of Baby's breath. Or to give it its proper name, Gypsophila. The bride then duly arrived, and she looked stunning. She was wearing an ivory dress. It was simple but also dramatic and show-stopping.

It had a detachable tulle and lace train, which could be removed to reveal a sleek and elegant stretch georgette silhouette. Thick floral embroidered lace provided gorgeous detailing to accentuate the V-neckline and low cut back. She also carried a bouquet of white lilies surrounded by Baby's breath to complement the bridesmaids' bouquets.

As Aoife and her father made their way down the aisle, Daniel looked back to see the bride. He turned and told Joseph that she was stunning but forbade him from turning to look to avoid any bad luck that it might bring their way. It seemed to take an eternity for Aoife to walk down the aisle, and Joseph began sweating heavily as he was getting very nervous. Daniel did his best to calm his nerves. Finally, Aoife arrived at the altar, and her father placed her hand on Joseph's. They both stared at each other with tears of pride streaming down their faces.

Now, the service could begin. Father Murphy started the service by welcoming everybody to the wedding of Aoife and Joseph. He gave the couple a lovely service. When the time came, Daniel gave the rings to Father Murphy. It was time for Joseph to place the ring on Aoife's finger and say his vows to which he finished with the words.

"I, Joseph, take you, Aoife, to be my wife, my life partner, and my one true love. I will cherish our friendship and love you today, tomorrow, and forever. I will trust you and honour you. I will laugh with you and cry with you. Through the best and the worst, through the difficult and the easy. Whatever may come, I will always be there, as I have given you my hand to hold, so I give you my life to keep."

Next, it was Aoife's turn to place a ring on Joseph's finger and say her vows which she finished with, "Joseph, today I stand before you, ready to start the biggest adventure of our lives. I know it will be hard, and some days will take a lot of work. But I also know there will be days filled with love, laughter, and pure bliss. I can't imagine sharing this adventure with anyone else but you. You're my best friend, the love of my life, and my soul mate. Today, I promise to stand by your side and to love you always."

Father Murphy then pronounced the couple husband and wife and told Joseph it was now ok to kiss the bride. The smitten couple duly obliged with a loud cheer coming from the packed church hall. The service ended, and the music played, sending the happy couple out of the church.

After they took the obligatory photographs inside the church, everybody walked outside to take more photos.

Dillon got his dad's car keys and ran to their car, coming back with three bags of rice, handing one to Lucy, one to Chris, and one to James. He told them they should throw rice at the bride and groom, as it was customary.

Joseph and Aoife were now posing outside the church for photos when Lucy approached and threw the bag of rice, hitting Joseph flush on the Jaw. Lucy's mother, Lisa, glared at her for being so bold. Dillon laughed aloud and said, "You idiot Lucy, you were to throw some grains on them, not the entire bag," before Lisa dragged her away.

Once all the photos were taken, it was time to go to the hotel. Garon, Dillon, and PJ all jumped into the backseat of his dad's car as they all wanted to travel together. The journey to the hotel would take approximately 45 minutes, and the three boys busied themselves talking about their favourite podcast. All three checked their pockets to ensure they had their mp3 players with the latest episode downloaded. "Phew was the collective sigh" once they all checked their pockets.

En route to the hotel, Dillon asked Lynne if she would like to dance with the best-looking guy at the wedding later that evening. Lynne replied that as she was married to him, he better make sure he asked her to dance later. Garon and PJ laughed while Lynne gave a cheeky wink to Dillon. The journey passed quickly, and it wasn't long until Garon's dad, Daniel, said, "we are pulling up to the hotel now".

The hotel was called Castleview manor, which had a long spiral driveway and looked out onto the lush rolling countryside. It had a truly magical setting, with a wonderfully rich history from the Victorian grandeur to the 15 acres of splendid gardens and gloriously wild woodland and trails.

Its grounds blended formal gardens, sweeping terraces, statues, and ornamental lakes with rambling walks. It also had walled Gardens, an ancient fountain, a pet cemetery, and a small round tower. Among other features and attractions were a paved patio, a gazebo, and a large bench. It was an excellent backdrop for the bride and groom to get their wedding photos.

Once they entered the hotel, it was a joy to behold. It looked like a private period property but with the twist of a modern hotel with all the conveniences of a luxury hotel. The bar and lounge were set with tea light candles for a pre-dinner drinks reception. The library lounge bar contained a cosy seated area for guests, while the open log-burning fires created a warm, comfortable atmosphere. They enhanced the design of the main Hall with a long rectangular table for the Bridal party. It also had seven round tables for the guests and a dance floor.

All the kids decided to explore the grounds while all the adults headed for the bar for some liquid refreshments. The bride and groom arrived shortly after and had all the customary photos taken. Dillon got some money from Gary as he wanted to buy some drinks, "Watch this, boys", he said to Garon and PJ as he made his way to the bar.

"I'll have three pints of beer, TA," he said to the barman. The barman laughed and said they were too young to drink. "Ok said Dillon, three pints of orange, instead please". PJ said, "That was close, I'm too young to drink" before Dillon slapped him around the ear.

The three boys sat there trying to decide what they would do once they had drunk their orange. They all took out their camera phones and started getting the adults to pose for silly photos so they could make up their own wedding album for the happy couple. They had great fun making the adults pull the most ridiculous faces they could think of. Each of the boys tried to outdo the other for the best photo before they were called in, as it was time to sit down to have dinner.

After they finished dinner, they started the speeches. After a lengthy speech from Daniel, followed by Aoife's dad and then Joseph, they moved on, as Aoife didn't want to give a speech. It was now time for the first dance. Aoife and Joseph chose a DJ for the day, and their first dance was "She moved through the fair" (an old Irish song).

When the song ended, all the kids sprang to their feet, exited the wedding hall, and headed for the gardens. Garon told the other kids to hide and that they would look for them in 10 minutes. "Are we really playing hide and seek with them?" asked PJ. "No way," said Garon, "but they don't know that". The boys all laughed as Garon had a plan to get away from the others. As soon as the kids ran to hide, the three boys ran straight for the fountain they had found earlier in the day.

Once they reached the fountain, there was a lane nearby they had planned on hiding in, but when they got to the fountain, they noticed what looked like a gold coin shining from the water. Garon leaned in to grab the coin, with the other two holding him so he wouldn't fall in. In the blink of an eye, they had vanished.

Lucy had spied on the boys and realised that they weren't playing hide and seek, so she called the other kids and told them. So, they all descended on the fountain to catch the boys out, but when they got there, they were nowhere to be found.

CHAPTER TWO
THE SALMON OF KNOWLEDGE

aron woke up and was pretty groggy. He looked around to see where he was and to check if Dillon and PJ were with him. He spotted the others close by and ran to check on them. The other two were asleep, and Garon tried to wake them up.

Once all three were awake and had regained their senses, Dillon quipped, "hey boys, what the hell just happened? It looks like we may have time-travelled or something." "Don't be silly. That's impossible, isn't it?" asked PJ. "Let's think things through," said Garon.

They scanned their environment to see where they were, as it wasn't the fountain they had reached into, to grab the gold coin. Close by, there was a large standing stone, and there was a mountain behind them. They found themselves at the bottom of a waterfall that poured from a gash in the rock. It had lots of vines growing down from the top of the waterfall.

A thundering sound emanated from it like a steady drum roll. It fed a river, which flowed like lifeblood to a forest downstream. It was a truly awe-inspiring sight. Lush green fields also surrounded them as far as the eye could see. "Well, boys, I think it's safe to say we are not at the fountain or the hotel," said Garon.

Garon's gaze returned to the river. The surface glinted like ice and looked refreshing. Bending down, Garon scooped his hand through the water and raised it to his mouth to quench his thirst. Dillon and PJ followed suit. "I wouldn't drink from a river in Clondalkin," said Dillon, and they all nodded in agreement.

The riverbank had lots of rocks lying loosely next to it, and the boys sat down on them to discuss their next move. Fish were jumping from the water, flicking their tails lazily before landing back in the water and darting back to safety into its depths. "They are trout," said Dillon. "They have lots of spots with rounded heads and a square tail. I catch them regularly back home," he said. "Thanks for the fishing lesson," said PJ. "Maybe it would be better if you could figure out how to get home" "now, now boys, we'll figure something out," said Garon.

It was a warm sunny day, and the boys lay down on the grass to relax, still confused by their situation. They could smell wildflowers growing nearby and marvelled at how clean the air was compared to back home. After a while, the boys decided they should go to the forest to see if they could forage for food. It was only a short stroll to reach it.

As they got nearer, they could get an earthy smell and the smell of pine cones and rotting wood. When they reached the forest, scents on the wind reached them, and there was no mistaking the smell of wood smoke. "There is someone close by," said PJ. "Let's see who it is". They could hear someone singing as they walked closer, but it wasn't in English.

The song was familiar to Garon, as his dad often sang Irish songs at home. Close by, the words bellowed out.

Trasna Na Dtonnta Dul Siar Dul Siar
Slán Leis An Uaigneas Is Slán Leis An Gcian
Geal É Mo Chroí Agus Geal Í An Ghrian
Geol 'Bheith Og Filleadh Go hÉireann
Chonaic Mo Dhóthain De Thíortha I Gcéin
Ór Agus Airgead Saibhreas A' Tsaoil
Éiríonn An Croí 'Nam Le Breacadh Gach Lae
'S Mé A' Druidim Le Dúthaigh Mo Mhuintir
Trasna Na Dtonnta Dul Siar Dul Siar
Slán Leis An Uaigneas Is Slán Leis An Gcian
Geal É Mo Chroí Agus Geal Í An Ghrian
Geol 'Bheith Og Filleadh Go hÉireann

The boys came to a clearing in the forest close to the water's edge. There on the riverbank was a male fishing away without a care in the world, while singing away to his heart's content, as his long, blond, shoulder-length hair swayed in the breeze.

He looked taller than all the boys by at least a couple of inches and had a very athletic build. He was wearing a green tunic-like garment that hung just below the buttocks with the sleeves rolled up to his elbow. He wore a belt around his midriff and brown trousers rolled up to the knee. Close by, there was a staff and a pair of shoes made from cowhide. As they got closer to him, they could see that he was a similar age to themselves, with a sun-kissed complexion, the kind that someone used to living outdoors would have.

"Hello," said Dillon, "What are you fishing for?". This startled the boy, who dropped his fishing rod, a branch with some string and a hook at the end. He grabbed his staff and lunged at the three boys, who were equally startled by his aggression. Garon put his hands in the air and said, "We mean you no harm".

"Cé hé tusa" asked the boy. "Ah, you're having a laugh, boys," said Dillon. "We must be in the Gaeltacht" (regions in Ireland where Irish is the spoken language). Luckily, Garon could speak the language. "I always knew there was a reason for learning Irish," giggled Garon.

"Garon is ainm dom, seo Dillion agus PJ (I'm Garon and this is Dillon and PJ).

"Cad is ainm duitse?" (Who are you?) asked Garon "Is mise Deinmhe," said the boy.

"Cad atá á dhéanamh agat?" (What are you doing?) Asked Garon. With this, the boy put down his staff and appeared much more relaxed.

He told Garon that he was fishing for a unique fish that his master had wanted him to catch, but he had been fishing for many hours and had not caught the fish his master required.

Garon repeated to Dillon and PJ what Deinmhe had said to him, and Dillon asked what was so special about the fish as he was a master fisherman. When Garon asked about the particular fish, he told him that his master had said it was a King salmon and that its flesh would have a deep red colour. "Nah," said Dillon, "Salmon aren't red". Deinmhe told Garon it was one of a kind and not to be damaged or eaten by anyone other than his master.

They looked at a pile of fish that Deinmhe had amassed during his many hours of fishing, and they were all trout. Dillon explained to the boys that the trout would have a round head, lots of spots and a square tail, but the salmon would have a pointed head with fewer spots and a forked tail. Oh, and the salmon they wanted would be reddish. Dillon sarcastically said that the fishing rod wasn't exactly a premium model like he was used to back home.

The boys broke off some branches and got some string and hooks from a bag that Deinmhe had with him. A little while passed, and no one was having any luck, so they thought they might need to revise their plan.

Garon came up with a plan. He remembered from a history class he once had about saint Brigid's well that there were rushes used to make the saint Brigid's cross. He recollected seeing some vines hanging by the waterfall and that if they interwove them together on a larger scale than the cross, they could make a fence or net of sorts.

The river was very narrow at a certain point, so they could make a fixed fence at this point in the river and weigh it down with some rocks they had sat on earlier and stop anything swimming by it. They then made a longer one for the widest parts of the river. The width of the river was about 11 feet wide, and the narrowest was about three feet wide.

It took a few hours to get the fences built, and the boys started at the waterfall, one boy on each bank with Garon in the water holding the fence down. He would stamp and bang the water with a stick to frighten any fish towards the fence at the narrow part of the river. There Deinmhe would wait with a third fence. Once a fish swam past him, he would raise the fence so the fish was trapped. The plan was to release any more trout caught as there were enough already caught earlier in the day.

The boys soon got into a rhythm, and the plan was working a treat. A few hours passed with many trout caught and released. The boys were all beginning to tire, but just as night fell, there was a mighty splash in the water. A large fish jumped out of the water and gave an almighty splash as it landed in the water again near the fixed fence.

Deinmhe raised the fence as quickly as he could. As the other three boys were close by, they all dived into the river between the two fences and grabbed the biggest fish they had ever seen. All four boys let out an enormous cheer, but as it was getting dark, they couldn't tell if this was the fish they craved so badly.

Deinmhe packed their prize in some large rhubarb plant leaves growing nearby to protect until the morning as his master, the druid Finnegas, would return then, and Deinmhe dared not do anything to the fish for fear of what his master might do. Instead, the boys put more wood on the fire and cooked the trout Deinmhe had caught earlier in the day. Once they all had their fill, they all lay down to have a good night's sleep with full bellies after their very eventful day.

The following day when they had awoken, none of them felt energetic or rested as they had each had a restless night as they weren't used to sleeping outdoors, especially in a forest where branches were creaking, animals chattering and howling in the distance, leaves were rustling, and the wind was whistling around them. It certainly wasn't the home comforts they were used to.

"I was hoping it was all a dream," said PJ despairingly. "Me too," quipped Garon. "Where's your sense of adventure, boys?" laughed Dillon. They then remembered that they now had a fourth team member, but where was he?

Just then, there was a rustling noise coming from some bushes and out walked Deinmhe. "maidin mhaith mo chairde codlatach" (Good morning, my sleepy friends) said Deinmhe. "Cá raibh tú" (where were you?) asked Garon. Deinmhe said he was out foraging for food to cook the fish in. Just then, the boys remembered they had caught an enormous fish the night before and never checked to see if it was indeed the unique salmon.

With that, Garon grabbed the bundle of rhubarb leaves they had packed the fish in. He let out a massive sigh in anticipation of what might be inside. As he opened the food parcel, he could see a forked tail. Then there were only a few spots and a pointed head, and there was undoubtedly a solid red hue from the skin. "Woo hoo, boys!" screamed Garon and all the boys danced in circles, chanting, "we caught the special fish!", while Deinmhe, slightly bemused by their actions, let out a roar of approval. The boys stopped dancing with the realisation that they didn't know why the fish was unique.

Suddenly there in front of the boys stood a wisened older man. Where did he come from? They thought, "máistir, tá tú ar ais" (Master, you're back), said Deinmhe. "Tá mé go deimhin" (I am indeed), said the stranger. Before them stood a man shorter in stature than any of them, and he was slightly hunched over.

He had long grey hair and an unkempt grey beard that dangled over his chest. He wore a long brown tunic that was all the way to his feet and cowhide sandals. Around his waist, on his right hip, dangled a small sack that also seemed to be made of cowhide. In his hand, he has a long staff with some reddish stone forged into the top.
Deinmhe introduced the man to the boys, telling them that this was his master, Finnegas.

He then told his master the strange tale of how the boys appeared from nowhere but had helped him to catch the King salmon. This brought an enormous smile followed by a cheer to Finnegas' face, and he shook each of the boys' hands, thanking them for their help in the almost impossible task.

With that, they inspected the fish, and Finnegas cheered loudly when he saw it, which confirmed to the boys that it was indeed the salmon of knowledge that he sought. Finnegas then instructed Deinmhe on how he wanted the fish prepared. They then set about lighting a fire to prepare for the cooking. Finnegas walked off into the forest, leaving instructions on how the fish was to be cooked but not eaten.

Then Deinmhe produced what seemed to be a large frying pan and filled it with water from the river. Next, he opened his sack from his earlier forage. It contained juniper berries, parsley & thyme, onions, and pine needles. He gently rubbed these onto the fish skin, then wrapped the fish and the other contents in the rhubarb leaves. He placed the large pan on the flames and put the fish parcel into the pan to steam in the leaves.

Not long after, Finnegas returned and told Deinmhe to open the parcel and check how the fish was cooking. Garon and Deinmhe took the fish off the heat and gently spread the rhubarb leaves apart. As they opened the leaves, they noticed two blisters on the skin of the salmon, and in unison, both tried to burst them. They each let out a cry of pain as they burned their thumbs, and both put their thumbs in their mouth to cool them down.

Finnegas let out a scream of despair as both boys fell to the ground. Dillon and PJ helped them both to their feet and asked them what had happened to them. Finnegas said, "NO, you have ruined everything" Garon was confused, as he could now understand Finnegas without translation. Finnegas, shouting angrily, explained how he had planned on being the first person to eat the fish as it would have given him untold knowledge but that the boys had ruined it by being the first to taste its flavours.

Finnegas said that his plans were ruined, and that he no longer had the appetite to eat it and stormed off to calm down. The four boys sat down on the ground and started eating the fish. As they ate the fish, Dillon said, "Oh, I wish I could understand what Deinmhe and Finnegas were saying as it's getting irritating with Garon having to translate for us all the time" "I wish I could understand you too" replied Deinmhe.

All the boys looked at each other in amazement. "I understood you then," said PJ as all the boys looked at the salmon and laughed. This brought Finnegas storming back, and he shouted that the salmon of knowledge could give the first person to taste it untold knowledge, but as the boys had all shared its meat, Dillon and PJ must have gained a little knowledge too!

The boys were overjoyed at their newly gained knowledge. They seemed to forget about their restless night and missing home. All four of them jumped to their feet and started dancing in circles, looping arms as they swung each other around. "Oh, thank you, mister salmon, oh thank you, mister salmon, for new knowledge, for new knowledge," sang the boys in unison before falling to the ground and laughing loudly.

WHAT'S IN A NAME?

nce Finnegas had calmed down, and rejoined the group to tell them what he thought had happened. He told the boys when he was a child growing up he had been told the legend of the Salmon of Knowledge and had searched for it in hope, more than in the expectation that he would ever catch it. He had thought that you needed to eat the fish to gain its knowledge, but once the boys dropped to the ground, it had proved futile, and the knowledge would no longer be his.

As the boys came to terms with their newfound knowledge, he would have to spend time with them. It amazed him that although Deinmhe and Garon had gained more knowledge, they could call on extra wisdom and knowledge by simply sucking on their thumb. As most of the plants and foliage were new to Garon, Finnegas had him walk the forest, and he let Garon tell him the names of all the plants and trees, etc., that they came upon to see if his hunch was correct. A few days passed, and he told the boys he could not teach them anything new as they would now be the master and him the student because of their newfound intelligence.

He told the boys that it was dangerous and that they would need to navigate their new world cautiously. Garon asked him if he knew why they had been transported there and if they could find a way home. Other than them finding a portal which the fountain they passed through obviously was. He had no other thoughts on how they might get home, though.

"Wait," said Finnegas suddenly. "If you ever get to the otherworld, you may find a leprechaun, and if you catch him, he may grant you three wishes, which may get you all home." According to legend, the King and most powerful of the Leprechauns was called

Fergus. He told them they were tricky deceptive creatures and explained that they weren't bad or good, they just existed, and if you did them a good turn, they might return the favour. He also said that if you capture one, never look away, as it could disappear if you did.

Garon asked Finnegas if there were any stone circles nearby as he remembered watching a tv programme about them. The programme said that stone circles used the earth's energy and that the natural acoustics and frequencies of the planet amplified the human cells harmonising the frequency with nature, possibly creating a tear in time and, therefore, creating a time portal. Once sandstone and granite that contained quartz and iron were used as they were needed to generate an electrical charge.

They could use the sun's power to generate energy if they were aligned to the north, south, east, and west and then aligned with the solstice and equinox. If humans touched the inner circle, the energy from the outer ring could create a field where the human body became harmonised and in sync with the earth's frequencies, creating a time loop.

"Wo! Wo! Wo!" shouted Finnegas. "I am going to like you, my friend! You didn't need the salmon's knowledge, and that is a fascinating concept," he laughed. "I have been in many stone circles where I felt energy, but never once thought it could be used to time travel." "Maybe we could build a stone circle to see if it could work," he said. "How could we build our own stone circle?" asked Garon, "it would take many people and many years to build one, and we want to go home now," he said.

"We build it the same way they built Stonehenge," said Finnegas. "As Garon said, that would take years," said Dillon, "and we want to go home now." "Not if we use this," said Finnegas, reaching into the sack he had tied to his right hip, pulling out a small copper rod. "There you are," he said. "What is it?" asked PJ.

"This, my young friend, is a levitation rod," replied Finnegas. "A what?" asked Dillon. "Surely you are joking with us?". "No, my young man," said Finnegas. "This is indeed a levitation rod." "How does it work?" asked Garon. "I cannot give you a proper answer other than to say that it uses acoustic effects from the earth, rendering anything you touch with it weightless," he said. "If an item becomes weightless, how can you make it have weight again?" asked Garon. Finnegas showed him the rod. It was broad on one end and narrowed on the other. Touching the wide end against an object made it weightless, and the narrow end gave its weight back. "Deadly," laughed PJ. "I can't wait to see that."

Finnegas then told the boys to pack up as they had some travelling to do. They set off northwards, and a day's walk later, they came to a large granite quarry. Finnegas looked into his sack again, pulling out four tiny pickaxes and giving them to the boys, telling them to break some large stones. The boys tried doing it, but it had little effect on the rock.

Finnegas then tipped his rod against the stone and told them to try again. Suddenly, a large stone was easily broken away from the bedrock, falling to the ground. Finnegas tipped the rod against the broken stone and told PJ to move it. PJ approached and pushed it. He could easily move the rock with little effort, to his amazement.

"This is cool," laughed PJ as all the boys gathered in a circle around the stone, pushing it to one another joyfully. "Come and join us," shouted PJ to Finnegas. "This is great fun!". Finnegas turned down the offer, saying, "the sooner we finish, the sooner we can try to get you back home". He tipped the rod on some more stones until they had five stones in total.

Finnegas and the four boys gathered behind a stone each and began pushing them effortlessly back to the standing stone where the lads had woken up when they travelled back in time. They then set about catching some fish for supper. The group all sat around talking and telling Finnegas stories from their lives back home until, one by one, they fell asleep.

The following day, they returned to the granite quarry and broke off another five stones before returning to the standing stone. They set up camp again, and this time Finnegas showed them some tricks and had all the boys transfixed and mesmerised until it was time to sleep again. Early the next morning, they all set off again to the quarry, breaking off five stones and pushing them back to the field.

The five of them sat around telling jokes and stories again until bedtime.

The following morning, bright and early, the group woke up, and Finnegas told the boys to raise all fifteen stones on their ends before moving them into a circular position around the standing stone. Once the boys had done this, Finnegas tipped each stone with the narrow end of the rod, and they crashed to the ground, embedding themselves in the soil. "This is just brilliant," said PJ. "What do we do next?". "Next," said Finnegas, "Next, we have some fun," he said. "All work and no play make it a very boring day."

They walked to the river, and Finnegas gave PJ the rod, telling him to use it on a rock. PJ did as he was told, and nothing happened. "Let me have a try," said Deinmhe, and again, nothing happened. Garon and Dillon also tried, but the rock didn't lose weight. Finnegas laughed loudly. "You are no druids, any of you." "I will need a new apprentice," he giggled. Just as he took the rod back, a fish leapt from the water and quick as a flash, he tapped it with the rod. The fish lay floating in the air as if frozen in time.

The boys and Finnegas all laughed and had great fun pushing the fish through the air to each other until Finnegas finally tapped it again with the rod and the puzzled-looking fish fell back into the water before darting away. For the rest of the day, Finnegas tipped different items, such as a small tree, and the boys could easily lift it from the ground and pass it around as if they were playing football. It reminded the boys of being back home, and they had a delightful day.

The following morning the group set off, only this time going southwards until a day's march later, they came to a sandstone quarry. This time Finnegas tapped the stone twice, low and high, and the boys could quickly break off larger stones than before until, again they had five large stones, before pushing them back to their new stone circle, then setting up camp for the night.

He told the boys they would need to make five trips this time, as they would need extra stones for the outer circle. The following morning, they set off and reached the quarry. Finnegas tapped twice on the stone face, but the boys struggled and made no impact on the stone. Finnegas laughed as he had intentionally used the wrong end of the rod to play a joke on them. He then tapped with the right end, and they easily broke the stones before returning them to the stone circle.

The third and fourth days were the same until the last day of their fifth journey. Finnegas tapped the stone face, and the boys all broke the stone. This time, however, PJ kicked his rock like a football and almost broke his toes as Finnegas tipped the stone with the wrong end.

The other three boys fell to the ground, laughing as a disgruntled PJ sat on his rock, arms crossed and sulking. Finnegas tipped PJ with the rod and lifted him into the air. This cheered him up completely, and he flipped and turned himself in the air until Finnegas tapped him, and he fell to the ground with a thump. This time, though, he got back to his feet and saw the funny side of it.

They all returned to the circle and set up camp for the night. They would start fresh in the morning. The following morning, they all woke, and as previously, Finnegas told all the boys to stand all 25 large sandstones on their ends before moving them into place. One by one, they fell to the ground with a thundering sound once Finnegas had given them a tap with the rod.

"What happens now?" asked PJ. "I am not sure," said Garon. "I think we need to touch the centre stone and wait until sunset." With that, Finnegas and Deinmhe said their goodbyes and returned to camp in the forest while the boys waited until nightfall.

Sunset came and went, and nothing happened. The three boys were all sad and disheartened by the non-event, that didn't take place and trudged off back to the forest in search of Finnegas and Deinmhe. Once they reached them, they told them the bad news. "Oh no, we're stuck with you now," laughed Finnegas. Garon asked Finnegas if he might have any other ideas on how they could get home. He told them that his teachers, the Tuatha Dé Danann, a supernatural race that lived in the Otherworld but could cross over to this world, may help if they could find them.

PJ asked Finnegas if there was anything in particular that they should look out for that might be of the most help or danger to them. With that, Finnegas sat there thinking for a while, rubbing his chin and scratching his head before finally telling them. "There are many things to look out for, but as with most things, there would be good and bad in everything," he said.

"There are Pookas, mischievous creatures that are changelings and can take on human or animal form and be good or evil". He also said that a legendary giant Benandonner in Scotland was heard saying he would come and conquer all of Ireland. Then there were hideous creatures like wolves, dragons and even vampires that could all be found in caves, swamps, mountains, forests, or anywhere.

"Last but certainly not least," he said, "there is the Fianna." Garon and Deinmhe both looked puzzled by this. Garon said to him, "I have read books in my time about the Fianna and always thought they were good people?", "Indeed, they aspire to be good people, my young friend," said Finnegas ", but alas, they have a leader who wants to bring a reign of destruction down on the land," he said. "I have a story to tell you about young Deinmhe," he said.

Once upon a time, some 19 years ago, there lived a girl named Muireann, who fell in love with Cumhail, the leader of the Fianna warriors. Her father was Tadg mac Nuadat, a druid who lived on the hill of Almu. He had foreseen that her marriage would lead to him losing his home, so he had never given his blessing to any potential suitors. This then forced her to run away with Cumhail.

Outraged by this, Tadg appealed to the High King of Ireland, Conn, to help him save his honour. Conn agreed and forbade the relationship between the two, sending his troops after the newly outlawed Cumhail. The armies of Conn and Cumhail met at the Battle of Cnucha, where Cumhail was slain by Goll Mac Morna, one of Conn's generals (who then became the leader of the Fianna).

Goll, an enormous man, who easily over six and a half feet tall and was almost as wide, lost his right eye in his fight with Cumhail. During the battle, Cumhail was winning the fight but was stabbed in the back by Luachra, one of Goll's soldiers. This gave Goll the upper hand, and he finally landed a fatal blow on Cumhail.

Muireann was returned to her father, but they discovered she was pregnant. Outraged and ashamed of her, Tadg rejected her and ordered his followers to have her killed. King Conn refused this and sent her to the Druidess Bodhmall, Cumhail's sister. Muireann gave birth to a son called Deinmhe, who, even as an infant baby boy, still had enemies because of who his father was.

Muireann had no choice but to leave her son with Bodhmall in Ballyfin, a small village in the Slieve Bloom Mountains. Bodhmall and her companion Liath, known to be skilled warriors and hunters, brought Deinmhe up in secret. They hid him in the forest and taught him to be a great warrior and hunter. They honed his skills, preparing him for the challenges ahead of him. Word of young Deinmhe was spreading, and Bodhmall and Liath were worried his father's enemies might find him, so she had to hide him to protect his identity.

They sent him to work in the service of several local kings, but he would be recognised as Cumhail's son each time. In fear of being unable to protect him, they forced him to move away again and again, until he eventually ended up with Finnegas. Together they had travelled the land for several years, hiding in the plains and the forests, waiting for the day when he could claim his rightful title.

"My friends," said Finnegas, "I give you Fionn Mac Cumhail." No longer would he be Deinmhe but Fionn or Fair one.

Finnegas then told all four boys that their time together had ended and that they must go out into the world and find their own destinies. First though, they needed to change a few things. "We need to start with these awful clothes you are wearing as you stand out a mile off," he said.

He took the sack he had tied to his right hip and said this is no ordinary bag. There are only two of its kind in existence. It is called a corrbolg, a magical purse that can carry an unlimited number of items, either magic or non-magic. I have one, and the other is held by Luachra, the fiend who stabbed Fionn's father in the back and robbed it from his dead body.

He then told the boys to reach inside and let the bag choose what they needed. One by one, the boys put their hands into the bag and out came clothing items in their favourite colours. Garon now had black trousers with a teal tunic and cowhide shoes. Dillon had grey trousers and black tunic, and cowhide shoes. PJ had black trousers with a white tunic and cowhide shoes. The boys all tried on their new outfits except Fionn, who was already wearing what the bag had chosen for him previously.

Next, they were told to grab a weapon, as they were currently unarmed. Garon leaned in and pulled out a sword, Fionn leaned in and pulled out a spear, Dillon pulled out a Staff Sling while PJ leaned in and pulled out a dagger. All the boys fell to the ground, mocking PJ over his little weapon. Though he wasn't amused in the slightest. The laughter soon ended when Finnegas said these weapons had chosen the individual for a reason and that they were no ordinary weapons.

The sword was called Mac An Lúin, and in times of the greatest danger, it would save its master, as one strike could take down almost any enemy. Fionn's spear was called Birgha and was a venomous spear that could poison whoever or whatever it touched, while Dillon's Staff Sling (which comprised a long staff with a short sling at one end for hurling projectiles) was called Crann-Tabuáll. The staff didn't have magical powers, but the slingshot could attack from a distance. Fergal's dagger, or Claíomh Solais, was a dagger that, when unsheathed, gave off an intense light, enabling the holder to see in the darkest of places.

Next, the boys should each reach into the bag and take a necklace and ring. The necklace for each boy was the same, and it warded off spells cast by druids upon them so they could not be corrupted or turned into animals (a popular druid spell). Garon picked a ring with a bear symbol, Dillon picked one with a cheetah symbol, and PJ picked one with a chameleon.

Finnegas told the boys that if they ever needed to use the rings, they should rub them clockwise once to unlock an extraordinary power, but only use them if required, as the spell would only last for one minute. Garon's bear ring granted extra strength, Dillon's cheetah ring granted extra speed, and PJ's chameleon ring let him blend with his surroundings. All very useful indeed, insisted Finnegas.

Fionn didn't need any of these as unknown to him as his mother was a druid, and, as part of his lineage, was immune to druidic spells. Still, if he said Goliath, it would give him great size and strength for a short period. He also had healing hands that could cure minor injuries. The boys were also given hip sacks to carry items in. (This was handy for their headphones and mp3 players especially).

Finnegas said that the boys would need to change their names as their actual names would draw attention to themselves. Garon would now be known as Darragh (strength, vitality, and wisdom.), Dillon would now be known as Shane (swift-footed warrior), and PJ would become Fergal (brave and courageous), While Deinmhe, as we knew, would be known as Fionn (The fair and wise one).

Finnegas told Fionn that he should visit his aunt Bodhmall as a matter of urgency. He then said his goodbyes to the four boys, but left them with some parting words. "It is hard to take a life, but sometimes it is unavoidable, and the gods won't hold it against you," he said. "Make sure you are prepared as it is coming, and you will need to kill, or be killed. I tell you this, as I know this is something you may struggle to deal with."

One by one, the boys all gave Finnegas a big hug and thanked him for all his help. As the boys walked away, they were all thinking about his last words. Could any of them possibly take a life? Would they have to? And could they avoid it? Only time would tell.

CHAPTER THREE
A BROTHERHOOD OF FOUR

With heavy hearts, the four boys looked back until they saw Finnegas fade into the distance. "Well, boys, what are we gonna call each other?" Asked Dillon. "Call me Fionn going forward," said Fionn. "Good call," said Garon. The rest of us should also call each other by our alternative names to get used to them. All four agreed and carried on with their journey.

After travelling for many miles, they came across a river and followed it for a bit until they came across a quarry. Shane noticed some metal fragments and nice-sized stones that would be ideal for his slingshot. All four boys looked around and gathered as many as they thought would fit into his hip sack. It began raining, and as night fell, they sought shelter for the night. Fergal came across a cave but noticed many bones lying on the ground outside, surrounded by what seemed to be many dog footprints.

He called the others to come over as the rain fell heavier and they all willingly stepped inside. They heard what they thought was the sound of crying puppies and moved further in to investigate. Shadows started moving inside, and they could hear low growls. Fergal unsheathed his dagger, and it lit up the tunnel. In front of them was a pack of angry wolves. The boys all drew their weapons and backed out slowly, keeping the now snarling beasts at bay.

When they got outside, the wolves followed and began encircling them. "Move to the river," said Darragh, "they don't like water". The boys stood back-to-back and moved towards the river, shouting and waving their weapons to frighten the wolves. Shane took some stones from his hip sack and threw them at the one that was closest to him. He hit it right between the eyes, and it let out a loud squeal before running away. They were still surrounded, though, and slowly edged towards the river. Once they reached the river, the boys carried on into it until the wolves stopped following them. Luckily, the river was just above waist height, so that they could get to the other side without difficulty.

Once they got out on the other side, they ran to safety. The rain pummelled down, and the boys had to get to shelter. They came across a small opening in a wooded area and set up camp for the evening. Fionn told the others to gather some dried leaves and twigs so he could start a fire. He reached into his hip sack and pulled out two pieces of wood. The first was flat with a hole, and the second was a harder, small circular piece of branch.

When they had the twigs gathered, he began by twisting the circular piece of wood into the hole in the flat piece between his hands as fast as he could. Suddenly, the twigs began to smoke and catch fire. "deadly", said Shane, "I have never seen that done before". The boys then began breaking small branches and throwing them onto the fire.

"Hey, boys," said Shane. "A pack of wolves chased us, so how about we call ourselves a pack or something?" he said. "How about a brotherhood?" he said. "Yes, that's a good idea," said Darragh. "A brotherhood of four." They all lay down to sleep, happy that they were now a brotherhood.

As they woke the following day, they noticed the fire still going, but Fionn was nowhere to be found. They then heard singing and crept over to check, and there he was, singing away at the river with his fishing rod in hand. Soon enough, he had enough fish caught, and they brought them back to the fire to cook. Once they all had their fill, they extinguished the fire and prepared to leave. "Where are we going again?" asked Fergal. "To see my aunt Bodhmall in Ballyfin," said Fionn.

As they continued their journey, they came across a small farm with what looked like a flock of birds flying over the house. A woman and three boys were wearing old tattered tunics and waving torches at the birds. As the boys got closer, they could see that this was no flock of birds. It was something else entirely. It looked like a mist of ghoulish heads snapping at the torches. Fionn began sucking his thumb and, in a transfixed state, said, "This is a sluagh there must be someone ill in the house". "What's a sluagh?" asked Shane. "It is a creature who collects the souls of the dead," said Fionn.

Darragh approached the woman, who was frantically shouting and waving the torch at the sluagh. He asked if there was anyone ill in the house. The woman told him that her husband had broken his leg and had a terrible fever. Darragh then told his brotherhood, who were all waving their weapons at the sluagh. Fionn entered the house, where he found a man in lots of pain writhing around on his bed.

He remembered Finnegas had said he had healing hands, so he set about getting the man to lie still. Once the man was calm, he rubbed his hands together to heat them, then placed them on either side of the break in his leg. After several minutes, the man's leg seemed to get better, and his fever had broken.

The woman came running in, shouting that the creature had gone. The man stood up from the bed, put his weight on his broken leg, and felt no pain. With that, the brotherhood and the other three boys came in. All seemed overjoyed! "Good on ye," said Darragh.

The woman thanked Fionn and said she wished she could repay them. He told her that a nice warm dinner and bed for the night would be great, to which the woman duly obliged by making a big stew for them to eat. They lay on some straw on the floor next to the fire and fell asleep for the night.

The next morning the woman gave them a loaf of bread, and they continued their quest to find Fionn's aunt. "How far is it to Ballyfin?" asked Shane. "It should take three days travelling through fields and forests," said Fionn. "What if we travel by road?" asked Shane. "Only a day and a half," said Fionn. "I say let's go by road," said Shane. Fergal reminded them that Finnegas had advised them to avoid the roads and travel unnoticed. "Let's take a vote," said Shane, to which he won by three votes to one.

As the day carried on, they got hungry, but as they were not near a river, Fionn set a trap to see if he could catch some food. They hid nearby to wait and see. Soon enough, they heard a loud noise and ran to check it out. There in the trap was a large hare. Darragh remembered Finnegas' words about killing and could not bring himself to kill it. Fionn had no problem, as he had done it many times before.

After a fire was lit, they cooked the prepared hare and sat down to have a nice supper of hare and bread. Once supper was over, they bedded down for the night. All except Fergal, who was still nervous that they might be too close to the road. He instead moved away a little to have a cold, dark sleep away from the fire.

Fergal was awoken abruptly by loud sounds of laughter coming from the camp, and he crawled over silently to check what was going on. To his horror, there was a group of six men all laughing, and as he looked closer, he could see Fionn, Darragh, and Shane were all hogtied and gagged, lying on their stomachs. One man said, "I'm sure this is the son of Cumhail, and he will bring us a nice reward." The men had some wine and began toasting each other while throwing logs on the fire.

Fergal waited patiently until the men fell asleep and crept quietly to release his companions. Once he reached Fionn, he took out his dagger to cut the ropes, but to his horror, he forgot it would light up, which woke up the six captors. He freed Fionn just in time. Fionn reached for his weapon, and just as he was about to be attacked by his captors, he shouted, "Goliath".

Suddenly he grew at least two feet taller and, with a swing of his spear, connected with three of his captors, knocking them off their feet. Fergal jumped on the back of another, trying to choke him while Fionn faced off against the other two with his spear. The other two boys squirmed helplessly on the ground, unable to help.

As one captor bore down on him, Fionn lunged forward with his spear, killing him instantly. The second got scared and ran off into the darkness. The other three got back to their feet and attacked him again. Fionn lunged forward, killing a second one, while the other two ran off into the darkness. Still struggling to choke his opponent, Fergal was tossed from his back, and he ran off into the night as well.

Fergal ran over and cut the ropes from Darragh and Shane. They jumped to their feet and thanked Fergal for his help. "Don't slag my little weapon again", grinned Fergal. Shane ran to Fionn and shouted "high five" while throwing his hand in the air. Fionn just stared at his friend quizzically, While Darragh and Fergal laughed out loud.

After such an event, no one could go back to sleep. Indeed, no one even tried to. They just sat there, taking stock of what had just happened. At sunrise, the boys decided it was only fitting to bury the two dead men, so they dug a large hole and put the bodies into it, then covered them up again. "result" shouted Shane, and the others rushed to check. Tied up close by were six horses. The horses had ropes around their necks as leads and cowhide blankets on their backs to be used as saddles.

The boys mounted four of the horses while setting the others free. "Maybe we should avoid the roads from now on," said Fergal. The others were all in agreement after the ordeal they just had, and now they had horses. It would be much quicker and easier to reach their destination than on foot.

Darragh quizzed Fionn about how he felt about killing a person, to which he answered. Finnegas was right to kill or be killed, and he felt no guilt as he was protecting himself and his friends. Darragh gave a nod of approval, and they rode on in search of their destination. "I wish I had a Goliath spell," said Fergal.

"With your little weapon, you might turn into a spear," said Shane as they all roared with laughter except for Fergal, who again was unimpressed at being made fun of. "Lighten up," said Darragh. "You know he's only winding you up, don't you? Let's measure weapons to see who's got the biggest," he said while nearly falling off his horse with laughter.

Onwards they rode through lush green fields and small woodland areas in search of their destination. They were all happy with the horses, making travel easier. All were in good spirits except for a moody Fergal, who was lagging behind the others. How could they treat him like this after his heroic rescue, a disgruntled Fergal thought to himself?

Bran And Sceolan

ight was falling when they reached the small village of Ballyfin. It had been several years since Fionn had lived there, and he was unsure where his aunt Bodhmall lived. It was only a tiny village and unlike any that the boys were used to.

The houses were oval-shaped with large poles placed into the ground to strengthen and support the structure of hazelwood branches and twigs that were interwoven to create the walls, which were then covered in white limestone to insulate them, while there was a conical thatched roof on top. They sporadically built the houses in a circular arrangement close to each other. There were torches lit outside each of the dwellings.

Darragh called to one house and knocked on the door. A man dressed poorly with a dirty appearance opened the door and greeted him, asking what he could do for him. Darragh explained they were looking for a woman called Bodhmall. The man told him she lived a half mile away up a hillside close to a forest and river. He warned him to be careful, as there were strange goings on up there. Darragh thanked the man and returned to his friends.

They mounted their horses and carried on slowly up the hillside, keeping a close eye out for any strange goings on. They soon came upon a house built the same as the ones in the little village, but there were also many wooden outhouses surrounding it. This house too, had a torch outside the door. The boys dismounted and cautiously made their way to the door. "Let me knock," said Fergal as he stood forward, leaving the others in the shadows.

He then gave the door a loud knock. He could hear heavy footsteps crossing the floor and the door opening.

There in front of him stood an Amazonian-looking woman, easily over six feet tall. She was broad with shoulder-length red hair. She was wearing a brightly coloured striped tunic with chequered trousers. There was a sword in her hand and she was wearing cowhide boots. "Who are you" she shouted. "We are the brotherhood of four", replied Fergal with a quiver in his voice. Loud laughter came from the shadows as the boys found his answer amusing.

Bodhmall leapt out the door to see who was lurking in the shadows. "My beautiful Deinmhe," she said as she caught sight of her now grown-up nephew. "I would recognise you anywhere, my dear nephew". "Liath", she roared ", come quickly and see who is here". With that, her friend Liath came out of the house. She was dressed similarly to Bodhmall and, although much smaller in stature, still looked like a woman not to be messed with.

"Our beautiful, grown-up boy," she said as she leapt forward to give him a big embrace. "You have finally come home to us after all this time." The three of them then hugged each other as Bodhmall shouted, "We must have a feast in your honour to welcome you home."

She was then introduced to the other boys by Fionn, who were all given great big hugs by the two women. They all entered the house, closing the door behind them. Inside the house was a gigantic fireplace with wooden chairs and a table in the main room. There were also three bedrooms with two beds made from animal hide covering a pile of straw. "Where is the bathroom?" asked Fergal. "What is a bathroom?" asked Liath.

This gave rise to Darragh and Shane again, hitting the ground in laughter. The two confused women wondered what was so funny until Fionn explained how the boys came to be there. The women started laughing and Fergal, seeing the funny side, also joined in. "We must get ourselves one of them," said Bodhmall. "It would be better than the stream we use", she mused as poor Fergal looked on, almost apologetic. It was getting late, so the women told everyone to get a good night's sleep as tomorrow they would have a party.

The following morning, bright and early, a lovely smell of cooking woke the boys early. Over the fireplace was a big pot of stewed rabbits with carrots and cooked potatoes. The boys were each given a wooden bowl full to fill their bellies. When the food was eaten, Liath showed the boys the outhouses, and there were pigs in one, sheep in another, while a third contained hens and chickens. There was also a stable that had two horses. Close by was a corral with some cows eating grass from a trough.

In the furthest corner away from the house, they could see Bodhmall entering another outhouse with some of the stew. "Don't go there?" said Liath sharply. She gathered the boys, and they set off into the forest to forage for food for the feast. They split up and searched for food, with Liath warning them to be careful as there were dangerous creatures about.

A short time later, Shane was bent down, picking up some mushrooms from the base of a tree, when he heard a noise above his head. When he looked up, stuck in the tree was Darragh's sword and Darragh rushing towards him. He had seen a giant python sneaking up on Shane and had slain it with a throw of his sword. Kill or be killed, he thought to himself.

Soon everyone had made their way back to the farm, armed with their loot. They had carrots, potatoes, mushrooms, turnips, a rabbit and even a snake. By now, Bodhmall had started a big fire in the centre of the yard. Above it was an enormous cauldron filled with water, awaiting the ingredients. A short time later, the rabbit and snake were skinned, chopped up and added to the water, followed by the vegetables.

Darragh quizzed Bodhmall about the outhouse in the corner but was told it was nothing to worry about. The food was ready soon after, and everyone had their fill. Liath, with Shane's help, entered the house and came back out carrying a giant harp. It was time for some music. It turned out that Liath was an expert at playing the harp and began playing some enchanting music, but when she sang, it was almost mesmerising.

Bodhmall came out with a small barrel of mead that she brewed herself. "Let's have a toast," she said, "To the brotherhood of four" she giggled as Fergal said, "I'm not old enough to drink". "What's your mam going to say?" asked Darragh with a giggle. Fergal saw the funny side (His mam wasn't here) as he took a big gulp from his cup. The mead flowed, and all had a good time. As Liath played the harp, the four boys and Bodhmall all danced in circles, linking each other as they danced.

Suddenly, a loud squealing sound brought Bodhmall to the outhouse, closing the door behind her. She returned, got a large bowl of water, and then returned once again to the outhouse. This increased the boy's curiosity, and they wondered what was going on there. "Well, everyone always says I'm a rogue," said Fergal as he sneaked over to look. Liath stopped him in his tracks and he returned like a scolded child. "Better luck next time," said Shane as Fionn gave him a high five!

"Off to bed with you now," said Liath. "I will see you in the morning". The boys entered the house, and all began talking about what could be happening. Soon they fell asleep but were awoken by a loud wailing sound. The boys crept over and peeped out of the door. Near the outhouse in the corner was a floating, spectral figure wailing and screaming. It looked like an old woman with frightening red eyes, a black dress, and long white hair. She carried on screaming and wailing while she was combing her hair.

"Holy shit, boys," said Darragh. "I never believed they were real, but that's a banshee." "A banshee!" screamed Shane, "but that means one of us is going to die tonight." "No," said Darragh, "but someone close by is going to die tonight." This brought Liath out of her bedroom, and she ushered the boys off to bed. The boys were worried for Bodhmall, as she was nowhere to be seen.

The next morning, the boys woke up and made their way to the main room. Liath told them to sit at the table while she made breakfast. They all sat there ashen-faced as they were worried, as there was still no sign of Bodhmall. Suddenly the door opened, and in she walked.

This brought a smile to the boy's faces, and they all jumped up and hugged her. "We were worried about you," said Darragh, as we heard and saw a banshee last night and thought you might have died. "You won't get rid of me that easy", she replied. "Although I have some news to share with you later".

They all walked outside to get some air, and Bodhmall brought Fionn over to the outhouse in the corner. They entered, closing the door behind them. The other boys were summoned a short time later and made their way to the outhouse. When they got inside, over in one corner of the room, on a bed of straw, lay a beautiful, tall, pale-looking woman who seemed to be asleep. In the other corner sat Fionn, cuddling two puppies. "Where did they come from?" asked Shane.

Bodhmall sat the boys down, as she had a tale to tell. The woman in the corner was a cousin of theirs named Uirne. She had fallen in love and had run away with a man. Her father, who was a powerful druid, hunted them down. Upon finding them, he killed the man only to find out that Uirne was pregnant by him. For bringing shame on the family, her father enchanted her and turned her into a Large Irish wolfhound dog and a dog she would remain until her death.

Sadly, the banshee wailing the previous night was for her, as giving birth to two puppies was too great an ordeal to survive. The spell her father had put on her meant she would never have children, and although she had returned to her human form in death, any offspring would forever remain as dogs. They could have human emotions and feelings but would never be human. Fionn had been summoned first as he would be their master.

All attention turned to Fionn, sitting in the corner cuddling the two dogs. There was a black male dog and a grey female dog. "I shall call my new friends Bran (Raven) and Sceolan (Silver) as he is black like a raven, and she shines like silver, and I will love them forever," said Fionn.

Soon after, Bodhmall asked Fionn to wrap Uirnes's body in a blanket, and they disappeared into the forest to bury it. Upon their return, they had some bad news to share. Fionn was returning to his master, Finnegas, while the other three boys would remain with Bodhmall and Liath. It turned out that the reason Finnegas said they had to visit Bodhmall was that the boys needed training, as they were unprepared for their new world.

Later that day, Fionn gave everyone a big hug as he prepared for his new journey; he then mounted his horse and said his goodbyes before riding off, followed by his new companions.

A WARRIOR I AM

ur brotherhood of four is no more," said Shane. "You're a poet and just don't know it, yet you speak in rhyme all the time," said Darragh. As the two gave each other a high five.

"I didn't see that coming," said Fergal as he sat on the ground with his chin resting in his hand. "No time for moping now," said Liath. "It's time to begin your training," she said. Bodhmall brought Darragh to a log pile, where she picked out the most significant log and told him to chop it with his sword.

He did so but made a minimal impression on the log. Next, Liath brought three hens out and let them free. She told Fergal to chase them and return them to the outhouse. He ran and ran, but the hens kept evading him while everyone else laughed loudly at his efforts. Next, Bodhmall brought Shane back down the hill and made him run back up.

The boys were very confused by how this would help them prepare for their new world. Next, Bodhmall brought Darragh out to the river nearby. It was a shallow river with some medium size boulders on one side. Darragh had to carry all the boulders from one side to the other. When he was done, he sat down, exhausted by the river. "We're only starting," said Bodhmall as she made him carry them back again.

This continued for the rest of the day until Darragh became quite frustrated at the monotony of it all. Shane had to race Bodhmall up the hill, which she easily won. He then had to run up and down again for hours while they gave Fergal a lot more hens to chase and capture while competing with Liath, who again caught them much more quickly than he did.

That night, the boys fell into bed with no supper, as they were so tired. After breakfast the following morning, it was the same routine until the boys collapsed with exhaustion again that evening. The same pattern continued for the next week until the boys finally approached their two trainers and said they had enough and wanted to leave. The next day, the boys were brought out into the forest, where they had to chop some logs.

They then had to return as they were to make a pigsty for the pigs. The following day, Darragh walked to the forest with Bodhmall to collect logs for the fire. He had to carry heavy logs while Bodhmall carried much lighter ones. In the pigsty, Shane and Fergal had to chase and catch all the pigs. It made it even more challenging running through sloppy mud while they kept sinking in it.

The same pattern followed for the next few days until the boys finally had enough, and again said they wanted to leave. Their trainers told them to be patient, as the next day would be different. The next morning, after breakfast, they all headed down to the river. "Not more stones," said Darragh, feeling dejected. "No," said Bodhmall, "today we will fish with our hands," she said.

All five of them got into the water and began looking for fish. There were plenty of laughs as they all tried and failed to catch anything but a mouthful of water. At least the boys were cheerful and spending time together again doing fun stuff. Although Liath said, it wasn't supposed to be fun as they were catching supper for later.

Darragh thought there must be a better way of catching them, and he began stacking the boulders across the river to make a dam. He told Fergal to stand near the dam and instructed Shane to wade down the river a bit until he spotted some fish. Bodhmall and Liath were fascinated and sat down on the bank to watch.

As soon as Shane saw a fish, he began running in the water, chasing the fish towards the dam. Fergal dived in and grabbed the fish, passing it to Darragh, who threw the fish over to the two women who were sitting there applauding their efforts. The boys repeated this until there was a fish each for supper. Once finished, they all made their way back to the farm, with the boys all singing a song. They all went to bed with full bellies that night, not suffering from exhaustion. They all woke the next morning feeling better and looking forward to the day ahead.

First, Bodhmall told Darragh to chop the original log again, which this time he did with ease. Next, she raced Shane up the hill, trailing far behind him, while Liath came a distant second behind Fergal, trying to catch the hens. All the boys gave each other high fives and danced in circles, linking with each other as they did.

"Well done to you all," said the women. As unknown to the boys, the boulder and log carrying was to increase Darragh's strength for wielding his sword. Shane had increased his speed as he needed to fight quicker with his staff, while Fergal had increased his agility for getting close to enemies with his dagger.

Now we can begin your next stage of training said Liath. They gave each boy a dagger and sheath to carry on his hip. "I already have a dagger," said Fergal. "Yes," said Bodhmall, "but this one won't light up giving you away". They also gave him a light shield to carry on his back without weighing him down. Bodhmall and Darragh proceeded to the forest, where they practiced with swords, and Liath would stay and train the other boys in using staffs and daggers.

Out in the forest, Bodhmall and Darragh armed themselves with their swords. Bodhmall raised hers above her head and kicked Darragh to the ground when he tried to block her with her sword still above her head. Embarrassed, he climbed back to his feet while putting on a brave face. Next, she raised her sword above her head again, and Darragh raised his sword to parry. Bodhmall sidestepped while pulling her dagger out, pretending to stab him in the leg. "You're good at this," said Darragh as he regained his composure.

Bodhmall then told him that there were eight main angles of attack with a sword when attacking, straight down, straight up, diagonally down to the right and diagonally down to the left, diagonally up to the right, diagonally up to the left and left and right strikes horizontally.

All of which could inflict deadly blows on the opponent. She also said it was best to be the offensive party rather than trying to counterattack, as it gave the upper hand and put the opponent on the defensive. They then practised all the best stances for stability and finished showing the best techniques for parrying a sword.

Meanwhile, Liath was busy with the other two boys at the farm. She took Shane to the side to teach him how to use his staff correctly. "Fighting with a staff is in your legs more than the weapon she said" "practice your stance to add force to your blows". "Move forward as you strike and sideways as you parry," she said. She also advised him to avoid backwards movement, as it was a disadvantage, and told him to avoid getting turned around, as turning his back on his opponent was not a good idea.

Then she showed him holding techniques, such as the most popular position, which was to hold the staff in thirds. One palm facing up and one palm facing down. There was also a narrow hold and a wide hold, which was used more for parrying than attack. They then had a sparring session, which didn't end well for the student, with him on the receiving end of a black eye.

Next, it was Fergal's turn to be trained with his dagger. Liath started by telling Fergal that a knife was one of the best and most necessary weapons he could carry as he could hunt, eat, fight and create with his dagger, which is more than can be done with a sword or staff. She told him that using a knife brought him closer to his enemy. It was essential to improve his agility, which was why he was chasing chickens and pigs.

She told him that while slashing moves were instinctive, the stabbing did the actual damage. She told him to make sure and put much practice and thought into his footwork and stance. "If you grip the knife on your right, your right foot should always be forward," she said. "Knowing how to dodge and check the knife hand of your opponent would be key to winning," she said.

She then showed him both offensive and defensive grips. While holding the knife in a forward grip allows for more finesse and a longer reach, a reverse grip allows for more power and less chance of taking damage. Last, she showed him how to parry although she avoided fighting in close contact to prevent either of them from being injured fighting at close quarters.

After a hard day's training, they all met again at the farmhouse. As the boys sat down at the table to wait for supper, a thrilled Fergal, with a grin from ear to ear, said, "I hope you know that my little weapon is better than yours". The other two boys laughed loudly and began teasing him again. After eating, all five sat down and talked about the day they had just had and what they would do the next day.

The following morning, Darragh had to train with Liath and daggers, Shane had to train with Bodhmall and swords, and Fergal wanted a day of relaxation as he didn't like handling large weapons. He left to lie down for the day by the river, enjoying the sunshine. As he lay there watching the clouds go by, he heard a low growling sound, only to look around and see an angry-looking wolf bearing down on him. Remembering his training, he took his dagger out of its sheath and turned head-on to face the wolf.

The wolf lunged at him, and he raised his hand and slashed the animal across the cheek. It squealed in pain as it landed, but turned to face him again. Once more, it lunged at him, but he remembered to stab rather than slash this time. This time, his blade sank deep into the wolf's flesh, and it let out an enormous squeal before running off.

That evening, as they all sat down to dinner, he told them of his encounter with the wolf and how his training had saved him. "Little weapons come in handy sometimes," laughed Shane.

The boys wanted to learn how to use a bow and arrow correctly, so they all set out in the forest the following day. The best practice they could do was to hunt, said Bodhmall. Each boy received a bow and quiver. They then set off searching for some prey, but all returned empty-handed. Lucky for them, Bodhmall and Liath had both killed some pheasants to allow for a substantial meal that evening.

For the next week, the days passed by in the same routine with their training, sword, staff, dagger, and bow. Defence, attack, parry and stance. Finally, Darragh bested Bodhmall in a sword fight, and Shane beat Liath with his staff. While Fergal just bragged that he fought a wolf. They were now ready to face the world. All they had to do was wait for Fionn to return.

A few days passed, and they were all sitting down to supper when the door opened, and in walked a stranger. Everyone jumped to their feet. Who could have the nerve to enter without being invited? He was tall with dark hair but wore clothing similar to that of Fionn. "What have you done with our friend?" shouted Darragh. Just then, in walked two Irish wolfhounds. "Tell us where our friend is", roared Shane. The two dogs lay down at the stranger's feet, and he laughed out loud.

"You had better have a good story to tell," said Bodhmall. "Relax", said the stranger. "I am only having a bit of fun", With that, he removed a small vial from his tunic and took a swig. Almost immediately, he had transformed into Fionn. He explained how Finnegas had sent him to spend some time with a witch. While there, the witch had created two batches of concealing potions.

One would change his appearance, while the other would return him to himself. Finnegas had devised the plan as he didn't see his future hiding out in the forests and wanted a better way to disguise him from his enemies.

To celebrate his return, Liath retrieved another barrel of mead, and they all shared a fun evening singing and dancing as they had done before they all retired to bed for the night. Bran and Sceolan slept by the warmth of the fire while the others all slept in their bedrooms.

Early the next morning, the boys woke early, only to find breakfast already waiting as Bodhmall and Liath had risen extra early to make a special breakfast. They had made some loaves of bread and cooked some chickens and eggs. When breakfast was eaten, Fionn informed the women that they must all be on their way, as their training was complete, and they now had a new mission. Reluctantly, they knew this time was coming, but they still asked all four boys to stay.

"What is our new mission?" asked Darragh excitedly. "I will tell you on the way," said Fionn. The four boys sadly said their goodbyes before mounting their horses. The women gave them some loaves of bread, chicken and eggs for their journey. They waved the two women goodbye as they slowly rode away. The two women seemed upset and hugged each other as the boys disappeared from view.

CHAPTER FOUR
THE FIANNA

After the four boys had travelled for many hours, they set up camp for the night close to a river's edge. They did some fishing and caught some fish (They were getting good at this now). They lit a fire and cooked their fish, along with some eggs. They heated the chicken, which had been cooked by Bodhmall and Liath, while giving some to Bran and Sceolan.

"Now, tell us our next mission," said Darragh as they all gathered around the fire. "Well," said Fionn ", We are going to join the Fianna". "What! are you mad?" asked Darragh with a puzzled look on his face. "Explain to me, who exactly are the Fianna, and why are we joining them?" enquired Fergal. "Well, boys," said Fionn. "Get cosy, and I'll fill you in properly", he said. He then began telling the others all he knew about the Fianna.

He started telling them what they already knew about his background. His father, Cumhail mac Trénmhoir, had led the Fianna before Goll Mac Morna took over after killing Cumhail, and Goll was still leading these warriors. The Fianna were a group of hunter-warriors who roamed the land, keeping peace and order as they saw fit. They were loyal to the high king of Ireland as he would feed and pay them regularly, but were also swords for hire in many disputes between tribes willing to pay them a wage. Their numbers were many, and they were stationed throughout Ireland.

There were never over 3000 in a battalion, and they had at least one battalion in each province (Ulster, Munster, Leinster, and Connaught). They had a robust code of ethics and were more than just hunter-warriors. They were required to have the highest intellectual calibre, be skilled in poetry and storytelling, and know music and genealogies and the histories of the provinces of Ireland.

Joining the Fianna wasn't a decision to be taken lightly. Those accepted into the group were members for life, and there was no change of heart allowed afterwards. Although you could marry, most of your time would be spent with the other warriors, with wives and families only allowed at times of feasting and rejoicing. There was an initiation that had seven stages to be passed before being accepted into the Fianna.

The stages were:

1. Intelligence

The first test that those looking to join the Fianna were given was one that put their intellect to the test. Men were required to be knowledgeable of twelve books of poetry, which detailed Ireland's legends, history and genealogy.

2. Defence

A person had to prove that he could defend himself adequately. He was required to stand in a deep hole and protect himself with a shield and a staff. He then had to defend himself from being struck by spears thrown by nine warriors.

3. Speed

The next test was to check speed and agility. You would be given a head start into a forest and be required to evade capture by a band of fierce pursuers. You must escape unharmed and escape the forest without breaking a single branch.

4. Movement

Next up was the movement test. You would have to leap over trees that stood at the same height as yourself, stoop as low as your knee, and make your way under the branch of a tree that stood just above shin height.

5. The Removal of a Thorn

The next test was a combined need for speed with a need to preserve oneself during battle. Candidates were required to sprint as fast as possible with a thorn stuck in their foot. It made this test more difficult by requiring the candidate to remove the thorn without slowing down at any point.

6. Bravery

The final physical test to become a member required a candidate to face many men without letting his bravery falter for even a second. This test ensured that the man would never back down, even when the Fianna were vastly outnumbered in battle. They could never run away.

7. Chivalry

The last test for becoming a member was all about character. As the Fianna were a very much-admired group, each member must act accordingly. They were required to accept several terms that, once agreed upon, would see them accepted as members of the Fianna. You must not marry out of greed for land or riches. They must marry only for love. They were also required to be courteous with women and never hoard something another needed.

"And that, my friends, is all we have to do to get into the Fianna," said Fionn with a grin on his face. "How do we even find the twelve books of poetry, let alone learn them off to even get past step one?" asked Darragh. "Well, it's funny you should ask that," said Fionn. "For when I was with the witch getting my potions, she had lots of books in her hut, and maybe we can find them there," said Fionn.

"Right," said Darragh ", after a night's rest, we will go straight to the witch's hut". The boys then bedded down for the night, but a restless sleep was had by all, just thinking about step one. None of the boys enjoyed the thought of having to learn and memorise twelve books, but they had to find them first.

Early the next morning, the boys set off to make their way to the witch's hut. They didn't even have breakfast and were eager to get there. When they were approaching a small wooded area, Fionn got off his horse and approached a small tree stump. *"Witch of the wood, witch in the trees, I beg you to show your home to me",* he called out. Suddenly, like a mirage, there in front of the boys was a little ramshackle of a hut.

It was ancient looking, almost falling apart, with old creaking timbers and smoke bellowing out of a small chimney on the roof. The door opened, and out came a relatively small, wisened old woman all dressed in black. She had a rather sizeable crooked nose and long white hair, but a friendly face. She had a large staff, which appeared to be made of oak, in her hand. It looked like she would fall over if not for the staff. *"Welcome friends, now please don't fear, to others we shall disappear"*. She had cast a spell, hiding her little hut from everyone except themselves.

She beckoned the boys inside and it was strangely bigger inside than out. A fireplace in the centre of the main living room had a large black cauldron hanging above it. There appeared to be bookshelves on every wall around the room except for a doorway into a single bedroom. There was also a large wooden table and chairs.

"Welcome, my friends she said, I have been expecting you. My name is Biddy, otherwise known as the witch in the woods." "Nice to meet you, witch in the woods," said Fergal. "Please don't turn me into a mouse." The old witch laughed as she spoke. "My dear boy, I am a white witch, I am a herbalist and a healer with some helpful spell's thrown in for good measure," "I don't mean to harm a hair on your head." She explained. "You've been reading too many books back home," said Shane.

"Now, my new friends, I was expecting you, and dinner is ready". With that, she cast a brief spell, and five full plates of food were laid out on the table. "I hope you like boar," she said. The plates contained boar, potatoes, carrots and mushrooms. They devoured the dishes in no time, and the boys thanked her for her kindness. With a wave of her staff, the plates were gone. "Finnegas told me to expect you," she said. "What may I do for you?".

"Well," said Darragh, "we hoped that you might have the twelve books of poetry that we may all read to gain entrance to the Fianna." "They are around here somewhere," said Biddy, again, casting a spell. One after another, all twelve books floated across the room and came to rest on the table. The boys all sat down at the table and began reading the books. "This is going to take forever," said Shane. "I'm never going to learn them off." "I may be able to help with that," said Biddy.

She walked over to one of her shelves and started rummaging around, picking up vials. "Ah, there you are," she said as she picked up one last vial. She proceeded to her cauldron and put three drops from each of the vials she had collected into it with some water. She then mixed the content in the cauldron and whispered a particular brewing spell. There was a puff of smoke from the cauldron.

"Here we go," she said as she filled four small cups with the brew. The boys all eagerly drank from the cup and felt a tingle inside. "What will it do for us?" asked Darragh. To which Biddy informed them they should each read a book, magically they could read and memorise it within a few minutes. Before the night was out, all four boys had read and learned all twelve books before falling asleep at the table, as there was only one bed for Biddy.

The next morning when they woke up, they quizzed each other, and sure enough, they all still knew the books by heart. All the boys shared high fives. Biddy arrived in the room, and they excitedly thanked her for her help. "You won't be the first people I have helped to join the Fianna," she said. "Ok, what's next on the list?" asked Biddy. The boys listed their requirements for defence, movement and speed and what was required for each.

Biddy cast her mind back and remembered making a special brew previously for a potential Fianna candidate that should be able to cover all these requirements. "Ah, here it is, in my potions book," she said. While going through the ingredients, she realised she needed a special flower called antirrhinum, which could only grow in the most demanding, dry, and rocky areas. It was renowned for its inner strength and power to overcome obstacles and challenging situations in life.

She knew it grew at the top of a mountain but could only be harvested at night as the bright blue flowers were only visible by moonlight. It would be a two-day ride to reach the mountain by horseback. She warned them that the mountain was supposed to be cursed and that the boys should be on their guard if they wanted to get the flower.

Anything that would help the boys in their quest needed to be done. They asked if they needed to say any words or spells to leave her hut, but she told them to get on their horses and ride east for two days until they reached the town of Kelshamore. This is a small town near the bottom of a mountain. They were to keep an eye out for three standing boulders with bullauns.

Once they came across these boulders, they should turn left, as the town was nearby. Biddy gave the boys some supplies and bid them farewell. The boys set off at a canter in search of their precious prize. The boy's rode, ate and slept for the next two days until they finally came across the three standing boulders. They took a sharp turn left and headed for Kelshamore.

THE ABHARTACH

hen they reached the town, it wasn't a pretty sight. It was covered in an eerie mist, and the people they saw moped about with their heads bowed, afraid to make eye contact with them. The boys heard a bell ringing and ran to investigate. There was a crowd of people gathered in the small yard, next to a sacred building, crying and wailing as they brought out a coffin to be buried. The boys all blessed themselves as a sign of respect for the unfortunate soul.

When the service had finished, the boys approached the druid, who was going into the building (nothing like the boys were used to back home). They asked him what had happened to the deceased person. The druid informed the boys that it was not a good time to visit their town as it had been plagued by an evil creature for the last few months. He said that people dare not leave their houses after dark for fear of being attacked.

The boys asked the druid where the mountain was, as it hid in the mist. He told them to go straight through the centre of the town, and they couldn't miss it. He warned the boys not to go as the evil creature had made its home in some ruins near the top. The boys then offered their services to the druid to rid the town of its problem.

The druid told the boys that the creature was an Abhartach. It was a dwarf-like creature and drank the blood of its victims. It sounded almost like a vampire. The boys said they needed to be very alert and keep their guard up.

They then set off into the centre of the town and onwards up the mountain. There was no let-up in the mist, and they could only see a few feet in front of them. Nonetheless, they travelled upwards, hoping to find the ruins and the creature. Night was falling, and the boys set up camp for the night and get a fire going.

Once the fire was lit, two of the boys would keep a lookout while the other two slept. This was to ensure their safety. Fergal and Darragh would keep the first watch. Fergal took out Claíomh Solais To light the surrounding area and give greater visibility. As Darragh looked at the two other sleeping boys, he drew his sword and lunged forward at them, taking the head clean off the Abhartach, a small pale human-like creature with large fangs that was kneeling over Shane, getting ready to attack.

The two sleeping boys woke up startled but grateful to still be alive. The boys took turns sleeping and watching the dead creature for the rest of the night. At daybreak, the boys buried the creature and returned to town to give them the good news. They stomped through the mist to tell the townspeople the excellent news. The druid was a little worried as the fog had not broken and had only appeared when the creature first appeared.

The boys stayed the night in town in case anything happened. That night, a local Shepard was indeed killed and drained of his blood, which meant the creature must still be alive.

"We never drove a stake through the heart," said Fergal as the boys shook their heads in disbelief, knowing they should have done that. They set off back up the mountain, but this time, they made it to the ruins where the creature lived. If it's a vampire, it must be in a coffin sleeping during the day, they thought.

As they entered the underground part of the ruins, the creature leapt forward towards Fionn. "Goliath", he roared as he instantly grew a few feet and gained his massive strength. He caught the creature mid-air by the throat and slammed it onto the floor. He stamped on its chest, crushing its heart, and again the creature lay dead.

The boys brought it back to where they buried it the first time, only to find the hole had been dug up. This time they buried it again, but not before forcing a stake through its already crushed chest. Then again, they made their way back down the mountain and straight to the druid to pass on their good news. The druid again shared his concerns as the mist had not lifted. So, the boys stayed another day.

Unfortunately, the boys were given the news the following morning that yet another Shepard had been killed during the night. This frustrated the boys. "What do we need to do to kill it?" asked Fergal. "Maybe we should burn it," he said. With that, Darragh stuck his thumb in his mouth and began sucking on it just as Fionn had started doing the same thing.

"Ah," said Darragh, with a big smile on his face. "Listen, lads", he explained. "It's not a vampire, it's actually a magical creature," he said. He then told the boys that the only way to stop it from returning to life was to prevent its magic from working.

It must be buried with its head down so that its magic couldn't work on resurrecting itself. The boys stomped up the mountain towards the ruins, not stopping for anything. When they reached the ruins, they could not find the creature. They returned to where they had buried it, and the hole was empty.

The best thing they could do was split into two groups of two and search for a greater area for the creature. Darragh was with Fergal, and Fionn was with Shane. As they approached a small stream, Fergal bent down to take a drink of water and saw in the reflection that the creature was perched on a branch on a nearby tree waiting to pounce, so he ushered Darragh away and drew his dagger.

As Fergal was still looking at the reflection, he watched as it leapt down at him. Just in time, he turned around and stuck his dagger deep into its chest, delivering a fatal blow. He shouted for Darragh to return, and they lifted the creature's lifeless body, carrying it back to the hole they had dug previously.

They called out for the other two boys, who swiftly returned. They would take no chances this time, so they dug the hole deeper. Darragh drew his sword and cut off its head, placing the head upside down in the hole. Fionn stamped on its chest, crushing it. Fergal forced a stake through its flattened heart before placing the body upside down above the head.

When this was done, Shane insisted on filling the hole with some nearby twigs and straw before setting the body alight. "There better be no coming back from that", he shouted as the boys laughed and cheered, thinking their job must be done.

When the flames died, the boys filled in the hole, burying the creature again. They made their way to the top of the mountain to search for their treasure as night approached. The boys spotted their prized flower growing and shining on a nearby ledge as the moon shone down. They all made their way over and gathered some to bring back to Biddy. They returned to where the creature was buried, and there was no sign of its body being disturbed, but they kept vigil until morning.

The following morning, Darragh woke to find a clear blue sky and the other three boys fast asleep. "Quick, Quick" he shouted as the others jumped to their feet, arming themselves. Darragh laughed loudly as he said, "the sky was clear, so the creature must indeed be dead, Gotcha, boys", he beamed.

They made their way back down the mountain to find a very different town than when they first arrived. The people were joyous and courteous to them and thanked them for their help. They made their way to the druid, who gratefully shook all their hands and insisted that there would be a feast in their honour.

Later that day, they made their way to a barn nearby. There was music playing, people singing, and Bards telling stories of their bravery. Pigs were being cooked over a spit, lamb and chicken were being cooked on fires and various stews, and the mead was flowing.

The boys thought this was the best day since they had been here. "I never get fed this well at home," said Shane as the boys did their usual high fives and danced in circles while linking with each other.

The party carried on until the early hours, until one by one the people left, safe in the knowledge the creature was dead. Eventually, the boys made their beds for the night and lay down to sleep.

The following morning, the villagers gave the boys a healthy feed as they received more thanks from their grateful hosts. They then mounted their horses and headed off toward the three standing stones. When they reached the stones and rode east for two days before reaching the little woods again. "Witch of the wood, witch in the trees, I beg you to show your home to me," said Darragh as Biddy's house appeared again.

The boys walked into the house, telling Biddy all about their adventure, explaining that it wasn't a curse but an evil creature tormenting the town. They handed over their prize, telling Biddy that the supply should last her a lifetime. Biddy nodded knowingly at the boys as they told their story before turning to her cauldron to make her latest potion. She stirred the cauldron, adding her ingredients and whispering her brewing spell. Before long, the potions were ready, and she filled eight vials for the boys as there was enough potion left over to make an extra one each.

"What's the next item on the list" she enquired. The boys told her it was the removal of a thorn followed by bravery and, finally, chivalry to finish it. Biddy told them there was no spell to remove a thorn, so they must figure this out for themselves, but the boys had shown by killing the creature in Kelshamore, along with other things they had done, that they needed no potion from her for bravery as they had it in abundance. As for chivalry, they could sell it by the bucketful, she told them, because of their generous natures.

Biddy then told the boys it was time to become members of the Fianna as their destiny awaited. The boys each gave her a big hug and a thank you as they exited her hut. "Don't be strangers", she called out as the boys mounted their horses and rode off with Bran and Sceolan in hot pursuit. (Fionn had left the dogs with Biddy when they had gone to Kelshamore).

"Where are we going to?" asked Shane. "We will go to Tara" said Fionn. "The Fianna have a fort there, and it is only a quick trip from here". The boys continued on their way and soon came upon the fort. Before they entered the fort, Fionn drank his disguising potion, and his appearance changed as before.

THE ENTRANCE TEST

he fort was built with outer and inner courtyards, each surrounded by large wooden fences made by standing debranched trees side by side, which were held together by interwoven hazelwood and the houses in the outer yard were built the same as they were in Ballyfin with oval-shaped buildings sporadically built with a large open courtyard in the middle.

The outer yard was for the Fianna of lesser standing, while the inner yard was built for the hierarchy. Most houses were made the same, but more significant than the outer ones. In the centre of the inner yard was a much bigger building, and the exterior walls were much sturdier and made by piling bricks on top of each other on the outer walls, which were lined inside much the same as the small buildings. The roof was supported by wooden poles that left a hole in the centre of the conical roof, as a large communal fire always burned in the centre of the room. This was the main hall and contained a large table with long benches on either side.

There were guards at the outer and inner courtyards to stop strangers from entering. As the boys approached, they were stopped by a guard who wanted to know why they were there. The boys informed him they were there to join the Fianna. He told them to go to the inner yard and ask for Cormac. As the boys rode through the outer yard, they could see many fires burning throughout the camp, with people heating themselves or cooking food.

They noticed that all the soldiers were dressed the same. They wore red and black tartan trousers, with yellow tunics just below the buttocks and a red brat (cloak) folded and hanging from their left shoulder, held on by a metal pin. On their feet, they wore pleated black cowhide shoes.

When they reached the inner yard, they told the guard they were looking for Cormac. When Cormac approached, he was dressed similarly, but had a blue brat held on by a decorated silver brooch. It seemed the colour of the brat depended on your position within the group. He asked the boys how he could help and was told they wanted to join their ranks. He queried whether they knew there was an entrance test, not for the faint of heart.

"Yes sir, when can we start?" asked Fergal. "Well, my good man, you're either very brave or very foolish," said Cormac. "I'm very brave," said Fergal before being poked in the side by Shane. "Quiet, or you'll make it harder on us," said Shane quietly. Cormac let out a loud laugh and spoke. "Men gather round, we have four brave heroes ready to join our ranks." "We shall start with the bravest one of them," he said, pointing at Fergal. Fergal gulped while the other three boys laughed under their breaths.

With that, Fergal was called into the large meeting hall, and Cormac and three others followed and sat opposite him at the large table designed to intimidate him. Each man told him to recite certain poems, which he did easily. He was told to send the next boy in on his way out. Next in was Darragh, followed by Shane, and then Fionn and again, all passed the test with ease.

"Right next to step two", said Cormac, "Defence," he said, "my favourite". With that, all four boys were brought outside and around to the back of the building, which had a small fighting arena with a waist-deep hole in the centre. Nine warriors were standing close by with spears in hand. "Who is first?" asked Cormac. Fionn leapt into the pit and said, "that would be me!". They gave him nothing but a shield and staff to protect himself. One by one, the nine warriors threw spears at him and parried them all away with his shield before climbing out of the hole.

"That potion worked well as he drank his vial," said Darragh. "Oops, I never drank mine," said Fionn before downing his own, with Fergal and Shane doing likewise. Darragh jumped into the hole and prepared himself. This time the warriors did exactly as they had done with Fionn, and Darragh also passed. Next, it was Fergal's turn, and he jumped in. Cormac gave the nod to the warriors, and as the contest started, two threw their spears at once, with one grazing Fergal's shoulder, and he let out a cry of pain. Cormac stopped the contest and asked if he wanted to quit, but Fergal shook his head as he wanted to carry on.

Fergal was getting brave now and put down his staff and shield as the warriors threw their spears. He remembered his training and weaved and ducked, avoiding being hit. Cormac gave a nod of approval as he exited the hole. Last was Shane, who threw his shield on the ground and easily parried the spears with his staff. (Thanks, Liath, he thought to himself).

"Onto round three, your speed test," shouted Cormac as they all left the fort and walked to a nearby forest. They showed the boys the course they needed to follow to get to the far end of the woods without being caught or breaking a branch. Shane offered to go first and quickly managed the course with the help of his training and potion.

He was followed quickly by Fergal, who was now very nimble after his hen chasing. Next up was Darragh, who rubbed his ring, giving him extra strength to help him run quicker. As he was doing it, the warriors questioned if he had broken some branches, but relented as they were only bent. Fionn was last to go and rustled a few branches again, but none were broken.

"Onto round four, your movement test," said Cormac. Again, the boys were shown a course they were expected to run, jumping over and ducking under obstacles. Darragh and Shane rubbed their rings before the challenge and, with extra speed and strength, could jump higher over the obstacles but had to come to a standstill to stoop under the branches that were balancing on two upright logs. As Fergal did his challenge, he rubbed his ring and blended into the environment as he leapfrogged over the tree whilst rolling under the branch and ran to the end.

As none of the warriors saw him, they didn't want to let anyone else know for fear of embarrassment and waved him on. Finally, it was Fionn's turn. As he was tall, he could easily jump over the trees, but as he stooped to go under the branch, it scraped his shoulders and dislodged from its holdings, but as it didn't fall to the ground, was given a pass.

"Next, we have round five," shouted Cormac. He placed thorns onto the ground, and one by one, the boys ran over them, and although feeling an initial burst of pain when stepping on the thorns, none felt any follow-on pain, so they ran to the end of the trail. Upon checking their feet at the end, they could find no thorns. Darragh saw the rustling of a bush and saw Biddy smiling at him upon looking. She had cast spells, removing the thorns from the boys to help them.

"All is going well so far, but we're now onto round six, your bravery test," said Cormac. "We are going to let you fight as a group", he said. "You will need to fight thirteen of us," he said. All four boys and the thirteen warriors put their weapons away and picked up wooden weapons, including shields, staffs and swords, and a little dagger. They made their way back to the fighting arena in the inner courtyard.

The boys gathered in a circle and prepared to fight. Cormac stood back and instructed four warriors to attack. Fionn raised his shield while the other three boys rubbed their rings and gained their powers. One warrior who was about to attack Fergal hit his sword on the ground as he disappeared. Fergal ran behind him, kicking and knocking him into the waist-high hole.

Darragh parried a sword attack with his shield before landing a massive blow onto one warrior, knocking him out cold. Shane quickly avoided his attacker and bludgeoned him across the back of his neck three times, knocking him out. Fionn picked up his attacker and threw him across the arena.

Cormac gave instructions to the rest of the warriors to attack. One by one, the four boys parried, kicked, struck, and threw their opponents until they fell, unable to get back to their feet.

Next, they had to fight Cormac. They gathered around him to defeat him to complete the challenge, but Cormac had seen enough. "My friends," he said, "you have proven to me and all the others that you are brave and strong, test six is complete." "We must make our way to the main hall for the last test."

Inside, the four boys sat next to each other as Cormac and his other beaten warriors sat opposite them. The door opened, and in walked Goll Mac Morna (The leader of the Fianna), who killed Fionn's father. He was dressed the same as the other Fianna members, but he had a purple brat held in place by a gold brooch.

He congratulated the boys on making it this far, but now they must swear an oath to the Fianna. They must agree that the Fianna were now their family, and they would defend them and the high king of Ireland above all others. Next, they must promise not to marry out of greed or covet land and riches. They must marry only for love, be courteous with anyone they should meet, and never to hoard anything from someone in need.

All four boys readily agreed to the conditions. With that, some warriors came forth carrying large tankards and mead barrels. When all the mugs were filled, Goll raised a toast to the latest members of the Fianna. "Hip-hip Hooray", he roared, followed by loud cheers from the other warriors in the hall.

They ushered the boys into a room, and when they emerged, they were wearing their newly gained outfits of red and black tartan trousers, with yellow tunics, and a red brat folded and hanging from their left shoulder held on by a metal pin. They were also issued with a standard sword, shield, and bow. "Let us have a feast this night", roared Goll.

Later that evening, there was an enormous feast held in their honour. There were the usual pigs on a spit with lamb, boar, and chicken vegetables, all readily available. The mead flowed, and the music and storytelling carried on long into the night. The only thing missing was a good bed, as the four boys were exhausted and just wanted to sleep. One by one, the boys found a quiet corner and fell asleep for the night.

The following morning, Goll summoned the boys. There was a task three days' ride away that he wanted them to take care of. He had received word that the people of Cradockstown near the Athgreany stone circle were having trouble that needed to be investigated and remedied.

The boys told Goll to consider it done and made their way out of the hall. They mounted their horses and embarked on their journey with Bran and Sceolan.

On their way, they took a slight detour to see Biddy. After they had said the verse and entered Biddy's hut, all hugged her and thanked her for all her help, including the sneaky trick of removing the thorns. She smiled and told the boys that it was her pleasure. She asked where the boys were going. They said that the people of Cradockstown near Athgreany stone circle were having trouble that they had to fix.

She told the boys that they should be wary of the lake nearby the town as less-than-friendly creatures inhabited it and that the stone circle had deep-lying magic associated with it. The boys said their goodbyes and left with the hounds in tow. Making their way to Cradockstown and the Athgreany stone circle.

CHAPTER FIVE
AND SO, IT BEGINS

Onwards they rode, making their way towards their target with nothing eventful happening on the way. They came across the Athgreany stone circle at the edge of a small forest and dismounted to see if they could sense any magic from it. None of the boys felt anything and continued on their way to Cradockstown.

When they reached the town, they searched for the town leader. He told them that there was a vicious creature living in the lake nearby and that it was killing people while they were out fishing and even strolling by the lakeside and that they needed to kill it.

The boys set off on foot towards the lake, not knowing what to expect. As they got closer, they saw a woman lying on the lakeshore and a creature beside her. As they got closer, Darragh began sucking his thumb. The beast was a half-otter and half-dog-like creature known as dobhar-chú or water hound. As the boys drew closer, the creature spotted them and ran into the water, swimming away. The woman on the shore was dead, having been killed by the creature.

Fionn climbed into a boat nearby and rowed out a small way. Suddenly, the creature climbed onto the boat. "Goliath", roared Fionn as he jumped into the water and swam as fast as he could towards the lakeshore with the creature in hot pursuit. He raced out of the water and ran towards the others. The boys drew their weapons and prepared for a fight. The beast came out of the water, grunting and snarling before fixing its stare and attack on Fergal. He drew his dagger, which temporarily blinded the beast, giving the others time to attack it.

Shane stayed back while firing metal fragments at it from his slingshot. Fionn prodded it with his poison spear before Darragh attacked with his sword, cutting the creature in two.

As the creature died, it gave an ear-piercing shriek, which caused the lake's water to ripple. Moments later, a second dobhar-chú, more prominent than the first, came out of the water just as some townsfolk arrived to help the boys. The creature leapt on the closest one, dragging them to their death into the lake.

The boys told the rest of the townsfolk to step back away from the water's edge, as it was too dangerous. Then the waters broke, as the creature had returned for more. The boys attacked with Fergal, jumping on its back and stabbing it with his dagger. It turned and jumped into the water, swimming away, leaving Fergal lying on his back. The water rippled again, making Fergal leap to his feet, but the creature didn't emerge.

Everyone kept vigil to see if the creature would return, but the water remained still. The creature leapt from the water just as people were leaving. Fionn threw his spear, striking the beast before Darragh cut its head off.

The townsfolk gathered the slain beasts and carried their bodies back to the town to put on display. The town leader thanked the boys while handing them a small pouch with some coins in it. "There would have been more if you came two months back as we requested," said the town leader. The boys wondered what caused the delay, but thanked him and carried on their way.

The boys were hungry and decided to hunt in the town's small forest. This was the first time that Bran and Sceolan were involved in a hunt. Soon they saw a deer running, and Fionn set the two dogs on it. They gave chase, barking and snarling at the deer, but they lost the sight and scent of the deer. Soon the boys caught sight of a second deer, and again the hounds gave chase with the boys in hot pursuit. Just as the deer reached Athgreany stone circle, it tripped and fell into the circle, and the dogs, instead of attacking, sat down beside the animal until the boys arrived.

When Shane approached the deer, Bran barked and growled at him. Fionn told the other boys to hold back and approached the deer.

He sensed something was different, and instead of slaying the deer, he placed a noose around its neck. He thought there was magic afoot and decided to bring it to Finnegas for advice.

The group set off in search of Finnegas, who never ventured far from where the boys first met him. Finnegas welcomed the boys like members of a long-lost family when they arrived at his camp. As always, food was the first thing on the agenda, so they prepared and ate a meal.

Finnegas wondered what brought the boys back to him. Fionn explained about the deer and how the dogs seemed to defend it rather than attack it. Firstly, said Finnegas, it was a doe (a female deer). But he agreed that there was magic at play and that the boys should bring the doe to his aunt Bodhmall as she would be better able to help with an answer as she too, was a druid.

The boys set up camp for the night to have some downtime with Finnegas. At first light, they set off, searching for Bodhmall and an answer to their riddle. As it was a two-day journey to Ballyfin, the boys needed to camp and hunted for food along the way. Fergal suggested they could kill and eat the doe, as it would be easier than hunting, but the other three boys scolded him. They hunted and slept along the way until finally they reached Ballyfin and onwards up the hill to Bodhmall and Liath.

It was mid-morning when they arrived at the outskirts of the farm and found both women out tending to the animals. As they got closer to the farmyard, both women waved and made their way to the boys. "What have we got here?" asked Bodhmall. "We found this doe", advised Fionn, "Finnegas said you could help, as magic is involved". Fionn and Liath had a brief chat before taking the doe and leading it into the farmyard.

As soon as they entered the yard, the doe transformed into a beautiful young woman who was not much older than the boys. There was a glow on her skin that radiated beneath her long, dark hair. She had a slight build and wore a purple silk tunic that hung just below the knee. She wore a belt around her waist and a brooch around her neck, with rings on three fingers on her right hand.

The boys dismounted their horses and ran towards the girl to find some answers. The girl fainted upon realising she was no longer a doe but had transformed into a human form.

"Quick, Let's get her to the house", shouted Liath. "Get some water and heat it on the fire," said Bodhmall as the boys ran in circles, not knowing exactly what to do. Fionn carried the girl into the house and placed her carefully on a bed. Bran and Sceolan sat down outside the bedroom door. Darragh left to fetch some water from the river and heated it on the fire.

Darragh brought the heated water to Liath, who dipped some cloth and began wiping the girl's face and forehead. Bodhmall fetched some stew that had been cooking away over the fireplace. Fionn sat on the spare bed, looking at the girl like a love-struck puppy. The other boys sat near the fire, waiting for news. Bodhmall and Liath told them to be patient, as they would get answers once the girl had awoken.

When the girl woke up, Bodhmall told her to take it easy and gave her the stew to eat. The puzzled-looking girl willingly accepted the food and scoffed it down, as if she hadn't eaten in a long time. (She hadn't eaten in days, as the boys never thought to do since they captured her as a doe). The girl gulped and tried to speak, only to be told to relax and talk to them when she was good and ready. The girl finally asked for a cup of water, and Fionn rushed to get it for her. She gratefully accepted and gulped it down.

"Are you ok now, my dear child?" asked Bodhmall.

MY NAME IS SADHBH

The girl finally spoke. "Hi, my name is Sadhbh," she said softly ", and it has been almost a year since I became enchanted." "How did that happen?" asked Darragh. To which Sadhbh asked, "Is this land enchanted in any way?".
Bodhmall told her she had been a druid since birth and had cast spells and placed runes around the outskirts of the farm, preventing any evil or magic other than her own from being used within its boundaries. "That explains a lot," said Sadhbh as she began telling her story.

She had grown up in Munster as the daughter of king Bodb Dearg of Teide (A small kingdom in the area). She had had a very happy childhood and never wanted for anything being in the protection of her family and her father's guards.

One day, she had asked to go on a hunting expedition with her father and soldiers when they happened upon a strange-looking, tall, thin man who immediately became besotted with her. He had begged her father for her hand in marriage, but her father had him bound and given 20 lashes for impudence. (How dare he ask to marry a princess?). They then carried on with their hunt.

A week passed, and again the girl went out hunting with her father and his men when they came across the strange man again. This time, he introduced himself to them, saying he was a significant person named Fer Doirich of the Tuatha Dé Danann. He could provide her with a lavish lifestyle and all the comforts she had become accustomed to living with her family. Again, the King had him bound and, this time, gave him thirty lashes before sending him on his way.

Sometime later, the strange man appeared at the gates of the family stronghold with a companion and asked to see the girl. When her father refused, the now enraged man held his staff aloft, casting a spell (as he was indeed a powerful sorcerer known for his reputation of cruelty and wickedness) that made the king and all his men fall asleep.

He then entered the stronghold, where he told Sadhbh's mother that her daughter's beauty and charm had captivated him, and the only thing he wanted in life was her daughter's hand in marriage. Her mother quickly refused his request, saying he was the most unpleasant of people and her daughter could never marry a man of his ilk. This enraged the strange man even more, and he cast another spell, sending her mother and the women of the stronghold into a sleeplike trance before turning his attention to Sadhbh herself.

He implored her to become his wife, as her beauty had left him enchanted, and he wanted nothing more in life than her hand in marriage. This time she herself had turned down his advances, and he grew angry and red in the face, almost exploding before he cast yet another spell.

If he couldn't have her as his bride, then no one could. The spell transformed her into a deer, and hounds or wild animals would tear apart her for refusing him. Unknown to him, the friend accompanying him cast a spell prohibiting wild animals from attacking her, but tame animals would protect her.

"And here I am now," she said. "Wow, that's a great story," said Fergal with a startled look on his face. The girl thanked them all and said she wanted to set off in search of her family, to let them know what had become of her. Fionn advised against it as Fer Doirich could still be watching her family home. Bodhmall agreed, saying it was best that she stayed living with her and Liath for the time being, at least.

Sadhbh thanked them for their kindness and agreed to stay with them. "Time for a feast", shouted Shane and Fergal. The women told the boys to go to the outhouse in the far corner and put on some old tunics, then to go to the forest for some food, but Fionn declined as he had cramps in his stomach. "Fionn's got a girlfriend", roared Darragh with laughter as he and the other boys teased him. Fionn blushed and shoved them out the door.

The women told the boys to avoid the river as they were bringing Sadhbh there to bathe. Fergal, being cheeky, sneaked to the river for a look. Shortly after, they could hear him shouting, "Ouch, you're hurting me," as Bodhmall walked towards the boys with a firm hold of Fergal's ear. "Be off with you, you little mongrel?" she said.

A red-faced Fergal returned to the others. "Well, did you see anything?" asked Shane. "Well," said Fergal. "I sneaked up as quietly as possible and got into a great hiding spot and just as Sadhbh and Liath were removing their tunics, an angry-looking Bodhmall grabbed me by the ear and dragged me back here." A less than impressed Fionn said it served him right as the others laughed out loud.

The boys changed clothing in the outhouse and ran to the woods to hunt for food. They successfully foraged mushrooms and carrots and caught pheasant and rabbit. They then returned to the farm with their haul. The women, now back from the river, told the boys to catch some fish while they prepared the food already there.

The boys strolled to the river and caught some fish before washing themselves in the river. They then returned and changed into their Fianna uniforms to prepare for their feast. They prepared dinner over the sizeable outdoor fire and cauldron, while Fionn and Liath fetched the harp from the house.

As soon as dinner was over, Bodhmall fetched a barrel of mead from the house. Liath played the harp and sang while Bodhmall, Darragh, Shane, and Fergal drank the mead. Sadhbh and Fionn danced together to the music. "He's gonna kiss her, he's gonna love her, he's gonna marry her", sang Fergal teasingly, which led to a red-faced Fionn chasing him around the fire while all the others laughed at the goings on.

That night Fionn and Darragh slept in the outhouse while the others slept in the main house, as Sadhbh needed to have a room by herself. Bran and Sceolan kept the two boys' company through the night.

The following morning, Bodhmall said that they needed to expand the outhouse into a small home to house their growing clan. She sent the boys into the woods to fell some trees and to the river for rocks. The trees were to expand the outhouse, and the rocks were the foundation of a fireplace. The women searched for the hazelwood branches and twigs to interweave the walls and white limestone to insulate it.

By the day's end, there was a newly expanded house with two new straw beds and a stone fireplace. It would take time to have the entire house finished. The group cracked open another barrel of mead to christen the house and bring it luck. Once they had finished drinking, everyone stumbled to bed for a well-deserved night's sleep.

The following morning, the boys were preparing to go back to Goll and hand over the purse of coin and tell him about Cradockstown and the dobhar-chú. Before they left, Fionn and Sadhbh left for a walk together down by the riverside. Darragh began to sing, "Love is in the air, oh yeah, love is in the air". "I fear you could be right," said Bodhmall.

Upon their return, the boys mounted their horses and, along with Bran and Sceolan, said their goodbyes and set off to Tara. They stopped to see Biddy on their way so Fionn could get a new brew to disguise himself. She was awaiting their arrival, as she had been monitoring their progress. She told them they should be careful of Goll as he was a treacherous man with evil in his heart.

After a quick break, they were soon on their way back to see Goll in the Tara stronghold.

It was nightfall when they arrived back at Tara. The guards were at the gate but bade the boys welcome, as they were in their Fianna uniforms. There were many fires lit around the camp, with many warriors drinking mead and singing songs, while others told stories or walked around in a drunken stupor. The Boys put their horses in a stable for the night and had some mead. Fionn drank some potion to disguise himself. As the boys neared one fire, they heard one warrior call the name Luachra. Darragh recalled it was the name of the man who stabbed Fionn's father and had stolen the Corrbolg from him.

A tall, hideous warrior answered the name, and the boys zoned in on their target. Should they call him out in a fight or try to rob the pouch from around his waist? Darragh feared there could be fallout from calling him out, so they would need another plan. Suddenly, chaos broke out at the main gate.

Three loud howls echoed through the darkness, and a monstrous, powerful hound-like creature with a black fur coat and the stench of 1000 corpses, the size of a donkey with burning fiery red eyes and paws the size of a man's hand, had attacked the front gate. There was great fear among the guards as they froze in place, while the beast devoured two of them. Other warriors gave chase, and the beast ran off into the darkness of the nearby marsh.

"It was a Cú Sidhe (hound of the Sidhe)", shouted one of the other guards. It was famed for the fear and terror it brought throughout the land with its howling and barking. It usually roamed marshes, bogs and caves.

Cormac came forward and put more guards on duty for the rest of the night. The ordeal soured the partying, and all the other warriors had to find a bed for the night. As the boys found a bed, Fergal shouted to Darragh that he had a present for him, as he threw him the Corrbolg that he had removed from Luachra in all the commotion.

The following morning, Goll summoned the four boys to the main building. They told him about Cradockstown and the dobhar-chú and handed over the coin given to them. They said there would have been more, but for the time taken to send warriors to the village. Goll ignored their comments and said, "Let me introduce you to his highness, Cormac mac Airt, the high king of Ireland|". The four boys bowed down before the king as he took his leave.

The king's stronghold was a fort on the hill of Slaine, a quick ride away, and he had been to the fort to pay coins to Goll for the loyalty of the Fianna. Goll told the boys they should be careful to hold their tongues in front of the king. He then handed them a new mission to hunt the Cú Sidhe that had attacked the fort the previous night.

The disgruntled boys took their leave and left to get their horses. They brought Bran and Sceolan to help hunt the animal. As they rode out across the marsh, they wondered why they seemed to receive punishment after their previous successful mission instead of being congratulated.

They set up camp, and Darragh took out the Corrbolg and was astounded when he opened the pouch, and found that inside it looked more like a chest, with various weapons and items inside. Fionn was silent and distant, so Darragh suggested he return to Ballyfin as he was obviously pining for Sadhbh. The other boys agreed, and soon Fionn, along with Bran and Sceolan, rode off to see her.

The other three boys sat and talked about home. They wondered how their families were and if they were missing them. They had been gone a few months now. They would be on their summer holidays back home and didn't even know what year it was. "Yeah, but on the plus side, we get to drink and stay up late," said Fergal. The boys broke camp and set off to find and slay the beast.

They travelled for a few hours, and night was falling when they came across a large cave. The smell of death was in the air, and they knew they had reached their target. The boys tied their horses up and readied their weapons. Fergal drew his non-magical dagger so they could remain in darkness. Darragh told the boys to put on their headphones to drown out the howling of the animal, and, being overcome with fear, they ran into the cave.

Inside the cave, the stench got worse, and the boys worried the fumes would overcome them. They wrapped their brats around their mouths and noses several times and carried on. They could hear howling and barking, but it was very faint and caused them no fear. Suddenly, right before them, was an enormous set of red eyes.

Fergal drew Claíomh Solais, and the cave lit up. The beast was in front of them and stood snarling at them. Shane jumped to his side while the creature lunged at Darragh, knocking him off his feet. The animal tried to bite him, but he blocked its mouth with his blade. Fergal jumped on its back and began stabbing it while Shane hit it repeatedly across the head with his staff. The creature fled further into the cave, with the three boys in hot pursuit.

The boys caught up with the beast and had it cornered. Darragh drew his bow and fired an arrow right into the beast's mouth while Shane and Fergal now attacked it with daggers. The beast tried its best to fight them off, and as they distracted it, Darragh lunged forward with his blade, taking its head clean off.

Darragh reached into Corrbolg, and it seemed to know exactly what he wanted, as there was a large pouch at the top when he reached in. He then gathered the beast's head into the pouch, and the boys exited the cave. The boys congratulated themselves with hugs and high-fives all around. They knew they dared not go back to camp without Fionn and set off toward Ballyfin.

The boys stopped and lit a fire and slept for the night. The following morning, they set off at first light to the farm. Along the way, they stopped in some woods and realised they were all becoming quite good and accurate with their bows as they killed some squirrels for lunch, which were small and needed some well-placed arrows. Then onwards, again, they rode until they reached their destination.

WE DO

n reaching the farm, it pleasantly surprised them as the outhouse appeared to be finished, with the white limestone now lining the walls and the thatched roof. There was smoke coming from the chimney, and the boys walked over to investigate. As they entered the front door, Fionn and Sadhbh jumped as the boys walked in and caught them in a romantic embrace.

The boys apologised and left, going to the main house instead. Liath and Bodhmall happily greeted them. "Did you happen upon the smitten couple?" asked Bodhmall. "We did indeed," said Darragh. "We should leave them till morning", advised Liath. The three boys should sleep in the main house.

The following morning, when everyone was together, Shane told of their heroic efforts in slaying the Cú Sidhe. Bodhmall and Liath congratulated them, as it was no easy feat. Fionn stood up and said, I have some news of my own. "I have asked Sadhbh to be my wife, and she has accepted," he said.

The rest of the group warmly congratulated the newly engaged couple. "He's gonna kiss her, he's gonna love her, he's gonna marry her", sang Fergal teasingly as the rest of the group joined in.

Darragh said they needed Fionn to return to Tara to turn in the beast's head. He agreed it was necessary, so the four boys set off without Bran and Sceolan, as they were only bringing the trophy back and then returning to Ballyfin for an engagement party.

When they reached Tara, the guards and warriors greeted them like heroes in the outer circle as they held their trophy aloft for all to see. Cormac congratulated them for a job well done. He took the beast's head as he would put it on display for everyone to see.

"Time for a feast," he roared. "Not another one," said Fergal.

There was a big celebration long into the night. The following morning Fionn made his way to the fort's blacksmith and asked him to make him two wedding rings. The blacksmith agreed to do it for the boy's heroic deed for free.

He told the boys to return in a few hours, and they would be ready. The boys busied themselves for some time and then returned to collect the rings. The blacksmith handed over two matching braided copper rings. "It symbolises never-ending love," he said, "as the pattern has no end and no beginning". An overjoyed Fionn thanked the blacksmith before the boys made haste towards Ballyfin.

A few days later, the boys arrived back at the farm, and Sadhbh was pining for Fionn, who was pining for her as well. When everyone greeted each other, Liath said they must carry out the tying of the knot. With that, she told the couple to cross their wrists and hold hands as she wrapped some cord around them in a figure of eight representing infinity. They must do this for a few hours a day until they are married.

Darragh wondered if they should let Sadhbh's parents know she was safe and well and about to marry. This overjoyed her, and Darragh said he would fetch her parents once Bodhmall and Liath thought it was safe to do so. The two women agreed, and Darragh, Shane and Fergus set off on a new adventure to find king Bodb Dearg of the Sidhe and his wife, as it was a few days' ride away.

The boys had an uneventful trip to the little kingdom, except for Darragh stopping to suck his thumb for directions. Then onwards, they rode again until they came to a forest with a tall, strange man. It must be Fer Doirich, they thought as they avoided crossing his path. They finally made their way to the fort before requesting permission to see the king Bodb Dearg with news of his daughter. Upon hearing the news, the king immediately had the boys arrested and bound for his wife's pleasure.

The king and queen had the boys brought before them. "If you are mocking me and giving false news of my daughter, you shall each receive 50 lashes," the queen said sharply. "We come bearing good news," said Darragh. "If you release us, I will tell you everything". The king waved his hand, and they released the boys. The king and queen were ecstatic as the boys told them the story of the spell cast upon Sadhbh by Fer Doirich. After their experience with him, the queen knew this to be the truth.

Upon hearing she was alive and to be married, they insisted they go to her at once. Darragh warned that they had spotted Fer Doirich still in the woods nearby and that the king and queen should travel in disguise to Ballyfin to avoid placing their daughter in danger again. They would travel incognito with the boys the following morning after breakfast.

The next morning, the king and queen dressed in dark hooded tunics and set off with the boys, without guards to avoid drawing attention, to go to Sadhbh to see if it was really her. After they had travelled for a few days, they reached the farm. Darragh called out as they approached. This brought Bodhmall, Liath and Fionn out of the main house. Darragh told them it was safe, so Sadhbh came out of the house too.

It overjoyed the king and queen at seeing their daughter alive. And they leapt from their horses and ran to her. The king lifted her off her feet and swung her around, rejoicing. Once he had stopped, the queen gave her the biggest hug a mother could give and began kissing her repeatedly on the face. When their initial joy subsided, they all walked into the house to talk.

They questioned Sadhbh about her life after Fer Doirich had cast the spell upon her and how she came to be here on the farm. Sadhbh told them how the boys were out hunting and the dogs protecting her, Finnegas saying to go to the farm and then the spell being broken once they reached the farm, as runes protected it from spells. She apologised for her rudeness and introduced their hosts, Bodhmall, Liath and Fionn, her beloved, whom she intended to marry.

The king and queen greeted and thanked everyone, but told Sadhbh that it would be foolish to rush into marriage with a man she barely knew. Bodhmall suggested that they should have a talk with only themselves, Sadhbh and Fionn in the room. With that, the rest of the group left the house. Sadhbh told her parents that she had her heart set on marrying him, as he was her one true love. Fionn swore he would love her forever and protect her with all his might.

The king questioned him about his life and his source of income. Fionn recounted the story of his life and his real name being Deinmhe and his intention to one day rule the Fianna, as his father had done before him. He said that his aunt Bodhmall was a druid, and that they had built a house to prepare for their marriage as no harm would come to Sadhbh while she was within the confines of the farm because of the spells and runes surrounding the farm.

They asked Fionn to leave as they needed to digest everything before deciding. He turned to Sadhbh, embracing and kissing her passionately before leaving the house to join the others. He told the rest of the others what was happening in the house and that whatever the decision, he would respect it, as Sadhbh was more important than his feelings.

Sometime later, the door opened, and Sadhbh ran out and jumped into Fionn's arms, rejoicing that they were getting married. An overjoyed Fionn spun her in the air while the others cheered on the happy couple. The king and queen came out and approached Fionn, who gratefully hugged them and thanked them for the decision.

Not for the first time, there would be a feast on the farm that night. The boys knew what was required, changed into their old tunics, and left for the forest and river to catch and forage for supper. That night was the most significant feast yet, followed by mead and music. The king and queen bedded down for the night in the new house while Fionn, Darragh, and the dogs slept under the stars.

The following morning, everyone sat around the large outdoor fire, as the king had something to tell them. He agreed to the marriage in principle but that the happy couple should tie the knot daily for the next month, and if after the month was up, they still loved each other that the wedding would have his absolute blessing. He insisted they must hold the marriage in his family stronghold as it had its own sacred building and great hall.

The others worried about this arrangement, as the farm would be a much safer place to have the wedding for fear of Fer Doirich turning up. The king and queen said they would take their leave under the protection of Darragh, Shane, and Fergal. Then they kissed and hugged Sadhbh and said their goodbyes to the others. "We shall return in one month," said the king as they rode off.

A few uneventful days later, the boys had the royal couple back in the safety of their stronghold. They were each given a nice cosy room for the night in the local tavern. Shane said they should go to the tavern to find some company as it bored him with being with the same people all the time. "Is there something wrong with me?" asked Fergal. "Yes, you're not female", came the reply.

The three of them made their way to the tavern. "It is nothing like the bar in Castleview manor," said Darragh. It had cut stone walls, with flagstone-type flooring, a wooden bar at one wall and a raging turf fire at the other. In the room's corner was a lone man sitting on a stool playing the fiddle. Some people were drinking while others were dancing. "Let's make the most of it," said Shane as he spied a woman sitting at the bar. "Check out my style," he said as the others followed him to the bar.

Flashing a smile, as only Shane could, he said to the woman, "Hey, how you doing?". "I'm doing fine if you have the coin", she replied. A red-faced Shane turned to the others, and they all laughed out loud. "Wrong kind of woman," said Darragh. They spied a table with two women sitting at it and, after getting a jug of mead and some cups courtesy of the king, made their way over to them. "Let me do the talking," said Shane as he flashed a smile at the women.

The women were smitten with his smile, and it didn't even matter what he was saying as they kept nodding and laughing at everything he said. Fergal complained of being tired and set off to bed for the night. Shane, now getting brave, invited one woman to dance. The other woman grabbed Darragh, and soon the four of them were having a great time together.

The following morning, Fergal was first down for breakfast. A beaming Darragh came down the stairs a while later, followed by an equally happy Shane. "Top of the morning to ye," said Shane. "We don't talk like that," said Fergal. "We know that, but they don't know that," said Darragh, pointing at other patrons in the tavern. After breakfast, the boys made their way to the main hall. They told the king and queen that they hoped to see them in a month, thanked them for their hospitality and set off for Ballyfin.

On their way back to Ballyfin, they set up camp for the night. As they sat around the fire talking about the tavern the previous night, they thought back to uncle Joseph's wedding day. What if they had stayed in the hotel and not gone to the fountain? How different their lives would be. "I miss my family", cried Fergal as the other two boys hugged him, and they all cried together.

The following morning before setting off, Darragh said, "I know Fergal loves his little weapon, but do you like your wooden weapon, Shane?" giggled Darragh. "Or would you like to upgrade it?". Shane laughed, too, before saying that he found his wooden staff to be useless against the Cú Sidhe and that since he was now proficient with a bow, it was better than the sling at the end of his staff. Darragh opened the Corrbolg and told Shane to let it choose his weapon.

Shane looked away and reached deep into the pouch. He felt something in his hand and withdrew it from the pouch. There in his hand was the most beautiful spear with a shaft made of shiny ash, while the blade had leafy foliage decorations on the blade's surface, with copper and silver on the rib. It had a woven strap attached to either end to carry on your back. "Tell me what it does?" asked an excited Shane. Darragh stuck his thumb in his mouth and began sucking.

After a few minutes, he took his thumb out and told Shane that the spear was called Gae Assail (Spear of Assal). He said the spear would always hit its intended target and return to the person who threw it. "Deadly", shouted Shane, "Let's try it out".

He spied a tree nearby and took aim, unleashing the spear with all his might. The spear flew through the air before resting in the tree's bough. "It's not coming back," he said. "Pretend you're Thor," said Darragh. Shane raised his open hand above his head, and the weapon returned to him. "This is awesome," he said.

"Are you still happy with your little weapon?" asked Darragh jokingly while looking at Fergal. "My little weapon is just fine", laughed Fergal in return. The boys then mounted their horses and carried on to their destination. They arrived back at the farm only to find Fionn and Sadhbh had gone to the forest for a walk with their hands bound. The boys looked forward to seeing them, as the round trip had taken almost a week.

Bodhmall told the boys to follow the pair out into the woods, as they would be happy to see the boys. When the boys ran out into the woods, they could hear shouting and thought it strange that the couple would be arguing. The boys approached with caution, and rightly so. The couple was bound to a tree, and they gagged the unarmed Fionn. There was a group of at least ten thieves beating Fionn as Sadhbh cried out for them to stop.

"We know you have riches," said one thief as he again hit Fionn. "I swear we don't", cried Sadhbh. "Anyone wearing such a fine silk tunic as yourself is bound to have riches", came the reply. Shane sneaked slowly and quietly around behind the tree with his new weapon in hand. He saw the rope keeping Fionn bound and threw the spear straight and true, and it split the rope in two before returning to Shane's raised hand.

With his hands freed, Fionn removed his gag and shouted Goliath! The rope binding him to Sadhbh burst, and Fionn leapt forward, attacking the thieves nearest to him, crushing them with his bare hands. Darragh and Fergal rushed out to defend against the other onrushing thieves. One by one, the thieves fell until all were dead. Fionn rushed to check on Sadhbh, who was unhurt but shaken by the attack on them.

The boys built a funeral pyre to dispose of all the bodies while Fionn brought the shaken Sadhbh back to the farm. When the boys returned to the farm, Bodhmall and Liath gave them great big hugs for being in the right place at the right time to save the couple from harm. Sadhbh had gone to bed to recover, while Fionn sat on the ground with his head in his hands, unhappy that he hadn't protected her adequately.

"It could happen to any of us," said Shane as he approached Fionn, showing off his new weapon to cheer him up. He told him to throw the weapon at something, and it would return to him. Fionn threw the spear at a tree, splitting it in two. "It's not coming back," he said. "Pretend you're Thor," shouted Fergal. "Who is Thor?"

Asked Fionn. "Long story," said Darragh. "Just hold your hand up". Fionn raised his hand, and the spear returned to him. A now happier Fionn handed the spear back to Shane.

The entire group sat down to supper that evening and discussed what had happened earlier in the day and the couple's impending marriage. Shane said that as it was only three weeks before the king and queen returned, there was no point in the boys leaving the farm. They should remain in case any new thieves show up. Liath thought it was a good idea for the boys to lie low, as they had had a hectic few months behind them and could rest up for a while.

Darragh proposed going to see Biddy and Finnegas to tell them about Fionn's impending wedding. Bodhmall thought it was a good idea and that Darragh and Fergal should go while Shane should remain at the farm with them. They agreed to the plan, and all went to bed for the night after another eventful day.

The following morning, the two boys said their goodbyes and sat off to tell Biddy and Finnegas while Shane stayed behind at the farm. That evening, Shane asked if he could go to the tavern in the Ballyfin village down the hill and was told by Liath that it would do him good. Bodhmall gave him some coin to have in his pocket, and off he set down the hill.

As he entered the tavern, it looked very similar to the previous tavern, except the singer was a woman. She was playing the most enchanting music on a tin whistle in between, singing some beautiful verses. When the woman took a break, Shane bought her a drink and flashed a smile in the woman's direction and said, "How you doing?".

She smiled and welcomed him to join her, as she had finished singing for the night. Shane introduced himself to her and asked her name, to which she replied it was Cred. Her clothing differed from anyone he had met before, she was donning a long purple and green dress with a long black hooded cloak. She was tall, slim, and had the most beautiful pale skin with lovely red lips encased by the shiniest long black hair.

He asked her if she lived locally, and she told him she was only passing through. He then told her she looked like his wife. "Are you married then?" she asked. "No", replied Shane, with a glint in his eye.

They laughed to each other and talked for the rest of the evening before she invited him to her room. The following morning, he woke up, but his mysterious companion had disappeared, so he made his way back up the hill to the farm.

He returned to the farm and thought he was in the clear before Liath asked how his night had gone as his bed hadn't been slept in. He blushed and told her it was nice. She prepared him breakfast and sat down to hear all about his evening. He told her about the woman he met and their lovely time together.

Nothing out of the ordinary happened for the next few days, as life around the farm was quiet. The loving couple left for their daily walks, followed by Shane in the shadows, while Bodhmall and Liath tended the farm.

A few days passed, and Darragh and Fergal returned to give the bad news that Biddy and Finnegas could not attend the wedding. Biddy had sent a necklace made of beads of gold and emeralds for the bride. While Finnegas had sent some new clothing for Fionn to wear on the special occasion. It was a white silk shirt with a short black jacket and a black and white tartan kilt he had taken from the corrbolg.

The group all carried out their daily chores and so on for the next few weeks. The boys would go to the tavern some evenings, as Shane wanted to see if his mysterious woman would return, while the other boys teased him about his imaginary friend.

Finally, the day came, and an excited Sadhbh woke and waited impatiently for her parents to arrive. The king and queen arrived surrounded by soldiers. They couldn't wait to see their daughter and see if the wedding would go ahead. An ecstatic Sadhbh told them her love for Fionn was stronger than ever.

The king and queen insisted that there was no time to waste then and told the entire party to pack up and prepare to travel. Bodhmall, Liath, Darragh, Shane and Fergal all mounted their horses, while Sadhbh and Fionn insisted they would travel on Fionn's horse together. The entire party then set off for the three-day journey with Bran and Sceolan in tow.

A few days later, whilst avoiding the forest, they made it to the king's stronghold. There was a big party that night to celebrate their arrival. To Shane's surprise and delight, Cred was the tavern singer who gleefully introduced her to the group.

That night Sadhbh spent the night with her parents in the main house while Fionn and the group stayed in the tavern, with Cred joining them. The following morning an excited Fionn was first up and washed before climbing into his new finery for the wedding.

A disgruntled Shane was next up as Cred had disappeared again. The rest of the group were soon downstairs dressed in their finest while Fergal slagged Fionn for wearing a skirt. "It's a kilt," said a frustrated Fionn. Once the group was ready, they set off to the Sacred building where they were to marry.

It differed greatly from the church, the one the boys had been in for their uncle joseph's wedding. There was a wooden roof and partial stone walls. It had a small wooden altar with two chairs facing it. There were six benches, three on either side, with a musician playing the harp at the side of the altar. They adorned the sacred building with floral bouquets adorning the walls.

A nervous Fionn took his seat at the front while the group squeezed onto the front bench on the right. The druid tried to keep Fionn calm while waiting for the bride to arrive. Suddenly two uilleann pipers played outside the sacred building, and the queen arrived with some maids taking the front bench on the left.

The bride, accompanied by the king, soon followed her. He escorted her to the altar and placed her hand in Fionn's before sliding in beside the queen. Sadhbh was a sight to behold, dressed all in white. She wore an embroidered dress with lace and a veil covering her face. She also wore a wool cloak with shamrocks and knots embroidered on it. To complete her outfit, she wore the necklace Biddy had sent her.

The loved-up couple couldn't contain their joy as tears rolled down their faces. The druid did a more unique service than at Joseph's wedding. It began with handfasting, an ancient tradition where the couple crossed their hands over one another, right hand to right hand and left to left before the druid wrapped a ribbon around their wrists as a sign of unity. He then asked the couple if they would care for and look after each other and promise to love each other forevermore. They placed rings on each other's fingers and then replied in unison, "WE DO". The druid then pronounced them man and wife.

There was a loud cheer in the Sacred building as the groom lifted the veil and kissed his new wife before being congratulated by the king and queen, and then everyone else. It was then off to the great hall for the biggest party the kingdom had seen. There was more food than the boys had ever seen, as well as many musicians playing the harp, the fiddle and the uilleann Pipes. The party lasted many hours until the bride and groom disappeared for the night.

The next morning, everyone gathered in the great hall, and the king and queen told the newlyweds that for their safety, they should remain in the confines of the stronghold for the foreseeable future. A stubborn Sadhbh insisted they would stay for only a week and then return to the safety of the farm. The king reluctantly agreed.

The boys agreed they, too, would stay a week to travel back to the farm with the newlyweds, but Bodhmall and Liath returned to the farm to tend their animals. When the week passed, the newlyweds said their goodbyes to the king and queen and returned to the farm with the three boys and the two dogs.

CHAPTER SIX

ONWARDS WE GO

odhmall and Liath greeted them when they reached the farm and had put the finishing touches to their new house. They even made new table and chairs and their own cauldron to cook their dinners. The boys ran to the forest and chopped down some trees for firewood for them, too. Then the boys talked to Fionn and said that although he was still getting used to married life, they had not been to Tara for some time now and should at least show their faces for fear of being called deserters.

Fionn sat down and talked to Sadhbh, and she reluctantly agreed that he should return to Tara but return to her as soon as he could. They agreed to spend their first night on the farm together as newlyweds before the boys should set off the following morning. Darragh, Shane, and Fergal spent the evening with Bodhmall and Liath celebrating Fionn and Sadhbh's marriage, but the happy couple were nowhere to be found as they spent the evening together in their house, leaving the others to celebrate without them.

The following morning at first light, they all said their goodbyes and set off to Tara, with Bran and Sceolan in tow. On the way, the boys stopped off to see Biddy and Finnegas so that they could congratulate Fionn on his marriage before they carried on to Tara. It was nightfall when they reached the fort, and as usual, Fionn drank some of his disguising potion. They then found themselves a bed for the night.

The next morning after breakfast, they searched for Cormac, who sarcastically said, "You're all still alive then". "We are indeed," said Darragh. They informed him that Fionn had recently married, and he congratulated him but said they should report to Goll in the main hall as he had been looking for them. The boys carried on to the main hall, where Goll was sitting, stuffing his face with a giant chicken leg. "Ah, the missing troupe return," he said sarcastically before ushering them over to him. He wasn't a nice man, so the boys didn't discuss Fionn's marriage.

"Let's get to business," he said. "I have a new mission for you." "You will need to travel to Kilmagoura and slay the giantess Eileen Óg," he said. "You seem to give us the hardest missions," said Darragh. "That's because I don't like you, and you don't belong here," replied Goll. "I will tell you what," he said. "I will send four more warriors to aid you since you're so scared." "We're not scared," shouted Fergal.

"What has she done that we need to kill her?" asked Shane. "You don't need to know anything," roared Goll, "but I will tell you she is an immense woman who has killed many travellers from nearby towns and needs to be stopped."

The boys left the main hall, shaking their heads. "Why did we even join the Fianna?" asked Darragh. "We just seem to be weapons for a tyrant". "Don't worry?" said Fionn "his time will come". "I plan on being the leader sooner rather than later". The boys all gave him high fives as they made their way out of the inner circle. In the outer circle, Cormac introduced the boys to the other four warriors that would accompany them. There was Aron, Sheamus, Padraig and Conan. The boys greeted their new companions, mounted their horses and set off out of the camp.

They were going to take their most extended trip yet. It would take five days to reach Kilmagoura to carry out their mission and five days back. Fionn wondered what Sadhbh would think, as she must indeed be waiting impatiently for him to return. Shane told him he could return home instead of the mission if he needed to, but Fionn said that as they needed four more warriors with them, every man would be required.

The group travelled for three days when the weather changed, and it began pouring rain. They came to a large lake with a dark hue and strong odour from the water. They noticed a cave nearby and made their way over to it. It was an enormous cave, and they could easily fit all eight men, the horses inside, and Bran and Sceolan. It wasn't a deep cave, however, but the group could see the partially rotten remains of a cow, a human skeleton, and many other bones in the back. They knew they had better not lower their guard, as some predator must be nearby.

They lit a fire in the cave and gathered some firewood to keep themselves warm for the night. The men were hungry and searched for some food. The rain was getting heavier, and they drew twigs. Whoever picked the shortest would be the one to go out looking for the food. Padraig was the unlucky one and had to go out into the rain.

His best option was to fish, he thought to himself. He wrapped his brat around himself and covered his head to protect against a now howling wind and rain. He picked up a small branch lying nearby, tying some twine and a hook to the end. Then walked and stood on the lake shore that gave him the most tree coverage from the weather.

He wasn't gone long when Bran began barking and ran outside. Fionn and Fergal ran out, with Fergal taking out Claíomh Solais to light the area up. There were some significant ripples in the water moving towards Padraig. Fionn let out a roar to him to be careful. This brought the rest of the group running out of the cave.

Suddenly, up out of the water came a giant serpent-like creature with large sharp teeth at the end of a long snout. It had rough scales on its body and began snapping at Padraig. He dropped his rod and started running back towards the others. The others ran towards Padraig to help protect him, but the creature rushed out of the water and grabbed him in its mouth, shaking its him furiously from side to side. Shane took out his spear and threw it at the creature, hitting a scaly fin on its back. Holding his hand aloft, the spear returned to him.

The creature dropped Padraig from its mouth and began snapping at the others. The beast's attack left Padraig severely injured and unable to return to the group. The beast was now entirely out of the water and at least twenty feet long, with a long, winding tail. Darragh ran to Padraig and raised him onto his shoulders to carry him back to the safety of the cave. Still, the creature lunged forward, knocking Darragh to the ground, grabbing Padraig in its mouth before turning and leaping into the water with Padraig screaming out in pain.

His screams didn't last long, and a dejected Darragh climbed back to his feet. "I had him", he cried out, "I am so sorry I couldn't save him". Shane approached him, wrapping his arm around him. "It's not your fault," he said, while cradling Darragh's head in his arm.

The boys returned to the safety of the cave as they would not be hunting for food now. A short time later, Bran began barking again, and everyone armed themselves and moved to the cave's opening. The creature had returned, but this time, Shane threw his spear, hitting the beast in the chest. When the spear returned to him, he let out a cry of pain and dropped his spear. The creature's blood, now on the spear, had dripped onto his hand and had burned like acid.

Fionn brought him to the back of the cave to use his healing powers on him. While the others stood guard at the cave mouth, keeping the creature at bay. Fergal took out his dagger, and the light caught the creature's attention. Darragh took Fergal's ring from him and placed it on his finger, telling Fergal to go to the left and keep the monster's gaze. He then began rubbing the ring, blending into the environment as he ran to the right. Just as the effects wore off, he was close enough to slice the creature clean in two.

He held the blade away from himself so the blood wouldn't burn him before rinsing it off in the lake. He then grabbed Shane's spear and did the same to it before returning to the cave. "What the hell was that?" asked Fergal as Darragh handed back his ring. Darragh started sucking his thumb before telling them the creature was called the Ollphéisteanna, or great worm. He checked on Shane, who was well on the mend with the help of Fionn's healing skills.

The group kept a lookout for the rest of the night, taking turns to sleep.

The following morning, the rain had subsided, and they all exited the cave to inspect the creature. It had dark green scales that were very sharp to the touch. Blood still seeping from its wounds, Darragh collected some in an empty vial and placed it into Corrbolg for safekeeping. There were lots of dead fish floating on the water as the creature's blood had killed those swimming near it. The boys then set the creature on fire and quickly left the area to avoid inhaling toxic fumes.

"Onwards we go", said Darragh. We need to reach Kilmagoura. "Surely it can't be any worse than that," said Shane. "Who knows?" said Fionn ", but we'll find out soon enough." They soon came across a small forest and river and decided to hunt and fish for the rest of the day to have some downtime.

As evening fell, they all gathered in a clearing in the forest and set up camp for the night. Once the fire was lit and food eaten, they chopped some leaves off rhubarb plants close by and wrapped the remaining food to keep it fresh. After a small breakfast, they set off to their destination.

When they finally reached Kilmagoura, they saw it was only a tiny little town of only ten houses and a tavern. They tried to get into the tavern, as it was the only building with smoke coming from its chimney, only to find the door barricaded. Fionn called out to see if anyone would answer. With that, someone opened a wooden window shutter and peeped out. "Who is there?" they called out. "We are here to rid you of your problem," said Shane.

There was then some noise coming from the tavern as they removed the barricade. Once inside, some local people who were very pale and rather smelly met the group. "It smells rotten in here," said Fergal. "Did somebody die?". "Yes, lots of people died and that's why we're hiding in here", came the reply.

"Sorry, awful choice of words," said Fergal. The people inside hadn't left the tavern in weeks and had no way of washing or changing clothes. The group escorted people to their houses to fetch clean clothes and then to the river to bathe. When everyone was done, they gathered in the town centre to discuss the problem.

The town leader stepped forward and told the group that some old castle ruins were nearby and that it had recently become occupied by a giant creature that seemed intent on killing all the people in the surrounding areas. The townsfolk heard tales that a dark fairy from the great woods of Kylemore had cast a spell on an unsuspecting female shepherd, Eileen, as she tended her sheep and had happened upon the fairy.

She ended up with the hooves of her sheep at the end of her legs instead of her feet after the angry fairy cast a spell upon her. The villagers had christened her Eileen Óg and, for the last few months, had been wreaking havoc, killing and eating local townsfolk.

"Surely, she doesn't eat people," said Fergal. "No one knows for sure," came the reply, "but how else would she have grown so big?"

The group set up camp in the town centre for the night before going to the castle in the morning when it was bright.

The following morning, they left the town searching for the castle, and it wasn't long before they came upon it. It was a great big building standing on an island-like property. The only way in was by crossing an old-looking drawbridge. The castle walls stood tall and proud and were the strongest thing for miles around. They had built the castle with stones of varying shapes and sizes, and had added battlements, towers, and a central courtyard.

The group cautiously made their way across the drawbridge and into the courtyard. So far, the castle appeared empty. They split into three groups, so there was Fionn & Fergal with Bran. There was Darragh with Shane and Sceolan. While Aron, Sheamus and Conan made up the third. The first group chose the battlements, the second looked for a dungeon, and the third chose the towers. There was an eerie sound of silence as not even birds flew overhead.

As Darragh and Shane walked down some stairs, they could hear the sound of hooves against the hard stone floors and eased back up the stairs. Suddenly, around a corner came the giant creature with greyish-looking skin and wearing the fleece of her sheep as clothing. She did indeed have the hooves of a sheep and carried a giant club. They ran back up the stairs shouting, "To us, to us," which brought the others running back in their direction.

They backed into the courtyard, and Shane threw his spear, but the creature caught it and threw it away. Shane raised his hand, and the spear returned. Aron, Sheamus and Conan came running down the stairs, roaring at the creature, but a swing of its giant club sent them flying through the air.

Fionn then threw his spear, and it struck the beast in the shoulder. Fergal rubbed his ring and disappeared, only to reappear between the creature's legs as it was that tall. He took out his blade and stabbed upwards into the groin repeatedly. The creature grabbed him, slamming him against the wall and knocking him out cold.

Now back on his feet, Conan attacked the beast again and, this time, it slammed him to the ground, crushing him with a swipe of the giant club. Darragh made his way up the stairs while Shane threw his spear at the beast again, hitting it in the chest before returning to him. Fionn ran to check on Fergal as Darragh carried on up the stairs. Aron and Sheamus again ran at the creature.

Shane threw his spear again, hitting the creature in the stomach before returning. Now on a battlement, Darragh was finally in a position above the creature where he was close enough to attack. He jumped down, hitting the beast straight on the shoulder blade, right down through its chest and groin. The creature let out a loud, piercing scream before falling dead on the ground, with each half of its body falling in different directions.

The boys all ran to check on Conan and Fergal, who was now awake and back on his feet. They could not save Conan as his chest had been completely crushed, though Fergal was groggy but fine. The boys then set up a pyre before putting the creature and Conan's remains onto it and setting it alight. The deed was done, and the beast would hurt no one ever again.

The group then set off back to Kilmagoura, where they informed the townsfolk that it was safe for them, as the creature was no more. The town leader gave Darragh a purse with coin in it as payment. Darragh spoke to the rest of the group before returning to talk to the town leader. He asked him how to get to the great woods of Kylemore. They needed to eliminate the dark fairy to prevent a repeat, as they didn't want another five-day journey back to the area.

The group then set off, searching for the dark fairy in Kylemore woods. It was only a day's travel from the town, but it allowed the group time to recover from their previous battle. They set up camp close to the woods to get a good night's sleep before taking on the creature the next morning. Unfortunately, their good night's sleep didn't go to plan, for no sooner had they set up camp and had a fire lit than a menacing-looking human-like creature all dressed in black, with a large pointed hat, appeared in front of them holding a large staff. He growled angrily at the group that they were trespassing.

Fionn stood tall and told the creature that the area belonged to anyone who wanted to use it. Without warning, the creature raised his staff, shooting a fire bolt at the group, which sent everyone running for cover into the forest. The creature shot more firebolts, which didn't hit anyone. The group had separated and hadn't got their weapons as they were in the camp, so they had to be careful in dealing with the creature. They stumbled around in the darkness, trying to find their way back to camp and their weapons.

Fergal rubbed his ring and disappeared before running to the camp to get his weapon. When he reappeared, the creature spotted him and shot a firebolt at him, and he had to jump out of the way just in time. As the creature focused on Fergal, Fionn roared Goliath and ran towards the creature, grabbing it, but it disappeared, before reappearing behind him and hitting him with a firebolt. This gave the others time to return to camp and regain their weapons. In his Goliath state, the firebolt didn't hurt Fionn seriously, but he ran for cover to avoid a second one.

The creature changed its focus towards the rest of the group, and again they ran for the safety of the trees. Sheamus ran at the beast with his sword raised over his head, and the creature cast a spell, turning him into a wild boar. The wild boar then ran at Aron, but Shane threw his spear, killing it instantly. The creature tried casting a spell at Shane, but his amulet protected him.

Fionn had recovered his composure and was hiding behind a tree. Darragh sneaked close to the creature and rubbed his ring of strength before attacking the creature. But the creature again disappeared, reappearing behind him and shooting a firebolt at him, but Darragh rolled out of the way in time. Fergal again rubbed his chameleon ring and disappeared while he also drew his dagger.

It took the creature by surprise, seeing the light from the dagger floating. This allowed Shane to throw his spear at the creature, pinning him to a tree. Then giving Fionn the opportunity to attack with his spear, hitting and poisoning the creature. Fergal and Aron ran at the creature, stabbing it repeatedly before Darragh attacked with his sword and beheaded the creature to end its evil reign. The group then dug a deep hole before burying the creature upside down to prevent any magic from returning the creature to life. They then set off to Kilmagoura to pass on the good news and then set off to Tara to tell Goll the excellent news.

After travelling for five days, they finally arrived back at the fort in Tara and searched for Goll. They spoke to Cormac and told him about Eileen Óg and the dark fairy. The villagers got it cheap, two for the price of one, he said. He was sad at the loss of the three warriors, Padraig, Conan and Sheamus, but praised them, along with the rest of the group, for their bravery.

He told them that Goll was away on business with the king and would take the coin purse from them for safekeeping before telling them to take a well-earned break. Fionn didn't need to be told twice, as he couldn't wait to see Sadhbh. With that, the four of them set off to the farm in Ballyfin. On the way home, Fionn stopped off in a field and picked some lovely flowers to bring home to his new wife.

A few days later, the boys arrived back at the farm to find a very excited Sadhbh running over and leaping into Fionn's arms and kissing him repeatedly as he dropped the flowers. Bodhmall and Liath made their way out, giving all the boys great big welcomes. Fionn and Sadhbh disappeared into their little hut while the others entered the main house. The two women sat there enthralled by the boy's story of their latest adventure. They couldn't believe how far the boys had come in such a short time.

That evening, instead of the usual feast, the women thought it would be a delightful change for them to go to the tavern down in the village. Both Fionn and Sadhbh stayed home with each other while the others all left to have some craic in the tavern. They all had a great night eating, drinking mead, and dancing to the music.

There were a lot of strange looks, when Shane got up and started singing Dirty old town. Fergal disappeared only to return brandishing a new knife with an ivory carved handle that one patron of the tavern had "accidentally given to him" as he walked by his table.

Shane was now standing at the bar chatting with some girls, and Darragh was dancing with Liath when an argument broke out over

Fergal's new knife. The patron who accidentally gave it to him wasn't happy and began shouting that someone had stolen the knife that his father had given him before he died.

Everyone in the tavern started looking under tables and chairs, trying to find the weapon. The man approached everyone, checking to see if they had it until he came across a red-faced Fergal, who swore he found it on the floor and offered to buy him a large mead and return the knife. The tavern grew quiet, waiting to see the man's response, but he accepted the apology and mead, and everything got back to normal, with people singing and dancing.

The other boys laughed, as usual Fergal had talked himself out of trouble. It wasn't long until Fergal and his new drinking buddy were laughing and joking together, before becoming dance partners looping each other as they danced. Liath and Bodhmall made their excuses and left for the night, while Darragh joined Shane and the girls at the bar. They all laughed and joked at Fergal and his dance partner's moves.

Suddenly, Fergal's new buddy stopped dancing and shouted, "where's my knife gone". The tavern grew quiet, and everyone stared at Fergal, who shrugged his shoulders, saying, "it wasn't me" before his dance buddy laughed and said, "oh, here it is in its sheath" Fergal let out a sigh of relief, and the tavern erupted into laughter, as the two of them began dancing once more. Everyone enjoyed the rest of the evening until it was time to call it a night. Shane and Darragh walked the girl's home while Fergal made his way up the hill to the farm.

THE LUGHNASA

The following morning Darragh, Shane and Fergal decided to explore a bit of the countryside as Fionn was too wrapped up in his new bride. They packed some food, said their goodbyes, and off they rode on their horses. They decided they should head west to see if they could find a way home or find a new adventure.

As evening fell, they came across a little town called Tailtin. The town itself was small, but there were lots of camps built up surrounding the town. There were campfires everywhere, with lots of festivities going on. People were singing, dancing, drinking, hugging, and eating. There wasn't much they weren't doing.

The boys thought this looked fun and galloped into the town to ask what was happening. They tied their horses up in a stable and made their way into a somewhat packed tavern. In the tavern, it was as wild as the surrounding areas. There were two big powerful men arm wrestling at a table in the corner. The boys made their way to the bar and asked the Innkeeper what was happening. The Innkeeper told them it was "The Lughnasa".

It was a time for the community to come together to celebrate the harvest of crops. He then offered the boys some mead and a loaf of bread. He told them it was the first loaf batch of the harvest season, and it was customary to bake a special batch of loaves of bread from the first corns picked and to eat them at a celebratory feast.

The boys ate the bread and washed it down with some mead while the Innkeeper continued telling them about The Lughnasa. It was a three-day feast in which everyone partook in the activities. There would be sports contests, horse riding events, matchmaking, singing, dancing and storytelling, and of course, lots of eating to be done.

The boys thanked him for the information and changed their focus to the two men arm-wrestling. There was a queue of people waiting to take on the winner. Darragh joined the queue while the other two enjoyed some more mead. Person after person took on the winner until it was finally Darragh's turn to arm-wrestle. He sat down at the table and, with of rub of his ring and with his extra strength, easily beat the reigning champion. There was still a long queue to challenge, and each time Darragh rubbed the ring, he easily won.

Shane and Fergal began laughing aloud at Darragh, as they were drinking mead and getting drunk, and he wasn't. He finally had enough and threw the next contest to a young girl (Aisling), making her the defending champion. Darragh got himself a mead, while Fergal, now getting drunk on his own mead, became infatuated with the girl, as being drunk and didn't realise Darragh had let her win.

The next contestant beat the girl, and Fergal rushed to console her. He introduced himself and asked her name. He told her she was the strongest girl he had ever met before, asking her to dance. Not long after, an exhausted and drunk Fergal slumped on a table and fell asleep. The others thought it was time to get him to bed. They rented a room for the night and carried him up to bed. As the night was still young, the other two boys left to see what was happening outside.

They came across an enormous bonfire with people dancing around it and singing. Lugh was the God of the harvest and the people sacrificed a cow to him. They had cooked the cow on a large spit, and close by, there was a big black three-legged iron pot over an open fire containing boiled potatoes, cabbage, leeks, with scallions and wild garlic. The boys made their way over and got two large portions for themselves. "This is the closest thing to a meal back home," said Shane as the two boys reminisced about life and their families back home.

They walked around, and no matter where they looked, there was merriment, with all the people having fun, singing, dancing, and getting drunk. They stumbled upon a campfire where the women were all dressed in long purple and green dresses with a long black hooded cloak. The men wore green tunics and purple trousers with a black hooded cloak. Shane remembered Cred.

Could she be here, and did she belong to this group? He checked around and asked, but got no information about her. A dejected Shane then told Darragh it was time for bed. Darragh put his arm around Shane's shoulder and consoled him as the two returned to the tavern and bed for the night.

The following morning, all the boys made their way downstairs for breakfast. Before leaving the tavern, the Innkeeper told them that people would make a day of it, setting off early for the festivities. When the boys walked outside, there were people on foot, horseback and even ox-drawn carts, bringing plenty of food, drink and musical instruments for the day ahead. The boys got their horses and followed them until they reached an enormous field.

In the centre of the field stood a large rock, called Cloghstuckagh Moyvoughly standing stone. Young girls picked wildflowers and made them into garlands, placing them around the standing stone. There were several stalls with people selling their wares. They were selling items such as livestock, vegetables, fish, meat, clothes and weapons, amongst other things. A large wooden door with a hole near the middle of the field looked out of place, but many people were sitting close to it.

They placed ropes around the outskirts of the field, making a racing track and separating the area from a river nearby. There was also a wild goat wearing a crown, being paraded around as the king of the festival. Walking close by was Aisling, the girl from the tavern. They had crowned her as queen of the festival. "Aisling, Aisling" shouted Fergal while waving at her like a madman. She blushed and coyly waved back at him. "He's got a girlfriend, he wants to kiss her, he wants to marry her," joked Shane and Darragh as they laughed loudly, giving each other a high five.

The boys heard that the first event was a horse-riding event and made their way over to the start. This was no ordinary race, though, as the tradition was that the race had to be run in the nude, although no one knew why. "I guess that rules you and your little weapon out, Fergal", teased Shane while he slapped him on the back. Fergal, however, didn't see the funny side and was the first of the boys to strip off and get to the starting post.

Darragh and Shane soon followed, telling Fergal to lighten up. Many people were taking part, male and female, all waiting for the flag to drop and unembarrassed by the lack of clothing. When the flag dropped, they all set off at a gallop around the racetrack on the outskirts of the field. The winner would be the first person to ride around the track three times.

The boys gave it their best shot, but none of them even came close to winning, but they all had great fun taking part. "Wow, did you see the girl with the red hair?" asked Darragh. "I don't know what you mean", giggled Shane, while Fergal said he had kept looking out for Aisling. The boys all dressed as they wanted to see what the next event was.

As they walked, they saw a group of children playing leapfrog close to the river while their mothers were throwing lumps of butter into it, as it was supposed to ensure that their cows would produce plenty of milk throughout the year. The old folk gossiped and amused themselves while watching the children and their mothers. "Strange tradition," said Darragh as they walked by.

The boys then came to the next event, a straight-line race from one end of the field to the next. This time it was different, as the women and men competed separately. Fergal cheered loudly as the queen of the festival, Aisling, won her race before the boys got ready for theirs. All the male competitors readied themselves and, as the flag dropped, ran as fast as they could. Shane gave a rub on his ring and dashed off ahead of everyone, winning the race easily.

Next up was a spear-throwing challenge. "Ah, it's not fair," said Fergal. "My ring makes me disappear, and I don't have speed or strength like you two," he said to the others as he sat this one out. Darragh romped the event with the aid of his bear ring. When this event was over, the boys decided it was time for food and looked around in search of something tasty.

They came across the same meal as the previous night and ate this, as Fergal had missed out the previous night. While they sat there eating, the boys overheard someone saying that two guards protected the king of the festival and that if anyone could steal its crown without being spotted, they would be the new festival king.

"Aha", roared Fergal. ", This one is for me". No sooner had he eaten his food than he ran off searching for the goat. He didn't have to look far. In the middle of the field, staked to the ground, the goat and two guards were next to the standing stone.

He approached the guards and started talking to them. He pointed to the oncoming Darragh and Shane and told the guards that they were two dodgy-looking characters. As the guards looked over at the boys, Fergal rubbed his ring, disappearing and grabbing the crown from the goat before running away.

When the other two boys reached them, they asked the guards where the crown was, while the embarrassed guards and onlookers didn't know what had happened. Suddenly, out from the crowd walked Fergal with the crown on his head, grinning from ear to ear with a big glint in his eye. The guards clapped and said he had beaten them, and they released the goat back into the wild.

Now that Fergal was the king, he looked for his queen. She wasn't hard to find as she was standing near the large wooden door with a hole. The boys made their way over to her, with Fergal excitedly telling her she was his queen. She told him she was delighted and had cheered him on earlier while he was in the horse race. The others teased him, telling him she had seen his little weapon. A somewhat embarrassed Fergal asked Aisling sheepishly what the door was for.

She told him they conducted trial marriages at the door and young couples who joined hands through the hole in the door entered a trial marriage that lasted a year and a day. After this time, they could make the marriage permanent or break it without consequences if either person wasn't happy to proceed.

Darragh and Shane looked on in astonishment as Fergal asked Aisling if she would like to join hands through the door. Aisling accepted, and the two of them made their way over, joining hands through the door. A person called the doorkeeper wrapped flowers around their hands, which began their trial marriage.

Before the others could pick their jaws up off the floor, Shane got a tap on the shoulder. As he turned around, he jumped for joy as a beaming Cred stood before him. "What are you waiting for?" asked Darragh. "Get her to the door". Shane didn't need to be told twice.

He asked Cred if she wanted to try marriage, to which she nodded yes. "You're the last of the romantics", laughed Darragh. "What kind of proposal was that?" he asked. Shane didn't even answer as he rushed Cred to the door. As the doorkeeper tied flowers around their hands, Darragh spotted the redhead from the earlier horserace and made his way over to her.

When he reached the girl, he introduced himself and asked for her name. She told him it was Cliona, and that she had travelled from Ballyfin along with Aisling, the festival queen, as they were sisters. Darragh said to her he, too, was from Ballyfin, as they often stayed on Bodhmall's farm. The other two couples made their way over and asked if they planned to use the door, but Darragh said it was too soon, as they had just met. Cliona said she didn't think her parents would be happy with two daughters returning from the festival with husbands in tow.

It was now evening, and the three couples spotted and approached an enormous bonfire, where they all sat down and drank some mead. There was a play about the struggle for the harvest between two gods, Crom Dubh and Lugh. Crom Dubh jealously guarded the grain as his personal treasure, but Lugh had to seize it for humankind. The play ended with Lugh defeating Crom Dubh, thus ensuring that all the surrounding villages and townsfolk would enjoy an excellent harvest for the year ahead.

When the play ended, all three couples left to go their separate ways, after they had agreed to meet back at the wooden door the following morning. Darragh and Cliona chose a walk down by the riverside. Where They sat down under a tree and talked until falling asleep. Shane and Cred walked back to her camp, where they spent the night, while Fergal and Aisling walked and talked until they ended up back at the bonfire, where they sat down and fell asleep in each other's arms.

The following morning, they all met back at the wooden door, except Cred, who had disappeared again before Shane had woken up. This was the festival's last day and the day's main event was a faction fight, whereby two groups of young men and women fought with sticks until one group came out on top. The rival groups had to build towers of sods topped with a flag.

The competition could last for the entire day, as each group tried to sabotage the other's tower or capture its flag. If too many team members got injured, that team had to give up the event. The three boys put their weapons aside and, along with the two girls, grabbed their sticks before joining the red team.

Each team had twenty members on each team. Before the event started, each team had to cut out thirty sods of turf from the surrounding fields, stacking them on top of each other to create their tower before placing their flag on top. At the sound of a horn blowing, the competition would begin. Vast crowds of young men, women, and children gathered to watch the festival's climax.

Darragh sat the troops down for a quick chat. As the strongest, he would stay and protect the tower from attack. The two girls would help him. It meant he could help to protect them along with the tower. He told Shane that as he was the fastest and best with a staff or stick, he should focus on the battlefield to defeat as many of the opposing team as possible to stop them from reaching their tower or flag. While Fergal was the most agile, he should make his way to the front of the battlefield, trying to evade the enemies and either knock down their tower or capture their flag.

The rest of their team would split up between the three positions. Two would stay with Darragh and the girls, three would join Fergal upfront, attacking the tower and flag, while the rest would make up the main body of ten people, along with Shane on the battlefield to fight and take out the opposition team. Each team member raced to their position once the horn had sounded.

The blue team weren't as well organised as the red team. They split their team in two, with ten in defence and ten in the attack. Darragh sent the other two members forward to give Shane more significant numbers in the middle of the battlefield. Time passed by with no team making substantial inroads on the other. Even with his agility, they struck Fergal many times, and he had to back off along with his three helpers. This gave them a more significant advantage in the middle of the battlefield, now giving Shane seventeen against ten, as the blue team rigidly kept ten back, protecting their base.

It didn't take long for Shane and his troops to get the upper hand, with many of the blue team dropping out injured. With their injuries mounting, they dropped back into a defensive stance. It blunted the red's attack as the other team repeatedly pushed back. The injuries then started mounting on the red team, and it turned into a bit of a stalemate. This led to Darragh calling Shane and Fergal back to their tower.

After a quick discussion, they gave each other high fives. Darragh gave Shane his bear ring and Fergal took Shane's cheetah ring. While Fergal stayed back, Shane made his way towards the front of the battlefield. When Shane gave the word, Fergal started running towards him, rubbing the cheetah ring and increasing his speed.

Shane rubbed the bear ring and linked his hands while crouching. As Fergal reached Shane, he stood on his hands and was thrown through the air, as he rubbed the chameleon ring, disappearing from view. He landed safely on top of the blue team's tower before raising their flag and claiming victory.

The blue teams' members all threw their sticks on the ground before storming off. The red team gathered on the battlefield, dancing and singing, congratulating each other. The boys gave the rings back to each other. After the win, each member had a winner's garland of fresh flowers placed around their neck.

This gave them a free pass for the day at the festival, which meant free drinks, food, and the best seating for musical performances. Potential partners who wanted to join hands through the wooden door courted the team, but the group accepted no proposals, as they were spoken for.

They made the most of their free passes, enjoying food and drinks for the rest of the day while also partaking in singing and dancing before finally getting the best seats to watch a repeat of the two gods, Crom Dubh and Lugh fighting over the harvest. This was the last deed of the festival and brought everything to a close. The three boys and two girls then lay down on the grass next to a bonfire and slept for the night.

The following morning, the girls asked if the boys would escort them safely back to Ballyfin, and they duly obliged, as they wanted to return to the farm. When they reached Ballyfin, Aisling insisted on Fergal meeting her parents, while Darragh arranged to see Cliona in the tavern that night before he and Shane made their way up to the farm. Sometime later, Fergal arrived at the farm and Bodhmall, Liath, Fionn, and Sadhbh greeted him with big hugs and congratulated him on marrying.

As Bodhmall and Liath didn't grow crops, they didn't need to harvest any, so that evening, the entire group made their way down to the tavern. They were all eager to meet Aisling and Cliona. Shane was hoping to see Cred but was disappointed as she was not there. The rest of the group met the two girls, and all had a great time together except for Shane. He stood at the bar drinking and moping.

Darragh tried to speak to him, and he blurted out, "How are we to see if our marriage works? when she is nowhere to be found?". Darragh hugged him and, with a smile, said it would all work out in the end. He told Shane to sing him a song, and with that, Shane jolted into life, jumping up next to the musician and singing an out-of-tune song.

The rest of the group gave Darragh a few slaps for subjecting them to a bag of singing cats, while the rest of the tavern just booed him. This made Shane raise his voice, singing out even louder. When he finished his song, he asked if they wanted another tune, to which he got a resounding "NO". Laughing out loud, he re-joined the others and carried on drinking. As the night ended, Darragh and Fergal walked the two girls home while the rest of the group made their way up to the farm.

DOWNTIME

The next day, Darragh suggested a break and that Shane, Fergal and himself should go camping for a day or two, just the three boys, like it was back home. The others thought this was a great idea, so they packed up some minor supplies, ensuring to have a supply of mead, and after saying their goodbyes, rode off out of the farm.

On their way, they set a snare in a small wooded area and then went fishing. When they returned, they had captured a grey squirrel, and this would go nicely with some fish they had caught and some mushrooms they had foraged earlier.

A short distance later, they came across a stone circle. The circle comprising seventeen sandstone pillar stones, each at the height of at least two meters. At the circle's centre, they found the cremated remains of a young person in an urn. There was also a cooking pit. The boys would need to stay alert.

They searched nearby and found some twigs and wood for their fire, which they built in the cooking pit they found. They stuck upright small branches in the ground and a vertical branch piercing the squirrel and fish stuffed with mushrooms and placed it on the upright branches as they had no pots or water for cooking.

The three boys then sat down to reminisce about home. Fergal, being the youngest, was finding it the hardest being away from home. He really missed his family. He said he could picture his younger brothers playing in their garden while his parents would worry about him. Darragh said he was missing his parents and his bed, while Shane said he could picture Lucy, who was a bit of a tomboy, telling his parents to keep it together as he would be home soon. Shane and Fergal both mocked Darragh for missing his bed.

He checked to ensure they had their MP3s with their favourite podcast downloaded. As they hadn't used them, the batteries should be fine. He hoped the stone circle didn't have any energy that would disrupt their mp3s. After their food was prepared and eaten, they all took out their headphones and mp3s and turned them on while placing them over their ears. They drank some of their mead while listening to the podcast. Suddenly Fergal started laughing out loud while lying down, thumping the ground. The other two looked at him and asked what he was listening to.

Fergal was listening to podcast episode 4 (laughable). It was about overlooked media news stories from the week. It had great comedy minds telling bizarre tales sprinkled with just the right amount of swearing, bickering, and laughter. The other two boys were listening to episode 3 (Haunted house). When a family moved into their dream home, it quickly became their worst nightmare when they talked about the Hoia Forest Haunting.

"You must be joking if you think I'm sitting in a scary place like this listening about haunted forests," said Fergal. "Good point," said Shane as he and Darragh switched to episode 4. Soon all three boys were rolling around the ground laughing. As the flames died, Fergal took out Claíomh Solais to light the place up, hoping to deter wildlife, as the boys slept for the night. They took turns keeping watch as the remains in the urn concerned them.

Luckily, there was nothing to worry about, and when they woke up the next morning, Shane thanked the other two boys for a great night, as it had taken his mind off everything. They then packed up camp before setting off. They soon reached a large wooded area and decided to play some games. First, they pinned a large leaf to a tree trunk and, at the count of three, had to take out their daggers and see who could hit the leaf first.

Darragh called out, 1,2,3, and as he reached for his dagger, it wasn't in its sheath. The same happened to Shane, while a laughing Fergal took out his blade, throwing it and hitting the leaf. "I guess I win", he laughed. "Oh yeah, here's your daggers," he said as he handed the boys back their daggers that he had stolen.

The boys then decided to see who could shoot an arrow closest to the centre of the leaf. This time, there would be no time limit in case anyone got ideas about robbing arrows. All three boys hit the leaf, destroying it, and they all claimed bragging rights. Next, they cut some branches and sat at the edge of a nearby river while attaching string and hooks. They would see who was the quickest to catch a fish.

Darragh pulled up a sod of turf and found a worm, which he attached to the hook before throwing it into the water. He was the first to catch a bite, so he claimed victory. "Right," said Shane, "let's see who can race to the nearby tree and climb it the quickest", before dashing off, leaving the others behind and climbing to the top, shouting victory was his. The boys all gathered around each other, having a group hug. "This is awesome," said Fergal, "just like back home".

Next, the boys had a horse race. They all jumped onto their horses and galloped off. First, to the far side of the large wooded area, would win. As they rode off, Fergal rubbed his ring and disappeared. The other two boys stopped, thinking he must have fallen off his horse. A laughing Fergal reappeared well in the lead before reaching the far side of the woods in a canter. "You little shit", the boys roared with laughter, as they were well and truly fooled.

That was enough fooling around for the day, and they decided to sit and drink some mead. Looking back at the river, Shane spied a woman sitting at the river's edge and approached to have a chat with her. As he got closer, he began rubbing his eyes as if it wasn't a woman but a black horse. The horse looked jet black and really fit, so Shane decided he had to own it. He picked up some grass and approached the horse, offering it something to eat.

As the horse began eating it, Shane jumped on its back, grabbing it by the main. The horse reared up on its back legs, neighing loudly, before running into the river, trying to buck Shane from its back. Shane wrapped his arms around its neck, but the bucking got wilder and wilder until he fell off into the river. Darragh ran over, laughing hysterically at Shane. "What's so funny?" asked Shane.

"That must have been a Pooka," replied Darragh. "A Pooka, what's a Pooka?" asked Fergal. "It's a shapeshifter," said Darragh. "A changeling that can take on animal or human forms like a horse, a donkey, a dog, a bull, a young man, or even a young woman. The animal Pooka is usually jet black with fiery golden or red eyes," he said. "Thanks for telling me," said Shane. "I just did", laughed Darragh. "But you didn't give me time to warn you." He said while helping the soaked Shane out of the river.

Shane had other ideas and pulled Darragh into the river, while Fergal, not wanting to be the odd one out, dived in after them. The boys splashed around before getting out and making their way to their horses. They then moved into the wooded area and took off their wet clothes, hanging them on low-lying branches to dry. They then lit a fire and cooked the fish Darragh had caught earlier, then washed it down with the last of their mead before taking turns telling stories until they all fell asleep for the night.

The following morning, the boys all readied themselves, mounted their horses, and set off in no particular direction. They came to the top of a hill and, while looking down, saw some corn fields with plough tracks going through it, and on the far side was a small wooded area. They agreed to have a race, and the first one through the cornfields and over to the wooded area would be champion.

They galloped off as fast as they could, each taking a separate track. Darragh was first out of the fields, followed by Shane and Fergal's horse came out last. They galloped until they reached the wooded area. Darragh proclaimed himself as champion. "You're not fooling anyone this time, Fergal," he said, but there was no reply, and he didn't appear.

They waited patiently for him, but still Fergal didn't appear. After grabbing his horse by the lead, they headed back towards the cornfields and up the track. They came across Fergal lying face down unconscious and leapt from their horses to help him. They placed him sideways on his horse and led him out of the field and over to the wooded area. There was a small clearing with a small creek running through it. They Lay him down and grabbed a sycamore leaf, filling it with water while raising his head to get him to drink.

Fergal woke up and started screaming in pain. A rat startled his horse, which threw him off and he had broken his lower left leg. Thinking quickly, the boys broke some branches and, with the help of some vines, tied them around his leg in a splint to stabilise it. "We better get him back to the farm so Fionn can fix him," said Darragh. When he was ready, the others lifted Fergal onto his horse and set off back to the farm in Ballyfin.

The boys headed straight for the farm, riding through the night to get him back as quickly as possible. When they reached the farm, they called out to Fionn, who came out and carried Fergal into the main house. Fionn lay him on the table while he placed his healing hands above and below the leg break to heal it.

Darragh decided he wanted to see Finnegas to see if he, too, could learn any healing spells. Shane said he would go too, so off the two boys set. A few days later, they met with Finnegas, but he could not teach them any spells and didn't have any rings or pendants that would help either.

Next, they visited Biddy to ask her if she could teach them any healing spells. She was low on ingredients for creating potions but told them there was a magical spring that only flowed once a month from Aghade, a curious flat stone with a circular hole in it 30 cm in diameter. It only flowed at midnight and for only a few minutes.

She gave the boys her biggest empty vial, so they could find the magical spring and get as much healing water as possible into the vial for safekeeping. Once the boys had the directions, they thanked Biddy and off they rode. They came across the stone as described and set up camp, waiting for midnight to arrive. When the water started flowing, Darragh filled the vial before placing it into the corrbolg. As they weren't far from Tara, they dropped into the camp to see if everything was ok.

When they reached the main gate, they spotted Cormac and went to talk to him. He seemed happy to see them, but warned that Goll had returned and had brought his brother Conan with him. He told the lads that they would either love or hate him, as he was renowned for his insults, lack of tact, and troublemaking. The boys thanked him and set off to the tavern to quench their thirst.

When they got inside the tavern, they spotted a bald, overweight man talking loudly and insulting some men that were there drinking. When he spotted Darragh, he made his way towards him, hurling insults at him while telling Shane he looked like a pretty little girl. "I guess you're Conan," said Darragh. "Your reputation precedes you", he said.

"What is that supposed to mean?" roared Conan while laughing loudly. "It means you're a bit of an obnoxious overweight eejit," said Darragh. "Right," said Conan, "I challenge you to an arm-wrestling match, and the loser must apologise to the other". "Deal," said Darragh as he readied himself while rubbing his bear ring, easily beating Conan. Conan then issued an apology and said the drinks were on him.

Conan spent the rest of the night buying mead for Darragh and Shane. As the night ended, the boys told Conan that he was all right, and they would look forward to crossing paths again, as maybe he wasn't an eejit after all. Conan laughed and told the lads he would look forward to it. The boys headed to bed for the night before setting off for Ballyfin the following morning.

When the boys reached the farm, they asked how Fergal was and indeed where he was., "Oh, he's up at the river, and his leg is better", said Liath. The two boys ran to check on him, only to find him lying by the river's edge. Aisling was with him with his head cradled in her lap while wiping his forehead with a damp cloth.

"Get up out of that!" shouted Shane. "What?" said Fergal. "I'm still feeling weak". "Get up, you plonker", laughed Darragh. "there's nothing wrong with you". A red-faced Fergal sat up and thanked Aisling for looking after him. The boys left them alone and headed back down to the farm. Fergal remained sitting, feigning injury and exhaustion while a concerned Aisling gave him her undivided attention.

That evening Darragh gathered everyone around the table in the main house. They needed to sort out what they were going to do next. He thought it was important that Fionn should make more friends and acquaintances within the Fianna, as the only people he knew were the boys. He would need allies within its ranks to become its leader. Sadhbh reluctantly agreed that this was the best course of action. Fionn should travel with the boys to Tara while she would remain at the farm with Bodhmall and Liath. There were also Aisling and Cliona to keep her company. "Right, that's it," said Darragh. "Tomorrow, we leave for Tara."

CHAPTER SEVEN

THE WILD HUNT

he following morning, the four boys took their leave along with Bran and Sceolan. Bodhmall, Liath, Sadhbh, Aisling and Cliona, who had made their way up the hill, all waved them goodbye. Onwards the boys travelled and, as always, stopped off to visit Biddy and Finnegas. Cormac welcomed them into the fort when they finally reached Tara. They made their way to the tavern, where Conan met them with a grunt. Darragh introduced Fionn and Fergal, while Conan introduced Aron, Diarmuid, Cailte, Aengus, Fiacha and Innsa to the group.

"You all arrived at the right time," said Conan, "for tomorrow we prepare for the wild hunt." "What's that?" asked Fergal curiously. "It is the greatest hunt you can take part in," said Conan. "No one knows how or when it started, but it is part magical, part creatures, but all self-preservation," he said.

When it comes, it is said it will arrive with the old witch Cailleach Bheara at its head. This really excited the boys, and they could barely contain their excitement. Conan told them they should drink and be merry, as the hunt was difficult and dangerous, and that tonight's drink could be their last.

The following morning, everybody had a big hearty breakfast to keep their strength up. Everyone sharpened their blades and ensured that there were plenty of arrows in their quivers. They then mounted their horses and set off out of the fort. They then rode off to reach the plains of Knockmullin. Once they had laid eyes on the Loughscur Dolmen (a tall standing stone), they would prepare for the hunt to begin. Suddenly, out of nowhere, a giant stampede appeared. It was like a spectral fog rolling out across the plains.

There appeared to be large elk, wild boar and horses stampeding wildly, with what looked like hundreds of sluagh flying overhead. At the front was a half spectral, ugly-looking woman. One side of her face was hideously disfigured, the other extremely wrinkled, her hair was like grey mist waving round her head. It had to be Cailleach Bheara. Goll, who had now joined the group with some more troops, roared at everyone to arm themselves, as the creatures were there to take their souls before storming off in chase.

With that, Conan blew on his great battle horn, and all the troops set off in chase of the creatures. In all the confusion, it was hard even to think what to do, as the mist and fog everywhere meant visibility was abysmal. The stampede seemed to stay within the Loughscur Dolmen and a similar Dolmen two miles away. Shane was the best hunter as he threw his spear, holding his hand aloft, and it would return to him to try again. While the others could only shoot arrows into the fog and mist, hoping to hit a creature.

However, they were all bored with this, and Fionn, along with Bran and Sceolan, charged into the mist. He roared goliath while turning into his giant form and grabbed one elk by the neck, hurling it into the path of some others, knocking them off their feet, before doing the same to another.

Darragh had charged in after him and was killing the fallen beasts with his sword, while Fergal, not to be left behind, charged in and was jumping from animal to animal while stabbing them a few times, injuring them. "I killed nine", shouted Shane, "sorry, make that ten", he laughed.

The stampede continued, and you could hear people screaming and animals grunting and screeching while they charged or died. Darragh's horse took a tumble and slammed into a fallen animal, sending him crashing to the ground. He jumped to his feet and rubbed his bear ring before lashing out at some oncoming animals, taking them down. Fionn was happily throwing animals at each other with his sheer strength, laughing as he did so.

An exhausted Fergal withdrew from the stampede to marvel at the spectacle of it all. While Darragh had to dive behind dead carcasses, overwhelmed by the sheer number of beasts charging at him. He called out to Fionn, who was close by, to come and help him. Fionn came and stood in front of the carcasses and kept hitting them as they approached, knocking them off their feet. Those who could return to their feet ran around Fionn and Darragh, thus saving Darragh from being injured.

After many hours had passed by, and just as quickly as it had appeared, the stampede, mist and fog, along with the witch, all disappeared. It had been a long day with many troops and animals injured or dead. All the uninjured troops travelled around the plains, checking on injured troops and picking up any weapons that were dropped. They skinned the elk and the boars for their furs just in time for the cold of winter. It was also time to stock up on animal meats for the winter.

Townsfolk, for miles around, had gathered to watch the hunt. They stayed a safe distance to wait until it was safe to collect the dead animals to feed their towns in the cold months ahead. In some parts of the plains, the sluagh swarmed down to take the souls of badly injured or dead men. While others tried in vain to chase them away.

When the dust had settled, Fionn called out for Bran and Sceolan, but they didn't come, so the boys scoured the debris of dead bodies in search of them. They eventually found them with Bran injured and Sceolan sitting with him, protecting him from harm. Fionn hugged the two dogs while telling Sceolan she was a brilliant girl for saving her brother. Fionn then got to work on Bran with his healing hands, and it wasn't long before he was back on his feet.

Some distance away, Goll thought he saw Cailleach Bheara and set off after her, bringing Conan, Cailte, Aengus and Fiacha with him. Everyone else stomped around, cleaning up the plains. Darragh, Fionn, Shane and Fergal set off after Goll and his men, but as night fell, they hadn't found them. They agreed to set up camp and look again in the morning. At daybreak, they searched for the others and came to a field full of black sheep grazing. In a corner of the field, they spotted a cave with horses outside of it and made their way towards it.

When they reached the cave, Fergal took out Claíomh Solais and strode into the cave. To his horror, all five men were stuck to the ground. He called to the others, who followed him in. Cleary in pain and discomfort, Goll said they had thought they had Cailleach Bheara trapped in the cave, but upon entering it, she cast a spell on them, sticking them to the ground. Darragh began sucking his thumb for ideas and suddenly realised that pouring the magical water from the spring on them could release them from the spell.

He took the vial of water out of the corrbolg and poured it onto the trapped men. First, he poured it onto Goll, who was the nearest to him, and then he and Fionn pulled him up off the ground. Next, it was Cailte, Aengus and Fiacha, with each pulled up successfully. When he tried to pour the water on Conan, there was only enough water to free his legs and arms.

Darragh said he would have to wait a month for the spring water to return. Conan insisted they get him up now. Darragh told the others to leave the cave and that he and Fionn would get him out. Darragh rubbed his bear ring, and Fionn shouted Goliath before grabbing him by the hands and feet, ripping him out of the ground.

Conan let out a gigantic roar and feinted as the skin on his back was ripped from his body. Thinking quickly and to stop the loss of blood, Darragh told the others to kill and skin one of the nearby sheep. They laid him down on the sheepskin, and there must have been some magic of adhesion still left on Conan's back because the sheep's skin stuck fast to him, and before long, it grew in place of his old skin. When Conan awoke, he was the butt of everyone's jokes, but he soon saw the funny side, as he could either laugh or cry, and he was just happy to be alive and not stuck to the ground.

Now that they were all back on their feet and out of the cave, Goll said they should return to check on the rest of the troops. So off they rode back to Tara. The Fianna had lost five men to the hunt, while ten injured soldiers were being taken care of. "That was not a bad day's work," said Goll, with so few casualties.

Though he was unimpressed with being put under a spell, so he put together a group of his best soldiers to pursue Cailleach Bheara to her den. The group comprising Fionn, Darragh, Shane, Fergal, Conan, Aron, Diarmuid, Cailte, Aengus, Fiacha and Innsa. They all had a hearty meal and prepared their weapons for battle before setting off out of camp. They brought twelve Irish wolfhounds, including Bran and Sceolan.

The group travelled across the plains in the direction where the witch was last seen. Autumn leaves were falling, and you could hear the wind playing like music through the trees. With rodents scurrying on the fallen leaves. As they strode further, there was an eerie silence as a mist crept over the plains. They strolled over animal paths into the hills. Then set the hounds loose to see if they could find anything. As they ran and chased through the mists for many hours, the group realised that they had lost track of their dogs.

As if that wasn't bad enough, they had got lost themselves and weren't sure where they were. Now in poor form, tired and hungry, they started grumbling and arguing amongst themselves. Suddenly they heard a distant, piteous cry, and soon the dogs reappeared, tired and wet and covered in bog-mire from head to toe. Bran lay before Fionn and howled a long and mournful howl. "I think," said Fionn, "he knows of some unknown danger which may threaten us from the mists, and would tell us if he could speak."

They all turned at hearing a rustling in the bushes, where a woman emerged from the moonlit mists. She was beautiful, with long fair hair flowing down to the hem of her silver-woven dress, and she spoke to their astonishment. "Surely you are Fionn?" She said. "There is a woman close by who wishes to meet you, and has prepared a sumptuous feast in your honour."

"At last, some good news," said Fionn, "I should very much like to meet her now!"

The woman smiled and courteously included the entire group in the invitation. They walked a short distance to a house built on top of a little hill overlooking an inlet on a lake. There, they all followed her into the house. Where they each had a fine and hearty meal.

Fionn asked about the woman who had invited them for he wished to thank her for the meal. Just then a woman came in, and Fionn recoiled in horror, for he had never seen a woman so ugly. One side of her face was hideous and the other extremely wrinkled, and her hair was long and grey. Surely this was their prey, Cailleach Bheara.

"Good evening," she said to Fionn, "I know you well, and your fame caused me to summon you, so I could have a look at you to see if I liked the look of you! And I do, so you shall be my husband and share in all of my riches." Fionn nearly choked, and the shock caused his normally polite nature to shout in anger.

"Not all the treasure in the world would make me take you for my wife", he said, and said. That he was already married to the most beautiful woman in the world. The witch said if he refused her demands, no power would save him or his companions from her wrath. Upon hearing this, Fionn and the others laughed scornfully, amused that this woman thought of not just fighting them but killing them too. He and the best of his Fianna warriors!

"Laugh," she said sharply. "For soon you will laugh no more, but I will play and sing for you before you rest."

She took a small ornate harp of a very ancient style from a chest and played to them, then she chanted a little song to them in an unknown tongue, which seemed strange yet familiar, and a peculiar helplessness relaxed their limbs. Although they felt something was about to happen, they had no strength to stop it.

Seeing that her witchcraft had conquered the men, she put aside the harp, and she took up a sharp sword instead. She jumped from one warrior to the next, slaying Fiacha and Innsa without mercy, mocking them. Seeing this, Fionn cried out to her. "Spare the men, but kill me if you like, for I was the one who scorned you!"

The woman only laughed and turned to continue, but Fionn said, "How can I take you for my wife? When Goll mac Morna is the leader and most feared man in Ireland, surely Goll would make a better, more fitting husband for you."

The witch considered for a moment, then she chirped, "I will go to Goll. In the meantime, I will restore to you and your group freedom to move, but do not think of escaping, for I have placed a spell upon you that holds you to this place."

The following day, Goll walked from his tent upon hearing a cry from his men and looked down at the nearby river, where a grey mist was receding. Several ships had appeared, and distant figures were looking back at him. He sent a soldier to speak with the strangers and find out what they wanted. "Go back and tell Goll I have come to take him as my husband, or kill him as I have done to those he sent after me," said the woman, and she glared at the soldier so venomously that he hurried away back to Goll.

After telling Goll what the woman wanted, they grieved for never again would they see the others, or so they believed, and the warriors gathered around and raised a battle cry of fierce vengeance. Goll sent a reply that she would have to kill him as he would never marry her. It was nearly noon when soldiers reported that a host of warriors led by the fog-haired woman were coming ashore in small boats, so Goll sent his warriors to stop them from landing.

There was a fierce battle, but Goll's men succumbed, and beaten by spear, sword, or witchcraft. When Goll saw how it was going, he called out to the woman that there should be peace between them for the night, and they could fight again in the morning. "I will let the last of your soldiers go free, Goll", she said, "if you agree to meet me in single combat. If you will not, I will fight on until you are all dead." Goll agreed and set the fight rules so that only one would walk away alive.

The next morning, he armed himself and rushed down to the strand, and the whole day he and the woman fought, neither gaining the victory they wanted. That evening, they called a temporary truce and would continue the next morning. When Goll lay down to sleep, he had so many bleeding wounds he feared he must surely lose the fight.

Back in the witch's house, one guard keeping watch over Fionn and the others had a beautiful daughter called Eithne, who would sit nearby and listen while they spoke of past adventures. She seemed gentle and kind, unlike the witch, and each time Diarmuid saw her, his feelings for her grew more and more deeply.

"If I were a free man," he said to her, "I would ask you to leave your people and come to be my wife. But no matter how we try, we cannot break the spell the old witch has laid on us."

"How can I be sure of your love?" she asked. "Am I not one of your enemies?" "I swear, I speak only the truth!" he said, and she sensed that he truly loved her. "I give you my love, and I will follow wherever you go," she whispered. "This night you will be free, for I have power unknown to the witch, and it will release you from her spell."

While all the guards slept, she approached them and, standing over them, lifted her hands and said a spell in a foreign tongue. The men stood up and were delighted to find that their strength had returned to them, and they were free. They thanked Eithne before gathering their weapons and readying themselves to leave. Suddenly and to the great horror of the others, Conan lifted his sword and, with a single blow, severed Eithne's head from her body!

All stood astounded by his treachery, as she had shown them all such kindness. Enraged, Diarmuid swiftly drew his sword to strike Conan, but Darragh stepped in and warned them it wasn't the time for infighting. Diarmuid dropped the matter with great reluctance, and they left and travelled through the night, reaching camp just as Goll painfully prepared for the next day's battle.

The group all wanted to fight the invaders, but Goll would have none of it, as he had agreed, and would stick to it. Ultimately, Goll was too weak to fight, so Fionn went in his place. The witch was astounded to see Fionn freed from the spell and standing before her, but her anger was greater, and she leapt into battle and they fought for the whole day.

Fionn was having the worst of it, and as the sun set, he tired, but Darragh and Shane called out to him to be strong. Suddenly, the witch let out a cry of pain and dropped to her knees. With that, Fionn roared "Goliath" before transforming and slamming his spear deep into her chest, killing her. Just then, Fergal appeared behind the witch. He had sneaked up on her using his chameleon ring and stabbed her in the back, which made her drop to her knees.

The witches' men retreated as quickly as possible to the river and boarded their boats in great haste, for fear of being pursued by the lads, and they sailed away as the troops, instead, raised Fergal on their shoulders and cheered him on as he was the real hero. That evening, the troops built an enormous bonfire and burned the witch's remains to ensure she never roamed the earth again.

The following morning after resting for the night, an injured yet grateful to be alive, Goll gathered his men and, taking Fionn and Fergal with him, walked amongst the troops raising their hands in triumph and a job well done. He pledged to Fionn and the others that he would never mistreat them again. He then promoted Fionn to captain and put him in charge of his elite group that had survived (Darragh, Shane, Fergal, Conan, Aron, Diarmuid, Cailte, and Aengus) as a thank you for the victory in battle.

Goll gave the orders to pack up camp and return to Tara for the most incredible feast they had ever seen. After the wild hunt, there was more food than anyone knew what to do with. The news spread rapidly throughout the countryside, and he invited all the townsfolk from near and far to Tara to partake in the festivities. It was a momentous occasion, to kill the witch and end the wild hunt once and for all.

There was plenty of eating, drinking, dancing and singing and storytelling that night, as it was a night like no other. The bards told great tales of the evil witch and the ferocious wild hunt being usurped by the fearsome Fianna warriors. They paraded Fergal and Fionn around the fort to accept the applause and gratitude of everyone. One by one, the group, overdoing it with their merriment, fell asleep, only to wake up the following morning with thumping headaches.

A NEW LIFE

As always, it was time for home. The group took their leave with the blessings of Goll, and with Bran and Sceolan set off for Ballyfin. On the way back, they dropped off to share with Finnegas and Biddy how they defeated the witch and the wild hunt and Fionn's new promotion.

Then onwards, they travelled until they reached Ballyfin. Fergal stopped in the town to tell Aisling of his heroics, while a very excited Fionn rushed to tell Sadhbh of his latest adventure and promotion. Darragh and Shane ran to Bodhmall and Liath, who were tending their animals, to tell them everything that had happened.

That evening, the group walked to the village tavern for a feast. They had arranged for Aisling and Cliona to meet them there. When he entered the tavern, Shane was overjoyed to find Cred singing and playing music in the corner. Bodhmall then raised a toast to the boys for their heroics and development since they first arrived at the farm.

A beaming Fionn then stood up and told the rest of the group that he had excellent news for them. With that, he grabbed a smiling Sadhbh by the hand, telling everyone that Sadhbh had made him the happiest man alive by telling him she had a new life growing inside of her and they were going to be parents.

All the others were overjoyed and took turns to hug and congratulate them both on their great news, before Bodhmall and Liath bought a round of drinks for the entire tavern as a celebration. The rest of the boys raised Fionn on their shoulders and sang out loudly, "He's gonna be a daddy, he's gonna be a daddy, tra la la.la, tra la la la". Carrying him around the tavern. A beaming but embarrassed Fionn tried to hide his face in his hands, but the boys were having none of it and sang out even louder.

A short time later, Fionn and Sadhbh made their excuses and disappeared up the hill to the farm for the night. The others carried on partying until late in the night. The boys and their girls spent the night in the tavern while Bodhmall and Liath returned to the farm.

Early The next morning Shane awoke and, to his astonishment, found that Cred had stayed the night. She kissed him passionately on the lips before leaving, telling him she would see him soon. With that, she said goodbye and left the tavern. He hurried downstairs, where the others were sitting, eating breakfast. Shane told them it was great that Cred hadn't disappeared as she usually did and maybe it was a sign that their marriage could work.

When the boys made their way back up to the farm, Bodhmall and Liath called them together and said that they should clear away some of the forest so that they could build another three smaller houses, for themselves in case they wanted to have the girls stay overnight instead of at the inn. The boys thought this was a great idea and set about felling some trees and creating a clearing to build them.

For the next few weeks, the group painstakingly worked hard on building the three new houses. They were built roughly the same size, and they each had two bedrooms with straw and animal hide beds, a fireplace, and a table and chairs. The boys then fenced off a space around the back of the farm, making it more secure.

When they were finished, Sadhbh told Fionn that she wished to travel and tell her parents the good news of her pregnancy, but Fionn forbade her, telling her it was too dangerous. He told her he would travel to them in a day or two to pass on the news so that her parents could visit her instead. Sadhbh agreed that this was the safest thing to do.

Bodhmall told the group that it was not safe to leave the farm as they were about to enter the Samhain festive period. Samhain was the end of the harvest season and the beginning of winter. They had passed tales from the Elders through the years. That the veil between this world and the otherworld was the thinnest at this time of year. Apparently, the decline in the sun's strength at this time of year was a source of anxiety, and the Winter Fires' lighting symbolised man's attempts to aid the sun on its journey across the skies.

Now that the sun had descended into the realm of the underworld. The underworld forces were in the ascendency, and creatures from there, now free from the control of the sun, could walk the earth. Ghosts and a host of other demonic creatures could freely roam this world. Liath told the boys they should build bonfires and light them every evening. This would ward off any of these creatures, even though spells and runes protected the farm.

Bodhmall said they should set an extra place at the table each evening. As they thought that the spirit of relatives who had passed on came to visit during the festival time to check on their loved ones. In the meantime, they set about building the bonfires and setting them alight.

The following morning, their plans changed as a messenger arrived at the farm informing them that Goll and Cormac mac Airt, the high king, required their presence at the king's stronghold at the hill of Slaine. No one was happy with the news but told the messenger they would travel there with the utmost speed and inform Goll and the high king of the same.

The group decided they should spend that day together and have a meal that evening. If the king had requested their presence, it must be something important. They invited Aisling and Cliona to the farm for a meal and drinks that evening. They brought the harp out from the main house, and as Liath played, Sadhbh sang the most enchanting, melancholic love song to Fionn, which brought the entire party to tears. Aisling and Cliona then sang a good auld fighting song, which had the boys dancing in circles, looping their arms. Liath and Bodhmall then sang a lovely ballad with the boys, except for Shane dancing with their partners.

The boys told them they needed a fast tune on the harp as they bellowed out "Rocky Road to Dublin". Everyone made their way to bed after the music and singing had ended.

The following morning, there was a sombre mood around the place as the boys readied their horses and said their goodbyes. Sadhbh and Fionn held each other and refused to let go of each other and had to be pried apart, as they did not know what the king wanted. They didn't know when they were likely to see each other again.

The group then hugged each other, and there were tears as the boys, Bran and Sceolan, set off to Slaine. They trod slowly out the gate and kept looking back as if they didn't want to leave. Finally, the farm and the girls disappeared from sight, and the boys began concentrating on the journey ahead.

As always, the boys called in on Biddy and Finnegas to talk and catch up. They told them that none other than the high king had summoned them. Biddy and Finnegas wished them well for their important journey ahead before the boys set off to Slaine.

As the boys rode on, in the distance, they could see the camp at Tara, and there were more fires lighting than the boys were expecting, but they paid no heed as they must be the Samhain bonfires being burned.

CHAPTER EIGHT

AILLEN AND LEADERSHIP OF THE FIANNA

pon reaching Slaine, they saw it was a well-fortified camp. It was much larger than the one in Tara. This camp had three inner circles. A high wooden fence surrounded the outer circle, much like Tara, and had small barracks all around it, and there were some small trading posts and taverns and stables and blacksmiths.

Then there was the inner circle for the more critical people. This consisted mainly of houses rather than barracks, but also had trading posts, taverns, stables, and blacksmiths. There were bonfires and fires for cooking ablaze throughout the camp.

Finally, there was the inner circle. This had larger houses, the main hall and a large house where the king himself lived.

The boys noticed Cormac at the gates and wondered why he was not at the camp in Tara. He welcomed them into the camp before telling them that Goll and the king were waiting for them in the main hall in the inner circle. The boys left their horses in the stables and headed to the main hall.

Upon entering the main hall, they immediately drew their eyes to the centre of the room. For Cormac mac Airt, Goll, Conan, Aron, Diarmuid, Cailte, and Aengus were all sitting around a large rectangular table deep in conversation. The guards quickly ushered the boys over to join them.

The king informed the boys that the fort in Tara was under attack. He ordered them to take immediate action to stop it. The king then told the entire group the story of the fires on the hill of Tara. And why Slaine had become the main fort of the high kings of Ireland. The king continued that,

Some twenty years ago, as the year was drawing to a close, the festival of Samhain had begun. On the first night of the festival, when the world grew thin. Beings from this realm and the underworld could walk through portals and walk where they did not belong.

It was then that a druid boasting of his prowess. Had somehow insulted the Sidhe (creatures from the underworld) and Tuatha Dé Danann, who were living close by. One such being Aillen (A nine-foot-tall human-like figure dressed all in black wearing a tall pointed hat) a son of Dagda (The legendary king of the Tuatha Dé Danann), took exception to what the druid said. He came forth from the otherworld to exact vengeance against the druid.

Twenty times now, Aillen had come to this world. And twenty times, destruction he had brought with him. He carried with him a harp and a large pipe. He would sing and play the harp, putting the locals and the men of the Fianna to sleep. Then, he would rain down fire upon them and their houses with his pipe. He couldn't destroy the entire fort as the previous High King, and his wizards had some potency spells of protection, which stopped him from destroying the whole fort.

The king then stood up, gave a rousing speech to the troops before him. He then asked, "Is there a man amongst you who will slay this beast tonight? Who shall be my champion?". Fergal, having helped to kill the witch Cailleach Bheara, jumped to his feet and said he would willingly accept the task at hand. Darragh tugged him back and told him to be quiet.

The king asked again, and Goll, looking askance while taking a swig of some mead, looked at the troops, saying nothing. While the troops looked on and grumbled to one another. As the silence grew longer, the king himself thought no one would be his champion. When Fionn leapt to his feet, he said that he and his elite group would carry out the task.

The king and Goll looked relieved and grateful that someone had accepted the mission. With this, the king told them they would have free use of the closest tavern for the night to eat, drink and be merry on their last night before the battle. The king said that if they completed the mission, he would grant them whatever they wanted in payment and gratitude. Fionn rallied his troops, and they all left the main hall to devise plans to fight the beast.

The group then entered a tavern close by, eating, drinking and singing along together. Conan jumped onto a table and said, "As I am the mightiest of the Fianna, I should be the one who slays the beast". Fergal said, "maybe you need to graze in the fields for a while", as the others laughed, and Conan took a seat and a swig of mead. The men all went to bed early as they had a big day ahead.

Early the next morning, the king, Goll, Cormac, and some more troops waved the team out of the fort. As they expected Aillen to appear that night, the troops would have time to prepare for the battle ahead. They set up camp close to the fort at Tara, and Fionn started sucking on his thumb. He came up with a plan that they should all keep the tips of their weapons in the campfire and when the time came, and Aillen played his harp and sang, they should burn their hands with their weapons to keep them awake.

As darkness fell, a loud thunderous noise, and flames spewed from the ground. The group looked on at the astonishing sight before them. For in the darkness, they could just about make out the colossal frame of a man in the centre of the camp at the top of the hill. It was Aillen, and he had emerged from a sidhe mound (portal). They then heard a harp playing and an unfamiliar tune being sung.

With this, Conan jumped to his feet and rushed forward. Leaping upon a boulder, he shouted, "I shall slay the beast with my bare hands, as I am by far the best warrior". With this, Conan fell off the boulder and crashed face-first onto the ground. He had succumbed to the sound of the harp and the singing. "If it weren't so serious, I would laugh", shouted Darragh.

With this, the troops backed off slightly for fear of being put to sleep. Darragh, taking his headphones from his hip bag, invited Shane and Fergal to do the same. He then told them to play their mp3 players at full blast. With this done, the three boys rushed to Conan, carrying his body to a safe spot.

Fionn and the others had regrouped while tearing at their tunics and stuffing some cloth in their ears. The boys, then joining them, placed Conan on the ground. Fionn then told Cailte, Aron and

Diarmuid to go up to the left of the fort using the houses for cover while he and Aengus would go to the right of the fort. Darragh, Shane, and Fergal would go through the centre of the fort. Fionn told Bran and Sceolan to stay put at the campsite.

As they carried on up the hill, Aillen continued to play and sing, stopping sporadically to shoot flames from his pipe, setting some buildings alight. The boys came to a well of drinking water, and Darragh told the other two boys to soak their shields in water before moving onwards. The air was full of smoke and the smell of burning timbers, but the boys moved on towards Aillen while he played and sang again.

Darragh spotted Cailte and Aron dropping off to sleep. Shane looked to the other side and saw Aengus nod off, too. Fionn placed him behind a wall for protection. Not long after, Diarmuid dropped off to sleep. With that, the three boys lay down their shields before going and grabbing Cailte, Aron and Diarmuid and carrying them away to safety before returning to their shields. Soon after that, they heard Fionn roar Goliath but to their amazement, he too, fell asleep while attempting to run at Aillen.

Again, the boys carried him to safety inside one house. The boys withdrew to a safe distance, and Darragh devised a plan. From the Corrbolg, he took out the vial of Ollphéisteanna blood he had kept previously and poured some onto the head of Shane's spear, as he thought if the weapons didn't hurt Aillen, the acid surely would.

Fergal, using his ring, disappeared and ran to the right before reappearing. Shane ran up through the centre and gathered the three shields, stacking them on a wall beside each other, while Darragh ran to the left. Aillen shot some fire at the three shields, but they fell to the ground, too wet to burn. Fergal took out Claíomh Solais and waved it in the air before sheathing it again and running for cover. Aileen focusing on him and failing to put him to sleep with his harp, reached for his pipe to shoot fire at him.

Shane threw his spear at him while holding his hand aloft. Aillen let out a scream of pain as the spear pierced his shoulder, burning him badly. As he winced in pain, Darragh took out his bow and arrows, dipping some arrowheads in the acid blood before shooting two quick rounds into the other shoulder. Aillen again let out an immense cry of pain before dropping his harp to the ground, unable to hold it.

Having made his way closer to him, Fergal again took out Claíomh Solais, waving it in the air. Aillen again focused on Fergal while Shane again threw his spear, hitting Aillen in the throat before it returned to him. Darragh shot two more acid arrows, hitting him in the arm and leg. Fergal, by now using his ring, disappeared, and Aillen couldn't see him approaching.

Aillen, who by now couldn't play his harp or sing, with a large spear hole in the throat, began backing off towards the sidhe mound he had come through from the otherworld. With this, Darragh and Shane charged at Aillen, roaring at the top of their voices. As he turned to face the boys.

Fergal jumped from the top of a wall onto his back, stabbing firmly down into the beast's shoulder as it fell to the ground in agony. Fergal stabbed again and again until the others reached him. Shane stabbed his spear deep into its chest before Darragh took the beast's head clean off its body with a swipe of his sword.

While removing his headphones, Fergal shouted, "Not bad for a guy with a small weapon". Shane removed his headphones and joked, "What did you say, Fergal?" "Never mind," said a dejected Fergal. While Darragh removing his headphones, giggled, "You did a good job for a guy with a small weapon Fergal," giving him a high five. "Group hug," shouted Fergal. As the boys all hugged each other to celebrate a well-done job. Just then, they noticed the sidhe mound had a large flat stone on it with an engraved symbol that was shining. As they approached it, they disappeared.

Meanwhile, Fionn was the first to wake up and rushed to the top of the hill. There, he found Aillen dead on the ground while the fort burned around him. He searched through the flames and smoke to see if he could find anyone else. But he couldn't spot anyone. He made his way out of the fort and found all the others the boys had carried to safety.

When the group woke up, he was still with them. They all re-entered the fort now that the flames and smoke had cleared, searching for Darragh, Shane, and Fergal, but alas, they were nowhere to be found. With nothing else to be done, Fionn gathered the head of Aillen and placed it in a bag, tied it securely to his horse and set off back to Slaine, along with his troops.

The troops greeted them with loud cheers when they entered the fort in Slaine. They slowly made their way through the fort, accepting the applause that came their way until they came to the king and Goll along with all the fort's troops who had followed them. Fionn stood in the centre of them all, taking the bag from his horse and throwing the head of Aillen on the ground. "He has played his last tune and shall hurt no one ever again, my lord. I give you the head of Aillen", roared Fionn.

The sight of the slain Aillen's head. lifeless on the ground drew even louder cheers from the entire fort. Warriors sang and danced with joy. Finally, after many years of destruction, the menace of Aillen had ended. With that, the king approached Fionn and said, "I congratulate you and your team, and as a man of my word, what can I offer you?".

Fionn stood tall and thundered, "My lord, there has been a great wrong done to me. And I only ask for what should be mine by birthright," he said, "I lost my father to murder many years ago, and was on the run for many more years as a result, you see your highness I was born Deinmhe, son of Cumhail and the previous leader of the Fianna. It is my birthright to be the leader of the Fianna. That is the reward I want for the service we carried out."

The king approached Goll, who had an angry look of thunder on his face. He drew his sword as if to attack Fionn, but the king leaned in and whispered to him. Goll put his weapon away and approached Fionn, kneeling before him. Then laying his weapon on the ground, he said, "I pledge my loyalty to the new leader of the Fianna, Fionn Mac Cumhail".

The king and the surrounding troops congratulated Fionn on his appointment. The king then told Fionn that he planned to move to Tara permanently now that the threat of Aillen was gone. He was giving Fionn the fort of Almhuin on the hill of Allen as the new base for Fionn's Fianna. Fionn thanked the king for his kindness as the troops chanted his name in celebration. Fionn finally acknowledged their cheers before giving the order for his troops and setting off for Almhuin.

Upon reaching his new fort, Fionn set about getting everything set up to his liking. The hill itself was in the middle of a large bogland. It was full of peat and trees and swampland. Its location allowed guards to see anyone approaching for miles in any direction. Fionn instructed they should make the fort more like the fort at Slaine. It now only had one inner circle, but Fionn wanted four circles. He wanted the outer circle to contain barracks, taverns, blacksmiths, trading posts, and stables.

The next level should contain the same, but smaller barracks for more essential troops. Then the third level would have houses for the Fianna's most influential members and a meeting hall, stables and tavern. The last level would have a sizeable three-bedroom house for Fionn, with a large table and chairs in the main room next to a fireplace. There were also to be four more houses built, as well as a large meeting hall.

A large stone wall should surround the fort, and a trench five feet wide and five feet deep should be dug outside the Outerwall, with a drawbridge the only access in or out of the fort. This would ensure better protection and fortification for the fort.

Fionn left Goll, Conan, Aron, Diarmuid, Cailte, and Aengus to run things in his absence, as he needed to return to Ballyfin for a few days before he, along with his faithful hounds, set off on his journey. He stopped off at Tara in case he could find the boys, and upon failing to find them and using his Goliath powers, he carried three large stones from a nearby quarry to the top of the hill and placed them standing near the sidhe mound in memory of his missing friends and their bravery.

CHAPTER NINE

THE WHITE WARRIOR

hen he left Tara, Fionn rode straight to Finnegas to tell him the three boys had gone missing. Although he had found the lifeless Aillen lying on the ground near a sidhe mound.

Finnegas asserted the boys must have slain the beast, and in one ultimate act of revenge, somehow killed or cursed them. He was sorry, but there was nothing in his power to help Fionn find an answer.

Fionn then rode off to Biddy, again telling her about the boy's disappearance. She, like Finnegas before, could not answer what happened to the boys. She sensed their presence, which meant they were alive. Fionn despaired as he had hoped Biddy might help him find his missing friends. Again, Fionn thanked her for her help before setting off for Ballyfin.

Upon reaching Ballyfin, he stopped off to tell Aisling and Cliona about the boy's disappearance. Before rushing up the hill to see Sadhbh and the others. When he reached the farm, he rushed straight to his house. He found Sadhbh wasn't there, so he ran to the main house to see if she was there. As he entered the house, he came across a very upset Bodhmall and Liath. "Oh Fionn", cried Bodhmall, "she's gone". "What do you mean she's gone?" roared Fionn. Bodhmall rushed to comfort him, but Fionn pushed her away. "What do you mean she's gone?" he roared.

A distraught Bodhmall then told Fionn. Every evening since he had been away, Sadhbh would march to the farm's boundaries, anxiously awaiting his return. The night before, after supper ended, she had gone to the gates. She shouted Fionn was approaching in the moonlight.

She was so thrilled to see him returning to her, and she ran out to greet him and take him in her arms. Bodhmall and Liath, too, had rushed from the house. Just as Sadhbh reached Fionn, but it became clear it wasn't him.

Instead, it was a tall, thin man, all dressed in black. It must be none other than Fer Doirich, who possibly learned that she had regained her human form and come to seek his revenge on her. As Sadhbh left the confines of the charms surrounding the farm, the man pulled a wand from beneath his cloak. Once she reached him, he touched her with his wand, and Sadhbh immediately turned back into a doe.

Before Bodhmall and Liath could reach her, he had put a rope around Sadhbh's neck and they disappeared into the night. No matter where they searched, she was nowhere to be found. Fionn just stood and stared at Bodhmall like a lost man. He then beat his chest with his fist as though he wanted to kill the heart within him. Which should be dead yet did not die. Fionn marched from the house, bidding Bodhmall and Liath good night, which they returned, but in truth, they knew they were bidding him goodbye.

Fionn mounted his horse and, along with his trusted hounds, set off through the dark of the night, through fields and forests, through meadows and over hilltops in a blind rage, looking for Sadhbh. Anytime they saw a deer or doe, his hounds gave chase, for indeed, if it was her, the hounds would know and protect her. When Fionn finally gathered his thoughts. He remembered where Sadhbh had grown up in Teide and made his way there. He hoped for the best, but expected the worst.

Upon reaching the fort of Sadhbh's father, guards welcomed him in and brought to the king and queen. Fionn told them the story of how she was pregnant with his child. And him having to battle Aillen before returning to find her gone. The only person possibly responsible must be Fer Doirich.

Her distraught parents said they would do anything for the return of their daughter. With Fionn and a band of his guards, the king set off to the nearby forest in search of Fer Doirich. For days they set up camp in the woods searching for deer, or Fer Doirich, but there was no sign of them. When a week had passed, the king and his men returned to inform the queen about the lack of progress.

The next day Fionn came across a tall thin man, all dressed in black, as if he had been waiting on the king's men to leave. He lunged at him, grabbing him by the neck. "Tell me where she is", he shouted. "What did you do with Sadhbh?". The man turned into a snake and dropped out of Fionn's grasp before returning to his proper form. Again, Fionn lunged at him, but he vanished before reappearing behind him.

Fionn roared "Goliath" and charged at the man, grabbing him and slamming him into a nearby tree. There was a puff of smoke, and the man disappeared, not to return. Nearing despair, Fionn roared and shouted, stamping on the ground and thumping a tree, knocking it to the ground. Bran and Sceolan cowered in the shadows as he became increasingly enraged. For the following week, day and night, Fionn searched the forest, hoping to find Sadhbh or Fer Doirich, but neither was to be found.

Weeks passed, and Fionn rode alone day and night with eyes like a wild animal, with only his trusty hounds and a bundle of noises to keep him company. For every patter of a rabbit, or scurrying of a hare, or rustling from trees or bushes, Fionn would call out for Sadhbh, but alas, she was well and truly gone.

Fionn regained hope when he remembered he was now the leader of the Fianna. He would make his way back to Almhuin. He rode and rode until his horse could carry him no more. After resting, he would ride again until he had finally reached Almhuin. The fort was a completely different place from the one he left some weeks earlier.

The guards greeted him, then he made his way up to his new large meeting hall. He summoned Goll, Conan, Aron, Diarmuid, Cailte, and Aengus. Upon entering the hall, his leaders were astounded, for in front of them was a different-looking Fionn. Gone were his long blond locks and clean-shaven face, and in front of them stood a man now sporting snow-white hair and a full white beard. He was now a white warrior.

The men all greeted him, but this was a different Fionn. His eyes were glazed. He had a distant look about him. His body was present, but his mind seemed absent. He told his men they must send troops throughout the land, looking for his beloved Sadhbh. The men shook their heads in disbelief. As they took their leave in search of an impossible task. Where would they look? As there were no leads as to her whereabouts, and they didn't know where to begin?

CHAPTER TEN

MAG MELL

eanwhile, somewhere else, Darragh woke with a thumping headache. When he opened his eyes, and it was as if a veil was covering them, making his sight slightly blurred. He rubbed his eyes and then his temples to ease his blurred vision and headache, but it made no difference.

He sat up and looked around to scan the area. Only to see he was sitting in a henge. (A prehistoric circular earthen enclosure, there was a ring-shaped bank on the outside. With a ring-shaped ditch on the inside that marked out a central, circular area, that had openings, that pass through the earthwork circuits into the central circle). Multiple standing stones surrounded this henge.

He realised he was sitting next to a large, flat stone. Almost like an altar with a large symbol carved into it, similar to the one on Tara. Tara, he thought, where is Aillen, but more importantly, where were Shane and Fergal? He leapt to his feet, forgetting about his blurred vision and headache, and looked around.

Nearby, he found some pottery, complete vessels and broken pieces. There were also small bones, antlers, some flint and wooden tools. Darragh thought people must have held sacrifices near the stone, like altar. As he continued looking around, he found his weapons and put them all on his back.

As he continued exploring, he spotted something red sticking out of the ditch and, as he approached, realised that it was Fergal's red headphones. Just as he spotted him lying in the trench. He rushed to him, placed his palm flat on his chest, and felt his heart beating. He rested his head in his lap and gently tapped him on his face saying, "wake up, Fergal".

After a few minutes, Fergal's eyes opened. He shouted, "who the hell hit my head with a hammer?". Darragh winced and said, "No need to shout. I have a thumping headache too". He sat Fergal up and told him to get his bearings as his eyesight, too, was blurry. Darragh walked around the entire trench but could not find Shane. He stepped outside the large standing stones, where he came across Shane's black headphones and weapons. He picked them up and carried on around the outside but couldn't find Shane.

Close by, he could hear the sound of running water and rushed to investigate. He found Shane on his knees, splashing water on his face from a little stream. He approached him and asked how he was feeling. Shane leaned back and said, "man, my head is thumping". "Mine too," said Darragh, as he knelt down to rinse his face and eyes. "How's your eyes," he asked Shane, who replied, "Not very good, to be honest".

"Mine and Fergal's are the same", said Darragh. "Fergal, where is he?" asked Shane. "Ah, I left him sitting in a henge over there," said Darragh. With that, Fergal came running over to them. "Lads, there are people over there staring at me!" he said. The boys got to their feet and steadied themselves before approaching the people.

As they made their way back to the henge, there were three people standing there looking at them. They were all wearing grey linen tunics and hats and were holding small sickles. They asked the people who they were and where they were. One man replied that they were simple farmers from a small nearby settlement called Trim.

It was raining heavily by now, and the farmers invited the boys back to their settlement to shelter from the rain. The settlement wasn't far away. As they approached, the boys could see that the farmers lived in some ring-fort. It was in a large clearing in a wooded area close to the little stream. A large earthen circular outer wall with a wooden fence on top to keep things out surrounded it. Inside, there were at least fifteen houses.

They constructed the houses out of wickerwork. They formed the walls from long stout poles placed in a circle. The houses were round and standing pretty near each other, with their ends fixed deep in the ground, the spaces between closed in with rods and twigs neatly and firmly interwoven with hazelwood.

The poles were smooth and polished. They plastered the entire surface of the wickerwork on the outside and made brilliantly white with lime. There were narrow slits for windows splaying inwards to let light in. They thatched the roofs and shaped them conically, bringing them to a point with an opening in the centre for the smoke from the fire to escape.

There were also two large two-storey wooden stables for the goats, sheep, cattle and pigs that were kept while storing hay overhead. Then there was a blacksmith's forge, some cereal drying kilns, and a turf and log shed.

The outbuildings were roughly made from light timbering and small tree trunks lined with mud. They kept a few chicken coops near the houses for greater protection. There were small woven hazelwood fences around them. They fenced off the area with a large wooden gate to prevent wild animals from getting in.

Outside the ring-fort, there were large fields freshly harvested for crops. A graveyard to bury the dead was in the corner of one field. As they approached the settlement, they saw smoke coming from all the houses. This was a welcome sight, as they were soaked and freezing by now. They were brought into one house and made their way straight over to a large burning fire to get some heat into themselves.

Inside the house were some women and children who looked quizzically at the new strangers in their home. The women and children welcomed the three and gave them a nice hearty meal and a bed for the night. The following morning, they thanked their hosts and made their way out of the house, surrounded by the residents who lived in the settlement.

They invited the boys to sit with the settlement leaders, where they told the story of fighting Aillen and waking up in the stone henge. The leaders told them they were only simple folk who liked to keep to themselves. They knew little about the henge other than it being used by magical beings from a large settlement about a day's travel to the south of the henge. If the boys wanted answers, it was there they could find them.

One woman then wrapped some bread and other food in some animal skin. The boys gratefully accepted before thanking their hosts and leaving the settlement in search of the magical settlement they were told to seek. After walking a short time, Fergal stopped and sat down on the grass. "I've had enough," he said.

"I miss my mother, I miss my father, and I even miss my brothers. Now I have come to another strange place, and I don't even have a horse." The others laughed out loud. "You never had a horse back home," said Shane. "Come on, back on your feet, or we'll never get home," said Darragh. A disgruntled Fergal rose to his feet and followed the others.

Darragh mentioned his eyes had not improved, and everything seemed slightly foggy. Shane and Fergal were also both having the same issues. It was rather annoying, and they hoped it would improve soon. They carried on until darkness fell and, finding a secure spot. They gathered some tinder and firewood and set up camp for the night. They opened up the food parcel and ate all the food the woman had packed for them.

The boys couldn't settle that night as they were in a strange new place and couldn't see properly. Although it was a clear starry night, with a full moon, glowing yellowy white. It loomed large above them, popping in and out of smoky clouds floating by.

They could hear wolves howling and the wind blowing through the trees. There was the patter of animals running and the rustling of the falling leaves. The boys just sat and talked long into the night. Sharing stories of their families, themselves, their friendships with each other. And the hope that they could find their way back home.

The wind grew stronger, and the howling of wolves got louder until Fergal became very spooked. He asked the others if they could move and find somewhere safer to spend the rest of the night. So, they put out the fire and set off. Having travelled a short distance, they came upon a derelict-looking farmhouse in a desolate clearing in a long dead forest. There was a light showing inside. The boys approached and knocked on the door.

The door creaked open, and there stood a tall, thin, grey-haired old man with dark eyes. "Come in," he said, "welcome to our home. This is my wife," and he brought them over to the fireplace, where an old thin, grey-haired woman with long, sharp teeth and a terrible glint in her eye was sitting. "You are welcome," she said. "it's time for supper. Sit down and eat with us." The boys sat down while the old woman stirred the pot on the fire. The boys felt uncomfortable because they thought she was watching them all the time.

Then a knock came on the door. And the old man opened it. In walked a slender black wolf, who immediately walked straight across the floor to an inner room. A few minutes later, a dark, slim youth came out and took his place at the table while looking at the boys. The boys became uneasy, but had their weapons in case anything went wrong.

Then came another knock, and in came a second wolf, who walked into the inner room like the first, and soon after, another dark slim youth came out and sat down to supper with them, glaring at the boys, who by now became really uneasy.

"These are our sons," said the old woman, "tell them what you want and what brought you here, for we live alone and don't care to have strangers coming to our place." The boys told their story of fighting Aillen and how they woke up in the henge. Not knowing how they got there, and were on their way to an old magical settlement, hoping to find answers. The boys thanked them for supper and were sorry for disturbing them before standing up to leave.

As they looked at each other, the others laughed. The old woman looked more frightful than before when she showed her long, sharp teeth. "We cannot allow you to leave," she said, "in case you bring others to our door". The boys grew angry and reached for their weapons before shouting for them to open the door.

Then the eldest of the young men stood up. He transformed into a snarling wolf with drool dripping from his fangs before lunging at the boys. Darragh rubbed his bear ring before drawing his sword and cutting the beast's head off. The other youth jumped to his feet, transforming into a snarling wolf. Before he could even attack the boys, Shane and Fergal drew their weapons, slaying him instantly.

The boys turned to the old man and woman, but the woman fell to her knees, begging for mercy. "My poor boys", she screamed, "My poor beautiful boys, what have they done to you?". The old man transformed into a large grey wolf, but the woman jumped between him and the boys, telling the boys to get out of her house. The boys didn't need to be told twice and ran out the door and across the field as fast as they could. They kept moving while keeping their wits about them until it was morning light.

They came across an old desolate hut and, having checked it thoroughly, went inside to sit down and gather their thoughts. "What the hell is going on?" asked Shane. "Let's sit here and think everything through," said Darragh. "First," he said, "We were at a wedding and fell through a fountain, which was obviously some portal! And as if that wasn't bad enough, we seem to have gone through another portal to a place even worse than the first place.

"Correct me if I'm wrong?" said Darragh. "But can things get any worse?". "Don't forget the werewolves," said Fergal. "They were bloody werewolves!". "We have fought worse than that since we got here, Fergal," laughed Shane. "What's our next step?" asked Fergal.

"Well," said Darragh while sucking on his thumb. "I believe we will get an answer. It might not be the right answer or the answer we want to hear, but we will get an answer at the magical settlement." He said. "Right," said Fergal, "Mam, I'm coming home," he said. "Let's go, boys," he shouted.

The boys then set off in search of the magical settlement. Along the way, they came to another small settlement with three small farmhouses. There was smoke coming out of all three chimneys, but adults and children were dancing around a small rectangular stone in the corner of a newly harvested field.

As the boys investigated, they noticed the stone appeared to have offerings of fruit, nuts and crops, milk and even butter, along with some candles lit on it too. One man was wearing a goat's skull on his head, and its hide draped across his shoulders while chanting. The boys interrupted them and queried what they were doing.

They were told that they were making offerings to the gods, the spirits and the sidhe's or fairy folk, hoping they would be there for them in times of need. To protect their families, homes, crops and their health for the year ahead. They invited the boys to dinner, as the offering of hospitality was necessary to appease the spirits.

Fergal grabbed some apples close by and placed them on the stone altar. I hope the gods and spirits send us home soon. He prayed to himself before following the others into one house for dinner. When they had eaten and drank. The boys discussed their plight with the elders, who told them they would offer more on the boy's behalf. They then told them how to get to the magical settlement. The boys again thanked their hosts and set off searching for the settlement.

The following day, the boys came across another stone ring-fort. Unlike the previous one with the farmers. They had made all the buildings from stone. They again had thatched conical roofs with a chimney hole in the centre and slits in the bricks for windows. Dead clumps of grass and ferns surrounded the old fort with its old foundations and Weather-worn stone pillars. Vine and other foliage weighed down the stone-sculpted archways that led into the city.

At the archways stood two guards. As the boys approached, the rain started falling heavily while cascading from the rooftops and arches. The boys could just about make out that the guards wore green tunics and purple trousers with a black hooded cloak while wielding large spears. The boys thought they seemed very familiar, but couldn't quite put their fingers on it.

The guards stopped them and asked what business they had. The boys told their story and how they came here searching for answers. The guards welcomed them to the city of Fálias, as they had been awaiting their arrival. They told the boys to go to the house at the very centre of the city, as the grand seer wanted to see them when once they arrived.

As the rain pummelled down on the windy, uneven cobble paths, the boys ducked into doorways for shelter from the rain as they made their way through the city. There was plenty to be seen on the way. They could see into a large hall where soldiers were training in many different events. There were long jumps, high jumps, spear throwing, contests of strength, sword fighting, archery, wrestling, and slinging, as well as taverns.

They passed by goldsmiths, jewellers, cobblers, and even tailor shops. The most beautiful smell of cooking wafting through the air overcame the smell of the damp rain that continued to fall. On another street, there was storytelling, music, singing, dancing and Fidcheall competitions, which is the ancient board game.

They carried on until they finally reached its centre. Again, a guard stopped and questioned them before allowing them entrance. Dripping wet from the rain, they made their way into a sizeable smoky room. There was a fireplace ablaze that brought a dancing glow into the heart of the room, and they made their way over to dry themselves off.

In the centre of the room. Two crescent moon-shaped engraved marble seats were facing each other. There was also a round marble table in between them, holding a large chalice full of water. The chalice was spectacular to see. The bowl and foot were crafted in silver. While they decorated the outer side of the bowl with gold, silver, glass, polished rock crystal, and enamel ornament. There were three empty cups next to it on the table.

Soon a woman appeared from the shadows wearing a black hooded cloak and sat facing the three boys. She beckoned them to approach and sit facing her. She then told the boys to each fill a cup from the chalice and drink from it. As the boys did so, they regained their proper sight and thanked the woman for her help.

The woman stood up and turned away while removing her cloak. As she turned to face the boys again, she said, "Welcome, dear husband. I have been expecting you". The boys all rubbed their eyes again and shook their heads in disbelief as there in front of them stood none other than Cred.

"What the hell are you doing here?" shouted Shane. "It's certainly not hell", she replied, "and there is no need to shout, my darling," she said. "There will be time enough for that. Now dry yourselves at the fire". Cred then left the room as she had business to attend to. The boys then warmed themselves by the fire until they were dry.

Sometime later, Cred came back into the room and called them

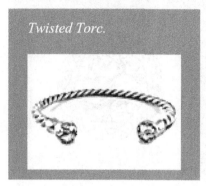

Twisted Torc.

into the next room. She then walked to the corner of the room and waved her hand. Suddenly, an exquisite wooden chest appeared decorated with bronze and polished rock crystal. She opened the chest and took out three twisted golden torcs. "Put these on", she said while handing them to the boys. Then waving her hand again, the chest was gone.

She then told the boys to sit down, as she was sure they had questions for her. These seats were the best they had sat on in a while, as they were crafted in wood, but with cushions made from animal hide stuffed with goose feathers. Shane was the first to speak. "It's great to see you, but why are you here, and where is here?" he asked.

"The simple answer is that this is my home," she said. "What do you mean, this is your home?" asked Darragh. "I live here," said Cred, "and to answer Shane's question, we are in Mag Mell." "What is Magna?" asked Fergal. "Magna is lava," laughed Shane, "but she said Mag Mell."

"Ok, what is Mag Mell?" asked Fergal. "Well," replied Cred, "There is the human world and the otherworld, which we call Mag Mell." "For want of a better word, you could say it is a mirror image of your world." "What do you mean, a reflection of our world?" asked Darragh. "That other place isn't our world. We come from somewhere else, but how can it be a reflection?"

"That I am aware of," said Cred, "yet I don't have an answer for you. Well, not entirely anyway," she said. "Mag Mell is an identical upside-down version of your world." "What do you mean?" asked Shane.

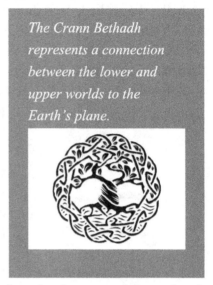

The Crann Bethadh represents a connection between the lower and upper worlds to the Earth's plane.

Cred told the boys that it was possible to travel between portals. Both external and internal portals existed. She then showed the boys drawings of two symbols. The Crann Bethadh, or tree symbol, was an external portal between worlds. Whereas the Triquetra, or intertwined symbol, was a portal within the same world. The symbols only shone at night and only shone to someone wearing an enchanted Torc.

Triquetra means Intertwined worlds.

"So, are you telling me I can travel through portals with this torc you gave me?" asked Darragh. "Well, that's where it gets complicated," said Cred. "Until you three came along, only enchanted people from Mag Mell, wearing these special torcs, could Portal jump," she replied. "The problem is you are human, yet portal jumped even without a torc."

"How can that be?" asked Shane. "That, my dear, is what brought me to you in the first place," said Cred. "When I first sensed your presence, I left Mag Mell in search of you." "I needed to see who you were and measure your powers, as you clearly arrived to the other world through a portal. Yet when we met, there were no obvious signs of power."

"I can still not figure out if you have powers or if it was by chance destiny that brought you all here in the first place."

"You have clearly travelled through time using a portal, yet we, as magical people, cannot time travel. Is there anything you can tell me about how you travelled through time?"

"Well," said Shane, "We were at our uncle's wedding, and after the marriage ceremony was over and we had eaten dinner, we went to the hotel grounds to have some fun." "We came to a fountain and saw something gold shining in the water. Darragh reached in to grab it, and here we are."

Darragh interrupted and said, "Now that I think of it, there was actually a symbol shining in the water. I thought it was a gold coin, but it looks nothing like either of the symbols you have shown us." Cred asked Darragh if he could describe the symbol, as it may help them return home.

He then described the symbol he had seen. It was like intricate knots entwined, resembling a tree. It had intertwined lines with no beginning and no end.

Dara Knot, represents destiny and endurance.

"Ah," said Cred, "Just as I thought, it sounds like a Dara knot, which is a symbol of destiny. Unfortunately, I have only ever seen one in drawings. If I knew where one actually existed, it could help transport you home."

Cred told the boys there was always a second or backup portal, like a front and back door. If they came through the front door and it is now closed. They may get home through the back door if they can find it. "Let's go back through the last portal," said Fergal ", So I can see Aisling again".

"It's not so simple," said Cred. "Whatever you boys did when entering Mag Mell, all external portals now appear closed. Now everyone is stuck here." "Our best scholars are trying to figure out what to do." "Now that is enough questions for today, as it's time to go to bed."

She then escorted Darragh and Fergal to their room, and she and Shane walked to her bedroom. "Oh," said Fergal ", this is the most comfortable bed I've ever been on". There was a pillow made of feathers wrapped in deerskin on top of a mattress made the same way. The boys fell asleep as soon as they lay their heads on the pillow.

The following morning, after Fergal's best-ever sleep, both he and Darragh entered the living room. They waited for Shane and Cred to join them. This seemed like an eternity before the grinning couple finally arrived. Cred then left to make breakfast while the boys sat and chatted with each other. There were still many unanswered questions that they had to ask. They were all really excited, as all they had to do now was find a Dara knot to get home.

Cred called them all in for breakfast, "Let's go, boys", said Shane, following Cred to the next room. "Why do you call each other boys," asked Cred. "We always have," said Fergal. "Well," said Cred, by my calculations, you have all missed a birthday since you arrived. Indeed, that makes you men. "What, I've missed a birthday!" Queried Fergal. "Yes, you all have," said Cred. Shane piped in and said, "if it's all the same to you guys, I'd rather say lads than men," and all agreed to do so.

Darragh asked what month they were in, and Cred replied it was November. "So, that means we're into our ninth month here," said Darragh. "My birthday was April, so I guess I'm 18 now." "Mine is August, so I'm 17," said Fergal. "I'm 19 now," said Shane, "I'm the elder statesman." "Can we have a birthday party later?" asked Fergal.

"We've had too many parties already," said Darragh. "I don't think we need any more". "Can we not have one more?" asked Fergal. "I will hold a party for you this evening," said Cred. That evening Cred held a big party and invited along many guests for company. Although Darragh was in no mood for a party, he still had questions that needed to be answered.

As the evening wore on, Darragh noticed everyone was wearing torcs on their wrists and couldn't help but wonder if they were all magical people. Cred sensing his unrest, called himself and Shane to her private chamber to check that everything was ok. "Let's take a step back", said Darragh. "You never answered our questions. Why do you live here? How is this your home, and are all these people the same as you?".

Cred told him they were all from the same tribe, but each had their own roles within the tribe. Her role was that of the grand seer, as she could see the past, the present, and sometimes even the future. Shane asked if everyone was magical.

Cred said there were many tribes and creatures, but not all were magical. She carried on and told the boys that there were different groups. There were the fairies, leprechauns, Spriggan's, Kelpies, and even their sworn enemies, the Fomorians. "But who are you?" asked Darragh.

CHAPTER ELEVEN

TUATH DÉ DANANN

e, she replied, we are the Tuath dé Danann. She then told the boys about her tribe. She said to them that many years ago, her ancestors had arrived on the shores of Ireland during a heavy storm led by their King, Nuada. The storm obliterated their fleet of three hundred ships, leaving them with no alternative but to make a new home for themselves. They were primarily peaceful people well versed in the art of music, playing instruments, and farming. They trained in combat, and the most gifted in mind and temperament would train in magic.

As they made their way inland, they came across two fighting tribes, The Fir Bolg and the Fomorians. They had taken no part in the battle, as they had no reason to interfere in a domestic dispute. They knew nothing about. The Fir Bolg were a smaller race of red-headed warriors originated in Ireland. They were predominately hunter-gatherers who had finally settled into farming settlements around the country.

Many years earlier, the Fomorians invaded the country, a darkly magical tribe known to be phenomenally ugly. They celebrated their ugliness, even driving out children who were normal in appearance. They took deformities as a mark of favour from their dark gods. For some of them, their forms became truly monstrous, while others were darkly beautiful. One might have a large and small arm, while another might have two heads and another three eyes. Some stories claim they were born whole but became strange in mind and appearance after exposure to the occult degenerative radiances and blasphemous smokes of their eldritch rituals.

In fact, one of their leaders, Balor, had become so powerful and monstrously distorted that he had to leave the tribe for fear of accidentally killing them. He left his wife behind with the rest of his tribe for her safety, only taking a handful of warriors with him.

After years of co-existing, they finally fell out with each other and went to battle. The Fomorians, with their more significant numbers and powers, drove the Fir Bolg out of Ireland. The Fomorians lost 800 troops in the week-long battle, but the Fir Bolg lost many more. So they emigrated to Greece and Scotland, where they lived in partial slavery for many years.

The Fomorians then turned their attention to the Tuath dé Danann in the battle of Mag Tuired. This battle was a long and bloody affair that waged on for weeks. When it seemed like there was no end in sight, they called a temporary truce and sent their best, most ferocious warriors to meet each other.

The Fomorians trying to intimidate the Tuath sent their strongest warrior, Sreng, who was big and fierce, out to meet them. He took with him a large shield, his two thick-shafted javelins, and his large two-handed sword. The Tuath then sent Bres, an equally ferocious warrior, although not as big out. He carried with him his shield and his sword and his two great spears. The two men drew near to each other until they were within speaking distance. Each looked at the other without saying a word, astonished at the other's weapons and appearance.

They then greeted each other, only to discover that they spoke the same language, as their origins were like that of their ancestors. The two warriors exchanged and marvelled at each other's weapons. They talked at length before deciding that the best result was to divide the country in two. To share it equally rather than enter a long, possibly unwinnable war.

Upon returning to their camps to recommend a truce and division of the land, the Fomorian leaders turned it down. Instead, they sent forth magic showers of sorcery and a furious rain of fire from the air onto the Tuath. The Tuath then gathered their armies and withdrew from the battlefield to regroup. Then, Nuada sent an envoy to the Fomorians, saying they should surrender half of Ireland to them. The response was for the Fomorians to send back the head of the dead envoy.

As the Fomorians would not share the land, they prepared for battle. The following morning, at the first glimmer of sunlight, the battle began, with troops facing troops on the battlefield. Mages from both sides rained down sorcery on each other while the best warriors entered the battlefield.

The Tuatha, with Nuada, their leader in command, formed a compact well-armed unit marshalled by fighting warriors armed with weapons and stout shields. Everyone pressed onto the man to his left, with the edge of his shield, the shaft of his spear, or the hilt of his swords, and began the attack on the Fomorians, cutting their way through them, clearing a path through their centre. Sreng also made an onslaught on the Tuatha and devastated their ranks, clearing a path for him and his men.

The battle continued, and great numbers of troops lay dead on the battlefield. Sreng encountered Nuada, who stabbed him in the stomach with his spear before retaliating with a blow of his sword on Nuada, cutting away the rim of his shield and severing his right arm at the shoulder. The king's arm, with part of his shield, fell to the ground.

They rushed the king from the battlefield and he later died from his injury. By the close of the day, both groups called a truce for the evening. The following morning, Sreng, refusing to rest with his wound, went back to the battlefield to carry on the fight.

Three Tuath soldiers sneaked through the Fomorian ranks and confronted their king Eochaid as he was washing his hands in a nearby stream, before killing him. The fighting was more ferocious than the previous day. With the Tuath wanting to avenge their fallen king.

Sreng and his troops advanced to the centre of the battlefield, where Bres and some of his most trusted warriors met them in battle. The fighting was fierce until only Bres and Sreng remained amongst the group of warriors.

After pausing and acknowledging each other, the two of them viciously attacked each other. The fighting continued for some time before Bres finally overcame Sreng with a swipe of his blade, removing his head from his body. Word of their king and the most ferocious warrior's slaying spread rapidly through their ranks, so the Fomorians retreated from the battlefield to regroup. Later that day, they sent an envoy to sue for peace, which was accepted and led to an uneasy truce between the two tribes.

When the battle was over, the Tuatha made Bres their king, and he remained their leader for seven years. He died after taking a drink from a well while out hunting. There remained an uneasy truce between the two tribes and the Gaels and other indigenous tribes throughout the land.

Many years passed when a Tuath seer dreamt that there would be an invasion from a new tribe called the Milesians. It would be on the coast of Kerry, so gathering their finest magicians and the best druids from around the country, set off to Kerry to prepare for their arrival.

When they saw them coming over the horizon, all worked in unison to create an illusion that there was no coastline. They then created a hurricane that covered the fleet, dispersing it in all directions. Several of the vessels sank, and many troops drowned.

When they did land on the shoreline, it was not in one combined force, but in detachments widely separated around the coastline. Some landed at the mouth of the Boyne, others on the Kerry coast, and even Cork. After the troops had regrouped on land, there was a short but fiercely contested battle.

The Milesians joined forces with the Gaels, deciding the battle's faith. In the great pitched battle, which was fought in a glen a few miles south of Tralee. The Milesians and the Gael forces, who far outnumbered the Tuath and Fomorians, were victorious. As part of an agreement, the Tuath and Fomorians agreed to surrender the human world. Using their magic and portals, they entered the safety of the otherworld. Only going back occasionally but never in large numbers drawing attention to themselves.

Many years had passed, but there was still an uneasy truce with the Tuath and the Fomorians within Mag Mell. There were little skirmishes now and then, but nothing major. Cred finished by telling them that her father, Dagda, was now the leader of the Tuath. While her brother Lugh was the general of their armies. Oh yes, and they had met her other brother, Aillen, who had become the family's outcast for his many evil deeds in the human world.

"You mean, Giant Aillen that we killed at Tara?" asked Fergal. "Yes, he was my brother," replied Cred. "Like the Fomorians, it depends on how we choose to use our magic," she said. "I try to use my magic for good, but Aillen used his for bad, and therefore, his appearance eventually changed." "I never even knew that you knew magic," said Shane. "That's because I try not to use magic in the other realm," said Cred.

Cred then explained that not all of their magic powers were the same. Her father, Dagda, had control over the wind and weather, livestock and the crops, the seasons and even time itself. Like Aillen, he had a magical harp, Uaithne, which had the power to sway human emotions, turn the seasons, and keep natural harmony and order.

While his cauldron Coire Ansic produced a never-ending supply of food for his tribe, ensuring they never went hungry. He had a large black staff, the Lorg Mor, which could end nine lives in a single blow. With a tap of the other end, it could restore the dead to life if done in time.

Her brother Lugh was a very skilled warrior and had no weakness with any weapon. He could throw his spear called Sleg, which none could stand against, a great distance. This spear was unbeatable in battle and would take the form of lightning when thrown. With one word ("Ibar"), it hit its target, with another ("Athibar!"). It returned to Lugh.

Lugh was a master of many talents. He was also a trickster willing to lie, cheat, and steal to overcome his opponents. He also carried a sword called Fragarach, or "The Answerer." The sword would force those it was pointed at to answer questions truthfully.

Then there was Cred herself. She was the grand seer who could see most things. She was a potent force of fertility, a source of great wisdom and poetry, and a dispenser of healing. Indeed, she had foreseen many things, and that was partly why she left for the other realm. She had seen Fionn and Sadhbh, and went to ensure that Sadhbh became pregnant. She could also see her future with Shane, and that was why she met him a few times.

"Why did you never spend the night?" asked Shane. "You see," replied Cred ", I told you the portals shone at night, and I travelled home to Mag Mell each night, so no one saw me using my powers." "But you spent the night once," said Fergal. "Yes, but I had other business to attend to before returning to Mag Mell the following night," said Cred.

"So, how do we get back home?" asked Darragh. "I don't have an answer to that," said Cred, "sometimes the timeline changes, and all things must right themselves." "There are other times where I cannot foresee what is going to happen." "Can you see what will happen to us?" asked Darragh. "Will we ever get home?". "I cannot answer that, as there are things I have seen that could change your timeline if I told you it would happen." replied Cred.

"So, are you saying we'll get home, then?" asked Fergal. "I am saying I cannot answer you," replied Cred. "Are you saying that you know but won't tell us?" asked Shane. "I am saying I cannot tell you," Replied Cred defiantly.

Cred told the group that Mag Mell was a much different and more dangerous place than the human realm. The main difference, she told them, was time. One year in Mag Mell was the equivalent of nine years in the human world. "How old are you?" asked Fergal. "You should know better than to ask a lady her age", came the reply.

She continued that although not all creatures there had magical powers, many of them did, and the group would not have the fortitude to endure and withstand the sorcery, ailments and sicknesses that existed there. She told them she would need to get them to bathe in the pool of endurance. They would have to travel through the Caves of Kesh Corran and across an abyss to reach the pool. Cred then gave the group heavier hooded cloaks. As with the season's change, it would now get colder outside.

Cred then ushered the boys out the door to a nearby stable. Upon entering, the boys could see four saddled and bridled horses waiting to go. All the horses were white with long flowing manes—their hoofs stamping on the ground in anticipation of what was coming. Cred and the others all mounted the horses, pulling on the bridles while exiting the stable.

Cred tugged gently on her horse's bridle and raised it's neck, which arched gracefully as he set off at a canter toward the caves. "Let's go, Lads", shouted Darragh as they followed suit. With the cool breeze coming through the air and the breath of their horses streaming out of their nostrils, fogging up the air in front of them. It wasn't long until the horses were at full gallop, with the steam flowing from their hides. They looked like a mist floating across the meadows.

Onwards they rode across fields and through forests, where the golden yellow leaves fell from the trees and crunched below the thundering hooves of the horses as they galloped. They splashed through streams and galloped over hills with the greatest of ease without ever faltering, as these were enchanted horses that had endless amounts of stamina. On and on, they rode with the miles stretching behind them until, eventually, Cred pulled up close to a stream.

"The horses might not be tired," she said, "but my bones are aching". After tying up their horses, the others gathered some wood and lit a campfire. The lads sat there and talked with Cred into the early hours about their lives back home and their lives with Fionn. Cred, in turn, told them about her life as a child growing up between the two worlds.

The following morning, they set off in search of the caves. They rode through the day and, as it was reaching nightfall, noticed a large white mountain gleaming in the moonlight in the distance. "That is the entrance to the caves," shouted Cred. As they rode closer, they could see massive limestone walls containing a horizontal line of cave openings in the cliffs.

"That's our destination", roared Cred to drown out the sound of the galloping horses. Soon they pulled up outside the line of caves. All separate yet inter-joining each other from the inside, halfway up the mountain, which was awesome to behold. The group then tied the horses to nearby branches and climbed up into the caves.

CHAPTER TWELVE

THE WELL OF ENDURANCE

hrough the darkened caves, they marched. In the darkness, they listened to the bundle of noises they could only guess at. There was the patter of a rabbit and perhaps the scurrying of a hare. A bush rustled, but that brief rustle was probably a bat hunting some food while hiding in the shadows. There was the usual howling of a wolf and the sound of scratching and scraping against the bark of a tree.

Yet onwards, the group walked further into the vastness of the cave. The cave was so vast that inside it was a forest whose trees got sunlight from large holes in its roof. There was a mountain and even a dark, what seemed like a bottomless lake. There were also prominent ridges and boulders to get past before they could reach the abyss and pool of endurance.

As they drove further into the cave, Darragh and Shane walked to one side of the mountain while Fergal and Cred chose the other side. Darragh spotted a doorway in the mountainside covered by holly. They approached it and inside, could see three women. Who, through the holly, looked like angels. They pushed through the holly, calling out to the women.

As soon as they walked through the holly, they fell to their knees, powerless and without strength, as the three women were actually old hags. Their hair was black and straw-like. Their eyes were bloodshot red, and their mouths were full of curved yellow fangs. They had long scraggy necks that could turn round like a chicken's neck, while their arms were long and skinny, with long claw-like hands.

They had cast a spell on the holly, which had poisoned Darragh and Shane, rendering their bodies lifeless. "What's the matter with us?" asked a nervous Shane as he tumbled to the ground. "I don't know," said Darragh as he fell beside him. The three old hags tied them up with some ropes. "We'll dine tonight," roared one hag, while another said there could yet be more to follow as they carried their prey further into the cave.

Luckily Fergal and Cred had changed direction to follow the others and had happened upon the unfolding events. They sneaked up to the hanging Holly. Within the cave, there was silence except for the voices of the hags planning what to do next. Luckily, they were busy and not too bright. Cred cut down the hanging holly with a long spear she carried with her without being noticed.

The three hags took their swords in their hands and prepared to slay Darragh and Shane. Before doing so, two of them had one more look out the door of the cave. Not noticing the missing holly, they peered out to see if any stragglers were coming. Cred stood back into the shadows while Fergal took a step back.

"We slaughter that one first," said one hag as she spied Fergal. She then moved forward in his direction. Fergal rubbed his ring before disappearing in front of her. He reappeared at her side before taking out Claíomh Solais and plunging it deep into her chest, killing her instantly. The second hag lunged at Fergal, and Cred stepped out of the shadows. She plunged her spear into her back before exiting her chest, killing her, too.

They sneaked into the cave and approached the third one from behind. They captured her, pushing her to the ground. She was bound with some ropes from the cave. They untied Darragh and Shane, who gingerly got to their feet. "Don't leave me like this", pleaded the last hag. After a lengthy discussion, they agreed they would untie the hag. Just as they did so, she lunged at them with her enormous claws, scratching Fergal down his cheek. Cred drew her spear and flung it at the hag, hitting it right between the eyes as she fell dead on the floor.

As Darragh and Shane had to regain their strength, they remained in the cave. They talked about the ordeal and explained how it had happened. A colossal figure strode down the side of the mountain towards the cave. The group all sneaked to the back of the cave to hide. Barely able to squeeze through the door was a fourth hag. If the other three had been terrible to look at, this one was more terrible than the other three combined.

She was wearing a heavy tunic with trousers and had a gigantic sword by her side and a giant club in her hand. She stooped down by the bodies of her three dead sisters, and bitter tears streamed down her monstrous face. "I am too late to save you, my dear sisters," she shouted, "but I will avenge you", she roared at the top of her voice. The group felt the floor tremble beneath them from the sheer force of her voice.

The giant hag was so inconsolable that she cried herself to sleep. Darragh told the others to grab a large cloth lying on the floor. Then, using their weapons, all of them gathered some enchanted holly. Placing it on the large fabric before upending it onto the giant hag and running from the cave.

They crossed the ridges and passed the boulders until they finally reached the giant abyss. There in front of the abyss stood a large standing stone as tall as each of them. It stood on four round boulders of sandstone, now partly buried in the ground. The abyss seemed bottomless and was at least 20 metres wide. It appeared almost impassable.

"This is pointless!" cried Fergal. "we've come all this way for nothing". "Don't let your eyes deceive you," said Cred as she approached the standing stone. "Do as I do", she told the others. As she raised her hand forward at the stone "oscailt" (open), she spoke as a Triquetra symbol began emanating brightly from the standing stone. She disappeared, only to reappear next to another standing stone on the far side of the abyss.

"Use your torc hand and imagine going through a door", shouted Cred from the other side. "Cool," said Darragh, as he approached the standing stone while holding his torc hand out. "Oscailt," he said before vanishing, reappearing next to Cred. "My turn next," said Shane as he approached, holding his hand out. "Oscailt," he said before it transported him to the other side.

"Come on, Fergal", roared the others as he looked nervously on. He finally approached the standing stone and said, "oscailt". Yet nothing happened. "It's not working", he cried out. "Point your torc at it!" shouted Darragh. BOOM, Fergal was standing next to them on the other side of the abyss.

The group soon made their way through a small tunnel covered in creeping ivy and holly. Before finally emerging to a partial muck and stone pathway and reaching a small grotto. The Grotto comprised stone-built walls with an engraved stone archway. Nearby, a small whitethorn tree was growing outside, with colourful ribbons tied to some branches.

Cred gave the lads a ribbon and a bronze tunic pin each. She told them they should each tie a ribbon to the tree. Once inside the grotto, to give the pin to the statue pouring the water. As it was an offering to the lady of the well, or earth-mother, as she was sometimes called. The lads, one by one, approached the tree and tied a ribbon to one branch, before returning to Cred.

Cred told the group to make their way through the archway individually before undressing. Once ready, they were to offer the pin to the statue, as the effects of the waters would emanate from the breast of the earth-mother. They should then bathe in the well. She also told them to duck their heads beneath the waters twice. The first time was for their healing and nourishing, and the second was for their fortitude and endurance.

Darragh was first through the archway before undressing. He could see the well was made from stacked stones, the same as the entrance to the grotto was. It was circular and at least six feet across. The statue was placed strategically on the side of the well. It was to collect water dripping from a stream trickling down the wall before emptying it into the well itself.

Darragh approached the statue, giving it the pin as an offering before entering the well. The well itself appeared dark except for the moonlight shining down on it through a narrow passage in the grotto's roof. He bathed in its waters, ducking his head twice beneath the waters. Once finished, He dressed and exited the grotto, telling the others exactly what he had done.

Shane was next, followed by Fergal, who one by one got into the grotto and did precisely as Darragh had done, before re-joining the group. Fergal noticed no pain in his face where the hag had scratched him as it had healed the wound while bathing in the well.

Once Cred was happy that the group had all given their offerings and bathed in the well, she walked them back to the standing stone. One by one, she made them travel back and forth over the abyss many times. Until she was happy and indeed, they were all content that they knew how to use the torc to travel through the portal stones.

They then set off back through the cave, over the boulders and ridges. They approached the mountain cave to check on the giant hag. The cave was in darkness, so Fergal took out Claíomh Solais to light the place up. To their horror, the giant hag was gone. They realised the hag must have been immune to the poison holly.

Cred walked over, picked up some of the holly, and was fine too. The lads were wary of touching it, but Fergal was brave and grabbed a bunch, and he fell to his knees, powerless. With that, the group heard the thundering sound of footsteps running down the mountain. Darragh quickly sheath Fergal's dagger, returning the cave to darkness, before lifting Fergal across his shoulder and moving towards the back of the cave.

Shane and Cred slid into crevices in the cave as the Giant hag squeezed her way into the cave carrying a torch illuminating the place. The group ducked for cover while Darragh rubbed Fergal's ring to make him disappear. "I know you're here," said the giant hag with a terrible laugh, but there was nothing but silence within the cave.

"Don't be shy?" she said, "we'll get this all over with swiftly". Suddenly, the power of Fergal's ring wore off, and the hag could see him lying at the back of the cave. She reached back and grabbed him by the throat, lifting him up and banging him off the cave roof.

Darragh reached for his sword, but where he had retreated, it was too tight to take it from its sheath. "Well, well", roared the hag at Fergal, "what do we have here? Surely you don't expect me to accept that you alone have slain my three sisters". She flung him angrily against a wall, with his limp body falling to the floor.

"That's enough" shouted Darragh as he came out of hiding. "I challenge you to single combat", he roared. The hag snorted loudly and shouted, "A skinny little morsel like you want's to fight me". "Yes, that's right", shouted Darragh, "outside of the cave, and you can lead the way". The Giant hag accepted the challenge and squeezed her way out of the cave. Darragh called on Shane and Cred to help once he had her attention. When he had her back to the cave door before he, too, left the cave.

"I will kill you first, followed by your little friend", roared the hag as she raised her giant sword to prepare for the fight. "Then I will eat your meagre remains for supper, as it certainly won't be enough for dinner," she roared with a terrible laugh. Moments later, Darragh drew his blade before rubbing his bear ring and attacking the giant hag as she swooped down on him with her giant sword.

There was an almighty sound of metal clashing as neither weapon gave an inch. Darragh was mindful that his ring would not last long and moved to the hag's right. Turning her and placing her back to the cave. It was hard to with-stand the terrific blows of the giant hag, and Darragh retreated slightly from her. He then lunged forward with all his might, with his blade hitting hers, forcing her to retreat towards the cave.

The hag let out a frightening growl as she prepared to move forward again. Just in time, Shane and Cred came out of the cave, stabbing the hag in the backs of her knees with their spears. The hag let out a wailing cry as she dropped to her knees before turning to see what had caused her pain.

Only for Shane and Cred to once again pierce her in the side with their spears. This allowed Darragh to rub his ring again before racing up to her. With the mightiest swipe he had ever done with his sword, he sliced the giant hag completely in two.

Darragh dropped to his knees, exhausted, just as the hag's upper body fell beside her legs. Cred ran into the cave while Shane checked on Darragh, who had exerted himself with the final blow. Moments later, Cred came out of the cave, linking Fergal with one hand and carrying some poison holly in the other. Fergal proclaimed the hag was lucky he hadn't faced her in battle. The entire group laughed as they made their way back out of the caves.

Outside the caves, the group found their horses waiting for them and, without hesitation, mounted them and set off back to Cred's house in Fálias. They could not get away from the caves quick enough.

As night fell, they pulled up to make camp for the night. Cred said that the rings the boys had would need to be upgraded. She thought they were not up to the task. Their effects needed to last much longer than they did, as poor old Fergal nearly got himself killed because of his one. She also noted that the holly had still robbed Fergal of his strength, which was curious. They all then lay down to sleep for the night.

THE POWER OF THE RING

he following morning; they set off for Fálias. Upon reaching the city and putting the horses into the stables. They then made their way to Cred's house. Cred waved her hand at a wall and a secret door opened and they all entered. It was a small gloomy room, and much like Biddy's, had shelves all around the walls with books and ingredients on them.

There was a small bronze cauldron on a tall slim stand, and Cred made her way over to it. She gathered chamomile, mugwort, lamb's cress, plantain, mayweed, nettle, crab-apple, thyme, and fennel and added them to the bowl before adding water and mixing everything together. She then chanted the following verse.

Ut lytel spere, gif her innie sie
Ut lytel spere, gif her innie sy
Ut lytel spere, gif her innie sy

The boys were told to drink from the cauldron. She told them it was the Nine Herbs Charm and would protect them from illnesses thought to come from toxins in the air. She then gave them the holly to hold, and none dropped to their knees or felt powerless. "That's great," said Cred, "One thing fixed, now let's sort them rings out".

She then grabbed some incense made from herbs and tree resin and set it alight. She burned the incense until the entire room filled with smoke and a pleasant smell and fragrance filled the air to create a calm atmosphere.

She then grabbed a small bronze bowl from the shelves. She then placed some charcoal in the middle of the bowl, filled it with sand, and set it alight. As soon as the charcoal had turned whitish, she put one more teaspoon of incense on it. She told the lads to throw their rings into the bowl. Then she threw a handful of Juniper berries into it and let it burn.

She then took three small embroidered drums made from wood and deer skin from a shelf. Then giving them to the lads, telling them to tap on the drum gently with both hands. "Don't worry about how you sound or whether you're doing it right?" she said. "Just play and feel the drum's vibrations flowing through your hands, arms, and body until your toes tingle". They tapped the drums until the flames died and their rings were cool enough to handle.

When they had their rings back on their fingers, Fergal rubbed his and vanished. It was easily 15 minutes before he reappeared. "I guess you could feel the power of the ring," said Cred. She explained Finnegas was a druid and had learned his craft from the Tuath. His spells and charms, though, would never be as strong as those of the Tuath themselves.

Cred told the lads it was time to go to Brú na Bóinne. "Where is that" asked Shane. "That is where my father and brother live," said Cred. "They live in a large Dun or castle within the city," she said. In the human world, it would be called Newgrange. Cred told the boys that on the Solstice, the sun was at its strongest and re-energised her father, Dagda, and imbued him with his powers for the year ahead. Which is why it is an important place in Mag Mell and the human world.

They all left the house and walked back to the stables, where the four white horses were again waiting for them, and off they rode to Brú na Bóinne. It wasn't too far to travel as the horses didn't tire, and it was a lovely crisp dry day. Before long, they could see the city in their sights.

The city was very like Fálias except on a much larger scale, and this time at its centre stood a sizeable dominating castle. A large gated archway led into the city, with inscriptions and carvings engraved on it. There were half-crumbled buildings, cracked blocks, and stones broken up by protruding tree roots.

There were towering spires rising into the sky, and smoke filled the air as it came from chimneys within the city. When they reached the gate, the guards waved them through as they recognised Cred. As the group made their way up the narrow winding streets, they saw many buildings with caved-in roofs weighed down by overgrowth.

Just like in Fálias, they passed sports halls where soldiers were training in many events. There were goldsmiths, jewellers, cobblers and tailor shops, as well as music, singing, and dancing. When they reached the castle, they saw battlements with blast marks and holes from earlier battles, and ash scarred the stone from past fires. There were birds nesting and flying close by, making their home on the battlements, while cobwebs and ropy vines were hanging from almost every brick in the castle walls.

As they entered the courtyard, they could see uneven blocks worn from the feet of many people and animals walking on them. Fire pits were blazing to keep the troops warm. As they made their way inside, they could see mould and mildew-covered walls. With spiders creeping along cobwebbed corridors filled with stone statues and animal totems. They passed by winding staircases leading to the battlements while making their way to the main hall.

When they reached the main hall, it had many statues and totems along with a stone altar and a large burning fireplace, which hardly heated the giant room. There, in the middle of the hall, was a huge wooden table big enough to fit thirty people. Yet there were only two people sharing the table. It was Dagda and Lugh.

"My beautiful daughter", shouted Dagda, "I was not expecting you. Come here and let me look at you". Dagda stood up and was a very tall, slim, pale-skinned man. He had shoulder-length white hair with a long white braided beard. He dressed from head to toe in a long white robe covered in gold embroidery. He approached Cred, hugging her while lifting her in the air and spinning her around.

Lugh then got to his feet, and he, too, was a tall man. Although he was much broader than their father. He was a pale, bearded man with his brown hair braided into a ponytail. He dressed in a purple satin tunic with gold embroidery around the collar with black satin trousers. He bellowed out in a deep voice. "Welcome home, my dear little sister". He, too, gave her a hug, lifting her off the ground.

"Who have we got here?" asked Dagda. "Dear father and Lugh," she said, "let me introduce you to my husband Shane and his friends Darragh and Fergal". "Ah, so you are the humans who come from the future," said Dagda. "That's us", said Darragh. Dagda and Lugh then welcomed the lads to their home. Lugh gave Shane a big bear hug, nearly squeezing the life out of him. Saying, "Nice to meet you, brother" "Eh, likewise," said Shane. Dagda, then gave Shane a big hug too. He then instructed a guard to bring more food and mead, as it was time to feast. They all carried on eating and drinking until it was time for bed.

Cred then guided Darragh and Fergal to their room while she and Shane went to hers. The bedroom was freezing cold, and the only heat came from two torches affixed to the wall to light the room up. Luckily, there was a blanket made of cowhide for the lads to cover themselves with through the night.

Darragh and Fergal woke the following morning feeling worse for wear, but made their way to the main hall, anyway. Cred and Shane soon joined them, and Dagda and Lugh not long after. After eating, Dagda told the boys that he had a little mission for them. A little skirmish had broken out between one of his regiments and a Fomorian regiment, a day's ride away. Lugh would accompany them, as he wanted to assess their fighting skills.

The three lads and Lugh made their way to the stables, where the lad's three white horses were waiting. A guard brought a magnificent pure white horse in from another stable. "This is Aonbharr," said Lugh. "Aonbharr, of the Flowing Mane, can travel on land or water and never tire."

They all mounted their horses, and away they rode on a day's journey to the east. They rode over hills, through forests and meadows, and streams. Aonbharr never slowed down in the water as his hoofs never sank below the water. He seemed to float across it until they eventually came to a small camp with Tuath soldiers in it, close to a river.

"Where are the enemy?" asked Lugh. "The other side of the river," said his captain. All four dismounted and tied up their horses. "What are their numbers?" asked Lugh. "Approximately thirty men, sir," said the captain. "There's no sign of any mages or druids amongst them," he said. "Right," said Lugh, "Tell your men to hold back as my new friends here are going to show me their skills."

Lugh turned to the lads and told them it was up to them now. Darragh turned to Fergal and told him it was time to see how good the improved rings were. Fergal waded across the river while rubbing his ring and vanishing. He returned a short time later and told Darragh and Shane that he had killed two sleeping guards and hid their bodies in some bushes.

Darragh then took the rings from both Shane and Fergal. He said, "let's have some fun," as he waded into the water. Once he reached the other side, he rubbed all three rings and ran into the enemy camp. Not visible to the enemy troops, he ran at full speed through the camp, slaying enemies with his sword as he ran.

Just as he was leaving the camp, he let out an enormous scream. He had been stuck in the back by something that burned through his clothes and burned the skin on his back. He then returned across the river. I killed at least ten men he shouted to Lugh before handing all three rings to Shane.

Shane followed suit, crossing the river and rubbing the rings. He stood in one spot and threw his spear as fast as possible at the enemies. Whilst holding his hand aloft, his spear returned for him to throw again. He easily killed many enemies before he, too, let out an enormous scream. He also had been stuck by something that burned through his clothes and burned the skin on his stomach and chest.

He made his way back across the river, passing the rings to Fergal and telling him to be careful. Fergal then made his way across the river and into the camp. There were nine enemies left alive, and they had all gathered together in a circle in the middle of the camp with their shields raised for protection.

Fergal drew his Claíomh Solais from its sheath and threw it onto the ground nearby, drawing their attention, with two men leaving the circle to investigate. Fergal quickly ran up and stabbed them with his other dagger. He Grabbed Claíomh Solais and ran away again. Like the other before him, he felt a sharp pain and a burning sensation while running away. He crossed the river back to the rest of the group.

Lugh congratulated the lads, but the job wasn't finished yet. He said that there was a druid or wizard hiding that must have caused their injuries, but he could not spot where they were. After crossing the river, he threw his spear at the enemy circle. He Shouted "Ibar" and the spear became a lightning bolt that struck the ground right in the centre of the enemies. It exploded on the ground, killing all the remaining enemies in one go. Then, shouting "Athibar", the spear returned to him. A line of flames hit him, but he did not sustain any damage. He threw his spear in the fire's direction, but it did not hit a target. Lugh then shouted "Athibar", and his spear returned.

Lugh then called all the troops across the river, instructing them to build a pyre and burn the dead's bodies. He tended to the three lads to ease their pain before telling them to mount up, and they rode off back to Brú na Bóinne. When they returned to the castle, they found Cred waiting for them.

Lugh explained to Cred that the lads had all received burns in the battle that needed tending to. Cred took them to her quarters to heal them. Once she had healed their wounds, she gave them all new Tuath outfits created with fire retardant material. This would protect them from fire and were warmer than their Fianna outfits.

They spent the next few days in the fort, getting to know Dagda and Lugh better. likewise, Dagda and Lugh wanted to learn more about the three lads from the future. They sat and talked, ate and drank, and then talked some more. Until they were all at ease with each other and each other's life stories. Cred eventually told the three lads that they had a new mission to go on.

CHAPTER THIRTEEN

THE LITTLE FOLK

hey returned to the stables, where their horses were ready and waiting for them. "Where are we going?" asked Fergal. "We are going to the enchanted forest of Avondale!" said Cred as they rode off out of the castle gates, down the city's winding streets, and out into the countryside. "What's in Avondale Forest?" Asked Shane. "An ingredient I need for a potion", said Cred.

They galloped off across fields and meadows, over hills and streams until nightfall, when they set up camp for the night. While they were sitting around a campfire talking, Darragh asked Cred what potion she wanted to make. She told him it was to help protect them from magic spells or weapons. If attacked again, their injuries would be less severe than the burns they received in their fight with the Fomorians.

The following morning, they set off for the forest. When they reached the top of a large hill, they looked down into a valley between two hills. There was a large forest with a lake nearby. "That is our destination," said Cred as they galloped down the hillside. On approach, they could see a special opening between the trees, almost as though they were inviting them into this magical place.

The branches overhead grew very close to one another, almost woven together. They seemed to form an enormous canopy over the top of the entrance, with hanging moss and giant cobwebs draping down around them. They heard sounds coming from the forest.

It was as if the wind, whispering through the trees, was emitting a call to beckon them in. Once they made their way in, there was an eerie silence; the only sound was hearing the cracking twigs and crunched leaves under their horses' hooves. The ground was uneven, with knobby tree roots protruding from the ground.

Many smells were wafting through the air, drawing everyone's attention for different reasons. There was an earthy smell, animal scents, and damp, rotting wood. While wandering around the forest, they could see large rocks covered in thick moss and trees covered in mushrooms. Suddenly there was a loud sound, and all of their hearts jumped in their chests, only for them to spy a deer jumping over fallen branches and scampering away.

As they moved further in, they came to a large opening close to the lake. The sweet smell of wild mint, lavender and pine was strongly present in the air. The forest floor was covered with fallen trees, branches, leaves, ferns, underbrush, moss, ivy and mushrooms. The moss was creeping over everything and looked as soft as cotton. Mushrooms were growing all over the place, on tree trunks, rocks, and everywhere the eye could see.

Then they heard the leaves on the ground rustling. It may have been the sound of all the forest animals scampering away into their hiding places. However, it sounded as though fairies or other magical creatures were trying to hide from them. There was a gigantic tree at its very centre. The leaves were all still in full bloom, and giant mushrooms surrounded it.

While around them, the other trees were losing their leaves. "This is a magic tree," said Cred. "It is said that you can take a leaf and whisper your wish on it, and it will come true. Although I am not aware that anyone's wish ever came true."

The three lads jumped from their horses and each grabbed a leaf, whispering into it. "What did you wish for?" asked Fergal. "I can't tell you, or it won't come through", came the replies from the others. "Well, I'm still here, so it didn't work," cried Fergal. "Right," said Cred, "It is here we will set up camp". "How long are we staying for?" asked Shane. "As long as it takes," said Cred. They then set off into the forest, setting traps for their dinner.

Cred told the lads to keep their wits about them as there was a tale that inside the forest, fairies that lost their wings had become bitter creatures responsible for creating confusion among anyone who crossed their paths, making them disoriented or even stealing their belongings. A short while later, they checked their traps and caught some squirrels and rabbits. When they returned to camp, Shane said he could hear whispering voices in the wind.

Cred said she needed a brave volunteer to sleep at the lakeside through the night. "Not me," said Fergal. "I don't want the angry fairies attacking me." "What for?" asked Shane. "I need to catch an Alp-luachra", came the reply. "If it helps, I'll do it," said Shane, "but how will I catch it?" he asked. Cred told him she would know when he caught one.

After eating dinner, Shane made his way over to the lake's edge. Cred warned him not to swim in the lake, for anyone who swam in it turned into a fish. The only way to change back into a human was to lure other people there to take their place. He bedded down on some giant ferns growing by the lake's edge and fell asleep for the night.

The following morning, Shane woke and joined the others. "Well, did we have any luck he asked?". "Not so far," said Cred. The group carried on with their camping and setting traps for the rest of the day until Shane again made his bed by the lake to sleep for the night. The following day and night were the same, with Shane again sleeping by the lake.

The next morning, when they were eating breakfast, Shane said he felt unwell and wanted to rest while the others went out setting traps and hunting. When the others returned with their food, Shane said he was starving, even after eating whatever food that remained in the camp. So, they cooked their day's catch quickly to ease his hunger. Shane grabbed the cooked food and started scoffing it down. "I think you have worms," said Darragh. "No, I think he has an Alp-luachra". Said Cred.

Cred sat next to Shane, and she stroked his face. "Are you trying to seduce me?" asked Shane as he lay down on his back. Cred shouted for Darragh and Fergal to jump on him and hold him down. The lads did straight away before Shane shouted, "What are you up to? Have you gone mad?". "No," said Cred, "I'm hunting Alp-luachra".

With the lads on his chest holding him down, Cred forced his mouth open and dangled some cooked rabbit above him, just beyond the reach of his teeth. Shane began choking, but Cred told the lads not to get off of him. A few minutes later, a little newt-like creature peeped out of his mouth, lunging at the rabbit. Cred then took a vial from her bag and captured the creature. "This is an Alp-luachra". Said Cred, "I need some of its saliva to make a potion", before putting the sealed vial into her bag.

Fergal jumped up and ran to the back of the gigantic tree, where he vomited all over the giant mushrooms. "Blaggard," a noise seemed to say, coming from the mushrooms. Fergal ran to the others. "I am sure I heard someone say blaggard", he said. "Oh no, you've annoyed the fairies", laughed Darragh. "It's not funny," shouted Fergal.

Cred told the lads to mount up, they needed to leave urgently. There was a tale that if anyone littered the forest in any way, a curse or a little unwanted friend might return home with them. Once ready, they all galloped off out of the woods as fast as they could. Not stopping until they returned to Fálias for fear of being chased or followed by evil spirits.

Upon reaching Fálias, they quickly left their horses at the stables and made their way up to Cred's house. With a wave of her hand, she opened the secret door once more, before they all went inside. She took the vial out of her bag and emptied the Alp-luachra into a large bowl without handling it, as there was a poison on its skin that could give off a large stinging sensation.

Cred approached the small bronze cauldron and gathered chamomile, mugwort, lamb's cress, plantain, mayweed, nettle, crab-apple, thyme, and fennel, then added them to the bowl before adding water and mixing everything together. This time, she grabbed the Alp-luachra with some thongs and pressed its mouth over the cauldron to get some of its saliva into the potion before chanting the same verse.

> *Ut lytel spere, gif her innie sie*
> *Ut lytel spere, gif her innie sy*
> *Ut lytel spere, gif her innie sy*

She then instructed the boys to drink from the cauldron. The lads all felt a slight tingle as they drank it. "That means it has worked," said Cred. She then gathered the Alp-luachra back into the vial and placed it on a shelf. The group decided it would be better to rest there until the following morning before setting off to Brú na Bóinne.

That evening they ate and drank before retiring to their rooms to sleep, with Darragh and Fergal going to one room and Shane joining Cred in hers. That night Fergal had a nightmare-like dream. He dreamt that an ill-mannered short, stout man dressed all in red with a pointed red hat, a long white beard on a hairy face, with a bulbous nose, carrying with him a sack large enough to fit a grown man into, had visited him in his room.

He shouted "blaggard" before grabbing & throwing Fergal into his sack and dragging him off. To his horror the following morning Fergal woke startled from the nightmare only to find himself bound, sitting in a dark cellar.

"Where am I?" cried Fergal. He then heard evil laughter coming from an unknown direction, "blaggard", came the reply. A very frightened Fergal cowered in the corner of the dark cellar. He could feel mice or rats running over his legs but wasn't sure, as it was too dark to see and too scared to move.

Meanwhile, Darragh woke from his sleep only to find Fergal missing. He searched for him but could find him nowhere. He then went to Cred's room, where he woke the startled couple from their sleep. "What's wrong?" asked Shane. "Fergal is gone," said Darragh. "He left his Claíomh Solais at the bedside, which is strange". "Have you looked everywhere for him?" asked Shane.

"Yes," said Darragh ", and it must have been on my mind, but I could swear I heard someone shouting blaggard," while I slept. With that, Cred leapt from her bed. "I was afraid of that," she shouted. "What do you mean?" asked Darragh. "A Fear Dearg has kidnapped Fergal," she said. "What's that?" Asked Shane. "Well," said Cred, "you know what a leprechaun is, right?". "Yes," said the two lads in unison. "This is his evil cousin," cried Cred.

Cred explained to them that the Fear Dearg was a mischievous and sometimes cruel little creature who gained pleasure from kidnapping and even torturing people who had wronged it. "How would Fergal have wronged it?" asked Shane. "Well," said Cred, "when we were at the large enchanted tree in the forest, Fergal vomited all over some large mushrooms. The Fear Dearg must live there, and Fergal's vomit must have upset it." Said Cred. "Then we must go there immediately," shouted Darragh.

Cred agreed they needed to go immediately, but she could not go with them. She gave the lads some gold coins and told them that if they were lucky, the Fear Dearg would accept this as payment for being wronged. They left immediately for the stables and set off for Avondale Forest.

Again, the lads galloped without rest, across fields and meadows, over hills and streams before they reached the hilltop and made their way down into the forest. Once there, they made their way to its centre. They tied their horses a short distance away to avoid drawing attention to them and sneaked up to the large enchanted tree.

They lay on the ground hiding to wait for the Fear Dearg to appear. After waiting for hours, there was no sign of him. Darragh sucked on his thumb for inspiration. "Aha," he said. "The creature likes gold, so let's leave him some." He walked over to the large mushrooms where Fergal had vomited and carefully placed a gold coin onto the ground before rushing to hide in some bushes. Soon after that, they heard a melancholy humming, and a little trap door opened beside the mushrooms.

A small pair of eyes peeped out to check that the coast was clear, then a tiny hand grabbed the gold coin and disappeared with the trapdoor slamming shut. The lads made their way over to the trapdoor before prying it open and sneaking inside. Once inside, some old stone steps led down into a tunnel. The lads had to crouch, as the tunnel wasn't tall enough for them to stand upright. They made their way down the stairs to the tunnel. Darragh took out Claíomh Solaris, which he had brought along for Fergal, and lit the way ahead for them.

When they reached the bottom of the stairs, there were multiple tunnels running off of it. Darragh put Claíomh Solais away, and they sat in darkness and listened closely. From one tunnel, they could hear evil laughter. Then they heard Fergal cry out, "please let me go". "Yeh blaggard, I will keep you as my prisoner forever", was the reply. "Please tell me what I have done to you," cried Fergal. "You're a blaggard", came the reply.

The lads crept down the tunnel and, in a room to the side, sitting in a small padded seat with his feet resting on a small stool, sat a little rather ugly red man smoking a long clay pipe and drinking a large cup of mead. "Blaggard", he shouted before giggling quietly to himself.

"Please let me out, I promise I will be good," cried Fergal as the Fear Dearg sat there giggling to himself. Darragh reached into his corrbolg and took out a large spool of string. With that, Darragh and Shane rushed into the room. Shane grabbed him by the feet, dangling him upside down while Darragh wrapped the string around his arms and legs repeatedly until the Fear Dearg, shaking like a caterpillar, shouted, "Let me out, you Blaggards, or I will make you pay dearly".

With the creature tied securely, the lads lay him on the floor and took out Claíomh Solais before searching the rest of the tunnels, looking for Fergal. They came to a small bolted wooden door, and Shane shouted, "Are you in there, Fergal?", "Yes, I'm here" came the reply. With that, the lads opened the door and untied a grateful Fergal, who hugged the others as he never had before.

They made their way back to the Fer Dearg. "You'll pay for this", snarled the little creature as they approached. "You are right, we will pay for this," smirked Darragh. Taking the gold coins from his pouch, he placed three coins on the table and said, "That is a coin for each of us. I hope that is enough to pay our way". "Untie me, you little Blaggard, so that I may decide," said the angry creature.

Shane untied him, and he sat on his chair, taking the gold coins from the table and biting on them to check they were real. The Fear Dearg then told the lads that he wasn't being serious. He was only having fun. "It wasn't fun for me," said a shaken Fergal. "I was bringing you home tonight," said the mischievous little man. "I think it is time you left," he concluded, before the lads made their way back up the stairs and out through the trapdoor.

Once outside, they sat down to chat and ensure Fergal was ok. Suddenly, a loud sound coming through the air reached their ears. The lads crept silently towards the sound. "What is it?" asked Fergal. "It sounds awful". "I think it is someone snoring," said Darragh.

"Yeah, that's what it sounds like," said Shane as they crept ever closer.

As they got closer to the sound, they could see two giant Fly Agaric mushrooms and suspended between them was a large dock leaf, being used as a hammock by a little human-like creature all dressed in green. He had a wizened old face, a red beard, a large top hat, and a cane resting on his chest. "It's a leprechaun", whispered Darragh as they sneaked ever closer. Shane ran over and grabbed the little man by the shoulders, lifting him into the air.

The Leprechaun woke with a fright and shouted, "Please let me go." "What will you do for us if I do?" asked Shane. "I will give you my crock of gold if you do," came the reply. "What is your name?" asked Darragh. "My name is Fergus, and I am the king of all leprechauns. If you release me, the treasure I have is mine to give."

"I don't trust you," said Shane, "for I know you are tricksters." "It is true we like to play jokes," said Fergus, "but you are very cunning, and I wouldn't get the better of you." "Take us to your treasure," said Fergal loudly as he reached over, grabbing his jacket. "Be careful, my young friend. If you don't hurt me, I will tell you all about my gold and where to find it, but I could hurt you if I choose, for I have the power to do so, but I won't. I will just be good and show you where the gold is."

"Come with me then, and I will show you the way to Lipenshaw, for there is where it lies," said Fergus, "but we better make haste, for when the sun goes down, the gold will disappear, and you will never find it again." Shane carried Fergus through the trees, and a few minutes later, they reached a large oak tree, and with a tap of his cane, a door opened in the tree, allowing them to pass through.

"I know you are quite clever and mischievous," said Darragh. "But I promise no harm will come to you if you don't try any tricks," he said as they made their way down a large stone stairway lit by torches. "I won't play any tricks on you," said Fergus. He then asked Shane to put him down, as it was embarrassing for the king to be carried like a child in his own kingdom. "Keep an eye on him," said Darragh. "He is cunning and will try his best to escape, so don't let him out of your sight".

When they reached the bottom of the stairway, they came to an extensive clearing, where they saw a great crowd of leprechauns gathered around a blazing fire, dancing and singing. As they made their way slowly towards them and into their midst, the singing and dancing grew silent.

Fergus shouted, "Let there be music," and they began singing and dancing once more. They asked the lads to dance with them. "It is foolish of you to ask me to dance," said Fergal, "when there is no music." Fergus lifted his hand and made a sign to the people, and instantly the sweetest music sounded around them, and the lads began to dance. When they had danced enough, they were invited to supper.

The lads saw an opening in the ground, and a flight of steps went further down than they already were. They came to a large hall at the end of these steps, all bright and beautiful with gold and silver, and the table was full of food for them to eat from golden plates, and golden goblets filled with mead for them to drink. When they sat down, they were told to eat and drink and be merry. The lads all woke up the following morning back at the enchanted tree, nursing sore heads as someone had drugged them.

"We've been tricked," said Shane, "that we have," said Darragh, "but we're not giving up yet". They returned to the large oak tree, where they hid in some bushes to spy. A little leprechaun came along a short time later and tapped the tree with a cane. Once the doorway opened, the lads all pounced on him. Darragh grabbed the cane in case it came in handy. Shane wrapped his arms around the leprechaun as they made their way inside. They followed the stairway down until reaching the next set of steps.

"Let me go," said the Leprechaun, "and look around you." Where there was a large table the night before, they had replaced it and the lads saw they covered the floor with gold and silver pieces. There were vessels of precious stones lying everywhere. "Now take what you want," said the Leprechaun. Fergal started filling his pockets. "Don't be impatient?" said Darragh as he called out to Fergus.

When the lads were distracted by the surrounding riches, the leprechaun disappeared, leaving only themselves and Fergus. "What do you want?" snarled Fergus. "You little rogue," said Darragh ", you broke your promise not to play any tricks on us". "But I never made you a promise," laughed Fergus.

Shane asked if he could see the actual crock of gold, as he had heard about it since childhood. Fergus ushered them down a hallway and into another room. With the wave of his cane, an enormous pot filled with gold hanging out over the edges appeared. The lads stood open-mouthed at the sheer size of the pot as it stood taller than any of them.

When they turned around, Fergus had vanished and as they looked back, so too had the large pot of gold. "I told you they were tricksters," said Darragh, as they made their way out of the room. They went down a tunnel near them and heard voices and laughter. One voice said, "They are looking for our crock of gold, but little do they know it is lying down at the bottom of the old well further down the tunnel".

"Aha," said Shane, "we've found it", as he rushed forward down the tunnel. Darragh shouted for him to stop. Once all three lads got to the end of the tunnel, they came face to face with a large stone well. As they peered in, they could see nothing, as the darkness seemed endless. "It must be a trap," said Darragh, taking a gold coin from his bag and dropping it into the well. The lads stood there silently, waiting for it to hit the bottom, but it never did.

Darragh began sucking on his thumb to seek advice before turning and making his way back to the room that had housed the large pot of gold. "What are we doing?" asked Shane. "By my reckoning, we need to say a verse for the crock of gold to appear," said Darragh. Fergal stepped forward and said, "Humpty, dumpty", before getting a slap around the ear from Darragh. "Not that verse, you idiot," he said. "It will need to be about the gold".

Fergal then dropped to the floor in a deep sleep and disappeared. "Golden pot, show me your lot!" laughed Shane, before he too fell into a deep sleep and vanished.

Darragh stood there silently for some time before he finally spoke out loud.

"Oh, crock of gold appear to me,
Please show yourself for me to see,

I wish you here for my pleasure,
Appear at once, leprechaun treasure."

"Ha, ha, ha," came a giant laugh as Fergus and the large pot of gold appeared in front of him. "It's not quite right, but I commend you for your effort," laughed Fergus. "I must also say you are very stubborn. Now tell me what you want." "What have you done with my friends?" asked Darragh. "Don't worry?" said Fergus. "You will find them fast asleep at the enchanted tree, for they mocked me with their verses, so will have no help from me."

"We want to go home," said Darragh. "Be careful what you say," said Fergus. "For your boldness and persistence, I will grant you, and you only, three wishes, one for each of you that were here today. I must warn you to be careful, as I am aware of your plight. You may wish to go home, but you may waste a wish for where is home?" asked Fergus.

"What do you mean?" asked Darragh. "I can see you come from a different time, but is that home? Or is home here in Mag Mell for your friend and his Tuath bride, then again home could be back in Ballyfin in the human world, where your other friend is also smitten with his bride,"—asked Fergus.

"You are wise," said Darragh, "much wiser than I am, please tell me, how do I use my wishes?". "Whenever you want to use a wish, just call my name loudly, followed by your actual wish, but again I caution you to word your wish correctly."

A short time later, Darragh woke to find Shane and Fergal eating by a campfire. "What just happened?" he asked. "Where we in the leprechaun lair, or was I dreaming?". "Well, if you were dreaming, we must have all had the same dream," said Shane. "The last thing I remember was Fergal falling asleep in front of us and then waking up beside him, then out of nowhere, you appeared,". "It's just amazing," said Fergal. "Just a shame we didn't get any gold or wishes from them," he said. "It is a shame indeed," thought Darragh. "Did I get three wishes or was I dreaming?"

When the lads had all eaten, Shane and Fergal mounted one horse and Darragh the other as they set off back to Cred in Fálias. Cred was delighted when she saw the three lads coming through the door. "We better have a little feast amongst ourselves this evening to celebrate Fergal's safe return," she said.

That evening, she told Shane to go to the cellar and choose her best wine for their feast, and Shane merrily strolled down the stairs. Just as he opened the cellar door, he heard glass breaking before bursting through the door. There on the ground was a smashed bottle with wine spilt all over the floor. Shane ignored it and grabbed another bottle, making his way back upstairs. He told Cred she must have rats, as a smashed bottle lay on the cellar floor.

A short time later, Cred again asked Shane to fetch more wine from the cellar. Again, Shane made his way down and could hear bottles rattling inside before rushing in, only to find an empty wine bottle, with others rocking on the wine racks. He grabbed another bottle and made his way upstairs, telling the others something strange was happening in the cellar.

With that, all four of them walked down to the cellar, and when they opened the door, they found a half-drunk bottle of wine. "I think I know what's up!" Said Cred as she told the lads to follow her back upstairs. She then sent Shane back down with a plate of leftover food, and he left it on the floor next to the open wine bottle. He then left the cellar, but could hear groaning and moaning coming from the cellar as he made his way back to the others before telling them what had happened. Cred said they should call it a night as it was getting late.

During the night, the sound of Shane screaming from the cellar woke Cred, Darragh and Fergal, and they all ran down to investigate. A battered and bruised Shane came staggering out from the cellar, screaming at the top of his voice. Cred brought him back upstairs while the others checked out the cellar.

As they found nothing wrong in the cellar, they rejoined the others. "What happened?" asked Darragh. "I do not know," said a shaken Shane. "I think I do," said Cred. She grabbed a large empty vial from a shelf and handed it to Fergal. She told him to sneak into the cellar and enter it invisibly if he could find anything to capture it within the vial.

Fergal crept down on his tippy toes and rubbed his ring before entering the cellar as instructed. There, in front of him, sat on a shelf, smoking a long clay pipe and drinking wine from a thimble, was a little man measuring only 6 inches tall, with a face like a withered apple. He had bloodshot eyes and a nose that was red and purple from heavy drinking. He wore a red cap, a short leather apron, light blue stockings, and shoes adorned with large silver buckles on them. Fergal sneaked over and captured the creature in the vial before sealing it and returning to Cred.

"I was right|," she said as Fergal handed her the vial. It is a Clurichaun. "A what?" asked Shane. "A Clurichaun," said Cred. He is a cousin of the leprechauns and must have followed us from the enchanted forest. She placed the vial on the table and asked the creature its name, to which it said, "Naggeneen". Cred said, "well, Naggeneen, I will make a deal with you. You may remain in my house as long as you hurt none of my guests again". The little creature promised to obey these rules before Cred released it from the vial, and it scampered away back to the cellar. "Why did you release it?" asked Shane.

Cred told them it was impossible to get rid of a Clurichaun once it had moved into your home. If you moved house, it would follow, and if you dumped it somewhere, it would return. The upshot to having them was they would protect your property. "Why did it attack me?" asked Shane. "Sorry, darling. I should have told you not to feed it scraps, as it likes to eat and drink well," said Cred. The others laughed at Shane before returning to bed for the night.

The following morning, Cred told the lads they had been ordered to return to Brú na Bóinne, as Dagda and Lugh had requested their presence urgently. After they had eaten breakfast to fill their bellies, the group all went to the stable, mounted their horses and away they rode to their destination.

CHAPTER FOURTEEN

THE BATTLE OF BOUOUINDA

pon reaching Brú na Bóinne, they left their horses in the stables and made their way to the castle's main hall. There they found Dagda and Lugh eagerly waiting for them. Cred wondered why they had summoned them so urgently. Lugh then told them that their recent little skirmish had not gone unnoticed. In fact, there was a druid Cesard, who had watched the entire thing unfold, before escaping back to the Fomorian stronghold of Dun Aengus, and telling their leader Faebar what he had seen, and now the Fomorians had declared war.

As they had been the wronged party, they could choose where the battle would take place and under what conditions. They had chosen the plains of Bououinda, and the battle would be between druids and wizards. "So why have you recalled us?" asked Cred, "the lads are far from being wizards." "You never know what will happen in battle, and if the tides turn against us, we may need to battle physically," said Lugh. "Well, we owe the druid Cesard a present," said Darragh. "As I'm guessing it was him who injured us."

"Make whatever preparations you need to," said Lugh. "We leave at dusk in the cover of darkness". The group went to prepare and readied themselves and waited to be summoned. Once again, they mounted their horses and set off out of the city. A hundred combat soldiers, a hundred druids and wizards accompanied them, along with Dagda, Lugh and Cred.

After travelling many miles, they came to a large forest. Instead of going through it, the leaders pulled hard to the left to go around it. "Why are we taking the long route instead of going through the forest?" asked Fergal. "Do you see the two white hawthorn trees at the forest's entrance?" asked Cred. "Yes, I do, but what's wrong with them?". She told the lads it was a fairy forest and the two trees signify a fairy path. They dare not cross the path and risk upsetting the fairies, as it would surely mean the loss of the upcoming battle.

"We haven't seen any fairies yet," said Shane. "What do they look like?". Cred told him that, like everything else, they had many forms. "Are they small with wings?" asked Fergal. "No," smiled Cred, "they certainly don't look like that." "Would it be safe to have a look?" asked Darragh, "if we avoid travelling on the pathway?". "That should be fine!" Said Cred, "just be careful, where you walk."

The three lads then broke off from the rest of their group and slowly made their way over close to the woods. They made sure not to enter the forest itself before dismounting and staring into the woods. They saw a large old oak tree, hollowed at its centre and hanging from its many boughs, were moss and ivy blowing in the gentle breeze and looked like waves hitting the seashore. The moon was shining brightly, and the lads could see there was a large group of little people dancing and having fun in its hollowed centre.

Cred rode over to the lads and told them they were falling behind the rest of the troops and needed to catch up. The lads, feeling happy for seeing the fairies but sad for having to leave without interaction, mounted their horses and rode off with Cred to catch the others, content knowing that they had at least seen some fairies. They all carried on riding and marching through the night until, at sunrise, they reached a small wooded area with a small lough next to it. "This is where we will camp," said Lugh.

He then sent some troops into the woods to cut some branches before returning and forcing the branches into the earth before placing animal hide across the top, making a tent for Dagda and Lugh to sleep in. Dagda had brought with him his large staff, his enchanted harp, which was kept covered, and the magic cauldron, which were all carried on a horse-drawn cart, and kept them close to him in the tent.

There was a fire built, and they placed the cauldron on it. Dagda then said some words, which filled the cauldron with a hot, meaty stew. All the troops then took turns to approach the cauldron and get themselves a good hearty meal to give them nourishment and vitality as they prepared for the upcoming battle.

Nearby was a large, mainly flat field with mountains on either side. The odd heather and fern were growing around the field. Some trees and swampy areas spread sporadically around, and on either end there were old stone ruins overgrown with moss and ivy. The druids and wizards made their way to the ruins to prepare for battle. Across the mist-veiled plain, they could see the enemy gathering at the opposite ruins.

The enemy wore what appeared to be goats' skulls, to cover their faces to induce fear in the Tuath. They covered their bodies in animal skins to appear more terrifying. Lugh gave the order, and the druids and wizards raised their magic staffs, casting spells that sent forth magic showers of sorcery, clouds of mist and a furious rain of fire from the air onto the enemy's heads.

The sky appeared to turn green and then red as fire and lightning flashed back at them from the enemy, although no one was injured. The druids and wizards watched as it faded away before casting spells back at the enemy once more. All strained their eyes in the enemy's direction, waiting and hoping that some of them fell. While some of them did, most did not, and they sent back more spells of their own, this time bigger than before. The troops stood behind the ruined walls for protection before again stepping out and casting more spells back upon the enemy.

In the meantime, Dagda, Cred, the lads and all the combat soldiers stayed back in the wooded area watching proceedings, keeping out of harm's way. They watched as the battle continued for most of the day. As evening fell, a customary truce was called between the two armies to allow each other to rest for the night. The troops were all well fed from Dagda's endless cauldron once again.

They carried any injured druids and wizards from the battlefield and placed them outstretched on the ground to check their wounds. Some had burns, while others had legs and arms that were broken or bruised. They placed these into the lough that was then filled with healing herbs and potions to heal their wounds and prepare them for the following day's battle.

There were many dead bodies recovered, and as darkness fell, shrill voices and screams mingled with loud, terrifying laughter could be heard in the darkness over the battlefield. These were the sounds of Bocanachs and Bananachs, fierce spirits of the air that were summoned by Badb (A member of the Morrigan, a trinity of witches, who were on friendly terms with Dagda, indeed all three were said to be his mistresses) who came upon the battle and offered her help, to unnerve and frighten their Fomorian.

At daybreak, the druids and wizards took up their positions and prepared for the second day of battle. It carried on in the same vein as the previous day's battle. This time, there were many losses on both sides. As evening fell, Manannan mac Lir (the most powerful of the Tuath druids, in fact, it was he who had given Lugh his horse Aonbharr) sent a single combat soldier to the battlefield, where he cast a spell on him. He then appeared as a thousand soldiers attacking the Fomorian wizards.

The wizards retaliated by casting more and more spells, but no soldiers fell, as they were merely an illusion to scare the Fomorians. The Fomorian wizards retreated from the battlefield to regroup. With that, the soldier left the battlefield and returned to camp, and a thousand soldiers disappeared immediately.

The following morning, the Tuath druids took up position for battle, only to be met with a large army of foot soldiers easily numbering two thousand troops. They began casting spells upon them, and some soldiers fell in their places (It was not an illusion). This panicked the Tuath, but Lugh told them to hold firm.

Suddenly, a large storm came out of nowhere, and the sky grew darker, almost as if it were nightfall. A strong gale lashed the battlefield in front of the Fomorian troops, and the winds grew ever stronger until the full fury of the storm unleashed against the Tuath.

To prevent the battle from being lost, Dagda intervened. He removed the covering from his harp, untied it from the cart, and made his way up the mountainside. When he had walked a short distance, he stretched out his arms and called out to his harp Uaithne! to the lad's astonishment, the harp left the cart and floated up the hill behind him.

His harp was his most treasured possession. It had been crafted from ancient oak and richly decorated with gold and jewels, and only the Dagda himself could play music on its strings. He could make anyone who heard it laugh for joy or weep with sorrow, and the playing of this harp made the seasons come in the correct order and control the weather.

He climbed upon a large bolder and began strumming the harp strings. Suddenly the storm died down, and the skies cleared. This, though, wasn't the only problem because the two thousand troops were edging their way up the battlefield towards his men. The Dagda played a different tune and called out the Music of Mirth. The Fomorians laughed so hard that their weapons slipped out of their hands, and they started dancing. But when Dagda stopped playing, they picked up their weapons and advanced once more.

Dagda strummed the strings of his harp softly so that it seemed as if it did not make a sound. This brought forth the Music of Sleep, and although they struggled to keep their eyes open, every Fomorian soldier fell into a deep sleep. Dagda then ordered his troops to flee the battlefield and return to Brú na Bóinne, for they had been lied to and were far too outnumbered to have a fair fight.

With that, all the troops packed up camp and, with Dagda's harp, cauldron and staff safely on the cart, left the area as quickly as they could and made haste back to the safety of Brú na Bóinne. Along the way, as they came upon the forest, the three lads broke off from the rest as they wanted to go back and spy on the fairies.

LEANNAN SIDHE

pon reaching the fairy forest, the three lads hung around until nightfall without entering the woods for fear of upsetting the fairies. As the evening grew darker, they moved in for a closer look. When they approached, a mist rolled out of the forest, and a beautiful young woman came out through it. "Don't listen to her", a voice whispered across the air. "Quick, lads", said Darragh. "Put your headphones on". A hare darted across the forest, away from them.

She approached the three lads, who could see her lips move but didn't hear her because of the headphones. She approached Shane and stroked his face. Shane took off his headphones to listen to what she was saying, and a voice whispered again through the air, "Be careful you fool".

Shane put his headphones back on immediately, but it was too late. He had succumbed to her spell. She turned her back to the lads, walking off into the mist. Shane followed, hot on her heels. "Come back, Shane", roared Darragh as he took off his headphones.

Suddenly the hare from earlier appeared in front of them and spoke, "I fear for your friend, for that is no beautiful woman; it is a Leannan Sidhe," said the hare, as it transformed into a friendly faced little person with a white glow emanating from it. "You had better follow to see where she leads him". "Thank you, good fairy," said Fergal as the two lads went in search of Shane.

They came across a little shack, and inside it was the creature, but it had no face, and was sitting next to Shane, who seemed besotted by her. His headphones were around his neck, and somehow, he was playing an instrument for her. Darragh began sucking his thumb for information on the creature. He told Fergal that the creature seeks a person's love, and if that person refuses, she must become their slave, but if they consent, they are hers and can only escape by finding another to take their place.

"Right," said Darragh. "The only option is to find someone to take Shane's place, for he is clearly besotted with her." "Who do you recommend?" asked Fergal. "I am not sure anyone would willingly swap places with him," said Darragh.

The two lads travelled back towards the battlefield, hoping they might come across someone to replace him. This time they kept off the roads in case the two thousand Fomorians were pursuing them. They even set up camp for the night but slept in the damp darkness of a cold bushy field, huddled together to keep themselves warm.

At first light, they carried on back towards the battlefield. They walked their horses instead of riding them to ensure they were quiet. Soon they came across a campfire with two ugly, deformed people sitting around it eating. Darragh told Fergal to sneak up behind them, using his ring to listen to their conversation while he hid nearby.

A short time later, Fergal returned and said, "I'm not sure who they are, but one is called Fathach, and the other is called Cesard". "Cesard," said Darragh ", We have our replacement, for he is the druid who burned us, and we owe him one". The two lads tied up their horses and positioned themselves close to the two Fomorians. Fergal was to sneak up close to them using his invisibility ring. When he saw Darragh was close enough to them, he should pounce on one of them to take them by surprise while Darragh would rush in a take care of the other.

Darragh rubbed his ring to gain extra strength before closing in. When he saw one of them fall to the ground, he knew it must be Fergal, so he rushed in, throwing his best punch onto the jaw of the second one, knocking him clean out. He then helped Fergal to subdue the second one. Darragh took a large spool of string from his corrbolg and tied up the two Fomorians.

He then questioned the one he had helped Fergal subdue. "What is your name?" he asked. "I am Cesard," came the reply. "Good", said Darragh, "you're coming with us". They then gagged and blindfolded him before allowing him to say another word, throwing him up onto one of their horses. They set off for the fairy forest.

When they reached the forest, they made a beeline straight to the shack where they had last seen Shane. When they peeped into the shack, Shane and the Leannan Sidhe were sleeping. Darragh borrowed Fergal's ring, then rubbed it along with his own to get stronger and invisible before entering the shack. While grabbing him around the mouth, he lifted Shane up to muffle any sounds before carrying him out. Fergal was waiting and tied him up, placing him on his horse and leading him away.

Darragh then took Cesard from his horse and carried him into the shack. He put on his headphones before waking the Leannan Sidhe. After taking the mask off his captive, he told Leannan Sidhe that Cesard was there to take Shane's place. He left the gag on so he could not speak and reject her.

Darragh saw her lips move, but not a word did he hear as he ran out the door. He grabbed his horse and rushed out of the forest after Fergal and Shane. The little hare raced after them and, as they removed their headphones, said, "I am glad your friend is safe from that evil sidhe" before disappearing back into the forest.

After travelling a short distance, the lads pulled over to the side of the road and took Shane from the horse's back. "What's going on?" he asked. "Let's just say you better not tell Cred that she's not the only woman for you", said Darragh as he and Fergal laughed. They then told Shane what had happened with his new girlfriend.

The lads then set off back to Brú na Bóinne. They wanted to let off some steam and, with the horses in the stables, made their way back to a tavern in the city rather than to the castle. The lads sat there drinking some mead and talking about their situation. They got up and sang a song or two, getting strange looks from people listening to their peculiar song choices.

As the hours passed, the lads got drunker and drunker and began reminiscing about life back home. They all agreed they missed their families enormously. Shane said it would be difficult for him to choose between his loving wife, Cred, and his family back home as he loved Cred but missed the comforts of home. Darragh said it was a straightforward choice for him. He'd love to see his parents again and be able to surf the net and play games on his computer.

They asked Fergal what his choice would be, and he started crying. "I miss my family, but I also miss Aisling desperately", he said. "I wish I could see her or hold her one more time before I get to go home to my family." They started singing sad songs and wrapping their arms around each other until they fell asleep, drunk at their table.

The following morning, they all woke up in the castle with thumping headaches. Some soldiers had found them asleep in the tavern and carried them there. Cred gave them all a cup of water with healing herbs to help with their headaches. She asked how they got on with the fairies. Shane made sure he was first to tell her about the Leannan Sidhe and being seduced by her. He told her not to worry, as nothing had happened between them.

Cred laughed as she told him she had nothing to worry about. The Leannan Sidhe was like a human husk. It was empty inside and had no feelings, as it was not human. It was a dark fairy that had taken a human form to seduce him. It might have taken a sheep's form if they had been sheep. "Baa", giggled Fergal to Shane. "Give it over," said Shane to his tormentor.

Cred said she would like to take Shane her home in Fálias to be sure he was okay. There was something there she could use to make sure everything was fine. The four of them went to the stable again, getting their horses ready and setting off to her home. As they were in no hurry, they were trotting along the road, all talking to each other. One thing led to another, and they began talking about their lives back home and their other lives in the human world.

THE SEER

red wondered if the lads would be happy if they never made it back home. Darragh told her he had made some great friends in his new life, including her but as he had lost friends back home and moved on with his life, he would be more than happy to go home. Although he would like to know how Bodhmall, Liath and Fionn especially were doing.

Shane said he would find it more difficult, as his feelings for Cred were really strong, and he wouldn't want to lose her. He asked if she would go home with him if the opportunity arose. Cred said she would have to give it some proper thought, as it was not something she could rush to decide. Whereas Shane knew his love for her and his love for his family. She didn't know if she could willingly give up the love of her father and brother and ideally would rather Shane stay and never return home. Shane gave out an enormous sigh of disappointment.

Fergal then interrupted by saying that he missed Bodhmall, Liath and Fionn, but he really missed Aisling and his mother. He told them he could always kidnap Aisling and carry her home to his own time through the portal if they ever get them working again.

"Aha," said Darragh, "how are they getting on trying to fix the portals?". "Not very good," said Cred. "Whatever effect you coming through had on them, they are still not working." "But they worked at the fountain of endurance," said Darragh. "True," said Cred, "but they aren't portals in the genuine sense; they are more like doors, connected solely to the abyss and fountain."

Cred then took the lads on a minor detour through a small forest and some old ruins to show them an ancient cave. It was only a shallow cave, and they could see a standing stone at the back as they went into it. They approached the stone, and it had an engraving on it. Cred held out her torc hand, and the engraving didn't light up. "But it's not night time," said Darragh. "No, but it is dark," said Cred. "If the portals were working, it would light up for us". As they exited the cave to carry on their journey, there came an almighty wind that blew them backwards.

As they looked out towards the forest, they could see treelike creatures almost blending into the woods, with their arms raised. "Quickly," said Cred, "They are Spriggans, and we must have upset them. They normally appear in wooded areas or guarding hidden treasures at cave entrances or forest ruins. They can be very hostile, so we must take cover," she shouted. With that, they all rode back into the cave for shelter. "There must be treasure nearby," said Shane. "What good is treasure to us now?" asked Darragh.

The winds died down, and the group left the cave, only for the winds to take up again. They looked at the forest again; the Spriggans were growing in size and almost as tall as the trees themselves. "We must hurry," said Cred as they turned away from the forest, riding away from it and the Spriggans. As the creatures grew bigger, the wind grew stronger, and as the group looked behind, they saw a swirling whirlwind swaying from side to side across the fields, throwing debris everywhere.

They pulled on their horse's reins and galloped away, but the whirlwind gathering speed seemed to chase them. They rode at full speed until they came across a steep ravine with no way down and had to pull up sharply. Just as they thought all hope was gone, the whirlwind abated, and the relieved group dismounted, and took large, deep breaths.

"I think we should find a different way to your house, Cred," said Fergal. "I think so, too," said Darragh and Shane in unison. "That's a first," said Cred, "I have been to the cave many times before but never have Spriggans attacked me". The group then thought it must have been multiple horses riding through the forest that had annoyed the Spriggans, yet none were brave enough to ride back through the woods to find out.

With that, they set off in a different direction from the one they came from, avoiding the cave and the small forest. They made their way back to Fálias. When the horses were safely in the stables, they made their way back to Cred's home. Upon entering, Cred went to the room and waved her hand at the wall with the secret door. Once it opened, they all entered the small, gloomy room. Cred made her way to the back of this room and waved her hand again, this time opening a door to a second room.

When they entered, they found a smaller room within, and all that was in this room was a large white marble bath. Many fragrant plants were growing on the walls, such as honeysuckle, lavender, jasmine, sweet peas, and mint. There was a small juniper shrub also growing against the wall. With another wave of her hand, some torches around the room lit it up. They could then see a trickle of water coming down into the bath.

She then grabbed some incense made from herbs and tree resin and set it alight. Again, burning it until the entire room filled with smoke and a pleasant smell and fragrance filled the air. Then she lit a large white candle and broke off a twig of honeysuckle, lavender, jasmine, sweet peas, mint and juniper berries before throwing them into the bath. She told Darragh and Fergal to leave before telling Shane to disrobe and get into the tub. She then said the following verse.

"Healing light that shines so bright,
to the person within, pass on your might
Make them mighty and healthy too
Dear spirit of the candle, I beg of you!"

A short time later, she told Shane to get out of the bath. She then blew out the candle and asked Shane if he had any lingering feelings for the Leannan Sidhe. Shane told her he felt fine, and Cred was happy that the druid Cesard must have taken her affections.

Later that evening, as they prepared for dinner, Cred asked who was going to the cellar for the wine. Shane sheepishly refused, so Fergal offered to go instead. Just when the others were getting worried about his welfare, he came back in the door, humming aloud happily to himself.

He said that he and his new friend Naggeneen had shared some wine and he learned a new song, but coming back up from the cellar, he forgot the words, only remembering the tune. When dinner was over, the group sat there talking and again. The talk turned to the lads' families and also to Fionn, Bodhmall, Liath, and Aisling.

"Follow me," said Cred as she led the three lads into the first room they had been in, with the two-crescent moon-shaped marble seats facing each other with the round marble table between them. The large chalice was still on the table full of water. In the corner, a small bronze bowl stood on a tall slim stand, and Cred made her way over to it. Once again, she grabbed some incense and set it alight, burning it until the entire room filled with smoke and a pleasant smell and fragrance filled the air.

She then sat down on the marble seats with the three lads and asked who the lads would like to see.

Fergal was the first to shout that he wanted to see his mother, Molly. Cred stirred the chalice and dropped some burning incense into the water, extinguishing the flame and creating more smoke from the chalice. Cred called out loudly!

"To the souls who have gone before us,
To the souls that are yet to be,
To those who wish to join us,
Please join so we can see,
Through the smoke, once it is clear,
I summon your presence to appear.
I call upon you as a mighty seer,
Please, Molly, to us appear"

When the smoke in the chalice cleared, the water was calm, and nothing happened. A disheartened Fergal gave out an enormous sigh of disappointment. Darragh jumped in and said "it must not work for our time, so it has to be Fionn for he was the first person we met, but it should be ladies before gentlemen, so I want to see Bodhmall and Liath". "Good call," said Shane. "What about Aisling?" asked Fergal. "We can do her next," said Cred.

With that, Cred stirred the water in the chalice again and dropped some burning incense into the water when the smoke in the chalice cleared. Cred called out loudly!

"To the souls who have gone before us,
To the souls that are yet to be,
To those who wish to join us,
Please join so we can see,
Through the smoke, once it is clear,
I summon your presence to appear.
I call upon you as a mighty seer,
Please, Bodhmall and Liath, to us appear".

When the smoke in the chalice cleared, they could all see within the water the farmyard at Ballyfin. They watched and waited until they could finally see Bodhmall and Liath tending to the animals. Fergal shouted, "it works, it works!". It overjoyed the lads that they could see what Bodhmall and Liath were doing. "I told you all I can see the past, the present and sometimes the future," said Cred.

As they all stared intently at the chalice. Watching until the two women finished work for the day. When they had washed in the river, they made their way back to the farm. They checked Fionn's house, then the other three houses, before shaking their heads and making their way back to their main house.

The two women sat together and began talking, wondering what happened to the boys. They knew Fionn was furious with them for what had happened to Sadhbh. But Darragh, Shane, and Fergal had never returned to them, and they had done nothing wrong to the three boys except to love, train, and feed them!

"We're here; we're here!" Roared Fergal, but the women could not hear him and sat there, getting lost in their thoughts. Darragh stuck his hand into the water to break up the scene and said he had seen enough.

"Can we do Aisling then?" asked Fergal. "Of course we can," said Cred, dropping some more burning incense into the water when the smoke in the chalice cleared. Cred called out loudly!

"To the souls who have gone before us,
To the souls that are yet to be,
To those who wish to join us,
Please join so we can see,
Through the smoke, once it is clear,
I summon your presence to appear.
I call upon you as a mighty seer,
Please, Aisling, to us appear".

When the smoke in the chalice cleared, they could see Aisling in a house preparing dinner. "Whose house is that?" asked Fergal. "I don't recognise it as hers or ours," he said. "Let's just watch said Shane". As they continued to watch, a strange man walked through the door. "Oh, my loving husband," said Aisling while rushing to greet the man. They then hugged and kissed passionately for several minutes.

Fergal jumped up and stuck his hand in the water, making her image disappear. "It can't be right," he said. "We're married; how could it be her?". "My dearest Fergal," said Cred. "The waters don't lie". "But we married, and I love her," said Fergal. Cred reminded Fergal that they had married at Lughnasa, and their marriage would last for a year, at which time they could make it permanent or break it without consequences.

"That's right," said Fergal, "but it's not been a year yet!". "I am afraid it has been more than a year Fergal," said Cred. "You were married for two or three months in the human world and are in Mag Mell nine weeks, which makes 63 human weeks or over 15 months, so you married her one and a half years ago." The tears poured down Fergal's face as he rushed out of the room. "Don't worry, I'll go talk to him?" said Shane. "You two carry on."

"We can stop for the day if you wish," said Cred, as Darragh was worried about Fergal too. "No, Shane's right," said Darragh. "Let's carry on. I want to see how Fionn is?". Cred, dropping some more burning incense into the water when the smoke in the chalice cleared. Cred called out loudly!

"To the souls who have gone before us,
To the souls that are yet to be,
To those who wish to join us,
Please join so we can see,
Through the smoke, once it is clear,
I summon your presence to appear.
I call upon you as a mighty seer,
Please Fionn, to us appear".

When the smoke in the chalice cleared, they were looking at a room Darragh didn't recognise. There was no one there, and Darragh questioned if the chalice was working. "Oh, it's working all right," said Cred. "We just need to be patient". Sure enough, a woman walked into the room that Darragh didn't know, followed soon after by Fionn (No longer wearing a white beard).

"Fionn's hair is white," said Darragh to Cred as they sat and watched the chalice. "Well, my dear Oonagh, how does it feel to be married to the most fearsome man in the whole of Ireland?" asked Fionn. "I will let you know if I ever marry him," came the reply laughingly from Oonagh.

"How does it feel to be married to the most beautiful woman in Ireland?" she asked. "I will let you know once I meet her," said Fionn.

CHAPTER FIFTEEN
THE GIANT BENANDONNER

ith that, Goll walked into the room and asked Fionn if he was ready for his journey. "Are you looking forward to our honeymoon, dear wife?" asked Fionn. Darragh looked away from the chalice towards Cred and said, "he's married again." Cred said, "Well, it is almost two years." "I am ready for our trip together," said Oonagh. "I cannot wait to spend some time with just the two of us by ourselves." "Well," said Fionn, "we are not travelling alone; we will take some troops with us to check out our new dwellings."

With that, they packed some bags and left the room (they were actually in Fionn's new home in Almhuin, which the three lads had never seen). Outside Goll, Conan, Aron, Diarmuid, Cailte, Aengus, and Bran and Sceolan were waiting for them to travel. "Where are we going to stay?" asked Oonagh. "First, we will travel to my friend Finnegas, and then to the white sandy beaches in Antrim", said Fionn.

With that, they all set off out of the fort and made their way to Finnegas, who was ready and waiting for his journey to Antrim. As they rode on, Finnegas whispered to Fionn, "Does she know anything?". "Shh," said Fionn ", She doesn't know anything". "Your secret is safe with me", said Finnegas as they carried on with their journey.

They carried on riding until they came across a large stone house near the beach, and it had fallen into ruin. "Do you expect me to stay here?" asked Oonagh. "That's why the troops are here with us," said Fionn. For the next few days, the troops cut down trees and brought stones from a nearby quarry to fix the house.

Oonagh insisted the house needed three rooms for sleeping, and also the main room for cooking and eating and the fireplace, too. Two rooms would need beds, and the third would need a cradle. "A cradle?" asked Fionn, "How long do you think we'll be here?" he laughed.

The troops built wooden outhouses for themselves to sleep in, and Oonagh queried why they needed to make them, but Fionn brushed off her question. Once the house was complete, Fionn had the men go to the nearby stone quarry, where they broke large rocks from the bedrock. Finnegas then took out his levitation rod and moved the blocks from the quarry to the beach, building a pathway out to sea.

When Oonagh asked Fionn what they were doing, he told her they were making a harbour, as he wanted to build a fleet of boats. "Are you sure you want to go ahead with this?" asked Finnegas. "Am I not the bravest man in Ireland" boasted Fionn.

For days the troops worked away, breaking large rocks in the quarry, and Finnegas levitated them into place out into the sea. Occasionally they would see selkies (half-human, half-seal creatures known as the seal folk) peeping up from beneath the waves to see what was going on.

They seemed to have great fun jumping out of the water and doing somersaults over the new pathway. There was also the odd Merrow (women and men from the waist up and a fish from the waist down) darting up and down the pathway. Finnegas had to be careful as these weren't as playful as the selkies and attacked if they felt threatened.

"When are you going to tell Oonagh about your plan?" asked Goll as the new pathway went out far beyond what would be required for a harbour and stretched out towards the coast of Scotland. "Once it's finished", said Fionn. As onwards and outwards, they built the new pathway.

When they had the coast of Scotland in sight, they could see a giant of a man marching in circles near the shoreline. He was at least twelve feet tall. Finnegas approached Fionn and asked if he was sure they should continue, for if this was Benandonner, the Scottish giant they had heard the tale of, he stood at least twelves feet tall, whereas Fionn, even with his Goliath spell, was just above eight feet tall. Am I not the bravest man in Ireland? Came the reply.

Fionn drove his men and Finnegas on until they finally came within reaching distance of the beach in Scotland. He then thanked Finnegas and his troops for a job well done before sending them away. "Shall we stay close to hand?" asked Conan, fearing for his master's safety. Fionn, who had become more arrogant since the lads last seen him, said. "Am I not the bravest man you know?" "No, that would be me", came the reply from Conan, who was equally arrogant of his prowess.

Fionn scalded him before telling them to leave. The troops and Finnegas left but camped just out of sight of Fionn in case he needed help. Once Fionn had sent the others away, he sat down with Oonagh to tell her his actual plan. He had heard the tale that Benandonner, a Scottish giant, had claimed ownership of all of Ireland and that Fionn was here to challenge him to a fight, to prove he was the greatest warrior in the land.

"You complete fool," shouted Oonagh. "I have married an idiot. I came here to spend our honeymoon with you, and all you want to do is get yourself killed". She then shouted at him, "Don't let me stop you", before storming out of the house. Fionn sat there, somewhat flustered. He had just been embarrassed by his petite wife, so what chance did he have against a twelve-foot giant? he thought.

Night was falling and as he was there by himself made his way across the new pathway to spy on his competition. He got to the beach and shouted, "Goliath" before gaining his extra size and strength and running across the new pathway. As he was running, a large male merrow jumped out of the ocean at him, knocking him off balance and into the water. He climbed back onto the pathway before making his way to the other side.

A little distance from the beach, he saw an enormous tower of stone with battlements at its roof and a huge stairway leading up to an entrance door. He made his way up the stairway, the biggest stairway he had ever seen, until he reached the door. The door was a huge, thick wooden door, and as he stood next to it, he felt like a small child. He grabbed the handle and struggled to push the door open before making his way inside.

As he made his way inside, there was a large open fire in front of him, bigger than any he'd seen before, and he made his way over to dry himself off. He could hear snoring coming from the adjoining room and made his way over to see if it was Benandonner and if he was indeed twelve feet tall. To his complete horror, when he got into the room, this enormous giant of a man was sleeping on some rugs. Not only was he at least twelve feet tall, but he seemed at least eight feet wide.

Even with his mighty Goliath spell, how would he overcome such a colossal creature? He turned to make his escape and knocked over a candle in the room, setting fire to the large sheepskin rugs the giant was sleeping on as he rushed from the room and out of the house. In his haste, he had even left the door open before running down to the beach and across the path.

Benandonner, woken from his sleep after being burned by the candle, ripped the door from its hinges and shouted a tremendous roar. "Fionn Mac Cumhail, I'm coming for you, and I'm going to eat your heart after I tear your limbs from your body". His voice could be heard for miles around, across the ocean to where Oonagh and, further still, his troops could hear.

Fionn then shouted, "Goliath," to hasten his way back across his pathway. Once he reached his house, he found Oonagh sitting there with a worried look on her face. "What have you done?" she shouted. "I could hear his voice from here, and I doubt, even with the troops you sent away, could you beat him?" "I am so sorry," said Fionn. "What are we going to do, for it is surely too late to escape?".

There was no sleep to be had as Benandonner constantly taunted and shouted at Finn from across the water throughout the night. Fionn began sucking his thumb to see if he could figure out a plan to defeat the giant and not have his heart eaten. After he had a few ideas, he sat down with Oonagh and concocted a plan to help them deal with the giant.

Oonagh went outside and gathered some large stones from the garden. She then mixed some dough to make some scones. She placed stones in some of them, then left the others as normal and began cooking them over the fire. She then told Fionn, "You mocked me for wanting a cradle, but now you must lie in it". Fionn squeezed into the cradle, and Oonagh covered him completely with animal hide, with only his face showing. Bran and Sceolan, never far from Fionn's side, lay beside the cradle. They then waited nervously for the morning to arrive.

Once morning arrived, they could hear Benandonner taunting Fionn again before making his way to the pathway. As he ran across the pathway, the ground began to tremble and shake like an earthquake beneath him.

The Selkies and the merrow, quite startled and frightened by the trembles, leapt out of the water through sheer fear. Even Finnegas and the troops camped nearby felt the trembling and stayed away from Fionn's house, as they feared not only was Fionn about to be killed, but they also would be if they tried to help.

As the trembling grew ever closer, Fionn and Oonagh braced themselves for the giant's arrival. The door flung open as the mighty Benandonner squeezed his way into the house. "I am here for Fionn Mac Cumhail," said the giant. "I am hungry and haven't eaten, for I plan to devour his heart, so where is he?".

A trembling Oonagh replied her husband wasn't home as he was out hunting. Benandonner told her he would wait until he returned and sat down next to the table. He told Oonagh to close the door, for there was a chilly draft blowing in. Oonagh replied the door was stuck, and that Fionn found it easier to slide the house around, away from the wind.

Not to be outdone, Benandonner got to his feet, putting his shoulder to the house and pushing, but it would not budge. He went back in and slammed the door shut. He then demanded food for his hunger while he waited for her husband to return. "I only have these scones cooking for Fionn and his son," said Oonagh. "So Fionn has a son?" asked the giant.

"Yes, he is in his room in the cradle", she said. With that, Benandonner made his way to where Fionn lay wrapped up. Upon seeing Fionn in the cradle, Benandonner thought to himself that if the baby was that big, his father must be enormous. "Who owns the dogs?" he asked. "Oh, the puppies belong to our son", she said. How can these be puppies for the child? He thought to himself as the wolfhounds were enormous.

He then made his way over to the cradle, poking his finger at Fionn, who bit down hard on his finger, biting the tip clean off. The giant let out a cry of pain and anger, pulling his finger away and demanding a cloth to wrap it in. "Where is my scone?" he shouted as Oonagh made her way to the fireplace.

She first took a normal scone from the fire and fed it to Fionn, and then grabbed some scones with the stones in them and handed them to Benandonner. He bit down hard into a scone, breaking his two front teeth. He let out another painful cry as he thought to himself. What kind of man must this Fionn be? He moves buildings rather than closing doors; his child is enormous and can bite my finger and eat scones that have broken my teeth.

Benandonner told Oonagh that he had other things to do rather than wait for Fionn to return. The giant made his way from the house and became scared that once Fionn returned, he might follow him back across the pathway to Scotland. He started running across the pathway, terrifying and provoking the merrows who leapt from the water barging into him.

Then he began pulling the pathway apart and throwing the large rocks at them. He then thought he should destroy the pathway behind him to prevent Fionn from giving chase. So, he pulled up all the large stones he could on his way back to the other side and therefore prevented Fionn from following him.

In the meantime, back at the house, Fionn crawled out of the cradle, suffering from cramps from being squashed into it for so long. He then hugged and kissed Oonagh for helping to save his life. The door burst open, and Fionn leapt back, fearing Benandonner had returned, but it was Finnegas, Goll, Conan, Aron, Diarmuid, Cailte, and Aengus. "I thought you were a dead man," said Conan. "Not a chance", boasted Fionn, "For am I not the smartest man in Ireland?".

"So that's how the Giant's causeway was formed?" asked Fergal as he and Shane returned to the room where Cred and Darragh were. "Well, you have seen it firsthand," said Darragh. "That's enough for now," said Cred, "we have seen all we need to see". Let us find something else to do today. Suddenly, there was a knock on the door.

Cred answered it and returned, telling the three lads that Dagda had sent word for them to return to Brú na Bóinne immediately.

CHAPTER SIXTEEN
THE BATTLE OF MOYTURA

nce again, the group all made their way down to the stables, where their horses were ready and waiting for them, and they hastily set off to see Dagda in Brú na Bóinne. Upon reaching the city, they realised the streets were empty, and no one was walking them. They promptly made their way up through the streets until they reached the castle.

To their amazement, the battlements were being attacked by what appeared to be large balls of fire. They dismounted their horses and rushed to the main hall to see Dagda and Lugh looking worried and in deep conversation. "What's going on?" Shouted Cred. "We are under attack from the Fomorian monstrosity known as Balor of the evil eye," shouted Dagda. "I thought he had left the Fomorians," said Darragh. "He has indeed left the Fomorians," said Lugh.

"But that is for their safety, rather than him being expelled", he said. Dagda interrupted and said that Balor was the former king of the Fomorians, and through his wickedness, had become so powerful and monstrously distorted that it was no longer safe for him to live amongst his people for fear of killing them or destroying their homes.

He had grown to the height of five men standing on each other's shoulders and had a huge destructive eye, which he never opened except for battle. It would take many men to raise his eyelid, as it was so heavy. His eye emitted poisonous fumes that could kill anyone who came too close, and it burned or turned to stone anyone who looked into it. He and a handful of men left and travelled to Tory Island to live out their lives with the sole job of raising his eyelid for him.

"So, how does that explain the battlements being attacked?" asked Fergal. "Balor's gaze can travel enormous distances," roared Dagda. "We need to stop him," shouted Shane. "That is easier said than done," said Lugh. "Balor lives on Tory Island for a reason, because of its location and the treacherous waters surrounding it."

The group then gathered around the large table to discuss a battle strategy to save the castle. In the end, they decided that the best way to save the castle was to attack the Fomorian stronghold of Dun Aengus. This would direct Balor's gaze away from the castle in order to protect his people. Darragh suggested they should make giant catapults, much like the Romans used in battle, to give them a greater attacking distance than the wizards and druids could provide.

Dagda and Lugh looked puzzled and asked Darragh who the Romans were, as they had never heard of them. Darragh realised his error and told them how the Romans had conquered many enemies and lands by having better weaponry and better-trained armies. He explained how a catapult was like a giant mechanised slingshot, capable of firing much heavier loads than handheld slingshots. He then began sucking his thumb and recited the instructions on how to make one.

Dagda sent word to his master engineer, and Darragh gave him the instructions how to build one. It should have a base frame with wheels at each corner to be horse-drawn in battle. There should be a vertical framework in the middle with a crossbar at the top. At the bottom, it would need a long beam of wood attached at the lower end to a tightly twisted rope.

This was to give the spring action to the catapult. At the other end of the arm, they would need a large container to hold the missiles they would use for firing, which would typically be a heavy rock or lots of smaller stones for a greater spread.

The engineer went to work straight away with his staff to make a prototype of the catapult. While Lugh sent word throughout the land to gather all the fighting men, they could for the forthcoming battle. A few days later, the engineer and his group summoned Dagda and the others to a nearby old ruin to view the catapult in action. They set the machine up facing the ancient ruins, and some soldiers loaded it with heavy stones and fired it at the old ruin walls.

After a few unsuccessful attempts, Darragh advised them to make some adjustments and, with one large rock loaded onto the catapult, fired at the ruins, pulverising the wall to the ground. It amazed Dagda and Lugh, the devastation it could cause. Lugh promptly told the engineer and his team to get to work on making as many as possible.

In the meantime, Dagda and Lugh drew up plans for when they should march on Dun Aengus. They decided it must be only three days, or Balor could destroy some of their battlements. They spent the next few days preparing for battle as troops gathered around the city in anticipation of the upcoming battle. Manannan mac Lir ordered the druids and wizards to use levitation rods to load as many carts as possible with heavy rocks to be used as ammunition for the catapults.

A few days later, the engineers had made 24 catapults and, with an army of 8000 troops, along with all their druids and wizards, set off for the three-day journey to Dun Aengus. As always, Dagda brought his harp, cauldron, and staff with him. Along the way, they travelled by some tar pits, and Darragh told them it could be used as oil to pour on the large stones and set fire to them before firing at the enemy, so they gathered as much as possible in any empty containers they had.

After they had travelled for two days, they approached the outskirts of Moytura, which was in Fomorian-held lands, and not too far from Dun Aengus, where they came upon many Fomorian druids and wizards at the far end of an enormous field.

Knowing that their catapults could attack from a greater distance than the enemy, they set up a row of ten catapults and loaded them with heavy stones before covering them with tar and setting them alight. A small group of wizards and soldiers operated them while the rest of the army stayed back a small distance.

They then fired them at the enemy, who were unaware of their power, with great success, killing many of them and burning their camp to the ground. While others, overcome with sudden terror, ran wildly away from the battle. Manannan Mac Lir then sent a single soldier onto the battlefield and cast a spell to appear as a thousand warriors, driving away the remaining druids and wizards.

Lugh gave the orders for the troops to advance the ten catapults further up the field, where they came upon the plains of Moytura. The plains were a vast area of relatively flat land that was barren, except for some sporadic grass tuffs and old dead trees. There were some ancient ruins strewn around its outskirts.

To their surprise, Fomorian cavalry ambushed them, attacking and destroying the catapults, and killing the soldiers and wizards too. Lugh sent some troops forward to intercept them, but they charged away before the soldiers reached them. Dagda sent word to gather the dead and brought them back to life with a tap of his staff, Lorg Mor.

Lugh then advanced his army up the plain to confront anything that might lie ahead. Manannan then sent a single soldier back onto the battlefield and cast a spell to appear as a thousand soldiers in front of the army. Some druids and wizards confronted them, with many thousands of troops behind them. They began casting spells of fire and lightning. One attack hit the soldier, and in the blink of an eye, the thousand troops disappeared from the battlefield to enormous cheers from the Fomorian troops.

Lugh gave the orders to set up the catapults behind his troops for protection and sent another barrage of rocks and stones towards the enemy, but they fell well short of their locations. He then gave the orders for his druids and wizards to advance further while casting spells, until they finally came within a distance that they could do damage to the enemy.

Each faction kept casting spells without a ceasefire, and for two days and nights, they each struggled with spells as mist crept in over the plains, making it difficult to see each other. Yet they carried on casting magic showers of sorcery and a furious rain of fire and lightning from the air on the enemy.

At daybreak, on the third morning, as the mists cleared, all cast their eyes in the enemy's direction, waiting and hoping that some of them fell. While some of them did, most of them did not, so Lugh gave the orders for the druids and wizards to withdraw from the battlefield, as it was now time to send in the troops. Dagda told him to wait as he would play a tune on his harp to turn the tide in their favour. As he took out his harp and began strumming, it had no effect, as the enemy troops were out of its range.

Lugh gave the order for his troops to advance, and an equal number of Fomorians came out to meet them. Dagda following closely behind his army began strumming the Music of Mirth on his harp, and the Fomorians laughed so hard that their weapons slipped out of their hands, and they started dancing, but as Dagda tired, they advanced more determined towards the Tuath.

When he regained his strength, Dagda played the harp softly, bringing forth the Music of Sleep, and although they struggled to keep their eyes open, the Fomorian soldiers closest to them fell into a deep sleep. Out of nowhere and using an invisibility spell, a Fomorian wizard appeared beside Dagda, drawing a knife and piercing him in the side. As Dagda fell to his knees, Lugh, standing close by, killed the wizard before removing Dagda and his harp from the battlefield and returning to camp to get Cred to heal him.

Seeing this as an advantage, Faebar, the Fomorian king, gave the orders for his men to attack. It created turmoil at the head of the army, as Lugh was no longer there. Darragh, Shane, and Fergal shouted at the troops to steady themselves as they all rubbed their rings and rushed into battle. The skies darkened, and it seemed as if it was night time again, but it wasn't. It was flocks of Sluagh, the soul takers who had entered the battlefield in anticipation of all the souls they could feast on.

Many soldiers began swiping their weapons at the creatures, but to no avail. Shane was the first to engage with the enemy through his swiftness. Darragh was close behind, and with stroke after stroke of his sword, he slayed enemy after enemy with ease. Fergal was the last to engage, but as he was invisible, could quickly kill some enemies without being injured.

The rest of the troops advanced, and their loud noises of metal clashing with metal could be heard for miles around. Lugh then rushed back to the battlefield to take charge of his troops, throwing his spear at the enemy before recalling it to throw again until he was in the thick of battle and drew his sword to fight at close quarters instead. Many soldiers ran from the battlefield because of the screams and shrills the Sluagh made as they devoured the souls of the fallen.

The sound of metal against metal and the excited Sluagh carried on for hours as the battle continued in a series of close combat and duels until evening fell. As mist again filled the land, it was time to call a truce for the night. With a significant number of soldiers dead on the battlefield, it was difficult to see if they could bring any injured soldiers back to camp to be healed. Yet the troops stuck to their task of bringing their comrades back to be healed.

Cred, along with the other healing druids, used healing spells and herbs to heal the injured. Dagda, who was himself healed, was now back on his feet and walked the battlefield with his staff tapping his fallen soldiers, but most were dead and he could not bring them back to life, as the Sluagh had beaten him to them. Instead, Dagda began playing the battle charge on his harp. It filled the warriors who survived with courage, took all the weariness out of their hearts, and let them forget their grief for their fallen comrades and think only of the glory they had won.

They then all sat down to a hearty meal from his cauldron before resting for the night to prepare for the next day's battle.

At the break of dawn, the troops gathered with Lugh, Darragh, Shane, and Fergal at the front and they set off to the battlefield. The battlefield was littered with the dead bodies of friends and foe alike as they made their way to battle before the sound of metal clashing with metal could be heard once more. The Fomorian wizards began casting spells, whipping up a storm, but Dagda strummed his harp, bringing calmness to the battlefield.

The Tuath wizards then cast fire and lightning spells on the Fomorian wizards, catching them off guard and killing many of them. This again brought swarms of Sluagh streaming and screaming across the battlefield to feast on their souls.

The soldiers clashed, and the fighting was brutal, as many soldiers fell with broken legs, arms and heads, while others had large gaping wounds from being struck with sharp heavy weapons. The casualties continued to grow, and it was only a matter of time before something had to give.

Dagda began playing the battle charge on his harp again, giving extra courage to his men, giving them the upper hand, before returning to camp. The Fomorian king Faebar noticed and decided it would be a significant blow to the Tuatha if they could get hold of his harp and keep Dagda from playing it.

And so, while the battle was raging, a few Fomorian warriors sneaked into the camp and stole the harp away from him. They fled as fast as they could and took refuge in deserted castle ruins close to the battlefield to hide the harp from Dagda's gaze.

When Dagda returned to his tent and found his harp was missing, he flew into a rage and, grabbing his staff Lorg Mor stormed onto the battlefield and, with a single swipe of his staff, killed nine enemies instantly, which brought the Sluagh rushing towards him to devour their souls. He continued through the battlefield, killing many enemy warriors as he went.

Alarmed by the swiftness of Dagda's destruction of his troops, Miach, the general of the Fomorian army, sounded the alarm for his men to retreat from the battlefield to regroup. The Tuath stood their ground and cheered loudly at their victory. But it was not a victory, as the Fomorians were merely regrouping to alter their attack. Dagda summoned Lugh, Darragh, Shane, and Fergal and informed them that his harp had been stolen and must be recovered at all costs.

Lugh said he needed to stay with his troops to prepare for a new onslaught, but the three lads were free to look for the harp. The three lads were wondering where they should search for the missing harp, and soon spied the deserted castle in the distance and thought it would be an excellent place to start. So, they set off on foot towards the old ruins.

As they made their way there, a group of Fomorian warriors intent on protecting the harp confronted them. Shane raised his arm and threw his spear, killing one of them, before holding his hand in the air for his spear to return. Darragh rubbed his ring and rushed forward into the group, killing many as he went. Fergal, not to be outdone, rubbed his ring and charged undetected into the warriors, stabbing them unseen to the naked eye.

No matter how many warriors they killed, there were more there to take their place until they finally had to yield their position and back away from the enemy. Fergal sneaked past them and into the castle ruins, where he found the harp, but it was too heavy for him to carry alone, so he sneaked back to the others and told them before making their way back to tell Dagda.

Dagda was delighted, and he said they must go immediately to retrieve his beloved harp. He summoned Manannan Mac Lir to accompany them, and as they neared the ruins, cast a spell on the lads to make it appear that they were many warriors approaching, but some Fomorian wizards appeared and cast down spells of poisonous mist, and the lads had to retreat. Manannan cast a spell of fire and dispersed the poisonous mist so that the lads moved forward again.

Suddenly, hundreds of Fomorian warriors rushed from the ruins. Far outnumbering the lads and Manannan, as Dagda had disappeared. The lads backed slowly away, although they still appeared to be a large force of warriors. Manannan cast a spell of fire and lightning, which dispersed the enemy warriors. Just then, Dagda came running from the ruins with his harp in close pursuit as he made his way to the lads and Manannan.

The Fomorian soldiers regrouped and charged towards them, and it seemed as if all hope was gone. Darragh roared at Dagda to play something on the harp quickly. Dagda immediately struck the strings and called forth the music of grief.

All the Fomorians began to weep and hide their faces in their cloaks, so that no one would see the floods of tears streaming from their eyes. The three lads rushed forward, attacking them, killing many, but when the music stopped, they took up their weapons again and began attacking the lads.

Dagda quickly played the soft music of sleep on his harp, and although they struggled to keep their eyes open, all fell into a slumber before the three lads, along with Dagda and Manannan, made their escape back to their camp. They placed the harp under guard at camp to prevent it from being stolen again.

In the meantime, having regrouped, the Fomorian general Miach sent his troops back to the battlefield. Lugh had marched his troops forward to meet them head-on. Darragh, Shane, and Fergal rushed forward into the fray. The Tuath locked their shields together and began pressing forward, pushing the Fomorians backwards on the plain.

Over the course of the day, many dead and wounded soldiers from both sides fell beneath their feet and had their souls devoured by the Sluagh hoards. Dagda again entered the battlefield and tried to heal or recover any of the fallen Tuath soldiers until a temporary truce was called once more, as night fell.

The fallen soldiers, now well into many hundreds, had to be gathered and piled onto a giant funeral pyre before being set ablaze to avoid spreading fever or disease among the living as the Fomorians did the same with their own fallen comrades. The lads sat around a campfire, having food to feed their hunger and regain their strength and wondered how long the battle could last as it seemed like there was no end in sight.

Dagda again played the battle charge on his harp, giving his men extra courage once more. Lugh then stood amongst his troops and congratulated them on the courage and conviction they had shown so far. He believed they were winning the battle, and it was only a matter of time before victory would be theirs. This gave all the troops and the three lads a massive lift as they lay down to sleep for the night.

During the night, the sound of an almighty thundering crash woke the lads. As they jumped to their feet, they heard Lugh shouting that the monstrous Balor was attacking them. As they looked around, they could see giant fireballs flying through the sky, crashing just out of reach of the camp. "I fear we will need to kill this beast," said Dagda. Lugh warned that if they succeeded in battle, Balor would turn his gaze towards Brú na Bóinne until he destroyed it.

There was little sleep to be had for the rest of the night, as it kept everyone on their toes for fear that a fireball might hit the camp. Instead of being too tired for battle, Balor's attack had the opposite impact. The Tuath warriors had a new steely resolve and fire in their bellies to beat the Fomorians as they made their way to the battlefield. This time Dagda joined Lugh, Darragh, Shane, and Fergal at the head of the army to give greater impetuous to the troops.

With Miach, the Fomorian general, as its head, the Fomorian army took to the battlefield. The Tuath troops banged their swords and shields against each other, creating a loud wall of noise in defiance of the Fomorians and started singing loudly "DAGDA, DAGDA" in unison. This brought nervousness to the Fomorians, who seemed to lose their nerve for battle. Fergal turned to Darragh and Shane and said, "This is deadly", before all three gave each other high fives. "Let's do this," shouted Darragh as Lugh gave the orders to advance.

The Tuath then advanced up the battlefield, protected by their wizards and druids scattered amongst them, casting spells of protection to ward off any incoming Fomorian attacks. The troops continued to bang their shields even louder as they marched. Miach, at the head of his army on horseback, fell from his horse as it galloped away from the thunderous sound. Once again, the skies darkened as swarms of Sluagh gathered above the battlefield.

Finally, Dagda roared out loudly, "CHARGE", and his army, with the three lads at its helm, charged into battle. There was again a massive sound of metal clashing with metal and soldiers roaring aloud as they hit each other head-on. With his large staff, Dagda easily knocked Fomorian shields and soldiers to the ground, making it easier for his men to overcome them.

The battle was ferocious, and each army inflicted brutal injuries on the other. With a tap of his staff, Dagda was healing and bringing his warriors back to life before the Sluagh could swoop, but it was not the same for the Fomorians. Their soldiers that fell in the battle stayed where they fell.

Darragh, Shane, and Fergal were in the midst of it all, not shying away from anything. All three-staying close to each other throughout to offer protection if needed. As Fomorian's attacked and killed Tuath soldiers, they too were killed before Dagda brought many of his men to life with his staff. The sound of steel crashing against steel got louder as the day went on, and the groans of injured soldiers filled the air. With the three lads, Lugh and Dagda, at its head, the Tuath army swiftly advanced through the ranks of the Fomorians.

As the ground beneath them turned red with the blood of the injured or fallen, and the excited screams of the Sluagh grew louder as they enjoyed feasting on the souls of the dead. Yet this did not deter the troops from the task at hand. The three lads hacked their way through the Fomorians, inflicting deadly wounds as they moved. Lugh could easily deal with many enemies because of his sheer might and endurance. The battle waged through the day until night fell, and a temporary truce was called again for the night.

As the two armies withdrew from the battlefield, the horrible crying and screaming of the injured warriors filled the air, with the excited screams of the Sluagh not far behind. Dagda again walked the battlefield, healing his wounded. He could clearly see that the Fomorian casualties were at least three times as many as those suffered by his army. His troops searched and carried the dead back to camp for another funeral pyre.

Once again, after all the troops had eaten, Dagda played the battle charge on his harp to give strength and courage to them. Guards kept a close watch on the fireballs streaming across the sky from Balor to ensure the camp was safe from where they landed. This enabled most of the army to sleep after a truly exhausting day.

The following morning, there was an eerie silence over the battlefield, and a heavy fog covered the land. There was not even the sound of Sluagh searching for souls, and such was the silence. You could almost hear yourself think. Eventually, Dagda took out his harp and played a tune which dispersed the fog from the battlefield. To their astonishment, all the Fomorian dead lay where they had fallen in battle and had not been gathered by the living to be cremated.

As the Tuath entered the battlefield, they eventually came to where the Fomorians had set up camp, only to find it deserted. "We've won, we've won", came the roar from many soldiers as they waved their weapons in the air in victory. Lugh stood tall and begged his men not to lose sight of their objectives, as while the Fomorians may have retreated, they were still an army that needed to be defeated.

With that, he gave the word to pack up camp, as they would now need to pursue them back to their stronghold of Dun Aengus, which would be no simple task. They marched through the day until they finally came within touching distance of Dun Aengus. It was lit up by torches to light the way for the Fomorians within as night fell. They camped out of the distance of the Fomorian spell casters and set up the remaining fourteen catapults at the front of the army, protected by their best troops.

Dun Aengus was a formidable fort set across fourteen acres and perched on the edge of a high jagged clifftop, with the wild stormy waters of the Atlantic battering the rocks below. It was built within four great stone walls, easily two metres thick and open on one side to the ocean, with a narrow stairway leading down the cliff edge to the rocks and ships below.

A circle of large jagged stones surrounded it, making an approach to the fort more difficult for any attacking forces. A giant standing stone. All around the enclosure were stone barracks, houses, battlements, stables, and taverns. Then there was the main hall where the king stayed.

"Let them have no sleep tonight", laughed Lugh as he instructed his men to load the catapults. Some with large stones and some with small rocks. They covered them in tar before being set on alight and firing them. They fired the large rocks at the jagged stones that surrounded it. One by one, the stones collapsed beneath the barrage of burning stones raining down on them. While the smaller stones were fired directly into the fort, causing widespread damage to the buildings within and causing terror and panic amongst the Fomorians.

There was no let-up in the barrage as some troops and wizards grew tired. Others replaced them to maintain a constant barrage down on the stronghold. All the Fomorians could do was watch from the battlements as the Tuath remained out of their wizard's spell range. As the supply of rocks dwindled, they sent other soldiers and wizards to a nearby quarry to replenish them with a constant supply. Ensuring that there was no let up for the enemy within its walls.

This carried on throughout the night, and when morning came, it was easy to see severe damage done to many buildings within the fort. Still, there was no let-up, as Lugh instructed his troops to carry on with the attack until they razed every building to the ground. All the Fomorians could do was hide behind their thick outer walls and hope they survived.

Darragh went to Lugh and advised him to concentrate all the catapults on one spot in the thick outer walls to weaken and collapse them. Lugh gave the order, and soon only the left-hand side of the wall was being bombarded with giant rocks pummelling it to smithereens until it had finally collapsed, unable to withstand another hit.

Suddenly the main gate opened, and out came a single woman waving a white flag and suing for peace. Lugh gave the order to hold fire, and the woman approached them, introducing herself as Caitlín, the wife of king Faebar. She was a horrid woman with booked teeth, a long nose and chin.

They brought her to Dagda's tent to discuss a treaty, and as Dagda reached forward to greet her, she drew a large poisoned dagger from her tunic and plunged it deep into his heart, shouting, "You shall play that harp no more". Dagda fell to the ground badly injured, while Caitlín was immediately cut down by one of Dagda's guards.

The guard rushed from the tent to get Cred and Manannan to save her father, but he was gravely wounded, and all they could do was to make him comfortable. Amazingly, Dagda did not die because of his powers, but he may as well have died as it left him in a deep, deep sleep.

In a rage, Lugh ordered his troops to aim the catapults at the main hall and destroy the cowardly king for such a despicable act of treachery when his father's guard was down, willing to talk peace. The catapults pummelled the main hall until there was nothing left standing. They then turned their attention to the taverns to destroy food supplies within the stronghold. After that, they turned their attention to the barracks to destroy any troops within.

Lugh strode forward and shouted that he would kill everyone inside the fort unless the king came and faced him in one-on-one combat. A short time later, the main gate opened and out came a warrior, but it was not the cowardly king Faebar, as he had sent his general Miach to fight in his stead.

210

This infuriated Lugh further, and he rushed forward, throwing his spear at him, piercing his shoulder before calling his spear back. He threw it again, hitting the other shoulder and calling it back. This time, he threw it straight through his left thigh and then did the same to his right thigh. Miach fell to the ground, unable to stand, and Lugh approached him, slicing his head off.

"See this people of Dun Aengus", he roared. "I have killed your mightiest warrior, and the same faith awaits all of you". He then returned to camp and gave the order for the catapults to destroy the main gates as they would enter the fort the following morning to exact his revenge on king Faebar. Through the night, they attacked the entrance and at the crack of dawn the next morning, Lugh rose from his sleep and rallied his troops before marching on the fort.

To their horror, upon entering the fort, the only people inside were the dead bodies of people, crushed by the stones of the catapults bearing down on them. The cowardly king and all his people had escaped down the narrow stairs on the cliff edge to their ships, sailing away, never to return. As all the troops entered the fort, they examined any parts or buildings still standing to check if any survivors were hiding out, but it was completely empty.

Darragh, Shane, and Fergal made their way to the standing stone. Amazingly, it remained undamaged. As the lads stared at the stone, they could see something engraved in it, but couldn't distinguish the symbol. Darragh said he thought it was a Dara knot. "A Dara knot", shouted Fergal ". We may have found our way home", as he danced around, cheering before Darragh stopped him, saying, "I am not sure, but even if it is, they still don't work".

With that, Shane went in search of Cred, who was still by Dagda's side, trying to nurse him back to health. Shane then begged her to accompany him to the standing stone, where she and the three lads inspected it, and all came to the same conclusion that it was indeed engraved with a Dara knot. "We're going home", sang Fergal as he danced around the stone. This time Shane stopped him, pointing out that the portals were not working.

Cred said that the best thinkers of the Tuath were trying their utmost to figure out how to fix the portals, but still could not figure out how to make them work again. The three lads eagerly expected that fixing the portals would give them a route back home.

When the troops surveyed the entire fort and were happy that there were no Fomorians left inside, Lugh decided to fortify the place and turn it into a new Tuath stronghold. He then gave the orders that all the troops, with the help of the druids and wizards, should help to rebuild the destroyed buildings within, along with the demolished parts of the Outerwall and gates.

For the next few days, everyone, including the three lads, busied themselves rebuilding all the destroyed buildings. It was made all the easier with the help of the wizards and their levitation rods until they finally rebuilt it to its original state. Once everything was fixed, Lugh gave the orders that there should be a large feast to celebrate their tremendous victory over the Fomorians.

They sent men out to hunt and forage for food as with Dagda gravely ill; his items were useless to anyone. The Cauldron remained empty. The harp made no sound, and it took three people to lift his staff, making it unusable, as the only person able to command them was the king of the Tuath. Lugh would need the rites of passage to become king, but Tuath laws meant the required old king to be dead before this could occur. Short of killing Dagda, there was nothing that could be done, and Lugh certainly had no intention of killing his father.

That evening, there was a bittersweet feast, while they celebrated their victory over the Fomorians, they mourned the loss of Dagda, as there was no sign of him improving, and he was still in a deep, deep sleep, and nothing seemed to help to heal him. The feast lasted all of two days, and there were many sore heads around the place as they woke from drunken slumbers.

The following morning, Lugh gave the orders to prepare for the journey back home to Brú na Bóinne. He ordered three hundred troops to remain behind and maintain the fort, and he directed that the troops' families to join them once the rest of the army returned to Brú na Bóinne.

With that, the rest of the army packed up and prepared to leave. They placed Dagda carefully on a wagon along with his cauldron, harp and staff, and they set off home, hoping that Dagda would regain consciousness.

After a few days of travelling, they finally returned to Brú na Bóinne. Once again, the streets were deserted, as Balor had set his gaze on it once more and attacked it with giant fireballs. Lugh called an urgent meeting in the main hall with Cred, Darragh, Shane, Fergal, and Manannan Mac Lir. They had to make their way to Tory Island to finish Balor off and save the city.

Lugh could not travel as he was the acting king of the Tuath and needed people he knew could carry out this most dangerous mission. With that in mind, he had chosen the three lads. Cred begged him to reconsider, but Lugh had made his mind up, and it was not for turning. Manannan Mac Lir would guide the lads and advise them of the perils ahead.

CHAPTER SEVENTEEN

THE MONSTROUS BALOR

anannan sat down with the three lads and discussed the deadly mission ahead. As the lads had already heard, Balor lived on Tory Island, surrounded by treacherous waters at least 246 feet deep and always covered in fog. Even if they got through the fog, it was almost impossible to reach the island as the waters were full of giant dangerous creatures of the deep.

First, there was the Muckie. It was a gigantic eel-like creature, measuring at least 50 feet long. It had large sharp fangs and would lash out with its long spiny tail if it felt threatened. Next, there was the Caoránach, a variant of an Ollphéisteanna, a massive serpent-like creature, but it had large sharp teeth at the end of a long snout, with four enormous claws at the end of its legs.

They must not under any circumstances break its thigh bone as a hairy worm, which would grow into a replica of the monster, would grow quickly from the wound but be more ferocious than the original monster.

If that wasn't enough, overhead, the skies were marshalled by Bocanachs and Bananachs, the fierce spirits of the air. Then, if they actually navigated safely across the waters, there were packs of wild direwolves roaming the island; they were larger than any ordinary wolves, with stockier legs, a wider head, and shorter ears than the standard wolf.

Manannan then told them they would have to deal with Balor himself if they had achieved the near impossible task of getting by all these creatures. He stood as tall as five men, one standing on top of the shoulders of the other, but much wider. He was an enormous creature whose single eye, in the middle of his forehead, was as large as the sun in the sky. As a child, he had seen his father's druids carrying out a ritual to lay a plague upon their enemies. Some vapours from the ceremony entered his eye, causing it to swell to a substantial size, granting it the power of fire and death.

His eye was so enormous that it took four men to lift the lid, and he kept it closed unless in battle. He kept it covered with several cloaks to keep it cool. They removed the cloaks one by one when it was required. The most important thing was the lads should avoid attracting his gaze, looking directly at them. If they were at a distance, they could burn; if they were close enough, his gaze would turn them to stone but if they were too close, his eye's poisonous vapours would kill them.

"Wo, wo, wo," shouted Darragh. "You are not selling this to me at all; we are being sent to our imminent deaths here." "I was thinking the same," shouted Shane, while Fergal screamed, "With my little weapon, I'll never get close enough to him." The other lads giggled to lighten the mood.

Manannan then told them that although he couldn't travel with them, he would help them cross over the waters by giving them his boat called Sguaba Tuinne. It was a magical boat which could sail itself across the water to a fixed point on the far shore. To help them travail across the waters, he would cast a spell, cloaking them and the boat in the mist of invisibility to prevent the dangerous creatures from being able to see them. He then gave them all a potion. Once they reached the shores, they should each drink theirs, which would mask their scent from the direwolves.

Lugh came onto the scene and asked if they were ready for their mission. Darragh told him they were as prepared as they'd ever be and would leave at nightfall, hoping to avoid any of the creatures in the darkness. Once night fell, the three lads readied themselves for the journey; Cred was inconsolable for fear of never seeing Shane again, but Lugh led her away, and the lads made their way to the water's edge where Manannan met them.

He had a small wooden boat, barely big enough to fit the three lads. It had a shimmering black effect to deflect the water back onto itself. As they entered the boat, he wished the lads well on their adventure. He told them that once he pushed the boat, it would not stop until it came to rest on the shore on the far side of the water. Then raising a wand above his head, he created a mist of invisibility around the boat to shield it from view before pushing it off the shore and sending it on its way.

The lads huddled together to heat themselves as freezing cold fog and wind encapsulated the boat. The lads all lay there shivering, clenching their teeth to keep them quiet. They didn't even know how long the boat would take to travel to the other side. They pulled some animal hide blankets over themselves that Manannan had left in the boat for them. It wasn't long before they heard the noises of Bocanachs and Bananachs screaming above their heads, and they dipped beneath the blankets to hide themselves.

After a while, the boat slowed down, and Fergal climbed from under his blanket to see what was happening but, in the darkness, could not see what the cause was. He took Claíomh Solais from its sheath to see what was going on and could see huge ripples in the water, most probably from a muckie swimming nearby. Darragh told him to put his dagger away and get back under the blanket, but it was too late. He had drawn the attention of a Caoránach, and it was swimming angrily towards the boat.

Fergal Jumped back under the blanket, but the beast attacked the boat, rocking it violently. The three lads pushed back their blankets and grasped the edge of the boat, holding on for dear life as the beast bit down hard on the boat.

Darragh took out his sword, hitting the beast on the head. It let out a massive squeal of pain as it withdrew from its hold on the boat. Shane threw his spear at the monster, piercing one of its eyes before the spear returned to his outstretched hand. The beast dived beneath the waters, and the three lads let out a massive sigh of relief.

Their reprieve, however, was short-lived as an even angrier wounded beast rose out of the water, grabbing hold of the boat with its two front claws. Fergal stabbed it in the thigh with his dagger, as Darragh shouted, "No, you idiot, don't do it". Instantly, the creature's leg burst open, and a hairy worm fell out onto the boat and began growing rapidly. Darragh rubbed his ring for extra strength before grabbing it and throwing it from the boat. The worm, however, grew until the lads now had two snarling beasts attacking the boat.

To make matters worse, this had drawn attention to the Bocanachs and Bananachs flying overhead, and they swooped down on the boat, attacking the lads from above. Darragh told Fergal to aim for the head and not its legs, to avoid creating more trouble for themselves as they fought off the creatures on each side of the boat.

Shane, with his spear in hand, was lunging at the Bocanachs and Bananachs to beat them back. The boat then started rocking wildly from side to side in all the commotion. To keep the boat afloat, the lads had to stop attacking the creatures. The creatures, however, didn't let up in their attacks, and the lads had to go back on the attack, trying to force the creatures away.

One creature grabbed Fergal in its mouth, and Darragh let out a huge war cry as he leapt into the air, slicing the creature's head off. Fergal fell from its clutches but carried on fighting. This time swiping his dagger above his head at the Bocanachs and Bananachs along with Shane, while Darragh fought to keep the Caoránach at bay.

Suddenly there was an enormous explosion from the water as, rising high from the shadows, was an enormous muckie before splashing down into the water again, almost capsizing the boat. The lads again stopped attacking and tried desperately to steady the boat. The colossal creature rose out of the water again, letting out a tremendous roar. It raised its large spiny tail from the water, swiping at the boat with all its might. This raised the boat, and the three lads clean out of the water before they crashed down onto the shore.

The boat broke into pieces, and the injured lads crawled under some nearby brush and waited, hoping the creatures would leave them alone. Fergal tried to speak, but Shane wrapped his hand over his mouth to keep him quiet as the angry creatures screamed and roared close by. They all lay there quietly until falling asleep.

The following morning, beams of sunlight shining in their faces awoke the lads, and they exited from the brush to see what faced them. It was a cold and desolate place with not much to see. There were some old ruins nearby, covered in moss and grass, and then there was a sizeable stony shoreline. They spied their boat lying in pieces on the shore. "What do we do now?" asked Fergal. "We have no way back by the creatures". "That's the least of our worries," said Darragh, "We still have the direwolves and Balor ahead of us".

Suddenly, in the distance, they could hear wolves howling. "Quick", shouted Darragh ", Drink the potion Manannan gave us". With that, all three of the lads drank the potion to mask their scent from the direwolves. They all ran to the nearby ruins and reached them just in time as a large pack of giant greyish-white-looking wolves arrived just where they had been standing before drinking the potion.

Fergal shouted to the others that they were lucky that they got out of there, but he heard growling over his shoulder, only to turn around and find one wolf standing above him, snarling with drool falling from its sharp fangs and foaming at the mouth. Just as it leapt at Fergal, Shane flung his spear at the wolf, injuring it in the side, before his spear returned to him. The beast limped off, squealing in pain, as the lads made their way into a more secure ruined building nearby.

The other two lads then told Fergal that he should be mindful not to speak unless he needed to, as they were in a perilous place, and it could draw attention to them. A sulking Fergal crossed his arms and skulked away to the corner to sulk. Darragh told Shane to get a fire going as he would go out and set a snare for some food. He returned sometime later with a giant hare for dinner. They then cleaned the animal and settled down for a good feed.

They then sat around and talked for hours about the past few days, fighting the Fomorians and getting to the Island. "Who'd have ever thought it possible?" said Darragh. "that we could have done what we have done since Joseph's wedding." "Yeah," said Fergal, "the closest I ever thought I'd be to real-life monsters and fighting was on my console." "If we ever get back home," said Shane ", I'll never look at a game the same way again."

The lads sat around talking, as they needed some downtime after the exhausting few days they had just had. They passed the day away, just talking and reminiscing about life back home. They then blocked themselves in for security so that they could sleep for the night.

The following morning, they removed the barricade and crept outside. Tory Island was a long, narrow island filled with large rock formations and not much else. At its centre, there was a sizeable mountainous hill, and at its top was the largest formation on the island called Dún Bhalair.

That was where the monstrous Balor lived, and they needed to avoid the direwolves and make their way up there. The lads didn't even have a plan on how to tackle Balor if they reached the top. They could hear loud noises above their heads and hoped it wasn't Bocanachs and Bananachs coming in search of them, but it was the giant fireballs shooting across the sky from Balor towards Brú na Bóinne.

Nearby, they could hear angry growling and snapping and quietly sneaking over to see what was happening. The direwolves were fighting over the corpse of the one that Shane had speared, as it had succumbed to its injury and died, creating a feast for the rest of the pack. The three lads decided now was the best time to make their way up to Dún Bhalair and put an end to the evil Balor.

They set off quietly in the mountain's direction, moving slowly as they went and ducking in and out of ruined buildings and rock formations to conceal themselves. If these weren't available, they crawled amongst the brush, growing sporadically across the land. Now and then, they could hear the direwolves howling or darting by their location in search of food, but luckily, the potions they drank continued to mask their scent.

They travelled throughout the day until finally coming to another ruin close to the mountain's base. They again set about snaring dinner and locking themselves inside for the night to keep themselves safe from attack. Now that they were closer to Balor, they could hear the thunderous fire balls roaring across the sky towards Brú na Bóinne. "We must put an end to this monster", shouted Darragh as they settled down for the night.

The following morning, the lads finished the food left over from the previous evening and removed the barrier to make their way out of the ruins. The lads each took a huge sigh! "Let's do this," shouted Darragh. as they gave each other high fives and began climbing up the mountain. Loose rocks and shale crumbling beneath their feet slowed their progress.

A few hours into their climb, they reached a secure ledge with a small cave that gave them the room and opportunity to sit down and rest for a while. Fergal took out Claíomh Solais and made his way into the cave before running back out screaming. "There are snakes, there are snakes", he roared. "Calm down", laughed Darragh. "There are no poisonous snakes in Ireland". "What do you mean, poisonous snakes? I thought Saint Patrick got rid of all the snakes," cried Fergal. "He might just do that," said Darragh ", but he doesn't yet exist".

Shane laughed as he made his way to the cave, throwing his spear blindly inside. When it returned to his hand, there were some snakes stuck to it. "Lovely," he said, "we don't have to snare dinner tonight", he laughed. They then prepared a fire and cooked the dead snakes before sitting down to eat and setting off again. The higher they climbed, the louder the sound of the thunderous fireballs roaring across the sky became until they finally reached the summit.

When they reached solid ground and tried to find their bearings, they could see badly scorched ruins and ground all around them. There were many corpses, badly burnt, lying around, while it had turned others to stone. They heard noises coming towards them and rushed to hide in the ruins nearby. As they hid, a group of blind soldiers led by one sighted one made their way past them.

The three lads followed closely, and when the warriors sat down to rest, they sneaked over to them and captured the sighted one before carrying him back to the ruins. They then tied him up and questioned him about why he was leading some blind warriors. He told them that the warriors who raised Balor's eyelid had plucked out their own eyes to avoid his gaze and therefore avoid being burned or turned to stone. He never got close enough to Balor, but camped nearby to help those who did.

"Aha," said Fergal as he reached into his hip sack. "I knew these would come in handy," he said, taking his mirror sunglasses out of it. "I don't believe you still have them," laughed Shane. "The last time I saw you wearing them was at Joseph's wedding." "That's cos that's the last time I wore them," said Fergal. "What good are they to you now?" asked Darragh. Putting on his glasses, Fergal said, "I can reflect Balor's eye on him and kill him." Darragh gave him a clip around the ear, saying, "that won't work; it would just get you killed."

"Let me prove it to you," said Darragh as he put the glasses onto the captured warrior before gagging him. He then led the warrior away towards Balor. As they got closer to the Monstrous giant, they could see that he was indeed a colossal creature, easily thirty feet tall. His skin was dark and rough like dried out cow's hide. He had long skinny legs with long bony feet and toes. His body was tiny compared to the rest of him, and he only had one small arm with a long bony hand with only three fingers on it. Then there was an enormous eye, easily eight feet wide.

He stood close to some scaffolding made of wood planks, making a stairway up behind him. Sitting above his eye, there were four blind warriors with hooks embedded into his eyelid. They were pulling with all their strength to keep his eye uncovered.

The lads and their prisoner stood behind a ruined wall, and Fergal took his shield from his back and banged it with his dagger, making a big sound. Suddenly the ground outside the ruins lit up, and Darragh pushed his prisoner out into the light. He burst into flames, but his screams were muffled as they had him gagged and died instantly.

Balor then cast his gaze back to Brú na Bóinne. Darragh told the others they should back off to a safe distance as he had devised a plan. When they were safely within a ruined house, Darragh told Shane and Fergal that he had noticed that Balor only had one short arm that was incapable of holding his eyelid open. He realised that Balor's only strength was the blind warriors keeping his eyelid open. He then told them their task would be easier to accomplish than they thought it would be.

It confused Fergal, as he didn't know how it would be easier. "It's quite simple," said Darragh. "All we need to do is to kill Balor's warriors and close his eyelid". Darragh then told Fergal to rub his ring, and once he had disappeared, Darragh sent the laughing Fergal up the wooden scaffolding to kill the four warriors keeping his eye open.

Once Fergal reached the top, he took out his weapon, killing the four warriors. This then dropped Balor's eyelid and he let out a loud, painful cry. As he was in the middle of shooting a fireball, it scorched his own eyeball. The other blind warriors, now without a sighted one to guide them, were aimlessly running around in circles. Shane took great delight in using them for target practice, throwing his spear, killing one before returning to him to try again. Once they were all dead, the three lads regrouped, with the giggling Fergal saying, "I love it when a plan comes together".

As they stood there watching, Balor tried in vain to raise his eyelid, but couldn't do it. Darragh then hatched another plan. He told Fergal to give him his ring and take cover out of sight. He then told Shane to take up a position with his spear, ready to strike. Darragh then rubbed Fergal's ring, becoming invisible before making his way up to Balor's head. Once he was there, he rubbed his own ring, gaining extra strength.

He pulled on the ropes with all his might, opening Balor's eye, but he grabbed his head, aiming it at the ground in front of him. Balor blasted a large hole into the ground, burning his own feet; as he fell to the ground, another blast made the hole in the ground deeper.

"Now, Shane, do it now", roared Darragh. Shane stepped out and threw his spear directly into Balor's eye with all his might. The monster released a huge, ear-piercing scream as he fell dead on the ground. Darragh, who was still on his head, fell to the ground before getting back to his feet.

Fergal came running out shouting, "We did it, lads, we did it". Darragh stood there exhausted, taking a deep breath. "Yes, we really did", he said before collapsing to the ground with exhaustion. Shane went in search of food to help Darragh regain his energy while Fergal stayed with him to make sure he was ok and prepare a fire.

Night was falling when Shane returned with a large hare, which they cooked over the fire and sat down to eat it. Now regaining his strength, Darragh scoffed at his portion of food while heating himself at the fire. Fergal got up to stretch his legs, and walked over to where Balor's body lay, and shouted for the others to join him. As they approached him, he jumped down into the hole created by Balor, for there, in its centre, was a buried standing stone that was glowing. "Look," he said, "it's a portal stone, and it's working". Its symbol is the Crann Bethadh, an external portal between worlds. "Don't do anything" shouted Darragh, but it was too late.

Fergal had raised his Torc to the stone, and all three vanished

The Crann Bethadh

before reappearing back at Tara, where they had defeated Aillen.

"You idiot," roared Darragh. "You complete idiot," he shouted in disgust. "What's wrong?" asked Fergal. "Are we not back in the human world?" "What's wrong?" shouted Darragh. "I'll tell you what's wrong." "When we were in Dun Aengus, we came across a Dara knot

on the standing stone, and that was our way home; if the portals were back working, we could have gone home," shouted Darragh in despair. "Now we have no way of reaching it." "Sorry," whispered Fergal, trying to atone for his error.

A group of spear-wielding soldiers suddenly surrounded the lads, and removed their weapons from them, then tied their hands behind their backs before leading them away to a barracks. A short time later, the door opened and in walked a senior soldier. "I am the captain of the king's guard", he said. "Who are you, and how did you get here?". Darragh told the soldier they were friends of Fionn Mac Cumhail and had helped him defeat Aillen.

All the soldiers in the room looked puzzled, and the captain left, arriving back a short time later with the high king Cormac mac Airt. "My captain tells me you helped Fionn defeat Aillen," said the king. "That's correct," said Shane. "How can it be correct?" asked the king. Darragh told the king they were members of the Fianna and had helped Fionn defeat Aillen a few weeks earlier before accidentally ending up in Mag Mell.

"Mag Mell," said the king ", Is only a myth, and they certainly aren't Fianna uniforms you are wearing, staring at the Tuath dé Danann outfits the lads had on, but it was over nine years ago that

Fionn had defeated Aillen,". "Throw them in the dungeon, and get me Fionn Mac Cumhail," he shouted.

They brought the three lads outside to a large pit in the ground, untied their hands, and threw them unceremoniously down into the pit before slamming a large wooden gate down above their heads, locking them in. The three lads sat in shock in the damp cold hole in the ground.

"Wow, nine years we were gone," said Darragh. "I completely forgot that we are wearing Tuath dé Danann uniforms". A short time later, the gate was raised, and they stood up, expecting to get out, but the soldiers threw food slops down on them to eat. The lads brushed themselves off, but just then, the heavens opened, and rain poured down on them. They all huddled together to keep each other warm.

CHAPTER EIGHTEEN

OLD FRIENDS, NEW ACQUAINTANCE

he following morning; the lads woke up cold and wet. They despaired at their predicament and sat there, too shocked to say anything to each other, until finally, the gate opened, and the soldiers lowered a ladder into the pit. "Out you come," shouted a soldier. One by one, the lads climbed the ladder before being led away.

They didn't recognise the place and wondered if it was even Tara that they were on. The soldiers marched them to the main hall and brought them inside. In the middle was a large blazing fire, and the lads each rushed over to warm themselves. "Well, well! What have we got here?" a voice boomed out. The lads turned around only to see Fionn standing there tall and proud. He looked older than they had remembered and he had once again grown a white beard. The guards stopped them as they rushed to greet him.

"Let them be," said Fionn, "These are my friends". The lads rushed to him, and he greeted them all with a big bear hug. "First things first," said Fionn, "let's get you some food in your bellies". They then moved to a large table in the centre of the room, where an enormous meal was lying on the table for them to eat. The king soon joined them, as he was indeed curious how these three strangers had got into his Fort.

The lads then began by telling them that once the battle with Aillen was over, they awoke to find themselves in Mag Mell, where the Tuath dé Danann took them in they had to fight monsters, werewolves, dark fairies, the Fomorians, sea creatures and the monstrous Balor. In the middle of all that, they could see Fionn besting the giant Benandonner. "And Aisling left me too!" said Fergal.

Fionn laughed out loud, "The giant is a tale to tell my grandkids one day," he laughed. Fionn told the three lads that when the battle with Aillen was over, he had brought the monster's head to the king and had been rewarded with the leadership of the Fianna and a new home called Almhuin.

He told them that the king had made Tara his headquarters, which was a lot different from when they were last there. He then said to them that Sadhbh and his unborn child had disappeared almost the same time as the three lads did. Shane asked how this happened and if they might help to find them again.

Fionn told them she was staying with Bodhmall and Liath, and somehow the Fer Doirich had captured her and turned her back into a deer, and they had not seen her since. "How are the two women?" asked Darragh. "I don't know," said Fionn. "I left them in a rage and could never bring myself to return to them". "We must go visit them," said Shane. "Yes, we saw them very upset when we were with Cred," said Fergal. "Cred", roared Shane, "my dear Cred, I wonder how she is and if her father is, ok?".

Fionn told them he and the king had heard enough for the day. "We must get you back to Almhuin and let you settle in, as well as get you some decent clothes", he laughed. The king then ordered his men to supply the three lads a horse each so they could travel with Fionn. Outside the door, Bran and Sceolan were sitting patiently for Fionn but leapt up on the lads, licking them furiously. "I think they missed us," said Fergal. Once the dogs finished slobbering over them, they made their way to the stables to collect their new horses before setting off to Almhuin.

On the way, Darragh asked Fionn if he had any news on Biddy and Finnegas. Fionn told him there was nothing to report. They were older and maybe wiser than when the lads had last seen them, but time hadn't slowed them down. "We will have to visit them once we've settled in," said Darragh as Shane and Fergal also nodded in agreement.

He brought them to the inner circle after they reached the fort. Fionn directed them to one of the houses he had built years earlier for them, and it had remained empty, waiting for them to return. He told them that once they had changed clothes into their Fianna outfits, they should join him and his wife, Oonagh, in the large meeting hall.

When the three lads had washed and changed, they made their way to the main hall. When they entered, there was an enormous cheer as Fionn, Oonagh, Goll, Conan, Aron, Diarmuid, Cailte, and Aengus were waiting to greet them. They then had an enormous feast to celebrate their return. The feast went on through the night with great fun had by all except for Shane, who, once he had drunk a few meads, started feeling sorry for himself and missing Cred. Darragh made their excuses and carried Shane back to their house, putting him to bed for the night.

The following morning Darragh spoke to Fionn and told him he needed to go to Ballyfin for Shane's sake. As Shane had often met Cred in the tavern there, she might turn up, and as everything happened so fast, they never made plans to meet up again. Fionn gave his blessing, and it wasn't long before the three lads were on their way to Ballyfin.

Darragh wanted to drop in on Finnegas and Biddy, but Shane was too eager to get to Ballyfin. When the lads reached Ballyfin, they made their way to the tavern and spent the day there drinking, hoping that Cred would turn up, but as night fell, Darragh helped a drunken Shane onto his horse and set off up the hill to Bodhmall and Liath's farm. He made his way to Shane's house, which had remained untouched for years, before putting him to bed.

As he tried to put the horses in the stable, one horse reared up angrily, and he pulled on the reins to calm it. This brought Bodhmall, Liath and Cred rushing from the house with weapons in hand. It overjoyed the three women to see Darragh and Fergal. "Where is Shane?" pleaded Cred, "please tell me he is ok". "Shane is fine," said Fergal. ", drunk but fine". With that, the three women hugged and kissed the other two boys. "Let me see your beautiful faces", shouted an overjoyed Bodhmall before they ushered the boys into the main house.

When they were in the house, the lads could see that Bodhmall and Liath had aged and their hair was growing grey, with a few more wrinkles on their faces. "Neither of you has aged a day in nine years," said Bodhmall, "Yes, life must have treated you well," said Liath. "Life has treated us anything but well," said Darragh.

"Well," shouted Fergal. "If you call the battle with Aillen, waking up in Mag Mell, joining the Tuath dé Danann, fighting monsters, werewolves, dark fairies, the Fomorians, sea creatures and the monstrous Balor, well, then I guess life has treated us well, but no it hasn't, and then I find out that Aisling left me so NO life hasn't treated me well!".

The women laughed as Bodhmall told him that Aisling had visited the farm each day for six months, hoping for Fergal's return, until one day, she failed to appear, and they never heard from her again. Cred told the other two women she was a seer and had let the three lads see what they were doing from her magic chalice.

Cred then told the boys that they had waited patiently in Brú na Bóinne to see if the three lads would defeat Balor, and when the fireballs through the sky ceased to come, almost instantaneously, the portals began working again, but the lads failed to return, and they feared the worst.

Darragh told the three women the story of Balor, and their boat trip, where the Caoránach attacked them, then the Bocanachs and Bananachs, before Fergal had stabbed the Caoránach in the thigh, creating a second creature, then the giant Muckie attacked them, knocking them clean out of the water and destroying the boat. Once they were on land, a direwolf attacked them.

"And snakes," shouted Fergal. "Yes, there were snakes", laughed Darragh. He told them that once they reached the summit, they found all but one of Balor's soldiers were blind, and they killed them before defeating the Monstrous Balor himself.

"Yes," said Fergal, "But the best part was that I found a working portal, and now we're here,". "That's a bit of a shame," said Cred. "Once we realised the portals were active again, I rode to Dun Aengus, where the Dara knot was glowing on the large standing stone, I tried to enter it, but nothing happened," "You idiot Fergal, I told you," Said Darragh. "How are Dagda and Lugh doing?" asked Darragh. Cred replied the same as when the lads had last seen them.

The two lads then took their leave and returned to their houses, as it had been a long day, and they needed sleep. The following morning, the three lads and Cred joined the other two women in the main house for breakfast. Shane kept hold of Cred's hand and wouldn't let go. Bodhmall told the three lads that Cred had updated them as much as she could on the lad's adventures, since they had last seen them. Darragh asked the women what they had done for the last nine years.

Liath told them that other than tending the farm, they had scoured the countryside hoping to find Sadhbh, or the dark man, but they had no success. She said they hoped Fionn would forgive them and visit one day. "Well, Cred, does he come and visit?" asked Shane. "I honestly don't know", smiled Cred. The lads spent the next two days hanging out at the farm until Darragh said it was time to return to Fionn. Shane spent a few extra days with Cred before joining them.

With that, the other two set off back to Almhuin. On the way, they stopped off to see an overjoyed Biddy, and they spent two days with her, helping her forage for ingredients and telling her about their adventures in Mag Mell. They then made their way to Finnegas and spent the next two days with him fishing, as Finnegas had a notion that there might be a second salmon of knowledge to be caught, but Darragh thought he might just be going senile. Finally, the lads left Finnegas and returned to Fionn in Almhuin.

The following day Shane arrived back and made his way to their house before telling them he had some news for Fionn. The three lads then made their way to the main hall, where they found Fionn and Oonagh talking to each other.

Shane rushed to Fionn and told him that Cred had said they should look to the forest of Cradockstown and the Athgreany stone circle. "Look for what?" asked Fionn. "She never said why", said Shane, "she just told me to tell you". Fionn jumped to his feet and said, "what are we waiting for? Let us make haste to Cradockstown to see what awaits us there".

They made their way to the stables, gathering their horses along with Bran and Sceolan, and rode swiftly out of the fort. Fergal let out a big shout. "The brotherhood of four rides together once more". "That's really corny," said Shane disapprovingly.

It was a three-day ride to Cradockstown, and the group was steadfast in their determination to reach the town. Never wavering or altering their course, except for hunting dinner and resting the horses and themselves. Fergal lamented the fact that their horses weren't as good as those in Mag Mell, whose stamina never waned.

After they had journeyed for three days, their first stop was the lake where they had previously slain the two dobhar-chú's. To their surprise, there was a shrine dedicated to them on the shoreline, telling the story of their bravery. They then made their way to the town and searched for the town leader, who remembered them for their bravery years earlier and gave them free food and a bed for the night as a thank you.

The following morning, they sat down with the town leader and asked if any other creatures had returned, but none ever had. Shane wondered if there was anything unusual they should look out for, as they had been told to make their way to the forest of Cradockstown. The town leader told them he had heard tales of a group of wolves occupying the woods that were supposed to be part wolf and part man and were called The Man-Wolves of Ossory.

He could not verify their existence, however, as no one had been attacked by wolves. There were, however, lots of livestock that had vanished in the middle of the night, with only blood trails leading to the forest as any evidence. They never contacted the Fianna because it was not a major issue, as nobody had encountered them or been harmed.

The group thanked him for his hospitality and information as they made their way out of the town, heading for the forest. The forest wasn't far from the town, and they reached it a short time later. They rode around the forest, not knowing what they should look for other than Cred had said to look there. As night fell, they came across a large house nestled in the forest and approached it, knocking on the door.

There was no answer, and they pushed on the door, which was old and creaked loudly, yet no one approached them from within.

Strangely, there was a fire in the main room lighting, and they called out to see if anyone was home. Still, no one answered them. They made their way further into the large house, and they came across a large room, and in the room were five tall, dark-haired men sleeping soundly. Fergal began shoving one on the shoulder, trying to wake him, but he did not stir.

This brought a small, angry old woman rushing into the room wielding a knife, shouting, "Leave my sons alone". The group were surprised and backed away from the woman. "Apologies," said Darragh, "We mean you and your sons no harm. We had heard a tale of a group of wolves occupying the forest and were just looking into it".

The woman calmed down and laid down her weapon before telling the group that they could not wake her sons before daylight. She said to them that a dark tall, thin man called Fer Doirich had cast a spell on her sons, and they must sleep each day from sunset to sunrise, or they would die.

"That's why Cred sent us here," shouted Fionn. "The Fer Doirich has returned, and I will have my chance to make him tell me where Sadhbh is." Fionn thanked the woman for her help and rushed from the house with the others in hot pursuit.

As they left the house, Bran and Sceolan ran off into the darkness, barking loudly as they ran until their barking faded into the distance. The lads mounted their horses and gave chase until they could hear them again, along with the sound of wolves howling.

They made their way to the Athgreany stone circle, and there was a small trembling deer in the centre of the circle. Bran and Sceolan circled the terrified animal as five giant, dark-haired wolves encircled them, snarling and snapping at the two dogs and the deer. As the lads rode into the stone circle, Shane, letting out a roar, took out his spear, throwing it at one wolf, hitting it on its rear left leg, before recalling the spear to himself. The injured wolf let out a large painful howl before fleeing away with the other four in tow.

Bran and Sceolan lay down with the deer, licking it in a caring manner. "Surely, this cannot be the same as what happened with Sadhbh," said Fionn as he leapt from his horse, wrapping the terrified deer in his brat. They decided they should camp for the night within the stone circle, with each one of them taking turns to stand guard.

The following morning at sunset, the lads decided it was time to set off. Darragh said they should call the large house in the woods and tell the mother and five sons that there were indeed a pack of gigantic wolves roaming the forest. When they reached the house and knocked on the door, the woman slowly opened it. "Are you here to brag?" asked the woman. "What do you mean?" asked Darragh, pushing his way past her into the house. There in the house were her sons, with one of them being nursed by the others.

"What's going on?" asked Fionn. With that, one son told the story of how they had, years earlier, been out hunting deer in the forest when they came across Fer Doirich, who cast a spell on them to hunt down and kill Sadhbh or any other deer or animals they encountered. Their bodies would remain where they lay, but their souls would turn into werewolves each day at sunset to roam the forest hunting. "Did you kill Sadhbh?" screamed Fionn as he grabbed him by the throat. "No, no, I promise," said the son. We never hurt anyone. Fionn let him go and calmed down before apologising.

With that, the lads said their goodbyes and left the house. As they mounted their horses, Fionn carefully tied the small deer to his back to stop it from falling off or escaping. He then asked the others what they should do next. "We need to visit Bodhmall and Liath," said Darragh. "I cannot bring myself to face them since the day Sadhbh disappeared," said Fionn softly. "Well, it's time you did", grinned Fergal as they turned and made their way towards Ballyfin farm.

As they drew close to the farm, Fionn slowed, unsure if he wanted to see the two women. The others reminded him of how Sadhbh had transformed from a deer upon entering the farm. And the same could indeed happen now. Fionn put his reservations behind him and galloped off towards the farm. As he entered the farmyard, Bodhmall, Liath and Cred came rushing out to greet them. Suddenly overcome with sorrow, Fionn jumped from his horse and rushed over to the women with tears rolling down his face.

The two women wept uncontrollably with joy at seeing their beautiful Fionn again. As the women threw their arms around him, there was a large scream, and when Fionn turned around, there was a small blond-haired boy on his back. "Who have we got here?" asked Bodhmall. "I am Oisín," said the boy. The group looked at each other, stunned by what they saw and heard. Could this really be Fionn's long-lost child? They each wondered without saying it aloud.

Bodhmall said that the child must be cold and hungry before grabbing and carrying him into the house, where she placed him sitting by the fireplace to heat himself. They then sat down with Fionn and talked for hours about their lives in the last nine years. Fionn spoke of his great exploits, and being the leader of the Fianna, his greatest accomplishment was overcoming this great giant with brains rather than brawn, but he had never given up searching for Sadhbh, even though he had remarried.

Bodhmall said that she and Liath had tried to follow Fionn's career from a distance and knew he had remarried. She told him they, too, had searched far and wide for Sadhbh and the dark man for many years without success.

"A dark man?" asked Oisín. "How can you speak our language?" Asked Liath. Oisín began telling them memories he had of being around a dark man. He had grown up in the wild. There were hills and valleys and forests and streams, but in whatever direction he roamed, he always came to a cliff that reached high into the sky. He had one companion, a female deer he took to be his mother, that would lead him to food and play with him daily.

Besides her, his only other company was a tall, dark man who was very mean, the way he used to speak with the female deer. Sometimes he talked gently and softly to her, but at other times he would shout loudly, in a harsh and angry way. But whatever way he spoke to the deer, she would draw away from him in fear.

"The last time I saw her," said Oisín, "the dark man was speaking to her. He spoke for a long time. He spoke gently and then angrily until he struck her with a hazel rod so that it forced her to follow him when he left. She looked back at me as if she was very sad. I tried to follow her, but I could not follow fast enough, and I cried until I could see and hear her no more. Then I began walking for days and was on the verge of being devoured when you and your dogs saved me."

"My dear child," said Fionn, "That indeed must have been my beloved Sadhbh". "How I wish I could find and help her". He then picked Oisín up and gave him a loving embrace, saying, "welcome home, my precious son". One by one, the entire group hugged the small boy and welcomed him home to his family.

Bodhmall said it was a long time since they held a feast in the house, but it was high time they had one to celebrate Fionn and Oisín coming home. That evening, there was an enormous feast held in the house. Oisín, accustomed to only eating grass previously and having never been in the company of so many people, sat quietly in the corner and ate only vegetables.

Fergal raised his cup and said, "A toast to my old friends and new acquaintance", as the others joined in. Fergal then dropped his cup, grabbed Oisín by his hands, and started dancing in circles, much to the bemusement of the small boy. As the rest of the group joined in, and all had a great night. Until, one by one, everyone made their way to bed for the night.

The following morning, they all gathered in the main house once more. Fionn said he didn't know of a cliff that reached high into the sky as described by Oisín, but he would send troops out with more vigour than before to find it and Sadhbh. Fionn told the group that Oisín was still asleep in Fionn's house as he had never slept on a bed before and was obviously enjoying his comfort.

He then sat down to discuss what should happen with Oisín in the medium to long term. He asked if it was ok for him to remain at the farm, where the two women could train him in combat and life skills. It overjoyed Bodhmall and Liath, as they would be more than happy to do this and have some more company around the farm.

Cred took a silver torc from her tunic and handed it to Shane. She told him that, she would need to travel back to Mag Mell and if ever, he was near a standing stone and pointed the torc at it, it would enable her to know where he was, so she could travel to him quicker, than meeting at the Ballyfin tavern. She then said her goodbyes and left the farm to travel home to check on her father, Dagda.

Fionn walked to his house and returned to the main house, lovingly carrying his newfound son. He sat him down and told him he would stay with his aunties while Fionn would visit as often as he could, but for now, he needed to go back to Almhuin.

He gave Oisín a great big hug, then thanked Bodhmall and Liath for agreeing to look after his son before hugging them both and making his way out of the house. Darragh, Shane, and Fergal all did the same before following him out. The four of them mounted their horses and, along with Bran and Sceolan, set off back to Almhuin.

As they travelled back to their base, they called in on Biddy and Finnegas to tell them the great news that Fionn had found his long-lost son. They were both overjoyed by the news and could see that Fionn had a newfound spring in his step. The four of them then made their way back to the fort, where Fionn rushed to tell Oonagh about his newfound son before telling his closest allies Goll, Conan, Aron, Diarmuid, Cailte, and Aengus, telling them to spread the word and to throw a feast in his son's honour.

That evening there was a grand feast held in the fort, with lots of singing, dancing, eating, and drinking. Bards were also telling stories of Fionn's heroics and the tale of finding Oisín in the forest. The party carried on well into the night, with every member of the Fianna celebrating, except for one person.

Goll had secretly never been happy about handing over the leadership to Fionn and was not very happy, as he still harboured thoughts that if Fionn were to die, he might once again become the leader of the Fianna. Now that Fionn had an heir that could scupper his plans. He kept his thoughts to himself, though, for fear of being found out and thrown out of the Fianna or, worse still, being killed by them.

TWO BECOME ONE

arly the following morning, Fionn gave the orders that they would go on a hunt as part of the celebrations for his reunion with his son, and a large party would ride out for a three-day hunting trip. They would then give any animals captured or killed to the local towns around the area to help them through the cold months ahead.

Fionn then named Darragh, Shane, Fergal, Goll, Conan, Aron, Diarmuid, Cailte, and Aengus in his main party, and they would choose the rest of its members, not numbering over fifty in total. Once everything was in place, they set off out of the fort with Bran and Sceolan, along with Lemaire, Brod, and Lomlu, who were all Great Irish Wolfhounds that could help with the hunt.

They set off out into the countryside and set up camp near a large forest. It was now Autumn, and leaves were falling from the trees, carpeting the forest floor with a red, yellow and orange carpet of colour. As they rode over these leaves, they made large crunching sounds beneath them, scaring any potential targets away. While riding further into the forest, there was no prey to be found. They could hear noises from animals darting away from them into the depths of the woods. In the end, they returned to camp for the night.

The following day they changed tact and split into four groups, each entering the forests from different sides, hoping to force animals towards each other. This time they were more successful, but it was a pitiful haul for the mighty Fianna warriors, and they packed up camp and move to a different location in the hope of more success.

They travelled many miles until they came to a distant forest surrounded by fields. It was near a long, winding river, flowing over a sheer cliff edge overlooking a ravine. They found a narrow pathway leading down into the ravine, which at its base was covered in large sharp rocks and a small stream. To be close to drinking water, they set up a camp close to the river.

They devised a plan that they should again split into groups and, if they couldn't capture or kill their targets, they should at least drive them towards the cliff edge overlooking the ravine. They then broke into groups setting off in different directions, with the purpose of driving any potential prey towards each other or the ravine.

After many hours hunting, with many beasts slain, either falling to their weapons or, in sheer panic, leaping from the cliff edge down onto the sharp rocks in the ravine below, while being chased by the wolfhound pack. This continued for many hours until, at last, they called it a day.

That evening they ate and drank and danced and sang around large campfires, they had set alight to warm themselves. There was much merriment to be had for their captures and people cheering Fionn and his son before the camp fell quiet for the night, with everyone having drank and eaten their fill then falling asleep.

The following morning, Fionn said that because of the excellent day's hunting, they should remain for one more day to gather as much food as possible for the local towns before returning to Almhuin.

This time Darragh, Shane, and Fergal decided it would be a good idea to fish in the local river; while the others could hunt wild beasts, they would hunt wild Salmon. Fionn thought it a good idea and gave his approval. As the day went on, Shane saw what he thought were two women close by.

The others warned him not to let his eyes deceive him, and as he made his way towards them could see it was indeed a black horse and a black boar drinking from the river. "Remember the last time", shouted Darragh, reminding him of a previous encounter with a Pooka. Shane returned to the others as he remembered only too well being thrown into the river during his last encounter.

As evening fell, the rest of the party returned to camp with many spoils from their day's hunt. Once again, they lit large fires around the camp to heat themselves and cook their food. Darragh told them to keep their wits about them, as they had seen two Pooka near camp earlier in the day, and they could cause some mischief. Once they had eaten their food, they broke out the mead, again raising a toast to Fionn and his son before toasting a successful few days' hunting.

A short time later, a boar darted across the camp, and Sceolan and Lomlu gave chase. Darragh shouted for them to return, but they took no heed of his words as they gave chase. Aron, who had become quite drunk, left the camp to relieve himself by the river when he spied a large black horse. He stumbled over, grabbing the horse by the mane, before climbing onto its back. To his surprise, it had a bridle around its head, and he grabbed it, trying to control it, but the horse sped off away from camp.

Darragh rushed to Fionn and told him about the two hounds and Aron, and the two Pookas. Fionn, Darragh and Conan jumped onto their horses and raced out of the camp to recall their companions. Suddenly a storm came upon them, and a great wind and rain, with bursts of thunder and lightning, lashed down on them. They chased through the storm, trying to recall the two hounds and shouting for Aron to dismount.

Aron had other ideas and pulled the bridle tightly, trying to control the animal as it galloped toward the cliff edge. It made it even more difficult, as the only thing to light their way was the moonlight, half hidden by the storm clouds. As Aron rode the horse into the dim light ahead, he thought he could see frightful faces, all glaring straight at him, with an evil laugh that grew louder while the faces drew closer to him.

He released his grip on the bridle and tried to jump from the horse, but unfortunately for him, his foot got caught in the saddle, and the horse dragged him along the ground. His limbs were torn from his body as the horse galloped wildly towards the cliff edge. When the horse finally shook off the last of him, it leapt into the air over the cliff's edge and plunged into the darkness of the ravine below.

The three riders pulled up close to the cliff edge but were beaten back by furious gusts of wind, coming back over the cliff's edge sweeping them from their horses. Fionn called out for Sceolan and Lomlu to return, but all they could hear were the faint cries of the hounds in the darkness. The three distraught riders made their way back to camp, where they drank large amounts of mead to console themselves, telling the rest of their camp mates what had happened until they fell into a drunken slumber.

The following morning, with heavy hearts, Fionn, Darragh, Conan, Shane and Fergal rode out towards the cliff edge, stopping every so often to pick up the broken limbs of their lost comrade Aron until finally they reached the cliff edge, picking up the last remaining pieces. Fionn called out loudly for the hounds to return, but heard nothing in reply. As they made their way to the cliff's edge and looked down into the ravine, lying dead on the sharp rocks below were the remains of his beloved Sceolan, along with Lomlu.

The group made their way down the narrow pathway, where they recovered the two hound's bodies. Fionn cried louder than the others had ever heard him cry at the death of his beloved Sceolan. A sobbing Fionn put the remains gently onto his horse while Conan did the same with Lomlu, and the sorrowful group returned to camp.

When they reached the camp, a sad and cowering Bran made his way to Fionn, where he licked the face of his lost sister Sceolan, then let out a loud remorseful howl that brought tears to the eyes of the entire party. Fionn sadly gave the orders to make a funeral pyre before cremating the remains of Aron Sceolan and Lomlu. He then told Conan, Goll, Conan, Diarmuid, Cailte, and Aengus to take the troops back to Almhuin while he, Darragh, Shane, and Fergal would return to Ballyfin.

Upon reaching the farm, Fionn tied up his horse, then he and Bran ran into the main house sobbing loudly. He picked Oisín up, hugging him tightly. Bodhmall and Liath went outside and asked the others what was wrong with Fionn. Fergal told them that Sceolan had died, and the women rushed back into the house to console him. The three lads sat in the yard, whispering amongst themselves. Losing Sceolan and Aron brought home to them about their own losses at being far from home and possibly never seeing their families again.

The three of them didn't feel much like talking to the others and left for the village tavern, where they drowned their sorrows and said they had to find a way home. Shane said he was still trying to convince Cred to go with him if the opportunity ever arose, but it might be even more difficult now that Dagda was in a deep sleep. As they talked, Fionn came in and said they needed to go to Almhuin to fetch his wife, Oonagh, as he was taking a break from the Fianna.

They made their way to the farm and slept for the night before setting off to fetch Oonagh. When they reached the Fort, Fionn summoned Goll, Conan, Diarmuid, Cailte, and Aengus, telling them he was taking a break and remaining in Ballyfin farm with Oonagh and Oisín. He left word that if anything urgent happened, they should come and get him, otherwise they were to assume temporary charge of the troops and look after the day to day running of the Fianna.

He then went to his home and told Oonagh to pack up as they were going to Ballyfin for a while. After Oonagh had packed, Fionn led the group back to Ballyfin farm and introduced her to Bodhmall, Liath and Oisín. Oonagh was delighted to greet her new family members. Fionn then brought her to his house on the farm where he used to live with Sadhbh.

Oonagh insisted that everything in the house must change so that it would not remind Fionn of Sadhbh, and until then, she would remain in the main house. So, for the next week, the three lads and Fionn, with the help of Oisín, stripped out the furniture, making new items to replace it all. They then had a big fire to burn everything before Oonagh was happy to move in.

For the next few months, a different group member took Oisín to spend the day with. He spent a day with Fionn, the next with Bodhmall, the next with Liath, followed by a day with Oonagh, then Darragh, then Shane until the last day was with Fergal. They agreed that this was the best way to help him integrate and become more familiar with different people.

Each of them took it in turns teaching him something new. They taught him the warrior ways with a sword, a spear, a dagger and a shield, as well as how to cook and look after the animals. They taught him how to fell trees, and they even helped him to build his own little tree house. They took him fishing and told him the story of how Darragh, Shane, and Fergal first came across Fionn while he was fishing for a great Salmon.

Oisín's favourite time, however, was with Oonagh, who was quite adept at being a poet and a bard. She could recite a poem or tell a story about anything while drawing everybody in. It fascinated Oisín the way she could tell tales. She would talk about the others in the group and their many adventures.

She would tell a story of the Salmon of knowledge, and as Oisín sat there amazed by it, she would recite a poem describing the same story sounding differently. She would tell the story of the Abhartach or even the giantess Eileen Óg. Oisín would sit there memorised by everyone, as she had a unique way of telling the stories that would leave a person wanting more.

As the months went on, Oisín himself became quite the poet and storyteller. He would often go missing from the farm, only to be found down in the village tavern telling tales or reciting poetry about the heroics of his father, Fionn, the bravest man, and his companions, the most fearless warriors in the land, Darragh, Shane and Fergal. (He always emphasised Fergal, as Fergal had told him he was the bravest of the four).

Fionn and his three companions would take him out hunting wild animals and foraging for food. They helped him master the bow and arrow by hunting pigeons and other animals in forests. They taught him to ride a horse and how to swim, and he actually became the most rounded of the entire group, such were the skills and talents he amassed. He even had great joy riding on Bran's back, such was the size and strength of the hound.

They brought him to Biddy to learn about spells and Finnegas to learn about magic. They took him to Tara and showed him where the giant Aillen had been defeated. When they brought him to Fionn's headquarters in Almhuin, all the Fianna warriors became enamoured with him, as he would disappear, only to be found by campfires or taverns telling tales of his mighty father and friends.

They brought him to every part of the Island that Fionn could think of, even where he had overcome the giant Benandonner in Antrim. Every story fascinated him equally. As the months went by, Oonagh became pregnant, and Fionn was reluctant to leave the farm, as he became very protective of his wife, remembering what had happened to Sadhbh.

One day, while the entire group was at the farm talking, Fergal asked how old Oisín was and when his birthday was. Everyone looked at each other in confusion, for none of them knew. They knew his mother had disappeared almost ten years earlier, so his next birthday would make him ten years old. "Hooray" shouted Fergal. "You're going to be ten tomorrow, Oisín," he said. The others laughed, as they thought it was a great idea.

The next day, the men set off hunting and foraging in the forest while the women set about preparing the house for a party. They even sent word to the locals in Ballyfin to join them in the farmhouse for the party. That evening, they spoiled Oisín rotten, as he was the centre of attention from everyone.

Fergal insisted on giving him the bumps, even though the others didn't know what he meant. Fergal told them what to do, and they threw him into the air ten times to celebrate his ten years of age, and so it was that the tradition of giving people the bumps on their birthday was born (Or so Fergal said).

For many more months, the group remained at the farm, with Cred visiting every so often. Each time they questioned her about Dagda, and each time, she gave the same answer that his condition remained unchanged.

Then one day, Goll and Conan turned up at the farm, telling them they had grave news for them. The high king Cormac mac Airt had summoned them to Tara urgently, and they would need to go with no time to spare. Fionn sat with the now heavily pregnant Oonagh, promising he would return as soon as possible, but he dared not risk the king's wrath. With that, the four lads, each saying long goodbyes to the three women and Oisín, set off for Tara with Bran in tow.

They travelled as quickly as possible to reach Tara, stopping only to rest the horses, eat, and sleep until they finally reached the High king's fort. Upon leaving their horses in the stables, they made their way to the main hall, where the king was in council. It quickly became apparent that Fionn would not get home to Oonagh any time soon.

For the king instructed them they were going to war. A king name Daire Donn, a descendant of the Fir Bolg, had mustered a massive army of men from continental Europe and further afield and he was intent on invading and conquering the whole of Ireland, and they must stop them.

The king convened a war council with his and Fionn's generals to find out how many troops he could muster. Fionn said that he could spare 8000 men, 2000 from each province, leaving 1000 men in each province to protect the lands and keep law and order.

The king himself could easily call upon 12000 men. While that was 20,000 warriors, they thought that King Daire was approaching with at least 40,000 troops on 400 vast ships. Darragh came forth and gave them plans to build giant catapults. Intrigued, Fionn and Cormac ordered as many as possible to be made locally in Kerry.

CHAPTER NINETEEN
THE BATTLE OF VENTRY

ing Cormac instructed them to make their way to Kerry, for that was where they expected the enemy to arrive at Ventry beach. Fionn sent messengers to the four provinces that they should each send 2000 of their best warriors to Ventry as soon as possible. Fionn, Darragh, Shane, Fergal, Goll, and Conan took their leave of the king as it was a five-day journey ahead of them.

For the next five days, they and Bran travelled from morning until night, only stopping to rest the horses and for food and sleep before they would be on their way again. They received water and food along the way from the people whose towns and villages they passed through en route to Ventry Bay, with the people cheering them on for the battle ahead.

They came upon a large standing stone near the village of Graigue, close to Ventry, and as it was dark, Shane pointed his silver torc at its shining symbol so that Cred would know quickly where to find him. He remained there in case she came to him. After their epic journey, they finally came within sight of the bay. Luckily for them, the enemy had not yet arrived, allowing them to prepare for battle.

Darragh told Fionn about the catapults that he had helped the Tuath to use to great effect again the Fomorians, and Fionn gave the instructions for as many as possible to be built. They also cut down many trees and sharpened them into spikes before forcing them into the sands along the bay's shoreline to thwart any ships from landing.

They sent troops to nearby quarries to gather rocks for the catapults. Others dug trenches along the beach again to thwart any troops who may reach the beach. Gradually the full might of almost 20,000 men had gathered, ready for battle. Cred did indeed come to Shane, and he told her of the great battle ahead. She said she had foreseen it and was trying to assemble some men to help, but Lugh forbade her from getting the Tuath involved in large-scale human battles.

After only two days, many sails could be seen on the horizon, and King Cormac quickly responded by ordering all the troops to ready themselves for battle. As the ships sailed ever closer, it became apparent that they could not all reach the beach at once and if the winds were not in their favour, they could crash into the sharpened logs, destroying the ships and giving The Fianna and kings soldiers an advantage over them.

As the ships sailed closer, Fionn gave the order for the catapults to be placed on the beach, and once they were in reach, began firing large rocks at them, but the troops using them were not very accurate, and the rocks landed close to the ships, but without hitting them. Suddenly, a tremendous cheer went up as they hit a ship, causing significant damage with the warriors jumping ship and swimming for the beach.

Fionn gave the order to attack, and Darragh, Shane, and Fergal didn't need to be told twice. They rushed to the shoreline, striking down the enemies as they reached the shore. Goll, Conan, Diarmuid, Cailte, and Aengus were all in the thick of it until all the enemies on the beach lay dead. The troops withdrew back from the shoreline to await the next foray with the enemy.

Daire Donn, having witnessed his first ship sinking, gave the order for his troops to get out their long straight oars with stiff shafts and hard blades, and with powerful, well-timed rowing, they crashed into the barriers, put on the beach to thwart them, before storming the beach.

The skies darkened as swarms of the dreaded Sluagh flew over the battlefield, letting out loud screams and shrills, excited for the feast of souls they could devour in the oncoming battle. Sligech, one of Daire's generals, jumped from his ship and urged his men forward, while Cormac and Fionn did the same.

The sound of loud roars filled the air as warriors from both sides raced towards each over before the sound of metal crashing against metal filled the air once more. The fighting was ferocious, and the sands turned red with blood as warriors attacked each other. The catapults were busy shooting large rocks to try and sink any incoming ships, but it wasn't long until thousands of the enemy were on the beach fighting.

Darragh was in the thick of it, with his sword cutting down enemy after enemy with a single stroke. Shane stayed back, while constantly throwing his spear, killing enemies before recalling it. Fergal would disappear before reappearing every so often while the power of his ring would run out.

Fionn, who had roared Goliath, rushed into battle along with Conan, Diarmuid, Cailte, and Aengus. Goll, however, stayed back from fighting in the company of King Cormac. The skies grew ever darker as a gale rose and lashed the battlefield, and the winds grew ever stronger until the full fury of a storm was lashing down on the warriors below. They gave the orders to retreat on both sides to give the warriors a breather and time to regroup. This time there was no Dagda or Cred to help the dying and injured, and many corpses littered the beach. And a truce was called until the following morning.

As dawn broke and the Fianna prepared for battle, they found that at least 100 ships had come ashore during the storm, and they had a more significant number of warriors to face. Yet they gave the orders to attack, and charged into battle, unwaveringly. The battalions dealt solid and mighty blows on either side, and they broke shields and armour as they were vigorously used to parry the impacts from the oncoming enemy.

In the midst of battle and hand-to-hand combat, swords broke on the splintered bones of the enemy, and fearsome battle cries were drowned out by the sound of the Sluagh, excitedly devouring souls. The battle continued in a series of combats and duels until the day's end, when a significant number of warriors lay dead before a truce was called for the night.

King Cormac instructed his warriors to gather the dead and build a wall from their bodies between themselves and the enemy, and when morning came, he gave the instructions to set the bodies alight, filling the sky with flames and smoke, before his archers and the catapults began bombarding the enemy troops on the beach.

When the flames died down, the enemy warriors made their way back up the beach to attack and were met head-on by the Fianna and kings' troops with Fionn, Darragh, Shane, Fergal Conan, Diarmuid, Cailte, and Aengus, as always, at the forefront of the attack. With Well-timed attacks, they cut through the enemy lines encouraging their troops forward.

Through the straining of spears and the shaking of swords, the shattering of shields and the battering of bodies, they fought long and hard, harrying the enemy, trying to dislodge them from their positions on the battlefield. They made their way across the battlefield and hacked down the enemy invaders until they reached the enemy general, Sligech, attacking him in unison, killing him and causing turmoil and confusion among the enemy ranks.

Yet again, the skies grew dark as night fell, and the ever-present Sluagh screeched across the battlefield. The troops called it a night and withdrew from the battlefield for the usual night's truce. King Cormac called his leaders together to talk about how they thought the battle was going. They could see that almost 150 ships managed to get the troops onto the beach, meaning nearly 15,000 troops had landed, and although they had inflicted heavy losses on the enemy, they also had suffered many casualties too.

The following morning Fionn, Darragh, Shane, Fergal Conan, Diarmuid, Cailte, and Aengus once again led the troops into battle on a mist-covered beach, making it very difficult to see the enemy approaching. Darragh gave the order for the troops to hold fast, where they stood and crouched down in silence, letting the enemy come onto them—which is precisely what happened as a line of the enemy, now led by a different general, Fagartach, approached them.

Fionn gave the order to attack, and all the troops jumped to their feet, taking the enemy by surprise, killing many, while others turned tail and ran away from the onslaught. They then pursued the enemy back to where they had come until they came to a wall of shield-bearing warriors and had to back off to regroup. General Fagartach gave his men the order to advance, where Fionn's troops once again met them.

They fought hard and fast on the strand for the whole day, and a number fell on either side. They continued fighting until they had injured each other's bodies or broken their weapons and called a truce for the night.

Fionn realised it was the Fianna at the forefront of the fight, and he was losing twice as many warriors as king Cormac and implored the king to push his men to fight harder in the battle. He confronted Goll for his lack of fighting, but the king said he was to protect the king himself.

Fionn spoke of his displeasure to Darragh, Shane, Fergal Conan, Diarmuid, Cailte, and Aengus about this, but he had no choice but to obey the king's command.

The following morning Fionn, Darragh, Shane, Fergal, Conan, Diarmuid, Cailte, and Aengus again took to the battlefield, rousing their troops into a frenzy, they charged forward towards the enemy lines, where they clashed head-on into a wall of shields and spears. Many men fell in the attack's first wave and withdrew to regroup. Darragh ordered the catapults to be focused on the enemy lines rather than their ships, which had landed at least 20,000 troops on the beach.

This gave Fionn's troops a slight reprieve as it caused panic and confusion in the enemy lines, enabling them to attack them again. They caught sight of general Fagartach, and Shane cut him down with a throw of his spear, causing even more confusion within the enemy ranks. Yet as they cheered, it mattered not for a new general, Bolcan, entered the fray, ordering his troops to regain their composure and forcing Fionn's men back.

Fighting carried on throughout the day with minor victories on each side until a truce for the night was called. All the while, the Sluagh swooped down, devouring the souls of the fallen. Fionn despaired and shared his concerns with Darragh, Shane, Fergal, Conan, Diarmuid, Cailte, and Aengus. They had lost almost 3000 of the 8000 Fianna who had arrived at the battle.

King Conan, meanwhile, had lost less than 1000, even though they had slain over 6000 of the enemy troops. He again approached the king, this time demanding more fervour from his forces. The king told him they would help more, but were not as used to fighting as the Fianna were.

Fionn was worried that the invaders were getting the better of the Fianna, as he had so many dead and wounded and, that morning, was finding it hard to motivate his men until the son of the King of Ulster arrived with 2000 men. This timely intervention prevented the defeat of the Fianna, and the Ulstermen entered the battle, fighting bravely throughout the day, enabling the Fianna to rest.

That night, to the delight of Fionn and the others, Cred, along with Manannan Mac Lir and a group of wizards, appeared at camp ready to help, and the following morning began casting spells on the enemy. They brought forth a tremendous storm, with strong winds and heavy rain.

The seas became so wild and angry with waves rising above their ships, sinking many and causing many to crash onto the beach. They then brought showers of fire and lightning onto the enemies on the beach, killing many, also causing havoc. This invigorated Fionn and his men, who charged at the enemy, dealing massive damage to those remaining on the beach.

The king finally gave the order for his men to engage and they stormed onto the battlefield, fully committed to destroying the enemy. The Fianna and King's men and the remaining Ulstermen and Tuath wizards dealt a deadly blow to king Daire's men, wiping out most of the warriors on the beach. They carried on fighting until, as usual, a temporary truce was called that night.

The following morning, another 50 ships had landed on the beach, and 5000 troops disembarked, ready for battle. Manannan sent Fionn, Darragh, Shane, Fergal, Conan, Diarmuid, Cailte, and Aengus to the battlefield and cast a spell onto them, creating the illusion of 1000 troops of each of them. Fionn roared "Goliath" and, as he grew to eight feet tall, so did his illusion.

He charged up the beach, followed by the others, and it created total panic when the enemy saw 8000 men attacking them, led by 1000 eight-foot-tall warriors. General Bolcan demanded his troops stand their ground, but as Darragh and his 1000 selves turned to run at him, he dropped his weapon and dived into the waves. The rest of the Fianna then followed the group into attacking and destroying the enemy army that was left on the beach.

Fionn instructed all the enemy bodies to be gathered and loaded onto the ships or wrecks on the beach, then set them on fire, cremating all the dead invaders. King Daire, who by now realised he had not only lost 250 ships but also almost 25,000 warriors, gave the orders to remain out of reach at sea until they planned their next move.

Shane gave a cheeky smile to Manannan, who gathered his wizards on the shoreline. They brought forward a colossal storm, creating giant waves and storm clouds above the ships. A lightning storm erupted overhead, setting many on fire, while others crashed into each other, sending the ships and the warriors within them to the bottom of the ocean.

A distraught King Daire had no choice but to order a retreat, and his remaining ships and troops sailed away over the horizon out of the view of the now jubilant troops, who began cheering and hugging each other for such a momentous victory.

Fionn gathered his troops, along with Cred and Manannan, and thanked them for their service. The King also joined and thanked them for their help. Cred and her wizards then took their leave and headed back to the standing stone near the village of Graigue and where Shane also joined them.

The wizards used the stone portal to transport them back to Mag Mell, but Shane could not use it. Cred held his hand and pointed her torc towards the stone, but nothing happened until she released his hand, and then she, too, was gone.

Shane returned to the beach and joined the others, who were busy gathering corpses to place them on a large funeral pyre. Once the task had been completed, Fionn gathered his Fianna troops and thanked and congratulated them for their service. He bade them farewell and sent them back to their provinces. He then gave instructions to Conan, Diarmuid, Cailte, and Aengus to lead their warriors back to Almhuin while he, Darragh, Shane, and Fergal made their way back to the farm in Ballyfin to check on the heavily pregnant Oonagh.

After several days of travelling, they finally reached the farm, where they saw Oisín standing alone in the yard. Fionn leapt from his horse and ran to his son, asking him why he was alone. This brought a concerned-looking Liath out of the main house, where she called Fionn to the side. She told him that Oonagh had gone into labour, and it wasn't looking good for the mother or child.

Fionn rushed into the house to check on his wife while Darragh, Shane, and Fergal took Oisín to the river and away from what was happening. Several hours passed, and they returned to the farm and could hear crying coming from the main house. They slowly entered and found Fionn, Bodhmall and Liath all crying and holding one another, as neither Oonagh nor the child had survived childbirth.

Fionn leapt up and grabbed Oisín, almost squeezing the life out of him, hugging him so hard. Once he regained his composure, he asked the lads to prepare a funeral pyre while he, Bodhmall and Liath prepared the bodies. Later that day, they all said their last goodbyes to Oonagh and the child before cremating the bodies.

Fionn slipped down to the town, where he consoled himself in the tavern, drinking for many hours. The others gave him space while they looked after Oisín. This was the first-time death had crossed his path, and Bodhmall sat him down and explained that one day death would come to us all, but that his day would be a long time away. The boy asked many questions so that he could understand it all clearly in his own head.

The next few days were a gloomy affair around the farm, with Fionn going to the tavern and the others spending time with his son. Oisín was worried for his father until Darragh explained to him that people dealt with grief in different ways and that Fionn would come back to him soon.

After a few days of the same thing, Darragh, Shane, and Fergal joined him in the tavern and shared a few Meads with him while talking about their previous adventures. Fergal jumped up and began singing, which brought a laugh to his face. "Let's go home," said Fionn as they returned to the farm.

The following morning, Fionn gathered everyone together. He asked Bodhmall and Liath to look after Oisín and Bran, as he and the lads needed to return to the Fianna headquarters to check if the troops made it back safely. Later that day, they made their way out of the farm. They stopped off on the way to tell Biddy and Finnegas the bad news about Oonagh and the child before riding onwards to Almhuin.

Upon reaching the fort, there was a distinct atmosphere around the place, and the guards were subdued. The lads made their way to the main hall, where they were met by Goll holding court and giving orders to Conan, Diarmuid, Cailte, and Aengus. Fionn approached and demanded to know what was going on. Goll told him he wasn't around often enough, and no longer deserved to be the leader of the Fianna, so he was taking the leadership back.

This enraged Fionn, who grabbed him by the throat, throwing him from the building, shouting, "Get out of my fort, and don't come back until you are ready to apologise". Goll jumped to his feet and stormed off while Fionn sat with the rest of his men and asked how they were and if things we ok around the fort. The others told him all was fine except for Goll trying to exert his command over them all.

Fionn called Conan to the side and asked if he was loyal to Fionn and the Fianna or his brother Goll. Conan assured Fionn that although he loved his brother, his loyalties were to Fionn and the Fianna. Fionn shook his hand and thanked him for his commitment and friendship.

After a few days had passed, a more humble Goll returned to the fort and made his way to the main hall. He apologised to the entire group for his behaviour. Fionn told him he accepted his apology, but he would no longer hold a position of strength within the Fianna. Conan, Diarmuid, Cailte, and Aengus would now run things while Fionn was not around. A disgruntled Goll made his way from the hall, murmuring under his breath and moving his belongings to one of the lower-ranked Fianna barracks.

Fionn, Darragh, Shane and Fergal remained in the fort for the next week, which was spent together talking about the adventures they had shared and even the adventures that were not shared when the three lads were in Mag Mell. Fionn laughed when talking about himself and Oonagh, and the giant Benandonner, and him being dressed like a child.

The others thought it was a great tale and an excellent memory of his time with Oonagh. Life was peaceful around the fort for the next few weeks until a messenger arrived telling Fionn that King Cormac had summoned him to Tara. Fionn feared the worst and thought it might be over him demoting the treacherous Goll that the king wished to see him.

He asked the others to accompany him, while leaving Conan and Aengus in charge of the fort before setting off to Tara. Upon reaching Tara, they made their way to the main hall, where the king was waiting. He warmly welcomed them, setting them all at ease, and asked them to sit down. They were then all served a large cup of mead, and the king called forth his daughter Gráinne, who reluctantly joined them.

The girl seemed quite shy and uninterested in their conversation, except raising her head to smile at Diarmuid every so often. When the niceties were out of the way, Fionn asked the king if something was wrong, that led to him being summoned. "On the contrary," said the king. "I have heard the sad news about you losing your wife and unborn child, and as a reward for your bravery in Ventry, I am giving you my daughter Grainne to be your new wife".

Fionn gulped loudly as he swallowed some mead, and silence fell around the table. "Well!" said the king. "Have you nothing to say?".

DIARMUID AND GRÁINNE

ionn stood up and took a deep breath, for he had never set eyes on the king's daughter before, and shared no feelings for her whatsoever, and thought her too young, yet he dared not offend the king, who had so generously offered him, his daughter's hand in marriage.

Finally, Fionn gathered his thoughts and tongue, then blurted out, "It is most generous of you, your highness. I don't quite know what to say?". "Say you except you idiot," laughed the king. "Yes, your highness, I accept," said Fionn, somewhat embarrassed, unlike his usual composed self. "A toast", said the king, raising his cup aloft. Everyone around the table cheered except for Diarmuid and Gráinne, who had eyes only for each other.

The king gave them leave to go about their business as he had a wedding to organise. A shellshocked Fionn and his men left the main hall, making their way to the stables. Fionn never uttered a word as they mounted their horses and left Tara. Upon reaching Almhuin, a still, quiet Fionn leapt from his horse for the others to put in the stable while he made his way to his house.

Sometime later, he joined the others in the main hall, finally coming to terms with what happened earlier in the day. "I don't know if we should congratulate you or not," said Darragh. "I cannot do that," said Diarmuid. He then confided with his close friends that he and Gráinne had been lovers for some time and were trying to find the right moment to approach the king for Diarmuid to request her hand in marriage, but their plans now lay in ruins. "I am so sorry, my dear friend," said Fionn. "For I know not what to do to help you".

Darragh advised that short of Diarmuid and Gráinne eloping and running away together, she would become Fionn's wife. He said that he could see no other option that would allow both King Cormac and Fionn to save face. Fionn agreed that this was the only way it could work and gave Diarmuid his blessing to run away with Gráinne, if that was what they both truly wanted.

Fionn then told Diarmuid that he should leave at once for Tara and put the idea to the princess. It may seem like a good idea, but she would need to be sure that she could leave her privileged life and family behind. Diarmuid rushed from the building and went straight to the stables, gathering his horse and riding directly to Tara. He sent word for Gráinne to join him privately in a tavern.

When the two were alone in private quarters, Diarmuid told her the plan put forward by Darragh and Fionn that the pair could elope together and therefore allow the king and Fionn to maintain their dignity and be clear of embarrassment in the situation. The princess was overjoyed and willing to leave her life and family behind to be with the man she truly loved.

Later that evening, as Darragh, Shane, Fergal, Conan, Cailte, and Aengus were sitting together in the main hall, Diarmuid and Gráinne marched into the hall to the other's amazement. Darragh jumped to his feet and ushered them out of the building, bringing them directly to Fionn's house. As they entered the house, Gráinne rushed to Fionn, giving him a great big hug and thanking him for his help.

It took Fionn by surprise at their boldness, for although he was happy for them, he did not think they would elope this very day. The princess told him that her father was busy preparing for the wedding to Fionn, and it would only be a matter of days until they pronounced her his wife as Tara readied itself for the wedding feast and an entire month of celebrations. Fionn, taken aback by the speed with which the king would have him married, agreed that maybe it was for the best.

He showed the couple to a spare room and told them they could sleep there for the night. There would be a lot of planning to be done the next day to help them escape safely as Fionn didn't even know where they could go to keep them from the king's reach or anger. He and Darragh sat together, pondering the dilemma they now found themselves in.

Early the following morning, a messenger arrived, instructing Fionn to come swiftly to Tara. Fionn told Diarmuid and Gráinne to remain hidden in his house and await his return before doing anything stupid. Fionn summoned Darragh to his quarters, and the two of them travelled promptly to Tara, fully aware of what the king would have to tell them.

When they reached Tara, Fionn and Darragh rushed to the king, who sat enraged, angrily banging his fist on the table. Fionn and Darragh approached him, and he shouted, "they have betrayed us" "Who betrayed us?" asked Fionn, pretending to be innocent in all of this. "my daughter, Gráinne and your idiotic friend Diarmuid," roared the king. "What do you mean?" asked Darragh.

"What I mean," shouted Cormac, "is that your friend has stolen my daughter away, and there is to be no wedding". Fionn pretending to be shocked, asked, "How could this have happened?". The king told them he had woken that morning to find his daughter missing, only for a servant to tell him where his daughter had gone.

The king told Fionn not to worry, for he would still have his wedding, although he didn't know when he would have his wedding. Fionn, relieved at not having to marry, told the king it was fine as he was not yet certain he wanted to marry. "What do you mean, not Certain?" shouted the king angrily. Darragh interrupted that Fionn indeed wanted to marry the king's daughter but was patient enough to wait for her to return.

The king told Fionn that he had a gift for him in the meantime and presented him with a new hunting horn (Dord Fiann). Fionn gladly accepted, hoping this was the end of the matter, but to his surprise and horror, the king gave Fionn and his Fianna troops a new mission. They were to hunt the couple down.

He said they could not run forever and that they would never be able to sleep in a cave with one opening or a house with one door. They would never be able to eat where they slept or sleep where they had eaten. They would have to keep running if they were to avoid capture and, in Diarmuid's case, torture.

The king then gave them leave to return and prepare his troops for the hunt. The king's anger shook both of them as they left and made them uncertain of how to continue pursuing the couple who were happily hiding in Fionn's house. The two of them made their way to the stables, collected their horses, and set off for home.

Upon reaching their fort, they made their way quickly to Fionn's house, where they found the happy couple awaiting their return. They were both holding hands and lovingly smiling at each other as Fionn and Darragh arrived. Upon seeing the unhappy faces of Fionn and Darragh, they let go of each other and asked what was wrong. Fionn sat there in shock as Darragh told them that her father, the king, had tasked the Fianna with hunting them down, and upon catching them, Fionn would still have to marry Gráinne and Diarmuid was to be tortured.

"What have we done?" said the princess as she despaired at their newfound plight. Diarmuid offered to surrender himself to the king straight away, but Fionn stopped him in order to protect his friend from punishment and himself from implication.

The four of them sat talking for hours until they agreed the couple could travel to places of safety while moving around regularly. They could camp with Finnegas, stay with Biddy and also with Bodhmall. They could also remain in the rebuilt house of Fionn and Oonagh in Antrim. All the while, Fionn would have to pretend the Fianna were indeed hunting them.

The couple left Almhuin that night under the cover of darkness, telling no one where they were going to, or coming from. While Fionn and his troops would patrol the country, pretending to be searching for the runaway couple. As night approached, Fionn and Darragh gave great big hugs to their friend Diarmuid and Gráinne before escorting them safely to the stables and then out of the fort.

And so it was that Diarmuid and Gráinne went on the run for the next two years, travelling from town to town, never sleeping in the same place for more than a night at a time. The Fianna warriors spent little to no time looking for them, but Fionn kept king Cormac updated, saying that they could not find them, no matter how hard they tried. The truth, however, was that they regularly stayed at the Ballyfin farm even while Fionn was there visiting Oisín, Bodhmall and Liath. Other times they spent the night drinking with Shane and Cred, who regularly met at the farm.

After such a long time, the king became impatient and began sending his own men throughout the country searching for the couple, as he still demanded justice. He received news that the couple were hiding out in a deep cave called Ben Edair on the Hill of Howth. The king sent some soldiers to Fionn, and they insisted on accompanying him to the cave, for the king had grown tired and did not entirely believe Fionn's heart was set on finding them.

There was a cold mist in the air as they reached the cave, and one of the king's soldiers, sneaked inside and returned a short time later and confirmed that there was a couple inside in the darkness, but he was unsure who they were. Gráinne spotted the soldier and warned Diarmuid that the king's men had found them. The couple fled the cave's darkness as fast as their legs could carry them. When they emerged onto the hillside, they saw Fionn and the king's men close by.

Diarmuid looked around in desperation and saw a small boat in the harbour nearby. They sneaked down the hill and into the boat before rowing silently away and evading capture. When Fionn and the king's men entered the cave, they found it empty, and Fionn questioned if the soldier's mind was playing tricks on him before sending them back to the king, saying they were not to be found.

The following day Fionn himself went to the king and asked if he could give up the chase, as he was tired of the endless pursuit of his friend and the king's daughter. King Cormac reluctantly agreed to give up his pursuit, but he still nursed silent anger in his heart. King Cormac sent out word he had forgiven his runaway daughter and Diarmuid, and they were welcome to return to Tara.

A few days passed, and a jubilant Gráinne and Diarmuid arrived back at the king's house, and he begrudgingly bid them welcome. Still, King Cormac harboured a hatred for Diarmuid inside of him that had festered since the day he had eloped with his daughter, and he wouldn't let go, although he pretended to put it all behind him.

After a few days had passed, the king invited Diarmuid to go hunting with him, for there was a mighty wild boar on the loose in a forest close to the fort. Although Gráinne was concerned for his safety, Diarmuid insisted it would help him win the king's favour and accepted the invite. So, the two men, with some guards, travelled to the forest in pursuit of the creature.

Once in the forest, they happened upon a dead deer lying on the forest floor. Diarmuid dismounted to investigate when a tremendous crashing and grunting suddenly erupted from a nearby bush. It was the boar itself, and it ran headfirst into the unsuspecting Diarmuid, ramming him with its tusks, gouging him in the back so that he fell face first onto the hard ground, bleeding heavily from his wound.

King Cormac, feigning concern for Diarmuid, jumped from his horse to tend to the wounded man when suddenly the wild boar appeared back on the same path while rushing the startled Cormac, spearing him in the chest with its tusks.

When he lay prone on the ground, the wild boar leapt upon him and ripped out his bowels, so they fell about his legs. The startled guards killed the beast before it could escape or wreak any more havoc, but there was no saving either the king or Diarmuid, and the distraught guards had the sad duty of bringing both bodies back to Tara.

There was pandemonium amongst warriors and townsfolk alike as upon reaching the fort. They made their way up to the centre of the fort until they got to the main hall, where they were met by the queen, Gráinne, her sister Ailbe and Cairbre Lifechair, the son of Cormac and heir to the throne. The women wailed like banshees and were inconsolable as they presented the two men's bodies to them. Cairbre Lifechair sent word around the kingdom that the high king Cormac was dead and that leaders from around the country should come and pay their respects to the fallen king while swearing loyalty to the new king.

When news reached Almhuin, Fionn, Darragh, Shane, Fergal, Conan, Cailte, and Aengus all wept at the loss of their friend but had to make ready and ride to Tara. Upon reaching the fort, they made their way to the main hall, passing condolences to the king's family. They then went to check on Diarmuid's body, where they all placed a kiss on their fallen friend's forehead and wished him well, wherever he may be.

Later that day, Diarmuid's remains were cremated, while they would hold the kings until all the tribal chieftains, who were expected to pay their respects, arrived. The group had to stay in Tara for the next week, as there was a three-day mourning period for the King's death and then a further four days celebrating Cairbre Lifechair's ascension to the throne until they could finally return to Almhuin.

Fionn lamented over life's hardships and took temporary leave along with the three lads, and made their way to the farm in Ballyfin, leaving Conan, Cailte, and Aengus in charge of day-to-day affairs. Upon reaching the farm, they told the others the sad news of their friend's death and also that of king Cormac. The four of them spent the next four weeks around the farm, spending some well-earned downtime together with Oisín, Bodhmall, Liath and occasionally Cred. They all enjoyed doing mundane things around the farm, as life had been hectic for almost as long as they could remember.

One day they sat talking and Oisín, who by now was at least thirteen years old, asked if he could join the Fianna and become a great warrior, like his father and the three lads. Everyone thought it a great idea, especially Fionn, who was extremely happy and made it his mission to train his son daily in all aspects of the seven trials for the entrance test into his beloved Fianna.

They spent every hour possible preparing for each trial, as Fionn could show no leniency towards his son, or it would cause great anger amongst the Fianna members. They weighed him down and made him run and jump to improve his running speed and jumping height. He chased the hens to improve his agility, and they even had Fionn, Darragh, Shane and Fergal all attack him at once to prepare for the standing in the hole trial. He was pretty good at memorising poetry, but Biddy could help with that, anyway.

They continued with the training until one day, the new king Cairbre Lifechair summoned Fionn to Tara. Fionn was disappointed but had to go until Darragh said he would go in his place, telling the king Fionn was ill. Fionn, being a man of honour, refused, and so the four of them made haste to Tara for the king's pleasure.

When they arrived, the king told them he had a most urgent task for them to carry out. His people were trying to build a new fort two days' ride away, and each night it burned to the ground. Fionn and his troops were to put a stop to the burning. Fionn told the king he would look after it, and off they rode to carry out their mission.

Darragh again told Fionn to spend his time training Oisín as Darragh, Shane, and Fergal would find out what was behind the burnings. Fionn was most grateful for the gesture the three of them showed and thanked them warmly before leaving them and making his way to Ballyfin while the three lads headed for the new fort near Tullow.

CHAPTER TWENTY

THE HAG AND HER SONS

he three lads set off on their newest adventure, curious about what lay ahead. They were mindful that they had promised Fionn that they would look after it for him, so they wasted no time in riding to the town of Tullow. There some soldiers and builders met them, and they joined them at a campfire to discuss what had been happening.

The chief builder told them that every morning at first light, a group of builders would set off to the site where the building was to take place, and each day, the first thing they set about the building was two guard towers, at what would be the entrance to the new fort. Darragh asked the builder to bring the lads to the site so that they could check for anything out of the ordinary.

The builder then escorted them a short distance away, where they could see the embers of the previous guard towers still glowing. The buildings were being built close to a Forest and a river, but nothing looked out of the ordinary. The lads thanked the builder, then sent him back to Tullow, and forbade the building of any new towers until they gave the all-clear.

The lads camped out for the night close to the river, where they caught some fish for dinner and then sat around talking. As they talked, they saw and heard nothing out of the ordinary. They could hear the wind blowing gently and water hitting the river banks, but nothing stood out to them. They slept for the night and, the following morning, made their way to the Forest.

The forest floor was covered in a layer of fog that crawled across the ground as if it had a mind of its own and was trying to reach a specific destination. They made their way into the forest, and beneath their feet, they could hear the cracking of twigs and crunched leaves being trodden on, and the branches overhead were very close to each other, almost blocking the sunlight.

They could hear the wind whispering through the trees as if it was calling them and readied themselves for battle, but nothing happened, so they rode further into the forest, where there were moss-covered trees and rocks covered in mushrooms that looked like fairies dancing in the wind.

The forest grew thicker, so the lads decided not to go any deeper. There was a peculiar smell like Sulphur floating through the air, but they could not see where it was coming from, so they left the forest and returned to Tullow. They told the builders to carry on with building the two guard towers. So, for the rest of the day, a team of builders went to the forest, chopped down some trees and built the two new guard towers. Sure enough, the towers were again burned to the ground that night. This infuriated the three lads as they had given the all-clear.

They gave the order for them to build two more towers, but as night fell. Fergal remained in one tower, while Shane stayed in the other. Darragh remained hidden nearby, waiting and watching to see if anything happened. In the middle of the night, they heard loud sounds of leaves being trodden underfoot and braced themselves for something to happen.

Suddenly, out of the forest strode a tall, skinny, monstrously deformed creature carrying a torch. He made his way to the tower Fergal was in, humming a tune as he strode. Fergal rubbed his ring and disappeared. In three strides, the creature had reached the top of the tower and began setting it alight. Fergal pulled out Claíomh Solais, startling the monster and stuck his knife into the monster's foot, pinning it to the wooden floor. It let out a painful scream as it pulled the dagger from its foot, throwing it from the tower.

The monster dropped its torch and leapt from the tower, running back into the forest. The three lads gathered together, with Fergal picking up his dagger, and gave chase into the woods, but as the forest floor seemed always to be covered in fog and they could not follow. They then made their way back to the two towers to wait out the night.

The following morning, the builders returned and were delighted to see the two towers still standing and began building the outer fence to the fort. The three lads, however, weren't so sure that it was safe, but they kept vigil throughout the day until the darkness of night fell once more. This time Fergal and Darragh climbed to the top of one tower while Shane climbed the other one. As per the previous night, the creature came walking out of the forest carrying a torch and made his way over to the tower.

This time, however, he didn't climb to the top. He instead set fire to the tower at its base. The two lads, unaware, became startled once they saw smoke and large flames climbing up through the tower. They had to jump from a height to the ground below. Darragh roared to Shane in the other tower to be prepared, and Shane, seeing the approaching creature, threw his spear at it, hitting it in the stomach, but it didn't stop the creature from setting fire to the second tower.

Now back on their feet, Darragh and Fergal ran at the creature, attacking it, as Shane made his way out of his burning tower. Darragh rubbed his ring for power and tossed Fergal into the air. Fergal, taking out his dagger, stuck it right into the monster's shoulder blade and slid down its back, ripping the flesh as he did.

The creature let out an ear-splitting scream, turned, trying to grab Fergal from its back, while Darragh rushed forward, cutting the creature's arm clean off at the elbow. The creature turned again, trying to flee to the woods, but Shane caught it in the leg with a throw of his spear, and the creature fell face-first onto the foggy forest floor. This gave Darragh and Fergal enough time to catch and slay the creature. They dragged the creature back to the burning towers, where they threw its remains onto the flames cremating it.

The builders returned the following morning, horrified to find that something had again burnt the two towers to the ground and began to despair until the lads showed them the charred remains of the creature they had killed during the night. This filled the builders with hope, and they cleared the rubble and began building again until it got dark.

The three lads had stuck around to see if anything would happen now that they had slain the monster. As they waited through the night, they again heard loud footsteps coming through the forest. "Oh brother, where are you?" came a voice in the darkness, as out of the woods stepped another tall monster, even taller than the one before, carrying a torch.

The three lads all rushed the creature at once, but the creature was powerful and knocked them all back onto the ground. All three took a tremendous sigh and rubbed their rings. Quick as a flash, Shane was on his feet, running at the creature, ramming his spear into its side. Darragh charged forward and cut one of its legs off at the knee. The monster fell to its remaining knee and let out an ear-piercing cry as Fergal Struck it in the neck with his dagger.

The monster stood up again, grabbing Fergal and throwing him away. Darragh picked up the monster's torch, burning it where its leg used to be, as the creature winced in pain as its clothing caught fire. Darragh and Shane then attacked the creature with all their speed and might until it was finally dead on the ground.

Meanwhile, deep in the forest, a grand old hag was preparing dinner for her three sons. Two were now missing, and the hag told her oldest son to bring his brother's home. He was taller and more robust than his two younger siblings and, amazingly, had the head of a giant cat.

He grabbed two big torches and set off from deep in the forest to find his brothers. Not long after, he arrived at the towers and found Darragh, Shane, and Fergal standing over his brother's dead body. "What have you done to my brother?" roared the creature as he threw the torches at one tower, instantly setting it on fire.

He rushed towards them, taking out a giant club and, with one swing, sent the three lads flying through the air before they crashed into the wooden fence beside the tower, demolishing it. The lads hardly had time to think and pick themselves up before the creature was on top of them, swiping with its big club, luckily missing them all.

Fergal rubbed his ring and disappeared before running to safety. The others also rubbed theirs before Shane ran to the safety of the forest. Darragh, gaining his extra strength, lifted the creature off its feet, slamming it on the ground, but it made the creature even more determined to hurt him. It leapt back to its feet, grabbing Darragh, and raised him above its head before throwing him hard at a tree nearby. Luckily, he had rubbed his ring of strength, or the impact may have killed him.

Shane, having composed himself, took out his spear, throwing it with all his might. It struck the creature through the left upper chest before returning to him. The creature let out a cry of pain and ran at Shane, swiping its club at him but missing by inches as Shane darted out of its way. Darragh struggling to get to his feet crouched over in agony as the creature once again charged at him. Just in time, Fergal took out Claíomh Solais, drawing its attention and allowing Darragh to step into the darkness of the forest.

The creature let out a scream of anger as it turned, looking for Shane. He, however, had raced to the top of the tower and flung his spear at the creature, this time hitting it in the upper back, before recalling his spear. This didn't stop the creature, and it ran straight at the remaining tower, smashing it to pieces. Shane fell to the ground, injured. The monster got to its feet just as Fergal rushed in, cutting it from left to right across the stomach. The creature let out a wailing sound as it tried to grab Fergal, but couldn't see him.

Now having got his wind back, Darragh rushed out of the forest before cutting both legs from the creature. It dropped to the ground and began clawing its way after them. This gave the three lads enough time to regroup, and they all charged at the creature, stabbing it with their weapons before Darragh finally beheaded it. To their horror, the contest didn't end, however, for as its body lay dead, the cat's head took on a life of its own. Attacking Darragh, chomping down on his leg, and dragging him around the ground.

Shane and Fergal stabbed it with their weapons, but it still would not let go. Darragh, mustering all of his strength, ran for the river and plunged beneath the water before surfacing again a few minutes later, struggling to remove the head from his leg. He scrapped for several minutes more before removing the head's grip from his leg and holding it beneath the water. He eventually exited the river, carrying the cat's head. He had survived, but luckily the cat's head had not.

Darragh, looking for guidance, sucked on his thumb before saying, "Ah lads, someone is taking the you know what". "What's wrong?" asked Fergal. "Gather your weapons, lads, cos we still have their mother, a giant hag, to kill before we're done here," said a disgruntled Darragh as he trudged into the forest. Shane and Fergal, letting out a deep sigh of despair, followed him in.

Fergal took out Claíomh Solais to light the way as they made their way through the forest. Although they were injured, they had no time to rest and made their way through the woods. When they reached the part where the trees got thicker, they discovered a side passage through a cave that brought them out to a clearing in the forest, where the smell of Sulphur was potent. There was a rather large ramshackle of a hut built next to an old bog, and that was where the smell came from.

The three lads sat down to take a break, for this could be their last break, judging by what they had faced earlier in the night. They gave each other great big hugs and said they loved each other, and then all gave each other a high five at the same time before yelling, "let's do this" and making their way towards the hut. Fergal rubbed his ring and crept silently to the hut before sneaking around behind it. He returned to tell the others there was a great big ugly hag cooking over a giant cauldron next to the bog.

Darragh wondered if there might be an easy way to win the upcoming fight. They all crept silently up and entered the old hut. Darragh told Fergal to sneak close to the Sulphur bog and wait for the signal. He told Shane to take up a position, ready to throw his spear, before he began crawling up towards the hag while rubbing his ring.

He then gave the signal to Fergal, who took out Claíomh Solais, drawing the hag's attention. Fergal then sheath the dagger and ran as fast as his legs could carry him back towards the others. The hag approached the bog to see what had lit up behind her while Darragh waved at Shane, who threw his spear full throttle at the hag, who let out an ear-piercing shriek while recalling his spear.

Darragh burst forward and, again, with all his might, pushed the hag as hard as he could into the sulphur laden bog. He then grabbed nearby torches, throwing them in after her, before running full speed back towards the hut. As the three lads were hiding safely inside the hut, there was a massive explosion in the bog, and they could hear debris falling around outside and onto the roof of the hut, where they remained until it had calmed down.

When everything seemed to have settled, they left the hut and ran to check on the hag. To their delight, she was nowhere to be seen except for an arm here and a head there. They found the hag's arm, head, and legs strewn all around the back of the hut, showing that the explosion had killed her. The three lads then set fire to the old house to put an end to the hag and her sons once and for all before making their way back out of the forest, where the builders met them waiting to see if it was safe to build again.

The three lads told them they had taken care of a giant hag and her three sons, so they would no longer cause any problems. They told the builders to build to their heart's content. They stayed close to the river, fishing and camping for the next few days to ensure the fort was no longer under threat, and once they were happy that everything was in order, they made their way back to Ballyfin.

OISÍN

hen the lads rode up to Ballyfin farm, they could see Fionn and Oisín hard at training. They put their horses in the stable as an excited Oisín called them over to tell them how they got on in their latest adventure, for he loved the art of storytelling. This brought Bodhmall, Liath and once again Cred out of the main house, and they all sat around, ready to listen to how the trio got on.

Shane took centre stage, eager to impress Cred, and began by telling the tale of turning up at Tullow and talking to the builders about the fort being burned down each night. The lads had patrolled the area and forest but could see no obvious answer.

They gave the builders the all-clear to build, but that very night, a rather tall ugly man turned up to set fire to the towers. While Fergal, hiding in the tower, stabbed him, and the monster ran off. "See," interrupted Fergal, "I told you I was the bravest". Oisín sat there, intrigued, while everyone else laughed. "Continue", said Oisín.

Shane carried on that the second night, the creature returned and how they overcame it. The following night there came an even bigger creature that took a lot more effort to defeat. "And close on his tail came his even bigger, stronger brother," shouted Fergal. "Wow," said Oisín. "What happened next?".

Shane carried on about the battle with the third creature. With a cat's head lifted Darragh above his head, throwing him full force at a tree and the effort it took to defeat it. Again, Fergal interrupted and told them of the head attacking Darragh and how he jumped into the river to kill it by drowning.

Oisín sat there with his mouth open, fascinated, as Shane told him about their journey deep into the forest, where they found a giant old hag busy cooking near a Sulphur bog. Fergal, again interrupted by shouting that they blew her up. Oisín jumped to his feet, clapping the lads for their heroics.

He told them all to wait there as he ran to the main house and returned wearing a cap. He said that he had a poem to tell the group. He told Shane to sit down while he took centre stage and recited a verse.

"From the future, three lads came,
To help my father garner fame,
First, there was Darragh, strong and true,
Then there was Shane, who knew what to do,
Last, there was Fergal, always quick to threaten,
Who liked to brag about his little weapon,
Then there was Fionn, strong and tall,
These four lads together survived through it all,
They fought many battles and monsters too,
And in every challenge, they knew what to do,
They solved every challenge and were very clever
And because of this will remain friends forever".

Everyone stood up and began clapping Oisín for writing such an excellent poem. But he told them to sit down as he had another. He then recited.

"I have a tale to tell you,
for this story must be told,
It is about four young warriors,
who were strong, brave and bold,
It is a tale of love and a tale of the fight,
and the warrior's cunning bravery and might,
It's a tale of men and a tale of woe,
How they faced each challenge as well as each foe
They have fought many creatures,
yes, this is true,
And the battles they fought,
their bravery shone through,
Through this, they have formed an unbreakable circle,
But their mightiest member, his name it is Fergal".

Once again, everyone jumped to their feet and clapped loudly as Fergal rushed over and gave Oisín a high five for telling the truth. Everyone laughed loudly, as Darragh nearly coiled over as he was in severe pain. He finally stood up and said that he was pretty sore and carrying a few injuries from the battle and needed to lie down. Cred and Fionn accompanied him to his house in order to heal his injuries, while the others prepared dinner.

A few hours later, Fionn, Cred and Darragh rejoined the rest of the group, as Darragh was feeling much better. They all sat down to dinner, washed down with mead, except for Oisín, who drank some cow's milk. Oisín then asked the three lads to tell him about life back in their time. Fergal jumped in and told them about his family, the school he attended and his comforts back home, such as his console and television.

Oisín couldn't quite understand the concept of television and consoles, so Darragh explained it was like fighting a battle while sitting at the table and that he could win the battle without fear of being injured. It fascinated Oisín at being able to do that.

Darragh told them they lived in large concrete two-story houses with running water and toilets. He told them that there were very few monsters living where people lived in the future, and because of this, no one carried swords or spears. He said they attended large schools and churches. Indeed, they were at an uncle's wedding when they were somehow sucked back in time.

Shane interrupted and said, "speaking of churches, my darling Cred, we've only ever married through a hole in a wall at Lughnasa, and I would dearly love to have an official ceremony to celebrate our love."

Cred began crying but turned down the proposal, saying that she would love nothing more, but that they would need to return to Mag Mell to marry in front of her father Dagda, who was still gravely ill and in a deep sleep. She thanked Shane for the proposal but didn't need a ceremony, as she was happy that they were actually married already.

Shane hugged Cred, and the two of them disappeared back to their house. Fergal told Oisín that he missed his family more than anything and hoped to one day see them again. By now, everyone was getting tired and returned to their houses for a night's sleep.

The following morning at first light, Fionn and Oisín were back training again to prepare for his entrance test for the Fianna. Darragh came along and told Fionn that the king needed to be told about the hag and her sons and that the fort was being built safely now. Fionn said he would travel promptly to Tara and inform the king before returning to the farm. In the meantime, the others took turns training Oisín while they awaited his father's return.

Once Fionn returned, they increased the training intensity for the next week. It was then time to visit Biddy in the woods. With that, Fionn, Darragh, Fergal and Oisín, with Bran, said their goodbyes and mounted their horses before riding off out of the farm. Shane decided to spend some valuable time together with Cred.

When they were approaching the woods, Fionn called out, "Witch of the wood, witch in the trees, I beg you show your home to me" as Biddy's house appeared, Oisín was amazed as it was his first time, seeing true magic.

Biddy came out of the house, giving them all a big welcoming hug, but she saved her biggest one for Oisín, who she said was by far the cutest of the group. They all made their way into the house, where Biddy called forth the twelve books of poetry and made a potion for Oisín to drink, enabling him to remember the books by heart. He asked Biddy for a batch of the potion to keep for the future, as he could see himself as a poet or bard before becoming a warrior.

He then recited the poems he had done for the others back at Ballyfin farm, and it quite impressed her, telling him that if he ever became half the warrior he was as a poet, he would be quite the warrior indeed. It flattered Oisín at the compliment of such a lovely woman. They then spent the night before leaving the following morning and riding onwards to Almhuin for the entrance test.

When they reached the fort, Darragh and Fergal told Oisín how they had used their rings of strength and invisibility to help them overcome the test previously, while they offered him their rings for the challenge, but he refused the rings saying he intended on being the greatest warrior ever. And so, his test began.

1. Intelligence

The first test that those looking to join the Fianna were given was one that put their intellect to the test. Men were required to be knowledgeable of the twelve books of poetry, which detailed Ireland's legends, history and genealogy.

Oisín quickly recited the twelve books to pass the test.

2. Defence

A person had to prove that he could defend himself adequately. He was required to stand in a deep hole and protect himself with just a shield and a staff. He then had to defend himself from being struck by spears thrown by nine warriors.

Once again, Oisín passed with ease after all the training and tips he had received back at the farm

3. Speed

The next test was to check speed and agility. You would be given a head start into a forest and be required to evade capture by a band of fierce pursuers. You must escape unharmed and escape the forest without breaking a single branch.

Oisín was light and nimble on his feet and got through the course easily.

4. Movement

Next up was the movement test. You would have to leap over trees that stood at the same height as yourself, stoop as low as your knee, and make your way under the branch of a tree that stood just above shin height.

Almost like magic, there appeared to be an invisible step in front of the trees. Oisín leapt over, and the trees seemed to move higher as he stooped to go under them, again passing with ease.

5. The Removal of a Thorn

The next test was a combined need for speed with a need to preserve oneself during battle. Candidates were required to sprint as fast as possible with a thorn stuck in their foot. This test was made even more difficult by requiring the candidate to remove the thorn without slowing down at any point.

The ground had thorns placed on it, and Oisín ran over it, wincing in pain as he did, but he ran full speed to the end and found no thorn in his foot.

6. Bravery

The final physical test to become a member required a candidate to face many men without letting his bravery falter for even a second. This test was to ensure that the man would never back down, even when the Fianna were vastly outnumbered in battle. They could never run away.

Oisín gathered his spear and shield and easily overcame the group of four warriors, who seemed to fall over each other.

7. Chivalry

The last test in becoming a member was all about character. As the Fianna were a very much-admired group, each member must act accordingly.

They brought Oisín to a room where he agreed the Fianna was now his family and would defend them and the high king of Ireland above all others. He promised not to marry out of greed or covet land and riches, only to marry for love, be courteous with whomever he should meet, and never to hoard anything from someone in need.

With that, Fionn, Darragh and Fergal came in carrying some large tankards of mead and a cup of milk for Oisín. They raised a toast to the latest member of the Fianna. "Hip-hip Hooray," roared Fionn, the proud father, followed by loud cheers from the others.

They then brought Oisín into a room, and when he emerged was wearing his newly gained outfit of red and black tartan trousers, with a yellow tunic and a red brat folded and hanging from his left shoulder, held on by a metal pin. He also had his new sword, shield and bow as he was beaming ear to ear with joy at his achievement.

Finnegas and Biddy joined them for drinks later that evening. Fionn raised his tankard and thanked Finnegas and Biddy for their help in secretly assisting Oisín through the entrance test without his son's knowledge. The entire group rejoiced at a job well done.

CHAPTER TWENTY-ONE

THE BATTLE OF GABHRA

he following morning, Fionn called the group together and told Conan, Cailte, and Aengus that he, Oisín, Darragh, and Fergal were going back to Ballyfin, and he was leaving them in charge once more. If anything needed attention, they should send word to him immediately in Ballyfin. They mounted their horses, and with Bran, set off to Ballyfin as fast as possible.

Once they reached the farm, they passed on the great news to the others that Oisín had become a proud member of the Fianna. That evening, they held a small celebration to congratulate Oisín on his remarkable feat. It overjoyed the young boy, when Fionn told him that his name would be remembered for his poems, stories and bravery through the annals of time.

The following morning Cred said that she had to return to Mag Mell, so Shane said he would accompany her as far as he could, which wasn't actually a great distance, as Cred always teleported through the Clonfinlough Stone, which was a large standing stone less than an hour from Ballyfin.

This was the first time Shane had seen the actual stone, and it amazed him at how large it was and at its many engravings. He had often wondered how Cred turned up so regularly in Ballyfin, and now he knew. He stayed with her until nightfall before they said their goodbyes, and she disappeared back to Mag Mell. Shane travelled back to the others at the farm.

The next few weeks carried on nice and peaceful, with farming, hunting, and training. Darragh, Shane, and Fergal would ride off every few days to different corners of the land, looking for ways to get home, but they always returned as they never found a way home. As time passed, they thought more of home as the thought loomed large that they may never get to see their families again. Darragh often thought he could use a wish given to him by the Leprechaun king, Fergus, if he did indeed get a wish from him, but the thought always left his mind as Shane wouldn't leave Cred, and they found fresh adventures to pursue.

One fine day Aengus arrived at the farm and told Fionn that the High King Cairbre Lifechair had summoned them to Tara, so the group, with Aengus, travelled promptly to Tara to talk to the king. Upon reaching the fort, they made their way directly to the king, who told them his daughter Sgiam was to marry prince Maolsheachlainn of Déisi.

Déisi was a small kingdom in the province of Munster, who were known adversaries of the king, and the Fianna were to escort her to his kingdom. For this, the Fianna would receive twice their regular payment, as it was his daughter's safety they were being charged with. Fionn gladly accepted and told the king that he would need a day to prepare his troops for the journey.

With that, the group took their leave and departed for Almhuin, where Fionn said he would need one hundred troops ready for the following morning to escort the princess to her new home. As luck would have it, that day, prince Maolsheachlainn's father, Oengus, had been killed by Cairbre's sons, Fíacha and Eochaid, in a skirmish between the two clans. The wedding was supposed to bring unity to the two warring clans.

Prince Maolsheachlainn had then cancelled the wedding, and the king sent word to Almhuin, telling Fionn that his troops were no longer required, so Fionn cancelled the travelling party. That evening Fionn, Darragh, Shane and Fergal were joined for drinks by Conan, Cailte, and Aengus. Fionn told them all what had happened, and that it was his plan to return to Ballyfin to his son once again.

Later that evening, as Conan made his way to his barracks, he was approached by his treacherous brother Goll, who heard the travelling party was cancelled. Conan drunkenly told him that the wedding had been cancelled, and they would not be entitled to a large tribute the king had promised them. And so, the devious Goll hatched a plan and set off for Tara for an urgent audience with the king.

It surprised the king to receive such a late caller to his home, and he thought it must be important. Goll told the king he had overheard Fionn saying that the tyrant king Cairbre Lifechair had reneged on an agreement, and he was going to demand his payment. It enraged the king at the insolence of the leader of the Fianna and thought that his power had corrupted him. Having sewn a seed of mischief in the king's mind, Goll took his leave before riding back to Almhuin.

The following morning word reached Fionn that the king had demanded his head and put a reward on him. Darragh, Shane and Fergal offered to talk to the king to see if it was true and when they arrived at Tara, they were dragged to the main hall, where the king promptly told them what Goll had said, and although the three lad's pleaded innocence on Fionn's behalf, the king would have none of it.

He told them to turn Fionn over to him or prepare for war. He gave them ten minutes to leave Tara, or he would have their heads. The lads didn't need to be told twice and were promptly on their horses, riding to tell Fionn the bad news.

When they reached their headquarters, they rushed to the main hall where Fionn, Conan, Cailte, and Aengus were in council and told them of Goll's treachery and that the king had demanded his head or war. A furious Fionn sent for Goll, and they dragged him into the main hall to answer for his crimes. Goll just laughed and said, "I will have control of the Fianna once I am rid of you".

Conan then came forward and slapped his brother across the face for his betrayal before swearing his allegiance to Fionn. Fionn gave the order for Goll to receive fifty lashes for his crime and that he was to be expelled from the Fianna forever. As news filtered through the fort, loyal Fianna members turned their backs on him as they dragged him through the fort before they gave him 50 lashes and threw him unceremoniously out of the fort with no item of Fianna clothing on his body. A few of Goll's loyal supporters stormed from the fort and rode away with him.

Fionn's heart sank, but he had become exceedingly enraged by now. He lost no time dispatching messengers to all Fianna members in the four provinces and also the Déisi prince Maolsheachlainn to join him at Almhuin and prepare for battle with the king. He sent

Darragh, Shane, and Fergal to Ballyfin to tell what had happened and gave the word for Oisín to join him.

Shane summoned Cred to the standing stone at Clonfinlough, where the lads waited for her. He told her what had happened and asked if the Tuath could help the Fianna. She said she had foreseen the upcoming battle and had already asked Lugh for help, but once again, he did not want to become involved in a fight between humans. She promised to return and try again as the three lads and Oisín made their way to Almhuin.

For the next few days, all the troops gathered around the fort. Darragh, Shane, and Fergal took some time out and decided to go fishing to help them relax, as they were worried about the battle ahead and what it meant for everyone. They returned to the fort the next day, just as Fionn was looking for them. They had mustered all the troops they could, and their numbers totalled 15,000 troops, but Fionn had received news that the king with over 40,000 troops was setting up camp in Gabhra to gain the upper hand on them.

Gabhra was essentially flat land. It had many fields separated by brush and trees and some ancient stone walls. At its centre was a large earthen mound with the ruins of a stone fort on top. At its base was the sizeable Sheebeg cave that seemed to have been purposely dug into its side. Fionn called his leaders, along with the Déisi prince, together and gave orders to march on Gabhra. He then blew the Dord Fiann his hunting horn and joined the troops as they exited the fort en route to battle.

After a few hours of marching, they came across the Glencullen Standing Stone, another large standing stone with engravings on it. Shane approached it, pointing his silver torc at the stone, enabling Cred to know his location, before they marched on to Gabhra, where the two armies faced one another in the distance.

The king set up camp on top of the mound, for he thought it an excellent place, solid and impregnable, and hard for the Fianna to reach. Fionn set up camp in a nearby field and gave the word for his troops to assemble and prepare for battle. The skies darkened with the familiar sight of Sluagh roaming the skies, excitedly waiting to feast on the souls of the dead that lay ahead. While a short distance away, the kings' troops also assembled and prepared to lock horns with the Fianna.

Finally, Fionn blew the Dord Fiann and his troops, led as always by Darragh, Shane, Fergal, Conan, Cailte, and Aengus, rushed forward as they braced for battle and charged into a wall of shields. The sound of metal against metal filled the air. The three lads all rubbed their rings and crashed into the enemy, harrying them and dislodging some of them, forcing them from their positions, enabling those behind them more access to attack. Many enemies fell before them as the fury of combat grew, and the sound of weapons clashing grew ever louder. Warriors swayed from side to side, each circling the other as they sought an opportunity for a deadly blow.

Sluagh swarmed from the skies and preyed on the bodies of the dead as they fell, yet the battle furiously continued. Warriors loudly cried out and groaned as they fought fiercely to the bitter end, none wanting to give an inch. The three lads were urging the Fianna on, fortifying their warrior's belief and encouraging them forward in combat. Many fought until their bodies were torn and their chests cut open from the mighty onslaught of the enemy blows. Even so, each army pushed forward, looking for victory.

The warriors pushed forward and dealt mighty blows to each other. Fearsome battle cries were drowned out in the multitude of sounds emanating from the battlefield. The battle continued for many hours until neither side was capable of attacking the other, and so a truce was called for the night.

That night, many warriors from either side lay dead, and the bodies were gathered and cremated, leaving the horrible stench of burned flesh filling the air. As Fionn sat with his leaders plotting the next day's battle, a soldier from the king's army, having made his way into camp, rushed forward, stabbing Fionn in the back, trying to assassinate him. Shane lashed out with his spear, killing the intruder instantly before Fionn healed himself. Once he had recovered, they drew up plans for the following day before trying to get some rest for the night.

Darragh, Shane and Fergal joined Oisín in Fionn's tent because they were worried that, although the king had lost more significant numbers of warriors during the day than the Fianna. They themselves had lost a great number of warriors. Fionn told them to stay strong, for was he not the greatest warrior in the land? Shane said to him that might be true, but if he, alone, was left to fight the king's army, he may no longer be the greatest living warrior in the land. With this, the three lads left to get some sleep.

They rose early the following morning and were greeted by a king's messenger asking if they wished to surrender, but he was swiftly rebuked and thrown out of the camp. As the Dord Fiann was blown, the army raised their shields against the enemy, and with a thick wall of javelins and swords in hand, they moved forward to engage the enemy once more.

Suddenly the rain came down, and the earth beneath them grew soft and slowed their advances. With their feet giving way, Darragh, Shane, Fergal, Conan, Cailte, and Aengus urged the troops forward until Fionn shouting; Goliath joined the fray, pressing forward, pushing the king's troops backwards on the plain. The Fianna warriors, buoyed by this, advanced up the battlefield, killing as they went, trying to dislodge as many enemy troops as possible.

Darragh, Shane, and Fergal gathered together and attacked the enemy on the left flank of the battlefield, cutting their way through and clearing a path that devastated the enemy ranks, allowing the Fianna to storm forward on that side. Conan, Cailte, and Aengus did the same on the righthand flank, with their warriors pushing forward that side, enabling the Fianna to encircle the enemy troops attacking from all sides.

The king, who was becoming alarmed, sent more troops to join the battlefield, pushing the Fianna back to where they started. Once again, skies darkened, and swarms of Sluagh rushed the battlefield in search of souls. Shane, having a clear head, realised that the king might be within reach and, taking Darragh's ring, rubbed it, gaining extra strength, throwing his spear full throttle at the king, piercing him right through the shoulder, before recalling his spear.

They withdrew the king from battle, and Shane gave Darragh back his ring before they charged at the enemy once more. The sound of steel crashing against steel got louder as the day went on, and the groans of injured soldiers grew louder and louder. With the three lads on the left and Conan, Cailte, and Aengus to the right, their troops swiftly advanced through the ranks of the king's army as their mood was grim with the news that their king had been injured and removed from the battle.

As the battle progressed, the closely packed Fianna warriors, urged forward by their commanders, advanced towards the mound. They formed a compact, well-drilled fighting machine, each warrior with deadly weapons and shields in hand, pushed forward until neither side was capable of attacking the other, so a truce was called for the night. Fionn sought to end the battle by killing the king, as they had tried to kill him the previous night. So, they told Darragh and Fergal to give their rings to Shane.

Shane sneaked as close as he could to the king's tent before rubbing all three rings; once he turned invisible and gained extra strength, he ran as fast as he ever had before, up the mound and into the king's tent. As the king's men rushed back and forth, wondering how to treat their ailing king, Shane rushed at him, plunging a dagger into the king's chest, killing him instantly, before making his way back down the mound and telling Fionn and the others the great news.

Fionn rejoiced at the news, predicting that the king's army would now be in disarray and disband, granting victory to the Fianna. Darragh worried that it could have the opposite effect and galvanise the king's army. He told Fionn that the Fianna may have lost some 5,000 troops and the king's army almost 12,000 troops.

However, they were still a formidable force that, under the right leadership, could still win the battle as the king's army still far outnumbered that of the Fianna. Darragh was so worried that he told Shane to summon Cred to see if the Tuath would send troops to aid them. Shane left the camp and rode to the Glencullen Standing Stone.

On the third day of battle, Darragh feared the worst was yet to come and told Fergal to stay close to him. At dawn, Fionn assembled his troops with himself, Darragh, Fergal, Conan, Cailte, and Aengus at its head. The king's army gathered to face them, and at its head were the slain king's two sons, Fíacha and Eochaid. They rode back and forth amongst their ranks, encouraging their men to fight.

Darragh told Fionn they needed to be cautious, as the enemy may have a greater appetite for battle with the king's sons now in charge. Fionn, being a little cautious and worried for his son Oisín, told Cailte to remain in camp with his son and to protect him at all costs if the tide of battle turned against them.

Fionn, being headstrong, took out the Dord Fiann horn, blowing it, and urged his men forward into battle. The king's sons gave the order to charge, and both sides rushed at each other, colliding with tremendous force.

Darragh and Fergal set out on one final glorious charge up the left flank, with many warriors behind them. Many dead and wounded fell beneath their feet and were trampled in the onslaught. The two lads hacked their way through the enemy lines, inflicting deadly wounds as they fought. Until finally, they were met with a large group of warriors unyielding in their efforts and had to retreat. In his Goliath form, Fionn was charging through the centre, slaying enemies for fun as he ran, while Conan and Aengus stormed forward on the right, making significant inroads into the enemy's lines.

Fíacha and Eochaid, again, urged their troops to stand firm, and they regained their composure and began pushing the Fianna back on their heels. As the fighting became more brutal, many warriors fell with broken limbs, while others had large gaping wounds and tried to crawl from the battlefield. The king's men pushed forward through their greater numbers, while the Fianna warriors withdrew slowly to regroup before making a fresh charge at the enemy.

As Fionn, Darragh, Fergal, Conan and Aengus gathered behind an old stone wall almost facing the Sheebeg cave. Darragh told Fergal to rub his ring and go into the cave to see if it could offer them any protection or advantage in the battle. Fergal, rubbing his ring, rushed forward into the cave as the others waited patiently for his return. They remained vigilant, shouting orders to their troops, who fought bravely against the onslaught of the king's men.

A short time later, Fergal returned and told them that there was a second entrance into the cave and that it appeared as though the king's men were preparing for an ambush, although there were no troops inside the cave. Wooden beams were holding up the cave entrances at both ends. He said that the king's men had horses with ropes attached to the beams at the far entrance, preparing to pull them down.

He excitedly told Darragh there was a large standing stone at the rear of the cave and that it contained what looked to him to be a Dara knot, and they may have found their way home.

Dara Knot, represents destiny and endurance.

Darragh was excited too, but now was not the time to think about home, as they had a battle to win. The skies suddenly opened, and torrential rain poured onto the battlefield, soaking all the troops and making the fight more difficult for the warriors, who were still attacking each other with all their might.

As they contemplated their next move, who should ride into view right in front of them? Only the treacherous giant of a man, Goll, marshalled by his ex-Fianna warriors. Fionn became enraged at the traitors turning up on the battlefield and moved forward to engage them. Darragh pleaded with Fionn to be cautious as Fergal thought they were setting a trap. Fionn, in his arrogance, told Darragh and Fergal to stay back, as Conan and Aengus would handle it.

As they moved forward on foot to engage them, Goll and his warriors turned and galloped into the darkness of the cave. Fionn and the others ran in after them, and Darragh worried he had made a mistake. A few minutes later, Goll and his warriors came back around the mound on their horses, tying ropes around the entrance beams, before pulling them to the ground collapsing the cave entrance just as they had the far entrance and trapping Fionn Conan and Aengus inside.

"No," screamed Fergal, "our Dara knot is in there". "So are our friends," shouted Darragh. He turned to Cailte, telling him to get Oisín back to the safety of Ballyfin farm and to tell Bodhmall and Liath what had happened before preparing to face Goll and his men.

Goll and his warriors had dismounted and were walking towards the old stone wall protecting Darragh and Fergal. Goll roared at the two lads that they would die a slow, painful death at his hands.

As the two lads braced for combat, Shane came charging back into camp accompanied by Cred and Manannan Mac Lir, who were the only troops Lugh was willing to send to help them. Shane charged forward, drawing his spear, throwing it full force at Goll, striking him just above the heart. Goll immediately pulled the spear from his chest and flung it back at Shane, hitting him in the chest before falling to his knees.

It knocked Shane clean off his horse, and he landed, gravely injured, on the rain-soaked ground. Cred and Manannan leapt from their horses to go to his aid. While Fergal screamed "NO" at the top of his voice, he ran forward, attacking Goll with his Claíomh Solais, stabbing him once more in the chest. Goll, as big and strong as he was, pulled Fergal's dagger from his body, stabbing him in the stomach and throwing him to the ground. "You're next," he shouted menacingly to Darragh.

Confused by what he had just witnessed, Darragh didn't know whether to help Shane or Fergal. Still, as Cred and Manannan were looking after Shane, he charged forward, drawing his blade and rubbing his ring, screaming with all the anger in the world; he took Goll's head clean from his shoulders as his body fell limp to the ground. Goll's men panicked and ran from the battle as Darragh lifted Fergal onto his shoulders and carried him and his dagger back to where Shane was lying. In all the surrounding carnage, the now leaderless Fianna warriors started fleeing the battlefield in a panic.

Now in floods of tears, Cred said that her healing powers were not strong enough and that with Manannan's help, she would need to get Shane back to her home in Mag Mell in order to save his life. Darragh rushed to his injured cousin, telling him he loved him dearly and would see him again soon while clenching his hand tightly and kissing him on the forehead.

Cred and Manannan prepared Shane as best they could, placing him onto a horse before all three galloped away from the battlefield. Darragh turned his attention to Fergal, who was crying in pain, rolling on the ground in agony, trying to calm him down.

"Garon," cried PJ. "I'm not enjoying this anymore," "That makes two of us PJ," shouted Garon in return.

As he looked up, he could see both the king's sons, Fíacha and Eochaid, charging in their direction with their swords raised. He tore the corrbolg from his waist, gathered Shane's spear, Fergal's dagger and his sword, and, taking Fergal's ring from him, put them all in the corrbolg. He pulled up a tuft of grass before carefully placing the bag and covering it with the grass tuft.

"FERGUS", he roared, and in the blink of an eye. There stood the smiling Leprechaun King Fergus. "So, you finally want a wish, do you?" He shouted out, "be careful what you wish for". "FERGUS", roared Darragh again. "We wish to go home to our own time".

Garon and PJ could feel they were wet through and thought it was from the torrential rain falling on the battlefield, but music had suddenly replaced the sound of battle. As they regained composure, they realised they were sitting in a fountain with kids laughing close by.

"Where are we, and what's going on?" shouted PJ, eyeing their surroundings.

"I think the wish worked," laughed Garon excitedly. "I think we're home."

"What do you mean, we're home?" groaned PJ in pain.

"Garon, PJ," shouted Lucy. "Why are you sitting in the fountain, and where is Dillon?".

"FERGUS", roared Garon

Appendix

CREATURES

Name	Pronunciation	Description
Abhartach	Ab-har-tach	A dwarf magical vampire
Aillen	Ale-lin	He was a fire-breathing goblin from the other world, Mag Mell
Alp-luachra	Alp- Lua-Cra	Appears in the form of a newt and crawls down a person's mouth, feeding off the food that they had eaten
Banshee	Ban-shee	A female spirit in Gaelic folklore whose appearance or wailing warns of a family death
Benandonner	Ben-And-Donner	A scottish giant.
Bocanachs and Bananachs		Shrieking airborne demons that haunted battlefields
Cailleach bheara	Call -E-A Bear-A	A mythicical Irish Goddess or divine hag.
Caoránach	Queer-hawn-nock	A great worm or mighty reptile that could multiply itself.
Clurichaun	Clur-E-Con	A mischievous fairy known for his great love of drinking and a tendency to haunt wine cellars.
Cú Sidhe	Coo-She	A spectral hound from celtic folklore.

Direwolf		Giant wolves that inhabited ancient Ireland
dobhar-chú	doh-war chew	A water hound or King Otter.
Fear Dearg	Fir -Jar-G	A trickster who doesn't just play practical jokes. Sometimes taking them too far.
Fer Doirich	Fer Dire-Ick	A villainous druid in Irish mythology.
Leannan Sidhe	Leannan-she	A figure from Irish Folklore. She appears as a beautiful woman but is an empty husk.
leprechaun	Lep-Re-Cawn	A small supernatural being in Irish folklore, who has a crock of gold and can grant wishes.
Man-Wolves of Ossory		Enchanted humans who turn into wolves
Merrow		A mermaid or merman in Irish folklore.
Muckie		A large loch ness type creature, living in lakes.
Ollphéisteanna	All-Pest-Anna	A great wormlike reptile.
Pooka	Poo-Ka	Shapeshifter who brings mixed fortunes.
Selkie	Sell-Key	Half human - half fish
Sluagh	Slew-Ah	preyed on the souls of the dead.
Spriggan		Shapeshifters who could cause storms

LOCATIONS

Name	Pronunciation	Description
Almhuin	Alm-uin	Ancient site in County kildare.
Athgreany stone circle		A circle of fourteen stones in County Wicklow.
Avondale		Location in Wicklow
Ballyfin		Located in Slieve Bloom Mountains County Laois.
Brú na Bóinne		A palace or the mansion of the Boyne Newgrange.
Caves of Kesh Corran		A series of caves located near Keash, County Sligo.
Cloghstuckagh, Moyvoughly		Irish Pillar Stones & Cross-pillar County westmeath
Clonfinlough Stone		A standing stone located near Kinnitty, County Offaly.
Cradockstown		A town in County Kildare.

Dun Aengus	Doon-An-Gus	A prehistoric hill fort in County Galway.
Dún Bhalair	Doon-Bal-Air	Balor's Fort is located on Tory Island Donegal.
Fálias	Fal-E-Ass	Mythical Tuath dé Danann city.
Gabhra		Thought to be Garristown in Co. Dublin or Keshcarrigan in Co Leitrim
Glencullen Standing Stone		Located in Glencullen, County Dublin.
Hill of Allen		Situated in the west of County Kildare.
Hill of Slaine		Found in Boyne valley, County Meath.
Kelshamore		A town in County Wicklow.
Kilmagoura	Cill Mhaí Gabhra	A town in County Cork.
Knockmullin		A town in County Leitrim.
Loughscur Dolmen		A portal tomb in County Leitrim.
Mag Mell	Moy Mell	The otherworld.

Moytura	Situated overlooking Lough Arrow in County Sligo.
Sheebeg cave	Hills outside the village of Keshcarrigan in County Leitrim.
Tailtin	A town in County Meath.
Tara	Found in Boyne valley, County Meath.

MISCELLANEOUS

Name	Pronunciation	Description
Aghade		Also, known as Cloghaphoill - Is a flat stone in Carlow
Aonbharr	Aon-Bar	A magical horse could travel like the wind over land and sea, created by Manamann Mac Lir
Birgha	Bir-Ga	Fionn's poisonous spear.
Claíomh Solais	Clave-Sol-As	Fergal's dagger of light.
Coire Ansic	Core-An-Sick	Dagda's magic Cauldron.
Dord Fiann		Fianna war or hunting horn.
Dùn	Doon	Stone fort or castle.
Gae Assail	Gay-Ass-Sail	Shane's spear of returning.
Lorg Mor		Dagda's magic staff
Lughnasa	Lug-Nasa	Festival marking the beginning of the harvest season.
Mac An Lúin	Mack-An-Loon	Darragh's sword, which could kill

		most creatures with a single blow.
Sguaba Tuinne	scuba twine	A self-navigating boat created by Manannán mac lir
Sleg		Lugh's spear, could turn into a lightning bolt and be recalled
Uaithne	Uath-knee	Dagda's magical harp.
Uilleann pipes		National bagpipe of Ireland

PEOPLE

Name	Pronunciation	Description
Bodhmall	Bogmall	Fionn's warrior aunt.
Cred		Shanes wife, seer Tuatha Dé Danann
Deinmhe	Dem-Na	Fionn's birth name
Fianna		A group of Irish warriors
Finnegas	Finn Eces	An ancient druid
Fir Bolg		Early Irish settlers
Fomorians		A hostile and monstrous race of supernatural beings
Lugh	Rhymes with hug	Tuatha Dé Danann general.
Manannan Mac Lir		Master Tuatha Dé Danann wizard.
Maolsheachlainn	Male-shack-lawn	Deisci prince
Oisín	Oh-Sheen	Fionn's son
Sadhbh (Sive)	Rhymes with hive	Fionn's wife.
Sgiam	Si-am	Kings daughter.
Tuatha Dé Danann	Thoo-a day Du-non	Supernatural race

Declan Biography/About me

Declan has a passion for fictional stories and characters. He debuted his first book, A Mythical Irish Tale, early 2023. Though he has been telling stories his entire life, his medium up to this point has been different. He wrote his book with a passion and desire to help those who've lost themselves in the fast lane of modern life by assisting them to escape and embrace their history and create a connection with ancient Ireland.

Declan's writing focuses on how he can connect with his readers and help them escape the rigours and stresses of everyday life – because writing is about 'escapism' to him.

He is the third oldest of six children, happily married, and is a proud father of one son. He lives in Dublin, Ireland and has worked in the purchasing, warehousing, and transport industries for many years, which has markedly amended his skills and expertise. He has always dreamed of writing a fictional novel about ancient Ireland one day. So, he took a break from his work to chase his dream.

His motto is simple: Writing should connect to the readers. Ideas are always easy, but implementation is complex, so he constantly challenges his words, creates art out of them, and delivers to his readers more than their expectations. Declan aims to carry on his writings with many more fictional books.

So, if you are going to be his friend or colleague, you should know that he admires the genuine quest for self-improvement and extraordinary imagination. Declan loves spending time with his family and is passionate about the great outdoors, Irish Folklore and world history. He values imaginative thinking, attention to detail, freedom of expression, peace, integrity and honesty in everything he does!